W9-CRA-123

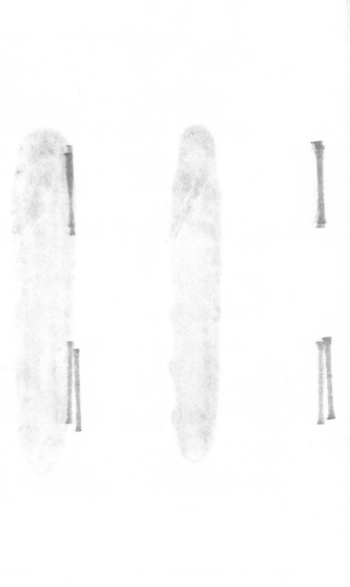

THE LILACS ARE BLOOMING IN WARSAW

THE LILACS ARE BLOOMING IN WARSAW

ALICE PARIZEAU

Translated by A.D. Martin-Sperry

NAL BOOKS

NEW AMERICAN LIBRARY

NEW YORK AND SCARBOROUGH, ONTARIO

NAL BOOKS TRADEMARK REG. U.S. PAT. OFF. AND FOREIGN COUNTRIES
REGISTERED TRADEMARK—MARCA REGISTRADA
HECHO EN HARRISONBURG, VA., U.S.A.

SIGNET, SIGNET CLASSIC, MENTOR, PLUME, MERIDIAN
and NAL BOOKS are published *in the United States* by
New American Library, 1633 Broadway, New York, New York 10019,
in Canada by The New American Library of Canada Limited,
81 Mack Avenue, Scarborough, Ontario M1L 1M8

Library of Congress Cataloging in Publication Data

Parizeau, Alice, 1930–
The lilacs are blooming in Warsaw.

I. Title.
Translation of: Les lilas fleurissent à Varsovie.
PQ3919.2.P3L513   1985   843   84-27322
ISBN 0-453-00481-4

Designed by K. E. May

First Printing, June, 1985

2 3 4 5 6 7 8 9

PRINTED IN THE UNITED STATES OF AMERICA

THE LILACS ARE BLOOMING IN WARSAW

1

THE SUN WAS not yet up, and in the fading night it was hard to make out the shapes of the houses.

Helena's footsteps faltered as she moved slowly forward. She hardly noticed her aching feet, scantily covered in rags, as she stumbled across the uneven ground. All her limbs felt out of joint. Sometimes the pain was worse in her back, sometimes in one arm. At times the echoes inside her head were so bad she had to close her eyes.

Helena would have liked to stop and lie down—anywhere. If only she could give up the struggle and let herself fade into the mist. But she couldn't. She *had* to get there. An inner determination, like that of some wounded animal, kept driving her onward. Her long blond hair fell over her eyes, brushing across her lips. She made no attempt to sweep it back; just to lift her arm seemed a superhuman effort.

How long had she been walking like this? She had no idea—weeks, months, years. It didn't matter, she *had* to go on. She remembered sleeping in a barn, where she had been warm. Her courage had almost failed her when the

time came to set out again; but then there had been the
sound of voices, and at once sheer fright had driven her to
continue on her way.

The mist spread itself out, then began falling in shreds
beneath the rays of the sun. As Helena knocked her right
foot against a big stone, the sudden pain made her stop to
see where she was. It was a strange place, neither town
nor country, a sort of vast wasteland all covered with
debris.

To her left lay the empty shell of what must have been a
house several stories high. One wall was still standing, its
presence somehow reassuring. It had managed to remain
upright, all alone in this wasteland; maybe, then, she
could, too.

The sun lit up a roadway, a stretch of paved surface
glistening with dew. Helena stared ahead. A little farther
on she could see other solitary walls, other ruins. And
then, far in the distance, seeming quite unreachable to
her, there stood a building still intact.

"Warsaw!" she shouted at the top of her voice. "Warsaw!
I've made it—I'm home!"

She broke into a run. Little by little the landscape took
shape. Farther off there were sure to be houses that were
inhabited. Helena threw her head back. The sun hurt her
eyes; even her eyelids hurt. She felt a salt liquid moisten-
ing her lips. Tears! It had been so long since she had cried
that these tears seemed to restore to her a part of herself
as she had been in former days.

Walking on, she saw more skeletons of houses. Without
realizing it, Helena began praying aloud. "O God, make
the next house be like the ones there used to be! With
walls, and floors, and ceilings, and doors! Let me go inside
and lie down on a floor. O God, please . . ."

Suddenly she saw a door. She touched it, felt it, stroked
the frame with her fingers; then she saw a strange notice,
half in Russian, half in Polish. Written in pencil, in big

block letters, the sheet of paper read: "NO MINES. CAPTAIN WLADYMIR."

Terrified, she started to run. It was happening again: she was being hunted down by men in uniform. She relived the scene that had taken place several weeks ago in that little village where they had pursued her to the edge of the forest. The stabbing pain came again, like some wild beast lurking in her belly. Bodies weighed heavily on her, brutal hands grabbed her arms, ugly, twisted, inhuman faces loomed over hers. . . .

Helena fell. She lay facedown for a long time, surrounded by an opaque mist streaked with spots of red.

"A child's fainted!" a woman's voice cried. As Helena was lifted up, she looked into a pair of fine green eyes beneath heavy, wrinkled eyelids. The woman, small and fat, supported Helena against her shoulder, dragging her over to where several people were clustered around the rusted hulk of a bus. She smelled something wonderful. A thin plume of smoke was rising from the body of the vehicle. Inside, where a portable stove had been set up, a younger woman was making sandwiches. Around her were others holding thick slabs of bread and hot sausage.

"Eat," said the woman, handing her some food. Helena chewed obediently, while the woman watched her with a tender smile. She felt like a little girl, as if nothing had happened to her. All she had to do was eat and drink and everyone would be happy. The coffee warmed her up, so she could think more clearly.

"What's your name?" someone asked her. "Where are you trying to go?"

Faces—too many faces. Helena turned to the old woman and huddled up against her.

"Let her be," the woman said. "The child's frightened. Come, eat up, dear. When you're ready to talk, I'll be here to help you. You needn't worry. These are all good people. You're not the only one, you know! There are people wandering about everywhere, in the streets, among the ruins. They're looking for their families, their friends, anybody. The good Lord's merciful. Little by little, everything will get back to normal. The Krauts have gone, the war's over. What more can one ask? Come on! Start by eating up your sandwich. Do you want some more coffee? It's not very good, I know, but it's hot, and that's the main thing."

Helena swallowed the last drop of coffee, gave a long sigh of satisfaction, and held up her face as the old woman wiped it with a strip of cloth.

"My word, you are dirty! It's time you got your color back. Come here a moment."

In privacy behind the bus, she brought a bowl full of water and a piece of soap.

"Give yourself a good scrubbing—you need it. I'll leave you to it."

Helena washed herself carefully, trying to disentangle her hair with her fingers.

"Wait, I'll help you," said the old woman, coming back. "Sit down on the ground." She took a comb out of the pocket of her brown apron and stood behind Helena with her knees pressed firmly against the girl's back. Chattering away nonstop as she worked, she plaited the long hair into thick braids.

"I don't know where you come from, or what your name is, but you look pretty poorly, my dear. We'll have to find somewhere for you to go. Perhaps your family's already back here. Many people have come back, you know. I came back as soon as the last Krauts had left, though it wasn't such a good idea—they'd laid mines, the bastards. Under the houses, in the ruins—everywhere. The merciful Lord protected me; I could easily have stumbled onto one of the filthy things. But I got back safe and sound to our own place. I live at Saska Kepa, right in the quarter that's still standing. Of course, the comrades are there, but all the same they're better than the other pack of swine. Hey, hold still! I can't do your hair if you keep wriggling about."

She bent down and whispered in Helena's ear, "Don't worry. I know very well they were in Saska Kepa, and they waited there quietly for our boys to get themselves killed on the barricades by the Krauts, so that they could move in in their turn. I know that, my dear, better than you. My two sons were there, and they went away as prisoners of war after the surrender. God is merciful, and they're sure to be coming back. Only one must never talk about the uprising anymore, you see! It seems they shoot those who say they took part in it. Otherwise, they're not too bad. They help us clear the mines away, and they've distributed supplies several times. So mum's the word, my dear! If you were there, don't talk about it. You never know who's listening, or who's reporting what."

The old woman straightened up and gave Helena a push. "Let's have a look at you," she said with a laugh. "You look pretty now, my dear, and quite presentable. Can you talk?"

"Thank you," said Helena with a big effort. "Thank you for everything."

"And she's polite, too. Well done, my dear! Now, what is your name?"

"Helena."

"And how old are you?"

"Thirteen."

"Thirteen—that's a fine age! Have you got any parents? A mother? Anybody?"

"I think so."

"Ah, you think so, do you? You must have been roaming around for a long time like this, all by yourself, to have forgotten your mother. That's not very nice. Come now, where do you live?"

Helena hung her head. It had been so long since anyone had asked her where she lived—before the Warsaw uprising, before the prisoner-of-war camp, before that autumn of 1944, when she'd kissed her mother for the last time before leaving with her rucksack on her back to rejoin her unit, the Rygiel Squad, which was forming up in a house opposite the Ogrod Saski. It was such a long time ago. . . . She tried to explain to the old lady, who quieted her, and put her arm around Helena's shoulders.

"You came back from Germany on foot!" she murmured as Helena finished. "No wonder you're in such a state! Can you still walk?"

"A little."

"Good. Listen, I'm going to take you to a quiet spot where you can lie down for a little while. I have to come back here, to feed everyone, and then I'll come and get you. At the other end of the bridge, right at the beginning of Paryska Street, there are several bulletin boards carrying the names of people who've come back. We'll have a look, in case your parents' names might be there. If they lived in Saska Kepa, chances are your mother's come back. If she's not there, we'll go to my place. I've just the one room, but don't worry, we'll manage all right. Now, here we are—this is the spot."

The old woman pushed Helena ahead of her toward a low building—a sort of toolshed. Behind the plank that served as a door were some jute sacks on the ground. Helena lay down, closed her eyes, and fell asleep immediately, as the old woman's tender hands covered her with other sacks.

Helena sank into oblivion. She no longer had to keep walking, to move forward, to try to find her way. She no longer felt hungry, or thirsty, or afraid. She was completely and utterly free. But the dreams came back. Her friend Jeanne was making her come along. They were leaving the hut. In the center of the camp parade ground, women were running. An infernal din made it impossible for her to hear what Jeanne was saying. The Russian Army was encircling the camp; they were going to be liberated. But the German soldiers, the guards, the SS, were still there, and they were shouting as they always did.

"Quick, quick, outside, outside, dammit—once again, outside with you!"

Jeanne started running with the others. A soldier stopped. He was holding his rifle as straight and rigid as his back; then suddenly it drooped forward at an odd angle, and several women fell down, as an explosion shook the ground. Helena threw herself flat and crawled toward the main gate where they left every morning to gather rotting turnips in the local fields and load them onto trucks. She got as far as the barbed-wire fence, when a body fell to the ground beside her.

"Oh, bloody hell! *Liebe Gott!*"

Oh no, not that—God didn't speak German. He couldn't speak German, not with Hitler and the SS, and the Warsaw uprising and the planes which swooped down so low to drop their bombs on the Poles. Surely God spoke Polish.

Suddenly, there was her grandmother, sitting up in her bed, "My dear," she said with a little smile, "in our day God spoke not only Polish but also the language of the Jews. Never forget that."

Helena wanted to answer that that couldn't be right, because her schoolteacher was always telling them that the Jews had crucified Christ; but her grandmother motioned her to be quiet, and then she left her bed, floating away into the void.

Helena kept on crawling forward; now the tall posts of the main gate were close. The noise stopped. The silence was quite surprising, even frightening. Flat on the ground, Helena raised her head and realized she was surrounded by dead bodies. How odd it was! During the Warsaw uprising, the corpses had been in civilian clothes, with

just red-and-white armbands on their arms; while here all
the bodies wore the uniforms of the German Army or the
SS. She would never get across this sea of bodies—there
were too many of them.

"Dirty scum!" a soldier shouted above her head. His
uniform was brown, not green.

"The Russians have arrived," she heard. "Our liberators."

"Come, darling, it's time to go." Helena opened her
eyes. The old woman stood beside her, smiling. Her teeth
were blackened stumps and one of them was missing in
front. But there was kindness in her eyes, and the movement of her heavy hand was gentle. Helena clung to her.

"You talk a lot in your sleep," the woman said. "That's
not good, dear. I only arrived a few moments ago, and I've
already learned you were liberated from your camp by the
Russians. Poor child! What else have they done to you?
Come on, let's go."

The sun was setting, and shadows were spreading through
the ruins. The old woman held Helena's hand, making her
walk as quickly as she could. Her knees buckled, and she
fell.

"Oh-oh! How weak you are," said the woman. "Don't
you worry, we'll soon put that right."

She lifted Helena from the ground, swung her uncere-
moniously up onto her back, and continued walking.

"Old Razowa's still pretty tough!" she said. "Tough as a
tree trunk. Can you see the good God from up there,
love?"

Helena opened her eyes. People were everywhere. Alone,
or in little groups, men and women kept stopping in front
of the flat surfaces of the ruins where little sheets of paper,
pieces of cardboard, or even planks had names written on
them—names of the living who were trying to find their
families, or names of the dead, indicating where they were
buried.

"Hold on tight, love!" Razowa called out. "We've got to hurry if we want to get home before night."

She clamped her arms tightly around Helena's legs as the girl sat astride her shoulders. Helena tried to make out her surroundings. There was the bridge—no doubt about that. The Vistula ran underneath it, and Saska Kepa lay on the other side. Beneath Razowa's feet lay planking that amplified the steps of the people passing in the other direction.

"The comrades have built us a temporary bridge," Razowa told her. "They're doing what they can to help us, of course, but if they'd only go away, things would be so much better. Well, it's no use grumbling all the time! While there's life, there's hope—isn't that right, love?"

Finally they reached the other side of the bridge. As Razowa bent down, Helena slipped off her shoulders onto the ground, and both of them began reading the names on a big notice board fixed to a post. Suddenly Helena cried out. Her mother's name was there—she was alive!

"Will anyone who has news of a blond girl named Helena, age thirteen, fairly tall, green eyes, snub nose, please get in touch with Irena Stanowska, at 49 Paryska Street, Apartment 3, Room 5."

"That's Mother!" Helena shouted.

She didn't want to be carried any longer. She could walk—it was just a few steps. She could run. She could . . . But Razowa kept her clasped in her arms, for her teeth were chattering and her body was shaking badly. Some Russian officers passed by in an open military car; others were walking in the street, and Razowa turned toward them as if to seek their help.

"Don't leave me," begged Helena. "I'm afraid."

The old woman caught the frail little body as Helena slumped to the ground.

Tears welled from Helena's closed eyes. Lost again, she dreamed of some hollyhocks growing near a house. Hungry, she drew closer. Surely it would be all right to eat the leaves of the hollyhocks. Suddenly soldiers in brown uniforms loomed up in front of her. They had been drinking, and staggered from one side of the road to the other as in a crazy dance. Their faces flushed, they burst into laughter again and again. One of them threw her something, which fell to the ground. Helena bent down. It was a piece of black bread. She couldn't remember when she had last seen a piece of bread as good and as big as that one. It felt warm to her fingers, and she put it up to her mouth, eager to sink her teeth into it. Suddenly there were hands gripping her shoulders, her waist, her thighs, her arms. She cried out, dropping the bread, and fought, butting out with her head. Everything went red. Faces, men's faces, and a pain she'd never known before, tore her apart. It moved up and gripped her stomach, attacking her chest, reverberating inside her head, pinning her to the ground. There was blood everywhere, even on the thick hand covered with hairs, which she bit as hard as she could—

"Helena darling!"

Helena couldn't open her eyes, but she recognized her mother's voice. Am I dead? she wondered. Am I in Paradise, with Mother? Then she's dead too—but where's Father?

The voice faded away. Helena found herself lying on moss. There were no longer any soldiers around her. Her arms, legs, and mouth hurt; but above all, her belly. There was a warm, sweetish liquid trickling down her throat. Blood. She tried to get up, but couldn't. Night lay around her; then suddenly it was morning again, warm and sunny, and once again she felt the coldness of the dew. Around her was the gloomy undergrowth of the forest, and above, the treetops waving in the wind. Helena started crawling. Grass, moss, a pool. The water was good, so fresh and clean. Helena drank, plunging her arms in, splashing her face. She got up onto her knees. A dog barked; was he going to bite her? Helena stood up and ran. Trees and bushes scratched her bare arms and hit her in the face. She passed a ravine, a clearing, a low-built house. A freckle-faced young boy spoke to her in German. Helena screamed and struggled, and then went limp. She no longer had the strength to get up when the boy returned with a woman. They blotted out the blue sky as they leaned over her.

A low-ceilinged room. A bed. The taste of milk in her mouth wiped out everything else—the voices, the people, and the words that flew round and round about her. Night. A cart filled with hay. Someone pushed her up, someone else gave her a helping hand. The hay smelled good. Once again, it was daytime, and then it was night again.

"If her temperature continues to drop, she'll be all right," a familiar man's voice was saying. "Let's get out of here. We have to be as quiet as we can."

Lying in the big bed, Helena was silent. Tears rolled down her cheeks, and she heard her mother's voice again.

"Helena, my child, nothing more can hurt you now. I'm here. Your mother's here. You're home, darling. It's all over, we're all together. Father's back and your Uncle Andrzej is here with us. We're going to take care of you."

Helena opened her mouth, but no sound came. She turned onto her side, buried her face in the pillow, and fell asleep. This time there were no dreams—or nightmares.

It was cold. Although the house was intact, the window-panes had been replaced with pieces of cardboard and the cool of the evening spread through the place. Andrzej Rybicki sat close to Robert Stanowski, who was silent in his wheelchair. Andrzej was tall, with twinkling brown eyes, and the gray in his curly red hair did not detract from his youthful air. Robert looked older than his friend, although he was not. His somber blue eyes and thin lips gave his face a look of severity.

"I'm going to the kitchen to make some tea," Irena called. "There's a bit of bread left, too."

The apartment had been divided in two: one room for Andrzej, the other for Irena and Robert. When the Russians had taken over, private homes had been split up into small apartments, often with communal bathrooms and kitchens. As a doctor, Andrzej had been able to get an adjoining bathroom, but they were forced to share a kitchen with the other tenants in the building.

"She didn't recognize me," Robert murmured. "My own daughter looked at me as though I were a stranger. I don't think anything hurt as much as that. Not the bombings, nor the charge against the German tanks, nor even being a prisoner of war. At least then I could pretend that one day we'd be free to rebuild our lives. But now—"

"Stop it!" Andrzej said. "Helena's back—that's the main thing." He ran his hand through his hair, shook himself, and got up. "A thirteen-year-old girl who's crossed Germany on foot all alone, in spite of what's happened to her—well, it is a miracle! And all her wounds are healing nicely. Robert, your daughter's really something! She was knee-high to a grasshopper when she started working with the resistance, and she was the only one in her class their chaplain was willing to enlist. We used to call her 'The Mascot'—we could send her anywhere. With her angelic air and her long blond braids, she knew how to sneak in wherever she was needed. It was Helena who saved my mother when they came to arrest me; she warned her to escape while the Gestapo surrounded the house, then found her a place to stay. She even got the news to me at the hospital, warning me to disappear. You were in your prisoner-of-war camp then, Robert. For you, everything came to an end in 1939. But Irena, Helena, and I—we went on resisting, somehow—"

"All right!" Robert said. "But *I'm* the one who lost a leg. I suffered hunger and cold, I got shot, before the Russians brought us back in cattle trucks. It was no picnic, believe me!"

"Quiet," said Andrzej. "The partition's very thin, and we'd better not be overheard. It's going to be hard enough, trying to explain Helena's presence to the Russian officers."

"A fat lot *you* know about them!" Robert said. "You leave early and get back late from the hospital, but I'm here day after day, stuck in this chair, and I hear them. They come in about seven in the evening, drunk, and they keep drinking and swearing. After that it's not long before their snoring sets the partition shaking."

Andrzej continued talking, as though Robert hadn't spoken. "Ah, Helena! The last I remember, she was creeping along in a pair of pants far too big for her, and a huge tank was moving forward. All she had in her hands was a bottle of gasoline, which she had to get as close as possible to throw. The tank blew up, but somehow she got away with nothing more than some dust on her face. Only children have courage like that—children and madmen. Helena is truly a marvel."

"Why are you telling me all this?" Robert stared into his lap. "You were there when Irena told me the whole story, and you saw me weep. It was you who predicted Helena would return, though I no longer believed it myself."

"Now you'll have to have even more courage than before," Andrzej said slowly. "My examination showed that Helena's been raped, and she's pregnant."

They stared at each other in the flickering light of the oil lamp. Then Robert pushed his friend aside and wheeled his chair toward the bathroom. He could barely get it open in time. Robert's body shook with spasms; he felt as though there would never be an end to this hot flood that surged up into his throat, filling his mouth. His eyes filled with tears as he spat out the foul yellow liquid.

Robert was a reserve lieutenant, and he had led his squadron's charge. It was the last cavalry charge in Europe—

horses against tanks, courage against force, carnage everywhere. When his horse had foundered, he'd continued to
run forward, revolver in hand. They'd had to club him in
the end, ten against one. He had woken up in a military
hospital.

Robert could remember every detail as though it had
happened only yesterday. The trip across Germany in
cattle trucks, the humiliation of doing one's daily business
squatting down like animals, the hunger, the camp at
Fallingbostel with its barbed-wire fences, the tunnels
they dug with their mess tins, the cigarettes passed from
hand to hand. His futile escape and recapture. And then
the amputation of his leg, the incredible pain, the troubled nights filled with dreams of the woman he loved
clasped in another's arms, and the shattering fear that
she'd never want him again.

Yet suddenly, all that seemed to mean nothing. Helena,
his little blond daughter, the joy of his life, his ray of
sunshine, whose tiny photo had been hidden underneath
his tongue through all the searches and identity checks—
Helena had been raped.

Blind rage swept over him. Irena hadn't been able to
protect her own daughter. His wife and Andrzej, his best
friend, had let a little girl play at being a soldier. They had
let her man the barricades and then left with the wounded,
without going to find her, without taking her with them.

"Here, drink this." Andrzej handed Robert a glass filled
with white liquid. Robert stared at him angrily; he wanted
to hit him.

"Try to control yourself," Andrzej begged him. "I know
what you're thinking. There was nothing else I could do,
or Irena either. Now Irena will need your help. It's better
that she doesn't know—not right now. She's her mother."

And he was only the father! "Andrzej, you've got to take
care of it as soon as possible. This child must not be born."

"It's too late. The pregnancy's too far advanced, and

she's too weak. It's possible that she'll have a miscarriage—she's had a lot of fever . . . Sh! Irena's coming."

Andrzej opened the door and helped Irena, who was carrying a tray. She seemed preoccupied as she put it down on the table. Robert wheeled his chair close to her, so that she wouldn't notice anything was wrong. Irena set out three cups, a plate with big slices of bread covered with white cheese, and started pouring the hot tea. She wanted to get back to her daughter, to gaze at Helena's face, if only to persuade herself she wasn't dreaming, that her daughter had been found and was fast asleep in a warm bed.

Her eyes met Andrzej's.

"I'm going to see how things are going in the other room," she said, getting up quickly.

"Stay here," Andrzej said. "I'll go check her pulse."

Robert remembered the Andrzej of yesteryear, the schoolyard with the big tree, and the gang of boys surrounding him. Once again, they were about to beat him up—for no better reasons than that he was a Jew and had red hair. At the end of the yard, another boy stood with clenched fists; it was himself, Robert. Fear had rooted him to the ground; he hadn't dared to move. It was the last day of school; tomorrow, the holidays would begin. Near the tree, some of them rolled on the ground—the fighting had started. Then suddenly he heard Andrzej calling his name. Robert plunged into the fight. All around him were arms and legs; then he and Andrzej were running at top speed along an alley, and between the benches in the park. They came to a stop, winded. There was no sign of the others. In front of them, a woman was pushing a baby carriage and a little boy was throwing pebbles at a swan.

"There were more of them than usual," Andrzej had said.

"Yeah."

Robert had protected him in those days; now it was his

turn. Or was Andrzej simply in love with Irena? They'd lived in the same apartment during 1944, when she hid him.

I don't have the right to ask, Robert told himself. I should have been here to protect my wife and child. Life was much harder for both of them than it was for me. For me, being a prisoner of war meant not having to struggle anymore. But they had to fight day in, day out to eat, to earn a little money, to avoid arrest, to keep believing that someday the Germans would leave and there would be a victory, that somewhere in the West people would find independence again, and freedom.

"Everything all right?" Irena's tone was anxious.

Robert hated himself for suspecting them. Even if they did love each other, he could do nothing but step aside. He was a cripple, incapable of satisfying a woman; Andrzej was useful, a doctor; he could save Helena.

A soft, warm hand closed over his. Robert looked up at a mischievous little smile, dimples, a pair of big shining green eyes, and an unruly mop of blond hair falling over her forehead.

"I love you, Irena," Robert murmured despite himself.

"I love you too—and you'll see, Helena will start getting better tomorrow. Andrzej knows what he's doing. Now that we're all together, something's bound to turn up. There's got to be reconstruction, they're going to need engineers. You're just being impatient. You've only been back home four weeks. I'm so lucky—all my friends are still waiting for news of their men. Till now, I've been thinking of Helena all the time. I was so afraid. Now everything's all right. You know, the wife of the Russian colonel who lives opposite us told me today they're going to try to get a concert hall going as soon as possible. Perhaps I could even give a concert or two."

She leaned forward, threw her arms around Robert's neck, and kissed him.

"We're going to be very happy, darling, now that all three of us are together again."

"All four," murmured Robert, thinking of Andrzej.

Helena was sleeping, her fever gone. Robert and Irena had spent the night in Andrzej's room; Andrzej had temporarily found a corner in the hospital. And Razowa, the splendid woman who had brought Helena back, had given them some panes of glass for the windows.

"You can't leave a sick little girl in a room where there isn't even any daylight, it's not healthy." She had seemed almost embarrassed to be lecturing them.

Robert had redeemed the family by expertly cutting the glass to fit into the window frames.

"Well, well!" Razowa had examined his work. "To look at you, I'd never have guessed you were capable of doing anything with your own two hands. If you like, I can bring you some bits of planking. You could make furniture and even sell it. I know people who'd give us a good price, either in cash or in kind."

"You're fantastic!" Irena told him after the old woman had left. "Not only have we got some sunlight in the house, but we're going to make money too. How did you learn all that, darling?"

Robert could hardly believe his wife's effusiveness. He supposed she was only now discovering him, the husband who once left even the most minor chores in their brand-new villa to the servants.

"Wasn't I the best engineer in my year?" he teased.

The strident noise of the doorbell broke in on them. Irena stood, her eyes wide with fear. How much longer would a simple ring at the door put her into shock?

Robert wheeled his chair over to the door, uncovered the spy hole, then lifted the hook.

"Holy Virgin, Jesus, Mary, it's Master Robert!"

Into the room burst a stocky woman with a happy

expression that lit up her round face. She displayed the
wicker basket beneath her shawl, which she carefully set
on the floor. "Mind the eggs!" Before anyone could stop
her, she threw herself to her knees in front of the wheelchair, seized Robert's hands, and covered them with kisses.

"Magda, how did you—?" Robert began, but she would
not be interrupted.

"It's Master Robert, it's my young master," she said
over and over. "I thought I'd never see you again! When I
used to bring the Old Lady cheese and pickled pork, she
read me your letters from the camp. If only she could
have lived long enough to see you again. But you're home,
and the little lass is home, so everything's all right. Oh,
Master Robert, I'm so happy!"

Robert tried to free his hands, while Irena drew up a
chair. They sat Magda down, relieved her of her shawl,
and brought her a cup of tea.

"That's a city habit! Haven't you anything stronger?"

"A glass of vodka?" suggested Robert.

"Wait, I've brought some of my homemade Wisniak."
Magda hunted through the deep pockets of her wide skirt
and produced a big bottle filled with dark red liquid. They
clinked glasses. Magda emptied hers in one gulp and
resumed her chatter.

"You can't imagine how we used to talk—the Old Lady,
Madam Irena, and I, and the doctor too, when he was
here. Every time I came here with my husband and a
basket, they always wanted to send everything to you. It
was no use my telling them it was little Helena who
needed it, while you were far away—your dear mother
simply wouldn't listen. The Old Lady had a will of her
own. You know that better than I."

Robert watched, moved, as Magda made the sign of the
cross. It was more than four years since he had last seen
the nanny who had protected him against the pedantic
ideas of his father and the constant fears of his mother. It

was Magda who had taken him on walks in the country when he was small; it was Magda's husband who had taught him how to use a fishing rod. He had spent many an hour with Magda in the cowshed as she milked the cows; he had ridden bareback with her children. So many questions came to him, and Magda answered them all.

Her husband had been killed during the war, but her two sons had grown into fine lads. The elder, Jasiu, had been a land worker who drank hard every Sunday. Ready for marriage, he'd never found the right girl and then the Germans had killed him before he ever could, for his work in the resistance. The younger, Wlodek, was a cowherd, and still only a boy.

Magda's three daughters were dead too; again, the Germans were responsible. In the winter of 1944, just after the holidays, they had organized a roundup in Celestynow. It happened in the middle of the night. The girls were home when the Germans came, while Magda, her husband, and the boys were out helping the resistance.

Magda's face revealed grim satisfaction as she recalled her resistance work. She was obviously proud that she had not stayed at home, like other women. She recalled an incident in which she and her husband helped steal a supply of arms that was being sent by train to the Russian front.

"My husband jumped up into the boxcar. The lads took care of the soldiers on guard, then threw everything they could out onto the side of the track. I picked up the heavy cases and carried them to the road, where the horse and cart were waiting. We put the arms on the bottom, buried them under a load of straw—and away we went!"

Suddenly self-conscious, Magda fell silent.

Robert thought of Celestynow, the little station where the Warsaw-Lublin express stopped. The sandy tree-lined road that led to the village, the main street, the church with the inn opposite it, the café next door, and the

bakery where you could buy a hot loaf of bread at four in
the afternoon for your supper. The smell of the pine
forest, the escapades in the woodlands, picking mushrooms,
and the first kiss he had exchanged with Irena under the
treetops.

Magda began talking again. To be sure, the Germans
hadn't managed to tear the trees down, nor had the
Russians. The house was closed because the president of
the local cell of the party had thought fit to requisition it,
while his deputy was doing his best to turn it into a public
library. The furniture, carpets, and everything inside had
all been stolen long ago, but the walls and the roof were in
good shape, and the windows had been boarded up.

Irena looked at Robert, who raised his head, as if feeling
her gaze.

"Is the Warsaw-Lublin express running again?" Irena
asked gently.

"Of course! It has to! With their stinking government in
Lublin, the coaches are crammed. There are people
everywhere, even on the steps leading up to the doors.
They can't get inside, so they stay hanging on outside.
They could fall under the wheels, or get their heads torn
off in the tunnels. But God looks after those who risk their
lives for nothing."

Magda heaved a sigh. "The more things change, the
more they stay the same. During the war, people used to
fight their way onto the trains till they were nearly
smothering. They all wanted to take their stuff to Warsaw.
Without us, the people of Warsaw would have starved.
Now that the Germans have gone, it's the same story.
True, it's brought money to Celestynow. For their food
the peasants have bartered pianos and jewels and books.

"I've bought some pictures," she went on proudly.
"They're so beautiful you can hardly believe they were
painted by human beings. I have a landscape that's the
spitting image of what we can see outside our own

windows—but it was painted in another country. Can you believe that?"

"Listen," said Robert, grasping Irena's hand. "Why don't we send Helena to Celestynow? She'll get fresh air there, space to run around in, and the forest for taking walks. The priest will agree to look after her, and while she's waiting to be accepted for school, he can give her lessons. That will let us organize our life and get ready for when she comes back. What do you think?"

"But she just got here," protested Irena. "She's so sick! She needs care, and Andrzej's right here. How can you ask me to send my baby to Celestynow, where I won't even be able to see her?"

But Magda embraced the idea. "Say yes, Madam Irena, say yes, and I swear you won't regret it," she said. "The little one will have fresh milk to drink every morning; she'll have homemade bread and cream cheese and honey from my own bees, and she'll get her strength back. This year the old apple tree gave me a bigger crop than ever, so I've got apples stored away for the winter, and lots of apple jelly in the larder. Here In Warsaw, you've got nothing. You can't feed a child properly on the little that I bring you."

"It's good of you," said Irena. "But now it's impossible."

Robert was having second thoughts. "I couldn't even come and see her," he murmured sadly. "In my condition, Magda, it's not very easy to make a train journey hanging on outside, on the steps."

"That won't be necessary, Master Robert," Magda protested. "You'll come with me in the cart. Look, while we're talking up here, Czarnula, the black mare, is standing outside in front of your house. She's a good horse, and she pulls well."

"But it would be putting you out, Magda—"

"No, it wouldn't! There will always be a place for you in the cart, both coming and going. And besides, you know

very well I'd love to have you come to my place. I have
plenty of time to look after you, and perhaps later on
you'll be able to walk again. The air's so healthy at
Celestynow, and with God's help we'll get you out of that
wheelchair. Well, Master Robert, what do you say?"

Robert felt moved. It had been years—*thousands* of
years—since anyone had spoken to him like that. Magda
was addressing him and him alone. To Magda he was "the
young master," just as in the old days when his father was
still alive. She'd known him when he could stand upright,
not hunched up in his wheelchair, incapable of managing
without Irena's help. In Magda's eyes, Robert was still a
man.

"Are you going to let me see the little one?" Magda
asked Irena. "Just a peep, that's all. I won't disturb her."

"Of course," Irena replied. "I was just going to look at
her myself. Come along."

The two women tiptoed into Helena's room.

"Water," murmured Helena. "Please, some water . . ."

"Oh, my God!" Irena cried. "How fortunate we came in
when we did, we would never have heard her from the
other room!"

Irena ran to fetch a glass, while Magda stood beside the
table. She fought the urge to stroke the disheveled tresses,
to braid them into a plait at the back of the little head. She
would have liked to repeat the familiar gestures of former
days, but she didn't dare. Helena had changed. This was
no longer the little girl she had known before the uprising,
who used to come to her house at night with other children
of her age to collect arms which they took into Warsaw in
rucksacks. How many times had Magda fixed her hair
before she left? In those days Helena had been like a
young animal sure of its own skill. She would jump onto
the steps of the coach at the last minute, when the train
was already under way, her heavy rucksack on her back.
Her hands clasped around the iron handrail were firm and

strong. Despite the weight of the rucksack, she would keep her balance for hours. She'd get off before Otwock, when the train began to slow down for the station, to avoid the police roundups. Other times, Helena had traveled at night in boxcars, lying down in a corner with her rucksack filled with cartridges. She would sleep peacefully until they reached Warsaw, where the brakeman would arrange for her to get off at the freight yard. The railway crewmen all loved the little girl and her radiant smile. They would stroke her blond hair with their sooty fingers, as though to protect her.

Magda took a step forward, then another, till finally she was sitting on the edge of the bed. She took the blond tresses gently in her hands and began plaiting.

Helena gave a little sigh, and Irena came and moistened her dry lips. How timid she felt in the face of her child's suffering! She hardly dared approach her, as if she were afraid of hurting her or upsetting her. Magda was much more at ease, touching Helena's forehead, patting the pillow to make it more comfortable.

Suddenly Helena cried out, "I've got to get there, I've got to get there, I've got to get there!"

The two women leaned forward. Irena remained silent, while Magda kept talking softly.

"You *have* gotten there, Helena. It's all over, darling. You hear me? It's Magda. It's all over, you're home, you're all safe and warm now."

Calmer, the girl turned onto her side.

"She's got to eat when she comes out of it," Magda murmured. "She's nothing but skin and bones!"

To Irena, her daughter had become a stranger, a heroine. To Magda she was just a child who had been hurt.

In the living room, Robert was wondering how he could convince Irena to accept Magda's offer of hospitality. When Helena's condition became obvious, the shock would be less for her at Celestynow. The peasants would be less scandalized than the townsfolk. Besides, she would be well fed, and at Celestynow they would have all the wood they wanted for their stove.

It was clearly the best solution. But before he could convince Irena of its merit, he would have to tell her about Helena's condition.

Robert buried his face in his hands. Alone, he could weep at last. If only he could fall asleep, forget everything, not have to make decisions.

"Irena," he said as he felt a cool hand stroking his hair, "I've got to talk to you. How's the little one?"

"She's calmed down and gone to sleep. Magda's at her side—she's going to sleep in the big armchair."

"Irena, promise me you won't cry!" said Robert abruptly.

"But, darling, why should I cry? Our little girl's back with us again. We're all together at last. If there are tears in my eyes, they're tears of joy. Darling, why do you look so upset?"

"Irena," said Robert gently, taking her hand, "Helena's pregnant. I'm sorry, my love, but our little girl was raped—by some Russian soldiers, she told Andrzej. He can't perform an abortion because she's too weak and the pregnancy is too far advanced. His advice is that we help her bring this pregnancy to term."

Irena collapsed onto a chair, staring at him with tear-filled eyes.

"You can't be a mother at thirteen," she whispered.

"Your grandmother had her first child when she was sixteen, remember? In the country it happens every day." Robert realized the lameness of his argument.

"But my grandmother was married to a man she loved," said Irena angrily. "Helena was . . . Oh, God! Robert, it can't be!"

Irena hid her face against his shoulder. Suddenly she leapt to her feet and began shouting.

"It's insane! You've all gone crazy! How dare you force a little girl to live through such a monstrosity? I don't want any Soviet bastard in the family. They were probably blind drunk—they usually are. That's no army! They're not men! They destroy everything in their path, they respect nothing. They're a bunch of animals! I won't have my little daughter carry the child of one of those swine. I don't want it! Do something, Robert!"

"Andrzej says it's impossible. Do you want to consult another doctor?"

"Please!" Irena wiped away her tears. "There must be a way. Everything can still be worked out. God will help us." Irena was sobbing like a child, her face buried in her hands.

"God has nothing to do with it." Robert sighed. "We have to find someone to do it—in the safest possible conditions."

"Abortion." Irena spoke as if the word frightened her. "Isn't there some other way? Tablets, injections—I don't know, anything else . . ."

"Darling, it's not as horrible as all that. It's simpler than taking out an appendix."

His words had no effect on Irena. "It's too atrocious," she murmured. "It's too inhuman! I'll fight tooth and nail to get rid of it. My father used to say if you wanted something badly enough, you could do it—and I want this with all my being."

"The little one's just woken up!" Magda announced, bursting into the room. "I'm going to make some tea."

Irena rushed into her daughter's room. Robert struggled with his wheelchair. The effort filled him with a strange satisfaction. Heroism, he considered, lay not in going off to the war, but in staying with his wife and child. And he was ready to do anything to protect them.

2

FREED OF THE winter's snow, the road had turned from white to black. Mud lay everywhere—thick, deep, and heavy with water. The wheels of the carts had cut deep ruts; people's feet sank into them, leaving ragged prints.

Helena lifted her head. She was alone on the road; for once she would not be the target of a curious stare, a half-cynical, half-pitying smile. She had been living in Celestynow since the beginning of the winter, but she was still not used to the constant attention.

Helena shivered slightly as she tried to avoid a puddle by stepping onto a stone. Thrown off balance by her heavy body, she slipped into the cold water, which leaked in through her old boots. Magda washed them every evening, because the mud built up both outside and inside and hardened into a crust which hurt Helena's feet.

How lucky she was to have Magda! Tough and simple, she understood everything without Helena's having to say a word. Mother, Father, and Uncle Andrzej asked questions, pitying her, but Magda was different. She talked to her, but she never forced Helena to talk.

Helena passed the church, its door wide open. Beside it stood a big tree, its trunk scarred with hearts. Magda had explained it to her.

"When you're young and hotheaded, you do forbidden things in the hayfields and in the woods. The girl thinks of the house, the big bed, the linen chest, and the children who will be running around her skirts one day. It's different for the man. He's looking for pleasure, and afterward he forgets. Carving their names on the bark of the tree is a way to increase her hopes of keeping him—especially when the tree's right in front of the church. Tomasz and I did it, and it worked." Helena wondered if her initials would ever appear on the tree. She glanced ruefully at her round abdomen.

Stopping in front of the tree, she found Magda's and Tomasz's initials, worn but still legible. Helena stroked the little heart, around which the bark had swollen up like a scar; then she turned back and went slowly up the wooden steps that led into the church.

The sunlight was dancing on the carefully polished floor, and the pews used by generations of faithful churchgoers stood empty. Light flooded through the plain glass that had replaced the broken stained-glass windows, illuminating the high vault, the walls, and the floor. Helena knelt and crossed herself, then turned and took the passage leading to the presbytery. The priest was waiting for her.

"You're punctual," Father Marianski said, rising to his feet. "Come, get rid of your shawl. I've lit a fire in the stove so you can warm your hands."

Helena thanked him with a nod, and sat down awkwardly. "I'm tired," she said. "It feels so heavy."

"In six weeks it will all be over, and you'll have a lovely baby in your arms. Magda will be happy to help you—and next autumn, you'll be on your way back to school. It doesn't do any good to keep thinking about yourself. There are other things in life. Have you done your homework?

Let's test you. When did King John III Sobieski beat the Turks?"

"On September 12, 1683, at Vienna. The battle was important because the King of Poland had thereby saved Europe from occupation by the barbarians."

"Well done, my dear," he said, smiling at her. "You've just earned a cup of tea."

His tall slim body disappeared through the door at the end of the room. Father Marianski was quite young. He had been appointed to Celestynow barely two years ago, immediately after the Germans had left, and had quickly become popular with the community. He was earnest and dynamic, not afraid of work. He would not hesitate to help an old man repair his barn, or a widow patch up her house. Old parishioners were scandalized when they saw him climbing up ladders in his cassock, or nailing floorboards down, yet it was their shock that shamed the young ones into action. The farmers took turns maintaining the field adjoining the church; they'd repainted the presbytery and repaired the roof. They brought sacks of potatoes, apples, chickens, bacon, and eggs, not only for him, but for the poor as well. They even brought flowers for the altar. During the winter, when there were no flowers, the women had decorated the altar with branches of fir.

Helena considered herself lucky. Father Marianski had found time to give her lessons three times a week, to prepare her for high school. The priest was kind to her and she found the work interesting. During the hours she spent studying, she stopped thinking about herself and the child she was about to have.

I hate this baby, Helena thought. I'd like to die, so that it would never see the light of day. Why am I condemned to carry it?

She went over to the stove in the corner of the room. She hoped her parents didn't come for the weekend. Their stricken faces and Uncle Andrzej's false confidences wore her down. Father Marianski was much franker. A baby was a miracle, he'd said, and the hope of the world, whoever its father or whatever the circumstances of its birth. She hoped he was right.

Father Marianski called out to Helena to open the door for him. He put a wooden tray on his desk and sat down. There were two glasses filled with steaming tea, and big slices of black bread dripping with honey poured over thick layers of cream cheese. Helena sank her teeth into one, feeling a sense of relief. The lump in her throat melted away; all her muscles relaxed. As though reading her thoughts, Father Marianski smiled. "So it's not so bad to be alive, to eat the daily bread the good Lord provides?"

Her mouth full, Helena nodded.

"Nothing like our country bread," the priest added with a laugh. "You see, young lady, we dwell on our woes, but we forget to give thanks for our joys. Prayer is saying thank you to the Almighty for what he gives us and for what we can hope to get from him. I'm sure it was much the same during the period we were studying today, when King John Sobieski conquered the Turks. Those were our country's days of glory."

Helena plucked up her courage and looked the priest full in the face. "You talk to me about glory," she said. "The trouble is, all that disappeared a long time ago. Since then, we've had a hundred years of slavery under Russian, and German, and Austrian occupation. We've had two world wars. Our kings all died long ago, and ordinary men make decisions now. Magda's son Wlodek went to a meeting yesterday. When he came back he said that Marx was right, because thanks to him, the peasants are going to get more land. Magda made a great fuss because Wlodek told me my parents' house is going to be his from now on. I love Wlodek and Magda, but our house looks so sad and abandoned. This winter, someone stole some of our floorboards, and one of the walls of our house has collapsed.

Why do things like that happen? My future isn't King
John Sobieski, it's here and now."

Helena's cheeks went red. Talking that way to a priest
was crazy, and now she was going to lose a friend.

The priest rose and began pacing, then stopped and
turned toward her.

"My dear, history lets us justify the present and sheds
light on it. You want me to talk to you about the realities
of today, and that's much more complicated. The past is a
reality that has been scientifically analyzed and screened.
Today's reality consists of facts deformed by individual
passions and reactions that can't be evaluated on the spot.
Before an event can be dealt with rationally, you need
some sort of perspective. Can you understand that? I
think you do, but you're not willing to accept it. You
believe I'm hiding something from you. That's not true.
I'm giving you these lessons so you'll learn to think and
decide for yourself. The facts are simple enough. First
there was the German occupation, through which you
lived, and the Warsaw uprising, in which you fought on
the barricades with other youngsters. Then came the
surrender, and you were sent to Germany as a prisoner of
war. In January, the Red Army entered Warsaw, while in
other European capitals—Paris, Rome, Brussels, London—
there were Allied armies: British, Americans, Canadians,
and Poles, all fighting under the same command. You
understand?"

"Yes, but after that . . ."

The priest rubbed his forehead. "You know that in the
struggle against Hitler, the Russians became the allies of
the Americans. Well, on February 11, 1945, while you
were a prisoner of war in Germany, Stalin met with President Roosevelt at Yalta, and together with the British,
they decided that Poland would lose part of her territory.
You know that Lvov and Wilno are no longer ours, that
your family's cousins had to leave everything back there

on pain of being sent to Siberia, and that the time when we could speak our own language and pray in our churches has come to an end. In exchange, they gave us some territory which had been 'conquered' from the Germans. And then the West withdrew recognition of the Polish government in exile in London. Since then, world leaders have dealt with the National Union government In Warsaw, which is the one we have now. This is a Communist government. In conformity with the theories of Karl Marx, it seeks to establish class equality. To do that, it must nationalize private property, the land, houses, factories, and banks. And to do that, it must also ignore the Church, or do away with it. Do you understand?"

"No! Are you saying there can't be a church in Celestynow any longer, and that you can't be there when the time for my confinement comes?" Helena's eyes were wide with fear.

"Come, my dear, you know people will never accept such a thing!"

"So we'll have to start fighting again." Helena carefully licked some honey from her fingers. "Organize another resistance—"

"No," Father Marianski said. "The war's over. We have to survive and hold on, and do our best to go on believing. Let me just tell you something important—something you must never forget. When you hear the Church and its priests being run down, when people mock religion, do not believe that God no longer exists. That's all I want you to learn for today and for tomorrow."

He moved over to tend the fire in the stove, turning his back on Helena, as if to say the subject was closed.

"I'm no longer a child," she said slowly. "I know priests have been arrested In Warsaw. Please, Father. You're the only one who explains things to me. How can Poles put Polish priests in jail?"

"It's because of Marx. He was a great philosopher,

probably an honest idealist, but he was wrong. Long before Marx, Christ taught us that the equality of mankind
must be respected. But Marx wanted to impose equality
through a system in which God doesn't exist. Well, God
does exist."

Helena wanted to cry out to him that if God did exist, it
wasn't fair that she should be forced to carry around the
bastard of a drunken soldier, but she held her tongue.
Someday, though, perhaps when she was back In Warsaw,
she would find an answer to that question.

"Now let's get back to work," said Father Marianski,
rubbing his hands. "I'll give you some dictation—a passage taken from Marx himself. Afterward, I'll comment on
it, and you can ask me questions if you want to."

The sun shone into the room, making Helena blink.
Bent over her exercise book, she wrote diligently. Sitting
opposite her, Father Marianski took out a tin of tobacco
and began rolling a cigarette. Helena felt happy. Only one
task faced her here—to learn. The world, her father's
artificial leg, the weight of her unborn child, her past and
her future—none of these mattered now. Her whole being
was concentrated on one goal: not to disappoint the father.
But her moment of peace was shattered by a movement in
her belly, which she could not control.

"Father," Helena murmured, "do you think one day I'm
going to be able to be like everyone else?"

Father Marianski looked at her for a moment in silence.
"You want me to tell you what I really think, don't you?"

"Yes."

"Physically, you're going to be relieved of your burden
before the weather becomes hot, and you'll become as you
were before, tall, slim, graceful, and very pretty—I promise you that. No, don't shake your head! God gave you
beauty, you might as well acknowledge it, the better to
thank him for his gift. Emotionally, Helena—how you
think, how you feel, the way in which you see people and

things—you'll never be like the rest of them. You're very gifted, you're mature beyond your years, and you lived your war years more fully than other children. You will be different, and that's an achievement. You've been through so much already, you'll be strong enough to do whatever you want to do. Have you any idea what you would like to do later on?"

"Yes! I want to become a writer," Helena answered without hesitation.

"Poor girl!" Father Marianski sighed. "It's not an easy job—and in this land of censorship you're bound to find it even harder. But that doesn't matter. You must write, if you really want to. It doesn't matter what you write— stories, poems, plays, romances, novels. Look, write me five pages about Celestynow—in verse or in prose, which- ever you prefer. Describe the village for me, the people, the forests all around—but describe it for me as though I didn't live here."

"When do you want me to have it finished?" Helena's eyes shone with anticipation.

"Let's say by next week's lesson. Now I've got to go read my breviary. Would you like to read a little while you're waiting for Magda?"

"She's not coming to fetch me today. Her legs are hurting her. I can get back by myself."

"I'll go with you part of the way," said the priest. "Then I'll be able to go and see the carpenter's wife, who's very ill."

Giving her no time to argue, he opened the door to the garden. That's a bit unwise of Magda, he thought. In the child's state, and with so many evil tongues in the village, this is no time to let her walk along the road alone.

The priest strode on his way, while Helena followed with her scarf pulled over her head so that her face was hardly visible. In the mornings, she was not afraid to walk the deserted road. But around noon, the village came to life. Even with Magda at her side, she had already had to take to her heels under a volley of insults. Fortunately, the father was with her; no one would dare harm her with him there.

Helena increased her pace, trying in vain to narrow the distance between herself and the priest, who was walking very quickly, despite the mud and the puddles. Deep in his own thoughts, Father Marianski paid little attention to his awkward companion. Suddenly a group of shouting children broke out onto the main road from the mouth of a lane, and Helena stopped to let them go by. The priest strode on, oblivious of what was happening.

"Helena, you look ugly with your big fat belly! Who did it to you, Helena? Who did it to you, you tart?"

One of the boys started chanting at her, and the others took up the refrain. The priest, his cassock swollen by the wind, seemed very far away to Helena. The children thought she was alone. One after another picked up a lump of mud and threw it, mixed with gravel and little pebbles, hitting her shoulders, her head, her face. Helena tried to run, but she couldn't. As one of the larger mudballs caught her in the face, her nose started bleeding, and she could taste the blood, almost sweet, in her mouth. She moved along more quickly, struggling to keep her balance—an ungainly, ludicrous figure, plunging into puddles at every step, the cold water splashing her legs.

Then she saw two men coming from the opposite direction.

"Well, Helena, you little tart, don't you recognize your friends?" one of them asked her. "I used to work for your father in the old days, when he was rich and had his summer house here. I even helped him build the veranda. What he paid us, me and my uncle the carpenter, wasn't enough to buy us a sack of potatoes. Not a good payer, your father, not generous at all!"

Helena moved to the left to avoid the man speaking to

her, but the other one blocked her path. He clapped her on the shoulder in mock-friendly fashion, pushed his face into hers, and said with a laugh, "Well, that little bastard of yours won't be long now!"

Helena put out both hands and tried to push him away. Her scarf fell into the mud. She bent to pick it up, and when she stood up again, she could no longer see the sun—only the mocking faces of the two men leaning over her. Helena was seized with panic. "Father! Father!" she shouted.

The taste of her own blood spurred her on. She ran between the houses, coming out into the railway station, where the midday train was just about to leave. There stood the stationmaster, his bearing proud despite his shabby uniform. Raising his right hand, which held his signaling staff, he looked as though all the power and all the authority in the world lay in his hands.

Helena ran past him, reached the steps of the coach, and pushed in among the people already clinging onto them. Someone swore at her, but friendly hands grabbed her and pulled her inside. The floor of the coach was already in motion as she felt herself swept by the crowd into the narrow corridor.

Father Marianski turned around. Saying his prayers as he walked, he had completely forgotten Helena. Only now did he realize that someone was calling him, and that it was her voice.

"Father! Father!"

It always took him a moment to realize this was how he would be addressed from now on. Tadeusz Marianski was in fact a different man from the one the world saw within the traditional setting of the cassock. At twelve he had been a brilliant but undisciplined student. His family was poor, proud, and rebellious. Tadeusz had decided to become a student, a seeming impossibility, but he had graduated at sixteen with honors and a special commendation from the Ministry of Education. He was the youngest graduate in his year, and one of the few who had paid for his own education by carrying heavy baggage about at the railway station. When he was seventeen he had met Father Marek, a man who accepted every challenge, whose enthusiasm was contagious. Tadeusz became a willing follower. Then came the seminary, the war, the prison camp, work with the young, philosophy, sports—and finally the priesthood. When he was appointed parish priest of Celestynow, he was much too young, too forceful, and too impatient to assume such a responsibility. But the bishop had said to him with a smile, "Our church needs soldiers, and I want priests who are able to fight, to resist pressures, to challenge propaganda and historical materialism."

Beneath the black cassock lay the muscles of a man. A few strides brought Tadeusz Marianski up to the two men about to pursue Helena. A flabbergasted child stood as though rooted to the ground as he watched the spectacle. Never before had Celestynow seen its priest give anyone a sound thrashing.

It was over very quickly. One of the men—the one who had first accosted Helena—found himself flat on his back beneath a tree, while the other was knocked into a puddle, unable to get up again. The child witness, a young boy, took to his heels at top speed.

Surprised by the sudden silence around him, Tadeusz shook the drops of water from his cassock. Running his hands through his hair, he looked around for Helena. She must have run off to Magda's. He'd better hurry there himself to calm her down.

A priest has no right to use his fists in anger, he thought as he hurried along. A priest should use persuasion. Father Marianski could already hear the gossips at work.

It was an effort to return the greetings of passersby. At

the crossroads, he met young Wlodek, Magda's son. Wlodek
had wheat-blond hair, and was too tall and too thin for his
age. With a timidity which bordered on sullenness, he
spoke with his head down and in a low voice. He already
knew what had happened, and he told the father that
Helena had been seen at the station as she jumped aboard
the Warsaw express. How on earth would she manage to
get to her parents' home? Without money, in her condition,
obliged to walk from the station to Saska Kepa? It was too
far. Unless she went to the hospital to find Andrzej . . .

"You know," Wlodek said, "that pair you beat up, Bolek
and Jurek, they're real thugs. They spend their time stealing and drinking. They were the ones who set fire to our
neighbor's barn. He didn't dare denounce them, because
he was afraid of them. The militiamen certainly won't do
anything. The last thing they want is trouble with those
two. Besides, the last time I saw Bolek at the tavern, he
told me he was thinking of joining the militia. You realize,
Father, what that'll mean for all of us here?"

Father Marianski did his best to reassure him, but he
knew that Wlodek was right. Bolek could very well become a militia officer and order the villagers around whenever he felt like it.

"By now all of Celestynow knows you beat up Bolek and
Jurek," Wlodek said, "and all by yourself. Because of you,
they've lost face."

Tadeusz Marianski smiled. "Don't worry. They won't
want to boast about it in the village. And we must never
let a woman be humiliated."

"Yes, Father." Wlodek made off as fast as possible. As
soon as the priest's cassock had disappeared from sight, he
retraced his steps to the tavern, where Bolek and Jurek
were at a corner table drinking vodka; they were the only
people in the gloomy, low-ceilinged room. Bolek, a bulky
man with a pockmarked red face, beckoned to Wlodek to

join them. Jurek, who Wlodek felt looked like a thin and devious rodent, was frowning.

"You know, that priest—" Bolek started.

"Stop going on about that black-skirted bastard," Jurek cut in. "We've got more important things to talk about!"

They had already emptied several glasses, which were littering the table.

"Can you keep a secret?" Jurek asked Wlodek.

"Oh yes!" Wlodek replied anxiously.

"Well, listen. There's been some fighting in the forest not far from here. You know about Bruno, don't you?"

Wlodek nodded. "Bruno and his men are in the People's Army," he said. "They steal and loot whatever they can in the neighborhood. They came from Lublin shortly after the Krauts left. They hardly even know how to speak Polish!"

"Shut up!" Jurek snapped. "Everyone knows it was the Communists who sent them to bleed us white."

"Jurek, you talk too much!" Bolek cut in. He turned to Wlodek. "Bruno and his band attacked some Russian who had a fair amount of loot. This happened last night on the Lublin road, just a few kilometers away. The Russian officers put up a poor defense because it was pitch dark, and they weren't expecting to be ambushed. They're all dead, or as good as. Now Bruno and his men want to get away, and he needs our help."

"Where do they want to go?" Wlodek asked.

"West, into the territory recaptured from the Germans," Bolek said. "It seems they all live like kings over there. Lovely villas, with stocks of vodka in the cellars. A proper paradise, eh? The Germans left with no time to take a single thing with them, so naturally everything is right where it was—just waiting for us."

"Why does Bruno need us?"

"He's got to get hold of some gas. The two of us can't handle it alone, but if you help us, everything'll be fine.

We'll load the drums onto a cart, take 'em to Bruno, and get handsomely paid for them—or maybe we go with him and his group. Get it?"

"Where do you think I'm going to find gas for you?" Wlodek wailed.

"The railway, of course! There are some tank cars standing on the siding at this very moment. Bring Magda's horse and cart and some empty drums. You'll help us take everything to Bruno and his boys. You'll get your share, unless you refuse. Otherwise, that black-skirted bastard priest of yours, your mother, and that stupid little whore that's nearly nine months gone will all be in trouble. I give you my word on that."

Wlodek thought things over in silence. "Okay," he said at last. "Let's get it over with."

A clearing, then another. Then a track that ran to the left, with the fence across the mouth half torn away, and finally the railway line. Jurek and Bolek came to a halt, then separated to search through the bracken.

"Over here!" called Bolek. The tank cars were there. Joining him, Jurek swore as he fiddled with something. Wlodek, straining to see through the darkness of the night, crossed himself.

"Got it! It's running out now," Bolek whispered. "Bring the drums."

How long did it last? Wlodek had no idea. All he would remember later was that his jacket got so soaked that it felt noticeably heavy.

The moon was starting to rise when Jurek began rolling the drums along the rails and signaled to the others to do likewise. The three of them moved along, one behind the other, bent double as they pushed the drums, sweating and swearing under their breaths. Finally they heard a cuckoo call over on their right.

"That's Bruno," said Jurek. "Wlodek, you wait here

with the drums while we go and discuss the details of the deal. We'll be back soon."

Wlodek sat down on the track. The moon was high in the sky. Everything was quiet—then suddenly there was a series of shots that sounded as though they came from an automatic rifle. Silence, and then yet another burst of firing.

Wlodek rolled down the slope at the side of the track, crawled up the other side into the bracken, and dived into the undergrowth. As he lay there on his stomach, he saw several shadowy figures moving about on the track. Cold and frightened, he stayed in his hiding place without moving, holding his breath. Hours passed. The shadows on the railway track had been gone for a long time before Wlodek finally dared to get up. His progress through the forest was slow. Branches snatched at his clothes, scratched his hands and face, and got caught in his hair. He was completely winded when he reached the clearing, but he ran without stopping to the road. The horse and cart were no longer there. Wlodek made his way home on foot, slowly and steadily, so as to give himself as much time as possible to think out a way of explaining to his mother the loss of their only horse and cart.

"Don't move. I want to talk to you."

Father Marianski woke with a start. A man stood in front of him in the darkness.

"If you're hungry, there's still some bread in the kitchen," the priest said quickly. "If you've come here to steal, you can go and hunt for yourself."

"You're a brave man, Father. But I'm not here to take anything. You've just got to hide me, that's all. My men and I have killed some Communists, and they're looking for me."

" 'They'?"

"The Russians. They'll be here any minute."

"All right," said the priest. "Go back to the door, and go along the corridor. You'll find a passage running from the presbytery to the church. Go up into the choir. There's a cupboard in the corner, on the left, where we store the vestments of the children who sing Mass. The cupboard has a double back to it. Just slide the boards to one side, slip in behind, and then slide the boards back."

"Thanks, Father." It was no more than a voice in the shadows, followed by the hush of retreating footsteps. Father Marianski closed his eyes and prayed.

Almost immediately the quiet of the night was shattered. A light danced in the window as men outside ran to and fro, shouting. Father Marianski forced himself to be still until the sounds moved away.

He lay awake until six o'clock, when his alarm went off. He rose and went to the church to check on the intruder. As expected, he was gone.

"They're all dead, Igor."

Jozef's voice was barely audible as he and his companion strode down the path through the forest.

The other man signed to him to be quiet. "Look!" he said. "Will you stop calling me Igor! My name's Janek now."

"Janek," Jozef repeated obediently.

"That's better. Now, where's Bruno?"

"In Warsaw."

"Good. No embarrassing witnesses?"

"Bruno swore there weren't any."

"And that damned priest—did Bruno manage to implicate him?"

"That proved difficult. He didn't want to know anything or hear anything. He told Bruno where he could hide, but he never left his bed. Bruno had to leave at dawn without even having seen him. He's a little embarrassed. Our

Polish priests are tough birds, and not easy to catch." The note of pride in Jozef's voice annoyed Janek.

It was amazing, Janek thought. Jozef was a Jew, and was convinced the Poles had handed his people over to the Germans. Yet he couldn't rid himself of an attachment to the Poles. Was it superstition or childishness? In any event, he was a good fighter, and he followed orders. He was perfect for the job of local militia leader.

"I've been in touch with the chief," he said out loud. "Contrary to what we wanted, there won't be any reprisals. Our orders are that the whole thing is to be kept secret. Can this fellow Bruno keep his mouth shut?"

"Sure," Jozef said. "He's a good Communist. You can trust him with any job you like. He's silent as the grave."

Fine light snow began to fall. "Filthy weather!" Janek said, shaking himself. "I'll leave now. Next time don't make me come down here in such a rush. Instead, you come to Warsaw and meet me outside my office. But do it discreetly—the less we're seen together, the better. Start collecting information on everyone in the village. I want to know what they do, what they think, what they say, and how they might eventually be of use to us. As for the other night—it never happened."

"But the bodies—"

"No one's going to find the bodies, Jozef, because you're going to arrange to get rid of them."

"Bruno's already removed their uniforms and burned them."

"Good—and I'll take care of things should their commanding officer want to know what's happened to them. The equipment, the automatic rifles, the cars—"

"I took the liberty," Jozef stammered, somewhat embarrassed, "of taking what Bruno left. If you agree, I'll say they're a gift from the glorious Soviet Army to our militia detachment, and I'll even ask the priest to bless them. That would be amusing, wouldn't it?"

"Very," said Janek without a shadow of a smile. "Speaking of that priest. He'll soon be getting visits from other blackskirts. Don't interfere, but keep your eyes peeled. I'll see Bruno when I get back to Warsaw, and make my mind up as to what the priest is worth. If we can use him, I'll offer him a job."

"He'll be a valuable agent," Jozef said. "There aren't too many of us, and we've got a lot of work to do!"

"More than you think," Janek agreed. "The army will be withdrawing soon. We'll have to rely solely on our own group and whatever militia force we can organize between now and then."

"There will also be the Polish Army."

Janek nodded his agreement somewhat reluctantly. As an agent of the party, trained by Soviet instructors, he'd learned the Polish troops were not to be trusted. How could one ever tell with these hotheaded Poles? It was no use trying to organize them, train them, threaten them—they were completely unpredictable.

Janek took a bottle from inside his jacket and swallowed a healthy slug of vodka. "Want some?"

Jozef forced himself to drink. He had learned early on to avoid being different. After all, he had just obtained a priceless piece of information. The Soviet Army would soon be leaving the territory of the new Poland. He knew there would be no lack of looting, stealing, and rape along their route. He might as well warn some of the villagers to hide their cattle, poultry, and horses.

Those he warned would be grateful, and it was best to have friends in every camp. Jozef had learned that lesson long ago, when he had left Lvov in a cattle truck. His mother had been with him. But six days later, after they had finally arrived at the forced-labor camp, and the doors had been opened for the first time, she was dead from cold and hunger. He was fifteen years old.

In his early days at the camp, he had learned to fight for

his tiny food ration like an animal, with no thought for others. It didn't take long for him to grasp the situation. The Poles were guilty of political crimes for the simple reason that they lived in Lvov, a Polish town condemned to become Russian. Jozef avoided them and applied himself to the task of learning Russian. Making himself useful, denouncing, when opportunity offered, anyone who deserved to be denounced, he had left the camp six months later for Moscow and the paradise of a student's accommodation.

He would never forget the transformation that school had brought. He and Igor—no, Janek—had been like brothers in those days.

"Don't come with me," said Janek. "It's better that we're not seen together. Long live Stalin!"

"Long live Stalin!" echoed Jozef, trying not to think how much the salute to Stalin reminded him of the Germans' "Heil Hitler!"

If one had to trust a Polish Jew, Janek mused, he supposed Jozef was more to be trusted than anyone else. Of course, he'd never be happy, never satisfied. That was a national characteristic of the Poles. It was thanks to Stalin that the Poles had gotten some German land; but did they appreciate it? Never mind, they would be brought to heel, even if it meant arresting them, shooting them, and sending them to camps.

As Janek disappeared around a bend in the road, Jozef hurried into his office on the village square. Everything seemed in order. Some Russian officers had been assassinated, the resistance men who had killed them had been liquidated, and Bruno—who had played his double role superbly—had managed to come out of it alive.

Yet as he thought back over it all Jozef felt a certain embarrassment. Janek had explained the operation. The Russian officers had dishonored their uniform by talking about news broadcasts from abroad. For the prestige of the army, it was preferable not to charge them formally and bring them to trial. They were to be liquidated as discreetly as possible, but their execution should also be used as a warning to the commandos in the forest, who were behaving quite intolerably. Those who had surrendered to the authorities had been incorporated into the militia, and had become valuable units. But others, like Bruno's group, had dared to revolt. Most were just young lads, out-and-out nationalists, who had wanted to fight against the occupation forces. When the Germans had left, they had turned against their Russian allies. A bunch of good-for-nothing criminals, Jozef had noted, yet he didn't like to think about their corpses, laid out in the bracken, which he had seen while he was helping Bruno collect the arms.

Jozef poured another glass of vodka, then another, until, drunk, he collapsed onto his camp bed. Sometime later, a young militiaman who admired him for the way he inspired fear in the peasants, gently took off Jozef's boots. Throwing a blanket over him, he backed out of the room without making a sound.

3

FREE!
   Helena turned around and around in front of the mirror. So this was what giving birth meant! A sensation of release and renewal. No more back pains, no more cramps in the legs—she was slim again!

Helena spun like a top. Her plain dark skirt clung to her hips; her pale green blouse, with its big pockets, made her shoulders seem broader; and the red tie provided an almost masculine touch. It was the uniform of a young girl who went to school every morning like all the others.

It was wonderful to be able to go to school. No more of the secret classes she had attended during the war; no more of Father Marianski's private lessons. A new life had started. She was no longer singled out, the student in Lieutenant Rygiel's group who learned math in Professor Szymanski's apartment—the depot for underground newspapers.

Being a patriot no longer meant transporting arms on the night trains, and getting good marks in Latin; instead, it meant singing at the top of one's voice, dancing in the school folk-dance ballet, and getting ready for the May Day show.

Helena grabbed her satchel full of books, kissed her parents, and was off.

The ranks formed up in the schoolyard, a red flag floating above their heads in the breeze. After the instructors took their places, the students sang the "Internationale." Then a poem was read over the intercom:

We are building Socialist Poland.
A great country is being born.
All of us are working together.
And everything we do
Is for the glory of the future.

"This poem," the voice announced, "was written by Kazimierz Skola, who has been awarded first prize."

Next month, they'll read mine, thought Helena. It too had been chosen as best poem. Kazimierz smiled at her, interrupting her thoughts. He was very slim, with a long and narrow face, and expressive eyes. He was Helena's best friend; they sat beside each other in class, and were inseparable. She was one of the few students who called him by his nickname, Kazik.

The sun lit up the corridors inside the building. Helena marched along in her file. Left, right, left, right. Her classmates had been chosen for the interdepartmental competition for best behavior, and they wanted to win it.

It was springtime. The school corridors had been decorated with special care, because the end of the school year was near, and official guests would be coming down for the awards ceremony. The best poems that had been read publicly during the year hung on the walls next to each other. There were also some colorful drawings, inspired by various regional art motifs, some songs, and publicity material for the ballets. Helena was featured as soloist: there was her photo in a Kujawy regional costume.

The group entered the classroom. After the usual noise of getting settled, absolute silence filled the room. Today the school director was coming to talk to them about the May Day parade.

At the very moment the bell rang, he opened the door. Zygmunt Wolkonski was a tall slim man, still young, with blond hair, green eyes, and a mischievous smile. All the girls had a crush on him—except Helena.

"He's a proper bastard, that director of yours!" her father had told her. "He was trained in Moscow, and he's more interested in getting you to report on your parents than in supervising your education. Bad enough it's a biased system of propaganda, but their main preoccupation is to produce informers."

Helena had to admit that her father hadn't been completely wrong. When she'd been called in to speak with the director, he had grilled her. Did her parents take her to church every Sunday? Were politics discussed at home? Did her parents get letters from abroad?

She had been careful not to tell the truth—not only in front of the director, but also with her best friend, Kazimierz. His father was a laborer, and had never read a book in his life. Her own faher devoured every written word that fell into his hands—and not because he had lost a leg. Uncle Andrzej had found him an artificial one, and he managed not only to walk like everyone else but also to work again. He made beautiful furniture, and earned enough money to enable Mother to stay at home. That also was something it was better not to talk about. Kazimierz's mother worked, and so did her other friends' mothers. Women who stayed at home were called "bourgeoises." And if people found out about Inka . . .

That little creature Inka. That tiny face creased like an old woman's. Baby Inka. Helena's mother had registered her as her own daughter. Andrzej had organized the delivery, the baby's baptism, the official papers—even an application for her own apartment when Inka turned nineteen.

Since Inka's birth everyone acted happier. Magda boarded the baby in Celestynow, refusing to bring her back to Warsaw on the grounds that there wasn't enough room in the apartment and that the city air wasn't good. Helena's mother looked younger, and her father dressed more sharply. Even Uncle Andrzej seemed more relaxed.

"Helena, to the blackboard!" It was the instructor speaking.

Helena jumped up as if jet-propelled. There she was, in front of all the class, reciting her poem. Then the director pinned a medal on her, and the whole class clapped. It was a red ribbon, neatly tied around a little card on which was written "Special Distinction."

"I have some good news," said the director. "Helena will be responsible for the troupe that will be dancing at Otwock tomorrow. You're excused from class today, Helena, and I'm making a small office available so you can get everything organized."

Flushed with pleasure, Helena thanked him. The students clapped again as she followed the director out of the classroom.

For the past several weeks they had been getting ready for this weekend, when the class would present a performance of folk dances at Otwock as part of the "Country Culture" program. Helena had not known that the great honor of being responsible for the troupe would fall to her. Of course she would have to obey their instructor, who was coming with them; but all the same, she was in charge.

Helena spent the day checking the costumes the boys and girls had made, updating the lists of names, and talking to each of her classmates to make sure everything was going all right. She felt important, grown-up, and loved.

In fact, Helena was very popular. True, the old lady who taught Latin often scolded her because she danced her folk dances better than she declined *rosa*; and the mathematics teacher—who wasn't young either—accused her of "intellectual idleness." Still, she was at the top of her class and her name always appeared on the honors board.

Everyone agreed she was the best dancer, and she was often asked to recite poems at the school shows and commemorative demonstrations. Her reports for good conduct, "community involvement," and "sense of comradeship" amply compensated for her reports for Latin and mathematics.

Happy and pleased with herself, Helena finished and made her way home after seven o'clock. Andrzej, Robert, and Irena were eating when she came in with Kazimierz, who was carrying her books as usual.

Kazimierz kissed Helena's mother.

"My father would like to know," he said, "if the apartment next door is still vacant. He told me to ask you."

A shadow passed across Irena's face, but Andrzej intervened quickly.

"It's never been free," he said. "The Russian colonel and his family have left, but the apartment's been allocated to the hospital by order of the militia and the city."

Kazimierz sighed, disappointed. "In that case, there's nothing we can do."

"I'm afraid not," Andrzej agreed. "I've got a copy of the militia order here. See for yourself."

He took a sheet of paper out of his wallet and insisted that Kazimierz look at it; then he refolded the document very carefully.

Kazimierz's eyes fixed on a piece of meat on the table.

"We've just gotten a little meat from the army pensioners' cooperative," Robert said. "I'd like to give you some for your parents, but that's all that's left, and Helena hasn't eaten yet."

"Well, in that case, another time . . ."

Finally Kazimierz left, bringing a sigh of relief from
Irena. Once the sound of his footsteps had died away
down the passage, Robert exploded.

"Will you stop bringing that informer here!" he shouted
at Helena. "Do you want us to lose that wretched room
next door, so Andrzej has to take your room, and you
come to sleep with us? With this young puppy under our
feet there's no telling what will happen. He's perfectly
capable of telling the party that we're getting food from
capitalist countries, in wonderful parcels that come to us
every day from the United States. That would be enough
to have us thrown into prison, all four of us. Obviously
you couldn't care less about it, because he's got a crush on
you, and you like the way he follows you around."

"Come now!" Irena protested. "Helena's got nothing to
do with it. It's not her fault he won't budge from her side.
Besides, if it weren't Kazimierz, it would be someone
else. They teach them denunciation a lot better than they
teach them Polish grammar. Do you want to stop Helena
from going to school and graduating? Is that what you
want?"

Helena bit her lip. At school, everything was simple,
cheerful, rewarding; here at home there was always tension.
She had hardly started eating before her father began to
talk about Inka.

"The little one's just got her first tooth," he said. "Your
mother and I, and Andrzej too, are going to spend the
weekend at Celestynow. Magda's organized everything.
Of course, you won't be coming with us. There's no such
thing as family life any longer—Mademoiselle's dancing
for the country bumpkins of Otwock. If that's getting an
education, I'm the King of Prussia!"

Helena knew her father. All she had to do was toss her
hair back and look at him in a certain way, and immediately he became gentle.

"Oh, well," he murmured. "You're so young. Don't mind me. I'm just tired."

"What did you do today, Father?"

"Oh, I spent several hours examining bricks the others were collecting, trying to see who could carry the most. It's all part of the salvage drive. We're going to rebuild Warsaw for you, and you'll have a fine city! It's amazing what one can dig out of that heap of ruins. Those prewar materials of ours were all good stuff, to have lasted so long. I have to admit that the Russian soldiers have done good work. If they hadn't cleared away the mines, not only would more lives have been lost, it also would have been impossible to carry out any salvage operations now. Do you know who organized the salvage drive? A former Polish Army colonel. He even managed to get hold of some trucks for us. While we're on the subject, I'm short of strong arms to collect bricks—"

"Oh, Father," Helena cried happily, "I can organize that for you! You'll see, the whole school will turn out to help you. Not this week, because we're already committed, but the following Saturday." At last she had found a way to help her father.

Andrzej bent his head over his plate. What strange times we live in, he thought. They've regimented the young. Their elders realize it but can't do anything about it. In the end they think enthusiasm for orders is good. I suppose it's the only way of surviving in this godforsaken country.

"I'm going to make some coffee," he said. "I'll wait for you on the other side."

"The other side" was the former drawing room, where Helena had slept during the war. It was the big room, so sought after, which the Russian colonel had requisitioned, and which had now become Andrzej's luxurious accommodation. They didn't dare remove the partition to make the three rooms interconnecting, and Andrzej still had to go around outside. But one day it would surely be possible. The main thing was to avoid arousing jealousy, because their official documents, which they had struggled so hard to get, could always be canceled. They had enlisted Magda's help, given an attorney two pieces of furniture made by Robert, and then brought the chief of the militia station a side of pork—but never mind! For the moment, they could enjoy the luxury of having coffee "in the drawing room," as they had done in days gone by. The ritual seemed important to Irena, Robert, and Andrzej. For Helena it was an amusing game.

They would go out into the corridor, as if they were going to pay Uncle Andrzej a formal visit, and later they would come back by the light of a pocket flashlight, a present from Kazimierz. That evening, they stayed together until late into the night, discussing the future of the world, while Helena sat down on the floor and fell asleep.

On Saturday morning Helena gobbled her breakfast and rushed to school. The trucks arrived on time. There was a lot of scuffling and laughter as the students loaded the costumes aboard, and then they were off. It was cold on the decking of the trucks, and their iron sidings were unpadded, but they were something to hold onto in the turns. To keep warm, the students sang at the top of their voices—scout songs, folk songs, everything they could think of.

Squashed between two boys bigger than herself, Helena was happy. There was no way she would have traded this moment to be at Celestynow instead, listening to Inka's babbling. Her father kept telling her it would be different once Inka started talking. "I wasn't interested in you either, when you were a baby. That came later."

Poor Father, he was just deluding himself. That child wasn't *hers*. It had been forced on her, and when she looked at it, her worst memories flooded back. She might as well admit it: she didn't love Inka. In fact she did her best to hide how much she hated the child.

The arrival of the trucks at Otwock was greeted with cheers. The boys and girls got out in front of the community hall, a former movie theater now put to a better use, where they were met by an Agricultural Youth delegation. As director of the troupe, Helena rated a bouquet of red and white carnations. They all sang the "Internationale"; then they unloaded the costumes, put up the backdrop, had a look at the alcoves partitioned off as dressing rooms for the dancers, and prepared a meal amid happy laughter. With tea and cheese sandwiches along a big communal table, they listened to speeches.

The first speech was given by the leader of the Agricultural Youth delegation. Then came the director of their own school; and then the local mayor. The priest hadn't been invited, but only one old teacher noticed his absence.

During a break, Helena remembered the promise she had made her father, and went to see the director. He was much in favor of the brick-gathering project, and he gave her permission to propose it after the show.

"Let your comrades vote by a show of hands," he told her. "I'll contact the appropriate authorities so that you can begin next weekend. I'll give you the details about the site as soon as I get them."

The director was very pleased. As a result of this initiative by one of his school's star pupils, the young and pretty Helena, he was practically certain to win the medal for the best school at the preliminary interregional competitions for "social preparation" and "patriotic behavior."

The first show was at two in the afternoon. The hall was packed. One of the couples made a mistake in the last dance, and instead of passing the other dancers on the left, passed on the right; also, a girl lost her crown of plaited straw. But otherwise everything went perfectly, and the audience applauded warmly. They danced encore after encore, until late into the evening.

Helena—tired, winded, covered with sweat, but beaming happily—got to bed at midnight. It was cold in the barn that was being used as the girls' dormitory, but the hay smelled good. She fell asleep quickly.

The next day, Sunday, there was a matinee, and then they left amid applause, shouts, and songs from the Agricultural Youth members, who ran behind the trucks until they disappeared around a bend in the road.

When she got down from the truck in Warsaw, Helena felt as if she were floating on a cloud.

Robert felt rich. True, his artificial leg wasn't perfect, and he'd had a lot of trouble getting used to it; true, his thigh often gave him a great deal of pain—but he refused to think of it. After all, he was alive, he loved Irena, and he was managing to earn some money. Magda brought them food, so they didn't lack the essentials. In this city raising itself so painfully from its ruins, their meager state of comfort was completely unexpected.

Robert finished sanding part of a tabletop, brushed the dust off his trousers, and decided to take a short rest and smoke a pipe. At that moment there was a knock at the door, and an all-too-familiar anguish overwhelmed him.

"Who's there?

"Militia!"

Despite the cold, Robert felt sweat running down his back. There were two of them, brusque men with angry faces. They came in, looked around, then asked several questions.

"Who lives here?"

"How many of you are there?"

"Where's your wife?"

The elder of the two pulled up the leg of Robert's trousers and examined his artificial leg. Robert, humiliated, plunged his hands deep into his pockets as the man asked him, "Who did that to you, comrade?"

"The Germans," Robert answered, somewhat reluctantly.

"Well, you can walk as far as the militia station," the man shot back. "Here's a summons for tomorrow morning, comrade. Report to office number ten at nine-thirty."

They took their leave. Robert locked the door, slumped down into the solitary armchair, and read the summons, which told him that one Bruno Zadra expected him for interrogation. What had earned him this pleasure? Was it Kazimierz's father, who after a year of representations, untimely visits, and denunciations to the Community Office had been obliged to abandon his hopes for the room next door? To think that Helena still let that boy come for her!

Robert sighed and lit his pipe. His hands trembled. Was he afraid? he wondered.

Yes, he was afraid. Not of death, but of suffering, of prison, of questions that humiliated and degraded. And of being separated from his family again.

Outside in the street, just beneath his windows, stood Razowa, the old woman who had brought Helena back home, ill and half-unconscious, so long ago. Since that day, Irena had given everything she could to the woman.

Razowa was fat and poor, and it hurt her to move about. Gone were the days when "her shop," as she called it, was in operation, and people crowded around the wrecked bus to buy her hot sausage sandwiches. Now Razowa sold newspapers at the corner of the street, clad in her thick jacket and boots stuffed with straw. She was cold, her rheumatism was excruciating, and she was alone.

Disabled as he was, at least Robert could make furniture without having to go outside and shiver for hours on end. And Irena had a man in her bed—a cripple, true enough, but a man just the same—while she herself was

just an old woman left to rot on the shelf. Little Helena
sang at all sorts of parties, the darling of the neighborhood,
while Razowa didn't even know where her children were.
Her sons had not come home from the war.

Razowa hung her head. She wasn't proud of what had
just happened. She had seen the plain-clothes agents coming out of the house, and she knew their visit boded ill for
Robert. She was already beginning to feel remorse. The
whole thing had happened so quickly that she hadn't had
time to think things over. Despite all the meetings she
went to—in warm halls, where she didn't have to shiver
for a few hours—she never heard any news of her children
or found a better job. But at one of the party meetings
everybody had been asked to give the names of people
who could be regarded as suspects. Those who complied
with the request were promised rewards: their names in a
special register, a little money—the kind of favor that
could make a big difference in a sick old woman's life. She
had reported Robert and his wife, because they were the
first people she had remembered that evening.

Razowa went along the Paryska Street sidewalk hugging
the wall as though trying to hide. She preferred to be
close to the houses, so she could lean against them when
her knees gave way beneath her. She was afraid of falling
and not being able to get up again. She had dreams in
which she was lying on the ground and the passersby were
stepping around her without responding to her cries for
help. Razowa took these dreams as a warning from God;
she was sure they would turn into reality. She knew how
to interpret dreams. A nurse meant serious worries and a
sickness in the family; a black cat, an imminent death.
And a black cat was precisely what she'd dreamed of the
previous night.

Razowa reached her door and went slowly up the
staircase, holding onto the rail. Once she was alone in her
little room, she lit a candle and looked at herself in the

mirror that hung over the sink. Wrinkles, rheumy eyes, a
twisted mouth, dirty gray hair—was that evil, sinister old
woman her? She stared until the features reflected in the
mirror blurred; then she sat down on her bed, took her
money from the pocket of her apron, and counted it.

Should I keep quiet, or should I tell him? Robert weighed
the pros and cons as he sat with Irena and Helena at the
breakfast table, drinking tea. When Andrzej burst into the
room and bade them a resounding good morning, Robert
pulled him into Helena's room and blurted out his news.

"If I don't come back from the militia station, you must
look after my two women. Promise me?"

"I promise," Andrzej agreed. "Didn't I do just that
during the war? Off you go now—you'll be back! You can
tell me everything this evening. We'll decide what to do."

"That's right." Robert spoke quietly, but the fear was
still there, lurking deep inside him.

"What's more, I'll come with you," Andrzej decided.
"It's on my way."

They left together, with a parting joke for Irena, who
promised them a good dinner that evening; but once in
the street, they fell silent. In front of the militia station,
Andrzej gripped Robert's arm. "Don't forget to speak
slowly," he murmured. "That will give you time to think.
See you this evening!"

Everything was gray: the staircase, the corridor, the
walls, even the faces of those standing in line. There were
a lot of people waiting: old and young, girls and boys,
women, and an ancient man whose body trembled as he
leaned on his stick, bent over nearly double and looking
ready to fall at any moment. No one spoke. Heads bent,
eyes riveted to the ground, they all looked as though they
possessed secrets they were afraid they might divulge by a
glance or a gesture. Robert tried to stir them up.

"Good morning!" he said in a loud voice. "Are they giving out numbers, or do we just have to wait our turn?"

The silence weighed so heavily that Robert could not bring himself to repeat the question.

Farther along the corridor, four doors opened from time to time. A name was called out from inside, someone appeared out of the grayness, then the door shut behind him. There must be another exit, since none of them ever came back; or perhaps . . . No, they weren't being killed; the others would have heard the noise. Were they being arrested and taken to the cells by a staircase running down toward a cellar, perhaps? Were they being finished off down in that cellar? Robert shook himself. This was ridiculous. The Gestapo had left, and it was inconceivable that the Polish militia were using the same methods on their fellow Poles. They were compatriots, after all.

It was after midday before his name was called. Robert's leg hurt atrociously, but the pain made him forget his fear.

He went into a small office. Behind the desk, a man was sitting in an armchair with his back to the window, which was covered with a makeshift grating. Robert leaned with both hands on the back of the chair in front of the desk.

"Your name?" The voice was neutral. He was a fairly young man, with curly brown hair, black eyes, and a sensual mouth.

Robert decided to brazen it out. "You're not in the militia, are you, comrade?" he asked.

"I am your referent, my name is Bruno, and I have some questions to ask you."

His tone was less abrupt. One point gained.

"May I sit down?" Robert asked. "I have an artificial leg."

"Well, it's not usual, but in your case . . ." Bruno muttered.

Robert let himself down onto the chair. As the pain in

his leg receded, his fear returned. He strove to speak slowly and to avoid mentioning names. That was the way they worked—they demanded names, then used them against others.

Andrzej had explained it to him. "Mentioning names is informing, without meaning to. It's betraying innocent people." He told him about a patient in the hospital, who had had both his jaws broken, and multiple bruises; in spite of his injuries, he had managed to get to the emergency ward in the middle of the night. No sooner had his wounds been cleaned and dressed than he disappeared down the lane at the back of the hospital. Twenty minutes later, secret-police agents came looking for him. Robert wondered if he, too, would have the strength to get himself to the hospital if they beat him up.

"You know that you must tell the truth," Bruno warned him. "So you were in the Fallingbostel prisoner-of-war camp?"

"Yes, that's right."

"Who were the officers who were there with you? Give me their names."

"I don't remember their surnames, just a few first names."

"Tell me them slowly, so that I can write them down."

Robert invented some names and recited them like a litany.

"There were also prisoners of other nationalities in that camp. What nationalities were there?"

"Americans, British, French, and Russians."

"Whom did you know among them, comrade? Give me some names."

Robert explained that the different nationalities had been separated by barbed-wire fences and that no communication had been permitted among the various groups.

"That's a lie!" Bruno was suddenly shouting. "You escaped, and you weren't alone. That was where you arranged your contacts with foreign countries, which you're still keeping up. Come on, admit it!"

He was hitting the desk with his hand. Robert realized that if he kept it up he would hurt himself; the thought helped him stay calm.

"I escaped alone. Nobody helped me. Unfortunately, I didn't get very far. The sentry shot me, and I woke up in the hospital, where they amputated my leg. I've answered all these questions already, when I was interrogated by a Russian officer after the liberation."

"Ah!" Bruno was calmer now. "So let's go right back to the beginning. When did you arrive at Fallingbostel?"

The man questioned him over and over. Robert answered carefully each time the same question was put to him. Bruno, half-asleep, scribbled on the sheet of paper, only occasionally looking up. Suddenly he stood up.

"We've talked enough!" he said. "I want you to meet someone." He rang the bell on his desk, and immediately a militiaman came in through a door at the back of the room.

So I was right, these offices do have two doors, Robert thought. One to come in, and one to go out—but go out where?

"Bring in the other one," Bruno said, "and be quick about it. There are people waiting."

Minutes passed. Bruno lit a cigarette. Robert reached into his pocket, took out his pipe, and filled it carefully. If Bruno stopped him from smoking, he would not let it pass. As long as he wasn't formally accused of any crime, they were equals; still, his hands were trembling.

A guard came into the room with Father Marianski. The priest's cassock was torn in several places. There were long scratches on his face, and his left eye was puffed up in an ugly bruise. Robert got to his feet, horror-stricken.

"You have no right to do this!" he cried. "We're citizens

of the Polish People's Republic—not of a country occupied by the Gestapo!"

No longer afraid, Robert seethed with indignation. Facing Bruno, he was once again the Polish officer who had fought for liberty on horseback against the German tanks. A blush rose from Bruno's stolid features.

"We only have communal cells," he said. "The prisoners can't always be controlled, I'm afraid. The answer is not to find oneself inside them. But when one commits reprehensible acts—"

"Reprehensible acts?" Robert interrupted. "But I know Father Marianski well. He's incapable of what you say."

"Watch it, comrade," Bruno said. "Our priest here has been preaching some real capitalist propaganda."

"He tells the truth," Robert said.

"Well, now! Not all scientific truth is fit to be disclosed to simple people. At their level, it becomes propaganda. Sit down, priest!" Bruno pushed his armchair over to Father Marianski and settled himself nonchalantly on the desk, with his legs dangling in the air. "Evidently you know each other, eh?"

"I have the honor of knowing Father Marianski. I am indebted to him for spiritual aid beyond all price, and I cannot conceive how he could possibly be detained in one of my country's prisons." Robert spoke slowly and deliberately.

"All right," Bruno declared. "You may go, comrade. I expect you here tomorrow at the same time." He consulted a sheet of paper on his desk as though giving the appointment serious thought. "No, not tomorrow. Next Monday. I'm too busy this week."

Robert hesitated, but Father Marianski shook his head, as though to caution him against resisting. As Robert left, heads turned, and the people waiting in the corridor followed him with their eyes. His artificial leg sounded sinister to his own ears.

*   *   *

In his little office, Bruno stared at the priest, wondering if Father Marianski would remember where he had heard Bruno's voice before. This holy man took me in like a friend in the middle of the night, but I have to torture him, Bruno thought. One of the beauties of the regime I longed to build. Dammit all to hell.

"I'm distressed about what happened in the cells last night," he said aloud. "But I've got some good news for you. From now on you'll be confined alone. I've managed to find a corner for you."

Tadeusz Marianski bent his head, hiding his joy. Alone! No more nightmare of a dormitory crammed so full that people had to sleep on the floor, squashed up against each other. No more fighting to protect the young lad who had been cornered by a group of prisoners, wild beasts with rape in mind. He had defended the lad with his bare fists until the noise had made the guards turn the lights on. The assailants had fallen back then, more because of the sight of his cassock than because of the strength of his muscles.

I have no right to accept this favor, he told himself. If I abandon that youth, he'll be turned into a beast like the others, because he'll have no other way of surviving in this filthy world.

As though he read the priest's thoughts, Bruno cut in coldly, "Don't argue—the decision has been made. Besides, the lad won't need your help anymore, he's been released."

This time Father Marianski couldn't hide his reaction. His relief seemed to bring out Bruno's spitefulness. To put an end to the priest's joy, he confided, "That young man's learned his lesson. At noon today he agreed to work as an informer."

The shock on the priest's face was too much for him; Bruno jumped to his feet and began pacing so he could keep his back to the other man.

"Now I want you to think things over. You're going to
be alone in your cell, and you'll have all the time in the
world. You must understand that the Polish tradition no
longer has anything to do with the needs of today. We
want to ask worthwhile people—people like you—to help
bring our customs up-to-date. It's stupid to expect our
people, tragically impoverished by the war, to support a
clergy which on the whole is completely unproductive.
We no longer want you to do any teaching, but you can
make yourselves useful just the same. Certain reforms will
have to be accepted, like marriage for the clergy, a more
civic concept of religion, turning the churches into halls
for party meetings. Think it over. If you could give me
some suggestions along these lines, who knows? You might
even become a cardinal. Other priests have accepted our
proposals. Why shouldn't you? I'll see you later this week.
For now, you can go and rest in the infirmary."

Bruno called the guard, who led the priest away. Then
the referent went over to the window and pulled the
drapes aside. Some workmen were busy in the inner
courtyard, fixing lengths of salvaged rail into the walls.
Similar work had been carried out at the prison. The rails
would be used as gallows from which to hang rebels, so
that all the prisoners could see them. The execution of just
one priest would be enough to persuade Father Marianski.
No matter how young and stubborn, he would give in. It
was merely a question of time. Yet somehow Bruno hoped
that Father Marianski would be able to hold out.

If this goes on, I'll end up swinging at the end of a rope
instead of him, Bruno told himself as he called a young
woman into his office. I'm worn out, that's all. I work too
hard.

"Come back tomorrow!" he shouted at the woman. Then
he regained control of himself, went out into the corridor,
and told them all to leave.

*   *   *

It was unbelievable. Helena looked first at her mother, then at her father. It was bad enough for her father to have to see the referent, and to meet Father Marianski there with his face all battered. But why was *she* summoned to an interview with the referent on the following day? How was she going to explain her absence from school at the very time she was to read her poem on the glorious and victorious Polish socialism? Would they remove her from the upcoming school play because she'd had to go and see the referent at the militia station?

"Yes," Irena agreed, "it's better that this doesn't get around at school. Andrzej will give you a medical excuse."

While they awaited Andrzej's return in somber silence, Magda arrived unexpectedly.

Irena made her a bowl of soup, while Helena unpacked the basket Magda had brought. She was almost cheerful as she saw the eggs, country bread, and piece of pork. There were even some potatoes—a veritable treasure trove. Robert told her about his interview with the referent.

"What was the fellow's name?" asked Magda in a quiet voice.

"There was a sign on the door, but I can only remember the first name," Robert said, rubbing his forehead. "Bruno something."

A gleam came into Magda's eyes. She listened without further questions; then she took a good look at the summons the agents had left for Helena.

With Magda there, everything seemed less sinister, as though her red cheeks, her baskets of food, and her hearty voice had the power to exorcise the threats that were weighing so heavily upon them. They ate, drank tea, and chatted. At ten o'clock they snuffed out the candles. Magda slept with Helena, who snuggled up against her instinctively.

"Maybe it's a mistake," she said as she dropped off to sleep.

"Don't worry, dear," Magda murmured. "I'm going to
go and see this Bruno, and there's a good chance he'll
decide to change his tune. Old Magda can do everything,
you know—just like the sorcerers!" Her rough fingers
stroked the blond locks, but Helena was asleep and didn't
notice.

"So, you were in the Warsaw uprising," Bruno said
slowly. "Who gave you your orders?"

"My leader."

"What was his name? How is it that you don't know it?
Well, his code name, then?"

"Rygiel."

"Do you know who he was? Another lackey for the
capitalists. This is exactly why we had to put the Home
Army into prison—because you all refuse to give us any
names. If you continue not to remember, I'm going to
have to keep you, just like the others."

Helena swallowed. She wasn't about to give any names.
When her parents had talked about the arrests of Poles
who—like herself—had fought on the barricades, she had
thought they were being paranoid. Now she realized they
were right. She was suddenly glad she had kept their
conversation to herself. No one—not her best friend, Kazik,
or her teachers—had ever gotten her to talk about her
family. She had learned to deflect their questions by talking about other things, like Uncle Andrzej's work at the
hospital, her father's disability, her mother's involvement
with her music.

It hadn't been easy. She had often yearned to be able to
speak as freely as her friends, repeating conversations
overheard at home or in the neighborhood. Such reports
had earned them strong commendations.

Even the school's director, after summoning her to his
office on the pretext of settling the details of a forthcoming
artistic display, had failed to get any information out of

her. If she talked, they would find out that she had a child; it was better to tell them nothing.

Bruno fixed her with a stare, drumming his fingers on the desk. Suddenly he stood and began shouting. "I know how to bring you to heel! How would you like to be thrown out of school? You'll never graduate, much less go to university. Of course, you'll be barred from all college activities—the dancing group, the choir." He leaned close to her, and she felt his breath against her cheek.

Helena felt as though she had been transported into the past, to the days when the Gestapo were all over Warsaw in their black cars. Frozen with fear, she was helpless to respond.

A militiaman entered the room and whispered something in Bruno's ear. Bruno regained his calm, smiled, and ordered Helena out.

"We shall meet again," he said. "Till then, I advise you to think things over."

Helena left quickly. Once out in the street, she broke into a run, desperate to get back to the orderly world of her studies.

Bruno turned to the militiaman. "Bring the old dame with her spring chickens in here. I want to know if there's any way I can get presents like that more often!"

The militiaman pushed open the door at the back of the room. Magda walked in, wrapped in her peasant shawl, her head held high, her boots thumping with every step.

"Well, my dear," Bruno greeted her with a smile, "it's good of you to come and visit us."

"Get him out of here." Magda pointed at the militiaman. "I want to be alone with you."

"Off you go!" said Bruno.

The militiaman disappeared behind the door. Magda made sure it was closed; then she turned to Bruno and murmured, "Some Russian officers were killed at Celesty-now, and I've got an eyewitness hidden away in a safe place, ready to testify that you were involved. You interested? Before they went to fetch you your gas, Bolek and Jurek spilled the beans, and . . ."

As Magda went on, Bruno's face grew pale. He gripped the edge of his desk to hide the trembling of his hands. The old witch wasn't lying—her information was too accurate for her to be making the story up.

"You come from Celestynow," he hissed at her. "You could easily have a little *accident*, you know."

"Of course." Magda stepped back. "A fire in my barn, animals suddenly dying, chickens disappearing—I know all about those things. I could also have a nasty fall in my bedroom and never get up again. But old Magda has her secrets—I have ways of pursuing you long after my own death. If you think you're smarter than I am, you'll find out otherwise. Your bosses will have your hide, and fast. Your own boys know all too well how to take care of you, you and that Igor who calls himself Janek!"

Bruno went over to the back door and opened it abruptly to make sure no indiscreet ear was pressed against the other side.

"You haven't told *him*, have you?" he asked anxiously.

"If it's a choice between foreign swine and local swine, I'll take the local bunch—and that's you!"

"What do you want from me?"

"Not much."

"Some land? You're welcome to it if you want—your neighbor's, and also the Stanowskis' old house, and a bit of money. That suit you?"

"No," said Magda slowly. "You're going to set Father Marianski free. And you're going to write a letter for me about Robert Stanowski, and another one about his daughter, saying you don't want anything more from them. A certificate of good citizenship, you might say, for them. Write them here and now in front of me. Then tell your assistant to fetch the priest, and we'll all go home together. It's that simple!"

"I can't."

"Why not?"

"The prison's too far away. We'd have to wait for the car to fetch that wretched priest of yours, and it'll take too long."

"I can wait all day."

"So you can tell the priest how you wangled everything? Never!"

"I'll be as silent as the grave. You have my word—and you know you can believe me."

Bruno thought for a moment. Father Marianski was very ill. He was in the infirmary, delirious, with a high fever. Bruno could free him, saying he didn't want trouble at Celestynow. There was a good chance that he'd die soon anyway after he was back at the presbytery—which would be much better than having to explain his death here at the prison. As far as Robert Stanowski and his daughter were concerned, too bad for that old witch Razowa. It was none of an informer's business what happened to the people she turned in.

"Okay, you win," said Bruno, taking a sheet of paper from the drawer. The only sound in the room was the scratching of his pen. Bruno filled out two forms, checked the spelling of the names, signed them, and then raised his head.

"Go now, Magda. Your priest will be at the presbytery this evening—and if he dies, it'll be your fault. He's got pneumonia, I believe, and moving him is likely to finish him off."

"If Father Marianski dies, he'll go straight to heaven," Magda said. "Unlike you. You'd better worry about not getting yourself killed, because you'll go straight to hell, and stay there till the end of time. Now, you just listen to me, my lad. If Father Marianski isn't at the presbytery by nightfall, I'll go straight to that Igor of yours and—"

Bruno silenced her and rang the bell.

"Deliver these two envelopes immediately," he ordered the detective who appeared.

The man curiously eyed first Bruno, then Magda.

"Get on with it!" Bruno ordered; then he picked up the telephone.

"Hello! Is that the infirmary? You're still holding that man Tadeusz Marianski?" He barked further orders, then hung up and looked at Magda. He felt a certain admiration for the old woman opposite him. "You're not rich," he said. "You could have done better by selling what you know. Why are you so keen on saving these imbeciles?"

"That's not your business—it's mine," Magda replied, getting up. "Anyway, don't worry. Magda's never cheated anyone in her whole life, and she's not going to start now. You can trust me. One word of advice, though. If you don't want to fry in hell for all eternity, try not to torture the honest folk you drag to your office. Sooner or later your bosses will look after you in their own way. All right, I'm off now."

Bruno shut the door behind Magda and sat in silence.

"Giddy-up!"

Magda urged her horse on as Andrzej sat silent by her side. She had dragged him from the hospital, and he had left by the back door, scribbling a note to his nurse to say he was sick. It was the first time something like this had happened to him, but after all, he had the right to feel ill, just like anyone else.

Andrzej was actually pleased with this unexpected trip to Celestynow. The collusion with Magda reminded him of the resistance and the war. He knew he could speak freely with her, for she would grasp his situation better than Robert or Irena would.

"I've got problems," he began, turning up the collar of his jacket to protect himself against the cold. "It seems there's some talk of removing the right to practice from all doctors of Jewish origin. You understand, don't you, Magda? That was why you hid me during the war, that was why I did all those operations over the years, scared stiff the poor wretches might develop gangrene. Remember the time I took a bullet out of that young man's thigh on your kitchen table? We disinfected it with your homemade liquor. I spent the next three days wondering whether I ought to have amputated it or not, but God was generous to him—and to us. The boy came out of it like a champion."

"Who told you doctors aren't going to be allowed to practice?"

"A colleague, a reliable man. It seems the regulation's just about to be approved by the party."

"What are you going to do?"

"Protest, of course. What else can I do? My friend advises me not to wait, but to go and work as a volunteer in the 'reconquered areas.' They're short of doctors over there, according to him, and they'll leave me in peace."

"Well, they're short of doctors everywhere. In your place, I wouldn't go. All you have to do is say it's wrong, you're not of Jewish origin, it's just a piece of slander, and you can produce witnesses to prove it."

"Where am I going to find these witnesses?"

"At Celestynow. The chief of the militia himself will be only too pleased to declare you're not a Jew. Trust me!"

"It's not a bad idea," said Andrzej, "but it revolts me to resort to lying."

"What must be, must be," replied Magda. "That's the way life is for us: truth is a luxury."

The cart bumped along the rough road. To the right lay woodland with pretty villas tucked away here and there among the trees. On the left, big snowbanks separated the road from the railway line.

"We're nearly at Otwock already," Magda exclaimed. "With you to talk to, the time passes very quickly. We'll be home before nightfall."

Andrzej agreed. "Your mare may be old, but she's in fine fettle. Do you remember how many times we did this road together, with cases of grenades hidden under the straw? You know, if anyone had told me then that you and I would find ourselves recalling the war in this somewhat nostalgic fashion, I'd have burst out laughing."

Otwock came into view, and soon they passed the railway station.

"When are you going to tell me the name of this precious patient of yours?"

Magda looked at Andrzej with a smile. "Good Lord, I'm not going to tell you anything! It's like the old days. No one must know anything in advance, so there's nothing to confess if one gets arrested."

"You're just as obstinate as you always were," Andrzej said. But he knew she was right.

They reached Celestynow as evening was setting in. The horse stopped in front of the presbytery, as if it knew their destination.

"Aren't we going to your place?" Andrzej asked in surprise.

"Later," Magda answered. Despite her outer calm, she was filled with fear. Would Bruno keep his word?

They entered the presbytery, which seemed dark and sinister. They fell silent, as ill-at-ease as thieves breaking into an unknown house.

God Almighty, grant that the priest has arrived, and that we can save him, Magda prayed. Grant that next Sunday he says Mass in this empty church. Please, God . . .

But the priest was not in his quarters.

Night fell. Andrzej slept on Father Marianski's bed. Magda sat near the window telling her beads until her eyes closed and her head dropped to the table, her two arms stretched along the bare wood.

After midnight, a car drew up in front of the gate. Its headlights shone into the windows. Magda woke with a start and ran into the garden, where she stumbled over the body of Tadeusz Marianski.

It was Sunday. After weeks of silence the bells at Celestynow were ringing, for noonday High Mass. People flocked in from all around, bringing their children, their elderly, even their babes in arms.

Today was a great occasion. The road had been cleared; since dawn, men wielding big brooms fashioned out of branches tied together had been clearing the water from the ruts. The women had decorated the altar with fir— there were no flowers in season—and waxed the floor of the church.

When Father Marianski arrived to celebrate the Mass, the crowd was so large that the big doors had to be left open for the people crowding outside to hear him. As they knelt on the steps, and down to the edge of the road, some of them exchanged conspiratorial smiles. News had spread by word of mouth. The priest, their priest, had been arrested, and beaten—but he hadn't given in. Like them, he was tough, resistant, and brave. Magda had brought the doctor from Warsaw, that Andrzej Rybicki, a man who knew his trade, and Father Marianski had recovered. It was a fine story for long winter evenings.

Jozef, the local militia chief, was there, right by the big doors. He had come, not to pray, but to be seen. It was no use having a title, or a revolver on his belt; they wouldn't mean a thing if he behaved differently from everyone else. All the militiamen were there, with their wives. This evening, perhaps, they would have to arrest someone or beat a man up without knowing why, but for the moment

the Sunday truce was in effect, the priest was back, and
Mass was being celebrated.

In front of the altar Tadeusz Marianski was deeply moved.

"I have not deserted you," he said. "I was taken away.
Now, with God's help, I am back among you again. Thank
you for everything you have done for me. I promise you
that Celestynow's church will never again stay silent. Next
time, another priest will come to replace me."

A low murmur rose from the crowd, swelling up toward
the altar; then everything was still. After Communion, the
parishioners broke into the old hymn to the glory of God
and country: "O God, you who for so many centuries
have protected Poland . . ."

Toward the end of this hymn there was a passage in
which two key words had been changed since 1945. Today,
instead of singing "deign to preserve for us the freedom of
our country," as the party insisted, the congregation sang
"deign to return to us the freedom of our country," as they
had done during the war and in the days of old when
Poland was divided among the Prussians, the Russians,
and the Austrians.

I'll have to put this in my report, Jozef said to himself.
Nevertheless, thinking of his boss, Janek, he felt a sense of
satisfaction and revenge as he sang along with the crowd.

4

IRENA LOOKED AT herself in the little mirror in the hall-
way. In her mind she could hear Robert's voice: *You
haven't changed. You're just as beautiful as ever.*

Since he had come back, Irena was no longer afraid of
her reflection. Her life was so full, so busy, it was as if she
had stopped growing old. True, she would never be a
great concert pianist, as she had wanted to be as a young
girl, studying at the conservatory.

She remembered being asked to play in Lille, France.
Irena had been nineteen but she remembered the trip as
if it were yesterday. Her mother's friends had felt that a
young girl's place was to stay at home and wait for a
husband. But she had gone—with a chaperon, of course.
How lucky Helena was to be able to come and go as she
pleased.

The trouble was, Helena preferred folk dancing and
writing bad poems on the great role of the party, to
playing the piano. Her last poem, a tribute to Bierut, the
chief of state, had made Robert so furious he wanted to
tear it up, but Irena wouldn't let him.

It had become known at the school that Helena had

been summoned to the referent. In order to prove her loyalty to the party, she was writing reams of patriotic verse.

Irena sighed. What distressed her most was Helena's indifference toward Inka. The little darling—now three years old—was so pretty, so clever, and so lively. Irena looked forward to the coming Sunday as if it were a present. Robert was taking them to Celestynow. She would have Inka's chubby little arms around her neck, and she would smother her with kisses. Inka had become almost a daughter to her. As time passed, she even found herself growing closer to Inka than to Helena.

Last week Irena had given a concert for the benefit of veterans. It was wonderful to find herself once again on a stage with the black hole of the concert hall lying at her feet.

"Why won't you play at the party festival?" Helena had asked her the next day. "You play so beautifully!"

Her daughter's naive admiration was touching, but Irena had found the question stupid. "I love music," she had replied, "but I don't want to mix it with politics."

Helena's silence had been a kind of condemnation. Irena wondered if the girl was still pouting about a similar recent incident. Zygmunt Wolkonski, the director of Helena's school—Andrzej said that the Russians had brought him along in their baggage to teach Polish children their "Marxist catechism"—had asked Irena to organize a cultural performance to be given in honor of Soviet students who had been invited over for the month of May. Irena had refused, saying she couldn't leave her invalid husband alone.

Communism, capitalism, Russian ascendancy—she didn't really care about any of them. As long as she and Robert were together, Magda managed to feed them, Helena brought home good grades, and Inka didn't fall ill, everything was fine. Her shoes might leak, her one pair of stockings might need mending every week, but she was content with what she had.

"Doesn't it mean anything to you that our elections are rigged," Robert would say, "that people are being arrested and left to rot in prison, that the Communists do exactly as they please, that we're all at the mercy of a bunch of despots?"

Irena tried to calm him down with kisses.

"This fellow Jakob Berman's trying to convert us!" said Andrzej angrily. "That 'man from Moscow' decides what we have the right to know and to think. We're becoming a nation of slaves!"

Irena was too happy to take him seriously. She rummaged in the kitchen cupboard and found a piece of dry bread to nibble; then she began getting dinner ready. Some carrots, three potatoes, and a bit of herring: a real feast! Once the meal was on the table, Robert would call her a miracle worker.

"Hi, I'm home early!" Helena came in. "And I've brought something!" She reached into her satchel and produced a piece of salt pork and some bread. "A present from Kazimierz," she announced. "It's my reward for the Polish homework I did for him."

"You mustn't accept presents from boys," Irena protested, for form's sake.

"It's not a present, it's payment for a debt," Helena teased. "Without me, Kazik would never get by!"

"Helena, we're going to Celestynow tomorrow, you know, and I'd love you to . . ."

The smile vanished from Helena's face. "You and Father go. I'm busy."

"You can't stay here alone."

"I'll be at school, and I won't be home till late, because we've got to get everything ready for decorating the classrooms."

"Don't you want to see your little sister?"

It was the first time since the baptism that Irena had spoken of Inka as her own daughter.

"My little sister," Helena said slowly, "will get along very well without me. I've things to do elsewhere."

Robert and Andrzej came in, looking happy. They had just come from a celebration for a house they'd helped put back in shape. The family, now able to move back into the second floor, had provided vodka for the teams of volunteers who had been involved.

"Good news," Andrzej announced. "I'm going to Cracow tomorrow, and I've got room for a certain young lady named Helena in the hospital van. It seems my specialized knowledge is needed to examine some patients over there. Want to come, Helena?"

"Oh yes! But I promised Kazik—"

"Sold!" Andrzej laughed. "There'll be a place for him too—if he can keep his mouth shut. It *could* turn out to be serious, something contagious—who knows? It'll be like Magda's last trick, when she refused to tell me who I was going to examine until the minute I laid eyes on Father Marianski."

Irena sat the table silently and efficiently, keeping an eye all the while on the potatoes that were cooking on the makeshift stove.

"Attention, everyone!" Robert announced, sitting in their one armchair. "We have a new marshal. No doubt about it, the Russians are our lords and masters now. Poor Marshal Pilsudski must be turning over in his grave. Our new marshal, war minister, and member of the Political Executive, is called Rokossowski."

"He was born in Warsaw," Helena pointed out timidly.

"Yes, but he was brought up, nurtured, and trained in the Red Army. I swear, nothing embarrasses them anymore—first arrests, then imprisonments, and now appointments!"

"We must protect ourselves against the reactionary forces

of the capitalist countries that left us at the mercy of the fascists in 1939," Helena recited. "It was thanks to Stalin that we were able to recover our frontiers on the Oder and the Neisse, and we ought to show our thanks to our Soviet friends."

A long silence fell in the room. Andrzej changed the subject, talking animatedly about their trip to Cracow. Robert and Irena held their peace. Once Helena had kissed them good night and gone to bed, though, Robert blew up.

"Wonderful! I can't even trust my own daughter! Bad enough they arrest anyone they please, they torture priests and nuns. Now they're taking our children from us."

"Quiet!" Andrzej warned. "The child can't do any differently. If she starts thinking like you, she'll never get into the university. Is that what you want? Let her get her education in peace. Don't you think she's suffered enough? Would you have preferred to see her settle down with Inka on her lap, so she could cry over her lost youth? She's a Communist—and so much the better! It'll make life much easier for her. For us, it's too late. We're stubborn individualists, and we knew life before the war, when our status as professionals gave us certain advantages. An engineer and a doctor—we earned a fair amount of money."

"Oh, enough, Andrzej!" Robert interrupted. "I'm tired, and I want to go to bed. Thanks for taking her to Cracow— but watch out for that Kazik. He's part of a different world."

Andrzej didn't respond, but on this point he didn't need to. Both men recognized that Kazik was a product of the times—and neither was prepared to say he was wrong for Helena.

"How beautiful our country is." Helena, sitting beside the driver, was enjoying the view. Behind her, Uncle

Andrzej and Kazik were dozing. She would have liked to talk with the driver, but he barely answered her, as if he only cared about his driving and wanted to forget she was there.

Her parents were wrong, Helena thought. They spoiled everything, the way they criticized and ran things down. True, Father Marianski had been put in prison for no reason, and Magda hadn't received the plot of land she had been promised—but there was so much to rebuild and transform that it was only natural that mistakes would sometimes be made. The essential thing was to work toward the building of a new Poland. This summer, she was going to help install electricity in two villages, and the prospect filled her with pleasure. Her parents wouldn't like it—but that was just too bad.

Deep in thought, Helena hardly noticed that a light rain had begun to fall. The poorly fitted window let in a thin spray of water, and the sleeve of her pullover got soaked. She shrank back in her seat.

"We're coming into Cracow," the driver announced. "Wake the others."

She obeyed.

"Where do we drop them off?" the driver asked Andrzej.

"At Wawel," Andrzej said. "Go for a walk, kids. When you've had enough, we'll meet at Wierzynek's. I'll be there at six. If I happen to be late, just have something to eat while you're waiting for me."

The van stopped. Kazik got out first and held his hand out to Helena, but she pushed it away. It was ridiculous to imagine that girls needed boys to do things for them!

A wave and a smile, and then they were alone at the foot of Wawel's royal castle. "I want to go into the center of the town," said Helena. "We can come back here afterward, if there's still time." They walked quickly to the marketplace, and then to the Cloth Hall.

"It's unbelievable!" said Helena. "A town where all the

houses are still standing! A real town, like in the books—
paved streets everywhere, and so clean."

" 'Cracow is a historic city whose origins go back to A.D.
995 and even earlier,' " Kazik read from a guidebook. " 'A
former capital, Cracow boasts more than 760 monuments
of inestimable architectural value.' "

"Oh, Kazik," she exclaimed, "you don't know how good
it makes me feel to be able to walk around with you like
this, without thinking of the Warsaw uprising, without
telling myself I ought to be helping with some reconstruction project! Here I can escape the feeling of remorse,
obligations, and urgent work to be done."

Helena stopped in front of shop windows, smiling at
people, going into raptures over the carved figurines displayed on the counters. She fingered the multicolored
cloths woven by craftsmen, tried on a highlander's felt hat,
and burst into laughter as she grabbed hold of a little doll
dressed in Kujawy regional costume, with long blond tresses
that looked like her own.

"Oh, Kazik! I'm so happy!" she cried, taking his arm.
"I'm happy, and I'm hungry!"

"I've got some money," Kazik announced. "I can buy
you a couple of pretzels. Come on!"

They left the marketplace and stopped in amazement.
Along the street that led into the square came a group of
nuns surrounded by militiamen with their rifles held ready.
Helena crossed herself mechanically; one of the nuns gave
her a reassuring smile.

"Let's go!" Kazik urged her. "It's getting late."

Helena and Kazik were silent as they walked down
Grodska Street, across Dominikanski Square, and into the
open door of the Dominican church. Helena freed herself
from Kazik's arm and went inside. The church was dark,
cold, and damp. Helena knelt down, and Kazik followed
her example. For a moment they were motionless, side by

side; then Kazik touched her arm. She turned toward him.
Something in his eyes made her blush.

"One day you and I are going to get married," Kazik
murmured. "I love you, Helena."

Helena shook her head. He was spoiling their friendship!
What could she tell him? That she didn't love him? He
might call her a tease—one of those rotten girls who
provoke boys and make them dream, and give them nothing in return. She was going to have to get angry and
refuse to see him. It was a pity; he was good-natured,
looking after her like a faithful dog, without asking for
anything in return. And unlike Jurek and Olgierd, he
never tried to get her into a dark corner and kiss her.

Helena felt a deep disgust for those boy-girl games that
brought so much pleasure to some of her female friends.
The touch of a man's hand on her own immediately brought
back the sense of being a trapped beast, desperate to
escape. But Kazik was tactful; he bided his time.

"One day, we shall get married," he repeated, a little
louder, "and if you want, we'll do it here, in this church."

Helena got up and moved away. She went out into the
street, and when Kazik joined her, she began to run. They
were completely winded when they reached Wierzynek's,
where Andrzej was waiting for them. As Helena came up,
he rose to his feet.

"So the mystery's been cleared up?" Helena asked with
a laugh.

"Oh, yes! The patients are really ill—but it's less serious
than was thought. However, I'll have to stay here overnight.
I've given them some medicine which ought to bring the
fever down, but I've got to look at them again tomorrow
morning."

"Hurrah!" cried Helena. "We're staying in Cracow!"

"Being happy makes you look even prettier," Andrzej
said as he took her hand. "I'd like to see you like that
always."

"Uncle" Andrzej was hardly like an uncle at all; he was still a young man, not at all unpleasant to look at. Till now, Helena hadn't noticed the little creases that formed around his brown eyes when he smiled, the attractive silvering at his temples, or his tall, slim, supple body. Moreover, Andrzej knew how to command. The old waiter, clad in a black jacket shiny with use, treated him as a distinguished customer.

Andrzej wanted to play the *grand seigneur*, the irresistible Don Juan seducing a wonderful young blond with big green eyes. He was disturbed by the presence of Kazik, that great gangling youth who never knew what to do with his overlong arms and legs. Kazik was young, he belonged to the present, to this confused reality dominated by fear, cowardice, and humiliation. He himself was old. It all seemed more than a century ago—life before the war; the German invasion; the occupation; the Warsaw uprising; the Soviet invasion. It wasn't champagne they were drinking, but vodka—but that didn't matter! He showered attention on Helena, his easy conversation creating an air of gaiety, a sense of confidence that tomorrow did indeed exist.

Kazik was ill-at-ease, and he was gulping down the vodka as though he hoped it would get him into a more relaxed mood. Helena, surprised and delighted, flirted with both men with all the innocence of her seventeen years. But there was no comparison between Kazik, the stammering clod, and this man she seemed to be seeing properly for the first time in her life—the charming companion whose savoir-faire dazzled her.

The waiter held a plate for her, his napkin over his arm, and Helena served herself daintily. Dinner was only a boiled potato and a piece of rather tough meat, but thanks to the smile of this doctor sitting opposite her, full of charm and self-assurance, everything seemed transformed.

I'm in love with him, Helena thought as she swallowed

her third vodka. It's marvelous, and it's insane! Poor Kazik—
how pale anything he can say or do looks in comparison!

The old pianist playing Chopin in the corner turned his
head toward her as though to do her homage. Andrzej's
hand was on hers, the tea was beautifully hot, and the
sweet wafers were delicious.

"Let's dance," said Andrzej as the pianist began a tango.

Helena felt herself floating on air. Her body seemed
light in Andrzej's arms as the two of them wound their
way in and out of the tables. He pressed her to him as
they went around the piano. Like magic, the electricity
failed, and the lights went out and now there was only
candlelight, the warm body close to hers, the male rough-
ness of his cheek against hers. Helena closed her eyes.
She wanted this moment to last forever. She wanted him
to caress her, to kiss her, to carry her off to some faraway
place where they would be alone to dance like this until
the end of time.

I can love, Helena told herself. She was thrilled to find
she was normal, like other girls—it only took a man who
knew how to please her, for her to stop being afraid.

Andrzej sang softly in her ear; his warm deep voice
made Helena shiver. He felt her agitation, and held her
more firmly, to make her realize how their bodies sought
each other.

The lights came back on, and the mood changed. The
candles were snuffed out. Andrzej called for the bill. The
pianist came up, and Andrzej slipped a banknote into his
waistcoat pocket as he left them. He was no longer a
magician, but an old man, tired and poor. Now there was
the driver's face, hard and closed; Kazik's low forehead;
Andrzej's encouraging smile—and her own tired feet, which
refused to carry her. Helena hung onto Andrzej's arm, and
refused to let it go until it was time to climb into the van.

Andrzej had booked three bedrooms at the Francuski
Hotel; hers was green. "To match your eyes," murmured

Andrzej as he wished her good night. "To match the most beautiful eyes in all the world."

Once she was alone, Helena got undressed, throwing her clothes down anywhere; then she buried herself beneath the eiderdown. She fell asleep with the taste of a kiss on her lips. Had Andrzej actually kissed her, or had she imagined it?

In the next room, Andrzej lay stretched out on his bed gazing at the ceiling. In a world of poverty, misery, and insidious terror, honesty's merely a matter of lack of opportunity, he thought to himself. This time, there's a chance for all of us. I've got an ace—it just depends on how I play it.

He ran over the day's events in his mind. First, there had been that death's-head of a driver, who had brought him the message. He was to get to Cracow as quickly as possible, to the bedside of a sick man. The driver—who claimed to be an experienced nurse—was to accompany him. Despite the generous reward promised, Andrzej had refused, saying he had too much work to do at the hospital. But twenty minutes later the director had ordered him to leave as quickly as possible.

Once at Cracow, the driver had taken him to a big private residence, surrounded by its own park, which before the war must have belonged to a noble family, or perhaps a rich industrialist. There he'd met a man—a Jew—who looked strangely like Jakob Berman, the prime minister's undersecretary of state, the strongman who controlled the secret police and all censorship. In certain circles he was said to be the Soviet agent who pulled all the strings behind the scenes.

But was that really Berman, or was Andrzej the victim of a mirage? Andrzej had examined his patient carefully. The man appeared to have a stomach upset caused by a dose of poison. Andrzej had discussed the symptoms with

his patient for a long time, watched all the while by the
sullen driver, who didn't move from his side. When he
had prepared an injection, the driver had stepped forward
and examined the syringe.

One false move and he'll kill me! Andrzej had realized.

An hour later, his patient seemed to have improved.

"Why did you choose me?" Andrzej had asked him.
"There are plenty of good doctors in Cracow."

"I chose you because you're a Jew, because you're said
to know your trade, and because you've got a fair number
of things on your conscience."

Andrzej felt as though he'd stepped under a cold shower.
"You're mistaken," he'd said. "I have nothing on my
conscience—except my folly in answering a summons as
strange as yours."

"Come now!" The man sighed, sitting up in his bed.
"On the table over there you'll find a file. Read it while I
rest; then we'll talk."

From the thick file with his name on the cover Andrzej
had learned that he, Andrzej Rybicki, was accused of
subversive and anti-Communist activities, of high treason,
and of espionage. During the German occupation, he had
been a lieutenant in the Home Army, and he had given
the order to open fire on a group of partisans from the
People's Army, a Communist group commanded by a
Russian officer. He had also communicated regularly with
agents of the government-in-exile in London, and had received money from them intended to keep his own unit in
funds. For these actions he was eligible for the death
penalty or for life imprisonment, but first he was to have a
public trial, as an example to other traitors who had carried out missions similar to his.

The more he read, the more Andrzej's repugnance grew.
He and his companions had risked their lives for four
years only to be accused now by their own fellow country-
men of treason and dealing with the enemy!

"Well?" the man had asked him.

"I've never seen such lies in all my life!" Andrzej was curt. "True, you hear talk of public trials, and reports of them appear in the press. But you really have to read your own file for an understanding of what it all means."

"Lies or not," his patient had said with a mocking laugh, "our prisons are overcrowded and poorly heated. Now, here's what I have to offer you. I have good reason to believe that someone's trying to poison me. They've failed this time, but they'll keep trying. I need to be able to count on you. As soon as anything happens to me, the same driver will come and fetch you. Come immediately, without anyone knowing where you're going or whom you're treating. In exchange, I'm offering you a passport and an exit permit for Israel in two or three years' time."

"I don't want to leave," Andrzej had replied, "but I've never refused to look after a sick man."

"We know that perfectly well. Even when it was a seedy priest just out of jail, you went to Celestynow in a cart."

"You're well-informed."

"It's my job."

The medicine was definitely working, Andrzej noted. The man was perking up nicely.

"Now think things over carefully," the man continued. "Your friends, the Stanowskis, don't have a very clear record either. The girl was in the Home Army with you. Her father's been put under surveillance because of his subversive ideas and his refusal to discuss his prisoner-of-war camp in Germany. I'm in a position to make them talk, both of them. And they'll confess, all right! Just trust me. If you agree to look after me, who knows? Perhaps we'll keep our eyes closed."

"Thanks in advance!" Andrzej had smiled. "For the moment, you must rest. I'll come back tomorrow. Here

are some pills—take one every four hours. I'd also like to
take a blood sample from you."

"Go ahead. The driver will take it over to the laboratory
and go and fetch it when it's ready. I think I'm no longer
at death's door, and I can eat a little now, can't I?"

"Yes, this evening—just some tea and bread. But not too
much. Now, why is somebody trying to poison you? Are
you sure it's not just your imagination?"

"I couldn't be more sure. The dog that ate the scraps off
my plate died."

"In that case, we must take certain precautions." Andrzej
rose to his feet. "We'll talk about it tomorrow."

"Friends?" The man held out his hand.

"Every patient is important to me," Andrzej replied.

Incredible, he thought now as he lay in bed. If I understand correctly, I can get a good many things out of this
fellow. I can get a few friends out of prison; and who
knows?—even go and live somewhere else one day. But is
he really Jakob Berman, or was I just having hallucinations?

Andrzej tried in vain to clear his head, to stop his mind
from racing. He couldn't get to sleep. When daybreak
came, it seemed like a deliverance.

That day, when he visited his unusual patient, he found
the man up and waiting for him in a book-lined study. His
manner was careful. This was how the former owners must
have received their family doctor in the old days. Because
he was only a temporary occupant and Andrzej a doctor he
was blackmailing, the scene seemed grotesque.

"You're better," Andrzej told him, "and your blood
analysis doesn't seem to show anything abnormal. A little
too much sugar, perhaps, but that's all. You have to be
careful not to drink any vodka for some time."

"You're a good doctor," the man said. "I hope I can
count on you in the future?"

"I've never refused to look after anyone who needs me," Andrzej answered.

"You're stubborn, like a Pole, instead of being flexible, like a Jew; but blood will tell!" the man said. "You'll realize in the end where your best interests lie. We'll have lunch together, and talk a little."

The driver brought them tea, bread, butter, ham, and a selection of cheeses. The spread represented such luxury that Andrzej couldn't stop himself from staring at it.

"There's also some salmon, and vodka, if you'd like. And Russian caviar too—that's the best. In fact, I'm going to have a small parcel made up for you."

"No—thank you!" Andrzej protested. "I wouldn't know how to explain such a present."

"Well, let's get back to business. How can I avoid getting myself poisoned in future?"

"There's only one way. Have everything you're going to eat tasted first by someone else, or by an animal. With dogs, the problem is hot drinks."

"I know a very pretty girl who'll take that task on," the man said. "Next time I send for you, it'll be for her. And don't forget—you owe me your hide in exchange for your freedom."

He rose to his feet; the interview was over. Andrzej made his way back to the front seat of the van.

"Forget this place, and your patient," said the driver, an underlying threat in his voice. "They gave me this for you."

Andrzej slowly picked up the envelope the driver had laid on his knees and opened it. Inside were several banknotes and a small card with a telephone number written on it. "That's my number," the driver told him. "Inform me whenever you leave Warsaw. You'll have to carry this card on you all the time."

What it boiled down to was that he had lost his freedom of movement and would be under surveillance. Andrzej tried to remain calm, but he was afraid. "May I at least know the name of my illustrious patient?"

"Why don't you ask him, next time?"

"Oh, I thought you knew it, comrade," Andrzej goaded. "Here, take this money back. I'm a doctor, and I'm paid by my hospital. Besides, it wasn't I who saved your boss, but the doctor who saw him before me and washed his stomach out."

The driver lost his temper. "Listen to me, comrade! If you want to see that girl who came with you again, or the boy—if you want to get back to Warsaw—just take that money and stop provoking me. *He* doesn't care for jokes, and neither do I."

Andrzej realized it was useless to insist.

Helena was hot. For more than two hours now she had been tossing bales of hay onto the truck. It was a mad race against time, with both boys and girls trying to outdo each other, like athletes coming up to the finish line. When the truck was loaded, all Helena could do was lean against the wall of the barn. She felt empty, and strangely lonely.

"You're better than most of the young farmers," said the man in charge of the rural development where they were working. "Congratulations, comrade!"

Helena gave him a painful smile and went to wash herself under the pump. The touch of the cold water on her skin made her shiver. Around her, others were chatting, laughing, singing. It was coming up to mealtime, the day's work was done, and everyone seemed to be in a good mood—except her. This trip to Zielona Gora, over which she'd had such a struggle with her parents, had turned out to be much less fun than she had hoped. None of her friends had come. The work group included some Poles, but more Czechs and Hungarians. Helena took her work so seriously that the others laughed at her. Unaccustomed

to such hostility, she was counting the days till the end of
the month and her return to Warsaw.

It was hot inside the tent, and the air was heavy and full
of the smell of sweat. Helena changed her blouse. Around
her, girls were contorting their bodies to hide their naked-
ness from each other. They took off regulation blouses to
put on regulation shirts, over which they knotted regulation red ties. Usually Helena enjoyed the atmosphere of
relaxation that preceded the evening meal; but now she
wished she were far away, alone in her own room,
daydreaming on her bed. She thought of Andrzej: his
smile, his big hands, his curly hair, the way he had of
looking at her, while she had to raise her head to return
his look.

"He's as old as your father!" Kazik had said angrily as he
left to go to his uncle's place in Wroclaw. He wanted to
see the "reconquered areas," he said; but in fact he wanted
to get away from Warsaw, and from Helena. He had
obtained permission to go there, as well as a means of
transport. Helena preferred not to speculate on how he
had managed that.

Robert and Irena were at Celestynow, at Magda's. They
must be spoiling Inka, and going for long walks in the
forest, thought Helena. Suddenly she realized she'd like
to be there with them. Especially if Andrzej spent his Sundays there.

Since their trip to Cracow, he had avoided being alone
with her, and a strange embarrassment had grown up
between them.

Helena left the tent and decided to take a short stroll on
the main road. Suddenly a cloud of dust hid the sun from
her eyes, a car stopped close to her, and she was clasped
in a pair of strong, warm arms.

"Andrzej! But how . . . ?" Helena was babbling in her
sheer joy at finding him, tall, strong, handsome, there to
take her far away, to a different world.

"How's it going, Helena?" Andrzej hid his happiness with forced lightness.

"Where have you come from?"

"As usual, from a hospital. I'm on my way to see a patient. As I was driving along, I suddenly remembered you, and I decided to make a little detour so that I could see you."

"Take me away," Helena begged him. "It's awful here!"

"You can't just leave. It would cause trouble. But if you like, I'll go and see the person in charge of the group, and try to arrange an outing for you. Okay?"

"Oh, yes!"

Soon Helena was collecting her knapsack and preparing to leave with her Uncle Andrzej. It was agreed that he would take her back to Warsaw, even though the change of plans would cut her stay by a week—but he had urgent work for her at the hospital. The group leader was impressed. An uncle who was a doctor, with a car, was clearly a good Communist.

The car coughed once as they started up; then it was rolling along the bumpy road. Helena felt as if she were floating on air.

"I have to see a patient, and then we'll have something to eat. You're not too hungry, are you?"

"No." She could forget about food for the rest of her life, provided he continued to smile at her like that.

It was getting dark when they reached an attractive house hidden away among the greenery. Andrzej parked the car. "This won't take long," he said. "Wait for me in the car, and don't talk to anyone."

Helena stretched out along the padded seat and closed her eyes.

"Dr. Rybicki," Andrzej introduced himself to the woman who opened the door. Inside, it was a lovely old house which must have belonged to several generations of wealthy and industrious Germans. From the drawing room came shouts and snatches of loud conversation in Russian and Polish. They're blind drunk, thought Andrzej, hoping his patient wasn't among them. He was taken up to the next floor and ushered into a room full of people. Here, too, was a lot of hard drinking and loud conversation. "Surely, comrade, you can't believe we're going to go on letting ourselves be taken for a ride!" a swarthy man was saying. "The party must defend our interests. We're good Communists, and we deserve certain advantages. I want this house . . ."

Nobody seemed to notice Andrzej as he forced his way through to the bed, put his bag on the little table, and leaned forward. His patient looked exhausted. The smoke was so thick he could hardly make out the man's features, and when he took his pulse, he found it weak and irregular.

Andrzej straightened up. "May I ask the comrades to leave us alone?" he called out.

There was murmuring, astonishment, and protest, until finally one of the men signed to the others to leave. Andrzej shut the door behind them, stepped over the empty bottles littering the floor, accidentally upset a glass of vodka, and finally sat down by the bed.

"My wound hurts," the man said. "Are you going to put a dressing on?"

The anxiety in his eyes was enough to command Andrzej's attention. His patient wasn't running a temperature, but his bandages were stained with blood.

"You're overexciting yourself, comrade," he said. "Try to get some rest. It's not very sensible to have so many people in here, to breathe in all that smoke, and to drink as you've been doing." The man stank of vodka, and Andrzej found the odor so unpleasant he went to open the window.

The patient reacted at once to the fresh air sweeping into the room. "Oh yes, that feels much better," he said.

Deftly Andrzej removed the dressing. Beneath lay a deep cut, obviously a slash from a knife.

"That's a nice little present, comrade," Andrzej murmured between his teeth. "Who did that to you?"

"A jealous husband," the man answered curtly. "You're here to look after me, comrade. I'll ask the questions."

"Why so?"

"Because that's my profession. And because I'm curious by nature."

This was yet another patient produced by the driver of that strange individual in Cracow who looked so much like Jakob Berman. Each month Andrzej got one or two calls. Everything was as easy as pie. He would go to the address he had been given, do his work, and then call the driver to make his report. Next day he would find an envelope in his room, filled with banknotes, gas coupons, special road passes, hotel vouchers. Even the car itself was a present from his invisible benefactor. One morning the driver had brought him a wallet containing the keys and the papers.

"It's always ready, comrade," he had told Andrzej. "Whenever you need it, I'll bring it. I've told your director that it's a vehicle on loan to you for urgent cases. Better not give him a fuller explanation. Understand?"

Oh yes! Andrzej understood all too well that it was in his interest to keep his mouth shut. He'd had a lot of trouble explaining to Robert and Irena the source of this providential vehicle, which from now on would enable them to go to Celestynow more frequently to see Inka.

Andrzej disinfected the wound and put a new dressing on. "You can get out of bed for a short while," he said, "and take a few steps around the room. I'll come back in a week's time to see that everything's going well. I don't foresee any complications between now and then. However, if you have any fever, let me know immediately at the hospital in Warsaw, unless you have another doctor locally. You understand, it takes a good long time to get here."

"I'm well aware of that, comrade, and I appreciate it."

"Here's my name and telephone number," added Andrzej, as he handed the man a scrap of paper torn from his notebook.

"It was a girl who did this to me," the wounded man said suddenly. "A little eighteen-year-old tart. She couldn't take a joke. Well, she won't do it again, the slut! We've settled her hash for her!"

Andrzej stood up and put his bag in order. His stomach contracted as he reflected what a fine bunch of assassins he was looking after. How long was this little game of hide-and-seek going to last?

In the long corridor the men were still drinking, leaning against the walls. On the steps of the staircase, a girl was sitting on a man's knee; she was laughing and crying, completely drunk. Her face was smeared with lipstick marks and black smudges where her mascara had run. Thinking of Helena, alone in the car, Andrzej hurried toward the front door.

One of the men in the hall below called out to him in Russian, "Hey, comrade! Come and drink with us. We can have a lot of fun together." Andrzej pushed him away and tried to make his way through to the door.

"It's the doctor," someone said. "He has to leave, comrade."

"Get out quickly, Doctor," murmured the woman who had opened the door for him when he arrived. She pushed him forward, Andrzej stuck his elbow into a body that was blocking his passage, and he found himself outside at last, in the night air that smelled of newly mown hay.

The car was where he had left it; and when Andrzej got in behind the wheel, Helena's head slid onto his shoulder. She was asleep. I have no right to love her, he thought. I was crazy to think that it might be possible one day. . . . The tanned face beneath the mass of blond hair was so innocent.

Andrzej touched the end of the tip-tilted nose with his lips, then her forehead and her hair. "I love you, Helena," he whispered. "But you'll never know it." Without waking her, he started the engine and put the headlights on. How wonderful it was to be driving through the night like this with her body pressed against his! The sudden image of the drunken girl back at the house made him grit his teeth. He had thought, despite the difference in their ages, that he could make this child-woman happy. But now he knew it was impossible; he was too afraid of bruising the world she was slowly rebuilding after all that had happened to her. He would never have the courage to face Robert or Irena, or his own reflection in the mirror.

He would have to go far away, abroad, someplace from where it would no longer be possible for him to return. He could ask the "death's-head" driver to arrange a meeting with his boss, and make a deal for a passport and an exit permit. The world was large. There were other peoples, other horizons. It was cowardly to abandon them all here; it was shameful to flee, but he had no other solution. Somewhere else, they might have robbed Eternity of a few years of happiness; but not here, not in Warsaw, not in the Poland that was now emerging from the ashes of war.

On the road, in the beam of the headlights, he could still see the face of the drunken girl back at the house. *They're going to turn us all into prostitutes and black-mailers! Only the young ones like Helena will manage to survive. There's no doubt about it—the only solution is for me to get out.*

He wanted to smoke, but he couldn't get his cigarettes out of his pocket without waking Helena. And his resolution was too new and too fragile for him to want it tested by the inquiring look of those green eyes.

Ahead he saw the black mass of a big truck standing

across the road. Andrzej braked sharply, and the car stopped
with a screeching of tires.

"Your papers, comrade."

There were a dozen militiamen, armed with automatic
rifles which they kept pointed in his direction. Helena
awoke and sat up in her seat. The militiamen surrounded
the car, opened the doors, and made Helena get out. How
fragile she seemed in the light of the headlights! Andrzej
got out, went over to her, and took her arm.

"You've stolen this car, comrade," one of the militiamen
shouted," and this girl's your accomplice. Come on, admit
it!"

"I'm a doctor, and I've just been visiting a patient. This
young lady is my niece, who's just come from the youth
camp at Zielona Gora. You don't have any right—"

One of the militiamen jostled him, as if by accident; but
Andrzej had seen it coming, and managed to keep his
balance. Another one stepped forward. Andrzej saw that
Helena had gone very pale. He thought of what all this
must mean to her, and what memories must be flooding
back into her mind. His muscles tensed, and his voice
became commanding.

"Where's the man in charge of this patrol?" he barked.

Two men came forward. With a swift movement Andrzej
produced the little card the driver had told him always to
carry on his person, and held it out under the nose of the
older of the two. The man examined it closely, then put
his hand out as though to take it; but Andrzej stepped
back. Now there was fear in the other man's eyes.

"Move that truck," Andrzej ordered him. "I'm in a
hurry!" The militiamen scattered. One of the officers
stammered, "You understand, comrade . . . we couldn't
have known . . . we were looking for a stolen car."

"Take the comrade back and see her into the car at
once!" Andrzej ordered him.

Andrzej got quickly back into the car and turned the

ignition key. The engine purred into life again. In front of them, the truck had been maneuvered off the road and was now parked on the shoulder.

"Phew!" Andrzej sighed with relief as he accelerated away. "We were lucky."

On the seat beside him, Helena was sobbing, her whole body trembling. Andrzej tried talking to her, putting his arm around her shoulders, but to no avail. I can't leave her, he thought. She needs me. He also reflected that the driver's boss must be a real bastard, if a simple little card with a telephone number written on it could keep his protégés out of the clutches of the militia.

"I'm afraid," Helena sobbed. "They're going to follow us. They're going to kill us. They're going to . . ."

But no one was pursuing them along the quiet road, and little by little Helena grew calm. When they reached the village where Andrzej had reserved two rooms in one of the houses, Helena was so exhausted that he had to carry her up to bed. She fell asleep immediately.

Andrzej retired to his room, resigned to the fact he would have to continue playing his role of "uncle," an amusing, protective, and paternal companion.

It wouldn't be easy.

5

BRUNO ZADRA HAD been sitting in his office for hours, listening to the silence. He knew that at that very moment, Wladyslaw Gomulka was addressing a crowd that had invaded the streets of Warsaw. If the Russian tanks didn't intervene, he was sunk.

At least thirty thousand prisoners had been released on the streets, and the horror stories of how they'd been treated had spread.

Bruno had hoped that Bierut would come back from Moscow and knock some sense into these rebels, but Bierut was dead. Had he been assassinated by the Russians because he knew too much, or because he was no longer useful to them? The official story was that he'd been the victim of a fatal illness. All Bruno knew was that his worst fears had come true.

Trouble had started in the spring. In June the metal workers had demonstrated in Poznan, and the militia had stepped in. The president of the Council had said the Poznan riots were justified. As a result, those accursed priests had not only been released from prison, they had also organized a pilgrimage to Czestochowa for the Assumption.

108   ALICE PARIZEAU

Since then there had been student riots more or less everywhere. Gilded youth! Not satisfied with the right to do nothing, a privilege Bruno had never had, they wanted still more—freedom of expression. Was he, Bruno, spending long days in this sinister office interrogating men and women who looked at him with hate, for nothing?

"If Soviet tanks don't intervene," Bruno said to himself, "I'm done for. I'll never get out of this hornet's nest. I'll end up paying for what others have done."

He lit a cigarette and paced. Haunted by a vision of clutching hands and bodies falling to the floor, he tried to calm down. He had just been doing his job; there was nothing else he could have done. But now there was no longer anyone who could help him.

"Oh God!" Bruno murmured. "If only that bloody Igor would show up, I'd know what to do. He promised he'd come this morning. Where is he?"

His wristwatch showed noon. It was a handsome gold watch from a Home Army officer who had hoped to buy his liberty. Bruno had accepted the watch, then called for the guards to take him away.

Bruno poured himself a glass of vodka from the bottle on his desk. Why bother to hide it? He was done for anyway. Vodka was all he had left. His hand trembled and he spilled some alcohol on his jacket, swearing.

The phone rang. Bruno rushed to pick it up.

It was Igor. "We're winding up," he said, his voice muffled as usual with a handkerchief. "I'll come for you in a few minutes."

"Where are we going?" Bruno asked.

"Home. Our friend's not going hunting, because his friends are too busy." That meant the Russians weren't going to send tanks in, because they couldn't count on the support of the Polish Army.

"The hunters propose a trip somewhere else," Igor added.

That meant the Soviet generals in the Polish Army were

going to go home. It was the beginning of the end. All they were offering Bruno was a trip back to Moscow—no doubt to some labor camp. When Igor said "home," he was talking about his own country; Moscow was Igor's home. Not Bruno's. Better to risk death in Warsaw, or anywhere in the country he loved than any other place in the world. He recalled all his days in the Siberian labor camps, and the cursed school in Moscow where they'd taught him their special brand of interrogation.

"Don't come for me," said Bruno. "Good-bye, and good luck!"

Bruno hung up, feeling strangely calm. He had already emptied his desk; all that was left was to take down his nameplate.

Outside, he walked quickly. Where would he go? He didn't have enough money to take a train and go to, say, Cracow, where he stood a better chance of vanishing into the crowd than he did in Warsaw. He would have to find a hiding place, shave off his mustache, and become a different man.

Razowa! Razowa, a widow who had so often brought him lists of names, the poor newspaper vendor whom nobody suspected. Why couldn't he have thought of her earlier? She was bound to have a nice little hoard tucked away; surely she could lend him the price of a railway ticket.

More cheerful now, Bruno jumped onto a streetcar to Saska Kepa. As the streetcar put on speed, Bruno lifted his head, and his eyes met those of a woman who had climbed onto the edge of the platform. Suddenly he had a premonition of danger. He wanted to jump off, but there was a truck just about to pass the streetcar. Bruno felt a dull pain in his lower belly: the woman had kicked him! He staggered back just as the truck drew level with him.

I'm done for! he realized in a flash. The truck driver jammed on his brakes, but it was too late.

The woman turned her head away and spat. "Just what you deserve, you swine," she murmured, riding away.

The panic-stricken truck driver searched the dead man's pockets, finding only a nameplate bearing the words "Referent Bruno Zadra." Almost without thinking, the driver climbed into his truck and drove off. With his free hand he opened the window and threw out the nameplate. The little length of painted wood hit the bridge, bounced off, and disappeared into the river. The last trace of the man who had just died floated away on the waters of the Vistula, and then nothing was left of him other than the contempt and hatred he had left in the memories of those who had known him, and to whom he had owed his two-room apartment and his staff car.

The crowd was so thick that Helena could hardly stand. Wladyslaw Gomulka was making a speech, and only when the wind was blowing in her direction could she hear what he was saying. However, the applause and cheers from those close enough to hear rolled back like ocean waves.

Gomulka had been in prison, and he had come out alive. He was a symbol of all of them who had lived through torment without crumbling.

Helena's heart beat faster. She was filled with a strange elation, and squeezed her companion Wanda's hand. Wanda, who had become her best friend among the first-year medical students, squeezed back in excitement. Together they joined in the singing of their ancestral song: "O God, who throughout so many centuries has protected Poland by the shield of power and glory . . ."

What did love matter compared to this? What did it matter that Andrzej was gone? She had loved him, but all he saw was a little girl. It seemed strange to think he had caused her sleepless nights. What was love compared to this? A coupling for procreation, the expression of ego?

But it was a new day. The Russians had failed, but

Helena felt a new sense of freedom and justice. All she had to do was work for it; to listen to Gomulka, to go forward with him and build socialism. As for love, it was just childishness.

Helena sang. Everything had become simple, easy, and clear again. She had decided to become a doctor and a party leader; she would reorganize the hospitals.

Gomulka had left the dais. The crowd stirred, dispersing. Bedlam disrupted the unity.

A woman fell to the ground. Worried that she would be trampled underfoot, several people cleared a path, finally helping get her up. A man hoisted her onto his shoulders. There was something heroic in this simple gesture.

Helena was uneasy. For the first time in years her parents were talking politics in front of her.

"This part's for Helena." Robert read Gomulka's speech aloud from the paper:

> The party should say clearly to youth: in the vast and vital process of democratization, march at the head of it—but do not lose sight of our instructions, which are those of the whole of Poland of the people: the unified party of the Polish workers."

It's now or never, Helena thought. I've got to tell them I want to join the party. Yet she couldn't bring herself to speak. A few moments later it was too late; a knock came at the door.

"Quick, hide the paper!" Irena whispered to Robert.

"Come now, darling!" Robert protested. "This is the party's official paper. Why should I hide it?"

"You never know—"

"Kazik!"

Helena had never been so happy to see him. She'd lost sight of him. For the past few years he had gone to live with his uncle. Some said he had been arrested, others that he was in Moscow. Helena had been afraid to ask his parents where he was. She was afraid his mother would blame her, somehow.

"Helena!" Kazik crushed her to him.

"Where were you?" She wanted to know everything.

Irena made tea and sandwiches and Kazik sat at the table. He had changed; he was no longer the awkward adolescent Helena remembered, but a young man with a self-assured air.

"I've been living in the 'reconquered areas.' " He weighed his words. "We lived well there—a house, a garden—"

"Who's 'we' ?" Helena interjected.

"My aunt and her children. When the Russians left, my uncle tried to hide some of the factory's tools, and ended up in jail. My aunt had to divorce my uncle in order to keep her job and the house we were sharing with another woman, who also had children."

"Girls?" Helena asked involuntarily.

"No, don't you worry! No fun for me—while you fooled around at school, I slaved away. I'm going to take night classes to make up for lost time."

"In what subjects?" Irena asked. During the occupation, Irena had never bothered to find out if Helena's friends carried underground newspapers, or grenades. She only cared that they weren't skipping their courses at school. She hadn't changed.

"I'm studying law now," Kazik said. "I graduated with good grades, so they took me right away."

They took you, my boy, Robert thought, because of your family. A workingman's son has it made over anyone unlucky enough to have been sired by a professional man. Helena had a time getting admitted into medical school— she'd probably never have done it without Andrzej's help, despite her wonderful record.

Kazik had barely been back a week, but already his

responsibilities had piled up. He'd met Wladyslaw Gomulka, who had shared a cell with his uncle.

"He's an extraordinary man," Kazik told them. "Although he's very suspicious, like everyone in prison, he accepted me very quickly. In forty-five, he was minister for the reconquered areas—he knew the problems there very well. He hadn't forgotten, and he taught me a lot."

Kazik gulped down a mouthful of tea. It was too soon to tell them everything. Anyway, if his plans fell through, he would look ridiculous. Yet, every word of Gomulka's was etched in his memory: "Many people have been compromised. They must be replaced by young people who, like yourself, have clean hands. Finish your law studies as quickly as you can. We shall meet again."

"He's a patriot," Kazik said, "a worker, a Pole, and an honest man."

"How times have changed!" said Robert. "Not so long ago Gomulka was being accused of being 'a right-wing anti-Soviet nationalistic deviationist,' and here he is now, rising to promise heaven and earth! Freedom of the press, and democratic elections—the Russians are never going to let that happen!"

"They won't leave of their own free will," Helena said. "Gomulka's a great man, but he won't have any more success than the others. We've got to fight."

"That's it, my romantic little daughter," Robert said. "The Polish cavalry's last charge."

Helena was silent. Against her father, she felt young and helpless. Even in her second year of medical school she felt fifteen in front of him.

"I've got to go," she said. "I've got a meeting."

"I'll go with you," Kazik said immediately, rising to his feet.

"I hope you'll have more practical work, and fewer meetings, thanks to Gomulka's reforms," Robert joked. "When doctors get certified on the basis of meetings, rather than being properly trained, the odds of dying under medical treatment are higher than being attacked by Soviet tanks!"

They all laughed, easing the tension. Soon after, Helena and Kazik left and Irena went to lie down.

Robert turned on the news from the BBC in London: "Workers in Budapest have organized a major demonstration of solidarity with Poland, joining students in a march. The situation remains highly explosive."

What would happen in Hungary if they didn't manage to calm the crowds down? What sort of repercussions would all this have in Warsaw? Robert, "the unbeliever," as his mother used to call him, whose only maxim was mind over matter, began to pray.

"I have to have that plasma right away!" Andrzej shouted.

The head nurse shook her head angrily. "This is completely crazy! We can't do a transfusion tonight."

"You're going to give *your* blood. You've got veins like everyone else. Now, come on!"

Andrzej picked up the case of plasma, then gestured toward the stock of bandages, cotton, and bottles of iodine. "Quick, put all that stuff in my car!"

The nurse stared; then her face softened. "Is this for the Hungarians? If it's for the people of Budapest, Comrade Doctor, I'm coming with you!"

So that's the way it is, thought Andrzej. She too listens secretly to the BBC in London—how else could she know that people are dying at this very moment in Budapest?

"You're a brave woman," he told her.

She smiled grimly. "If one has to die, it might as well be for a good cause."

They loaded the car and set out as night fell. Would the little card with the telephone number on it prove as successful as it had in the past? Would it get them through any obstacles they might encounter on their way to the airport where the commercial pilot awaited them, having promised to carry anything useful to the insurgents in Budapest?

Everything went smoothly, but the pilot was pessimistic. "There won't be any next trip," he said. "It's going to be like when we transported ammunition along the canal system to help the Jews in the Warsaw ghetto. This time the Russians are doing the torturing. But it's just the same. They open fire on anything that moves, and they hang anyone who falls into their hands alive, on the spot. There are thousands of dead in Budapest, and they'll have to give in within a week. They have no ammunition, no equipment, and there's nothing left to eat."

Andrzej drove back, parked, and walked to the doctors' quarters, swinging the car key around his finger. Despite everything, he felt good for the first time in weeks.

Kazik was embarrassed. Standing at the platform, he faced a crowded room expectantly waiting for him to speak.

"Student comrades," he cried, "we must remain calm. Comrade Gomulka will work with Comrade Khrushchev for all of us, but we must wait. Our enemies are eager for us to make a mistake out of impatience."

"Down with the invaders!" someone shouted. "We want freedom! Down with the foreigners! Down with the secret police! Outside, everybody, outside!"

Kazik lost control of his audience. But if the students took to the streets, they'd be dispersed—and worse. The man who had made him speak had warned him. He had to obey; the man was probably one of Gomulka's boys. Falling out of favor with the "Old Man," Gomulka, put his own future in jeopardy. And someday he wanted to walk up to Helena's parents and show how he had made something of himself and ask for the hand of their daughter.

"Comrades, listen to me!" Kazik shouted. "You're the victims of *agents provocateurs*. Don't go outside, I beg you!" The rest of his words were lost as the students jumped up onto the platform, seized Kazik, and dragged him into the hall. Hands were everywhere. He shook himself free and managed to escape, running as fast as he could.

The street was empty. Suddenly a mass of workingmen in blue overalls appeared around the corner. Kazik slipped into a doorway to avoid them, watching their unsmiling, resolute faces and their chests which were thrust out with the domineering air of conquerors. But Kazik knew they all worked seven days a week, twelve hours a day, to keep from starving. Their placards said they were "workers of the Zeran automobile factory."

At the end of the street, in front of the university, the students threw their caps in the air, shouting: "Down with the Ivans! Long live freedom! Long live the independence of the Polish people!"

The workers came on as though they didn't see them.

"Comrades," someone shouted, "I beg you! Don't attack us students! We're on the same side!" But nobody listened.

"Long live a free and sovereign Poland!" the students shouted.

"Profiteers!" the workers shouted back. Some of them raised their fists, as others pressed past their comrades as if to take vengeance for their lost youth sweating behind machines instead of reading books.

The students reeled back, trying to take refuge behind the iron gates of the university, but they were surrounded and overwhelmed at once. The end came quickly. The workers struck out with chains and within a few seconds all the students scattered.

Kazik came out of hiding and ran. Quite a brainstorm on the Old Man's part! he thought. He knew he was popular with the workers, so he used them against the students.

The street was empty of passersby; it seemed as though

life had come to a halt. Kazik ran through the ruins. His father was waiting for him outside the door.

"I was worried," he said in a low voice. "They warned me this morning that the Zeran workers were ordered to put the fear of God into the students. They've been handing out free bottles of vodka to them since this morning, for courage."

They walked along a lane where the year-old road-surfacing work still hadn't been finished. It wasn't very easy to walk like this in waterlogged sand; but it was the only way they could talk to each other without fear of being overheard.

"I don't like it," his father continued. "It wasn't a good idea, sending the workers in against the students. There are prejudices on both sides. The students regard the workers as brutal, ignorant, filthy drunkards. And on the other side of the coin, we still think of students as a bunch of parasites who read books for pleasure without ever learning anything practical and useful."

"It'll change one day, Father."

"I hope so, because as long as things go on like this, the Ivans'll always have us where they want us."

They turned back toward the house. Between them there was now a mood of distress: for each of them was afraid in his own way of what the future might bring, and neither of them dared admit it, lest he should appear cowardly.

Helena was cold. It had been years since she had walked around the streets aimlessly like this, with time hanging heavy on her hands. She felt as if her life had come to an end; without her dreams of becoming a doctor, what did she have to live for?

The verdict had been clearly spelled out: "Guilty of participating in demonstrations against our glorious Russian ally. Unworthy to continue her studies and become a doctor in the People's Republic of Poland."

Helena, the darling of the Polish Students' Association, the best student of her year, was no longer anybody! She had been rejected by society and branded a traitor. What was to become of her?

There was a man on the corner selling hot buns. He had set up a little stove on the sidewalk, with a fire inside, which kept shooting sparks out into the wind. A couple of men were warming their hands at it while waiting to be served.

Helena came closer. The scene reminded her of something—a moment she had lived through long, long ago. Suddenly tears started running down her cheeks, and she ran off, not wanting the men to see her crying.

I can't believe this is happening to me, Helena told herself. I've got to find some sort of solution. I can't just wander around the streets like this, with nothing to do and nowhere to go. To go home seemed to be out of the question. Irena would be there, and perhaps Robert too. She would have to tell them everything. And they had been so proud of her during these past few years at the university!

I've got to get them to let me back into school. But who's going to put in a good word for me? Uncle Andrzej can't do anything; since the campaign against the Jews, it's all he can do to hold on to his practice in Cracow. Kazik, perhaps? He seems to have been doing very well since he started work as a lawyer in the Ministry of Justice. It was a long time since she had last seen him, but after all, they were good friends. And hadn't he told her years ago in Cracow that he loved her?

Helena dried her eyes. Yes, she'd fight! She'd fight with every weapon she could lay her hands on. The only thing she wanted now was to find some way of being readmitted to the School of Medicine. Nothing else mattered.

*   *   *

The guard at the front entrance of the Ministry of Justice building paged Comrade Kazik Skola, then turned to the young woman who had asked for him, studying her inquisitively.

"Comrade Skola's coming down."

Helena wanted to walk around to shake off her uneasiness, but the uniformed guard's presence held her rooted to the spot. People were coming and going around her, stealing furtive glances at each other. There was an air of distrust and suspicion about the place, the awareness that arrest was always possible, no matter where, no matter when, without reason and without justification—

"Helena!"

"Kazik!" Helena bit back a cry of joy.

"Come," he said as he took her by the elbow and pushed her gently ahead of him toward the street. For a moment they walked in silence side by side. Kazik looked back several times to make sure they were not being followed.

"How nice of you to have come to see me!" he said finally. "But tell me, is there something on your mind?"

Helena nodded pensively. "I've been thrown out of the School of Medicine for anti-Soviet propaganda."

"I see!" Kazik frowned. "Well, don't worry about it; that can be fixed. Just let me have all the details—the date, the place, the people who were there, everything. But you're trembling! Come, let's go and have dinner, and you can tell me all about it, okay?"

Helena shook her head. "I've got to get back; my parents will be worried."

"That's all right, I'll just ring Razowa and tell her to let your parents know."

"Razowa has a phone?" Helena was taken aback. "She must be the only one on our street who has—probably the only one in our district."

"Maybe, but the facts are that she has a phone and that I, Kazik, have her number!"

Helena couldn't really understand how Kazik happened to have Razowa's telephone number, but she was too cold and too tired to go on asking questions. They had reached the Grand Hotel. Kazik led her in and settled her at a little table covered with a spotless white cloth; after ordering two vodkas, he went off to find a phone.

He came back to the table sooner than she expected. "It's okay," he said. "She's gone to your parents' house. She's going to tell them that she met you in the street and that you've gone to visit a friend." He added, "And, by the way, this business about Razowa's phone is just for your ears alone—it would be better not to talk about it."

"Yes, I understand." Did she?

Several waiters came to life and hovered around the couple's table; the rest of the big dining room was empty. Kazik studied the menu, then asked the maître d' which of the long list of dishes was actually available.

"We have some *paupiettes de veau*," he replied.

"Then *paupiettes de veau* it is!" Kazik said with a laugh. "And bring us a bottle of Bikaver wine, some bread, and some butter; that'll be a real feast. Does that suit you, Helena?"

"Yes." She'd agree to anything he suggested, provided they could talk. But that would be difficult to do in the Grand Hotel, where all the staff was in the service of the Polish secret police, known as the UB. Kazik seemed to be of the same opinion. They ate without speaking, listening to the orchestra, which had started playing on the dais.

After dinner, Kazik stood up and held out his hand. "Come and dance. It'll be easier that way." Once they were out on the floor, he lowered his voice. "Go on, tell me."

"The students of the Polytechnic School were supposed

to have a meeting, and we were being criticized for not helping them. So I organized the meeting at our school, in the lab. Then a group of workers turned up. There was a confrontation, and they forced us to break the meeting off. I wonder whether they really were workers, or whether they were UB dressed up in dungarees. Anyway, I was sent for by the dean, who asked me a lot of questions about my activities; there was somebody else in his office during all this, but I'm not sure who. When classes started again in January, after the holidays were over, I could see at once that something was wrong; and then one morning he sent for me."

"Who did?"

"The dean. He told me I was an 'undesirable element' and he showed me a directive to that effect from the vice-chancellor."

Kazik shook his head. "Helena, we're going to fight; we're not going to give in just like that! I don't know if you realize how damned stupid the whole thing is. You see, the government has been using *agents provocateurs* to create clashes between the intellectuals and the workers, so that they would have an excuse to step in and impose even more restrictions than before. I was caught up in a demonstration not long ago where that occurred, and the same thing must have happened at your school. It's all just a big political game, a gigantic mix-up. But don't worry, Helena, I can get you out of it."

Helena nodded wearily and closed her eyes. *My father was right. There is no point in working hard or struggling for anything, when it all just comes down to politics and more politics. This is what it comes down to for me: getting thrown out of medical school for reasons beyond my control, and then having to turn to an influential friend to save my neck.*

"Helena . . ." Kazik was leading her back to their table.

"You know that I want more than anything to help you and take care of you."

"Of course."

Kazik didn't detect the irony and despair in Helena's voice; all he could see was the smile on the red lips parted over the two rows of dazzlingly white teeth. He wiped his mouth with his napkin and pushed his chair back. "Finish up your tea like a good girl. I'll be back in a few minutes."

The dining room was still as empty as ever, except for a couple of men at the other end who kept stealing glances in her direction, and the maître d', who was somewhere behind her chair with another man, who pretended to be a customer. UB agents, no doubt. Everywhere there were agents, a constant reminder of the unheeding oppression.

Kazik came back, settled the bill, and ushered her out. Outside the door stood a black automobile, one of the cars that belonged to the UB.

"Well, what do you think of it?"

"Splendid," Helena replied as she leaned back against the cushioned seat. They drove awhile in silence, and it wasn't until they reached Helena's house that Kazik turned to her and took her hand in his.

"Helena," he murmured, "I'm going to get an apartment soon, big enough for the two of us. You know that I love you, and I want you to be my wife." Helena stared at him and opened her mouth to speak, but Kazik quickly shook his head. "No, please, don't say anything yet—just think about it for a while. In the meantime, I'll do what I can about medical school. Don't give up hope—it can be fixed."

Helena bade him good-bye hastily and got out of the car. She was confused, frustrated, and tired, and wanted desperately to be alone, to think things out.

She turned the key very quietly in the lock and pushed the door open. When she got inside, she saw Irena and

Robert sitting together on the sofa, looking tense and nervous.

Robert spoke up. "Darling, we have some bad news. Magda's broken her leg; she's in the hospital. What's more, Inka has run away. We haven't the faintest idea where she's gone, but it's been two days now and we've had no news of her. Father Marianski managed to get a letter to us; according to him, she didn't want to stay with Wlodek, so she ran off—God knows where and with whom. She just left very early one morning, and she hasn't been seen in Celestynow since."

"And she's only nine," Irena murmured.

"At that age," said Helena, "I was transporting underground newspapers and grenades. You're really getting worked up over nothing. She'll be just fine on her own."

What Helena really wanted to tell her parents was that Inka's disappearance was of minor importance compared to the fact that she had been thrown out of medical school and that a man she didn't love had just asked her to marry him.

Inka was afraid. They had taken Magda away, and Wlodek would soon be back. Inka had no desire to be alone with that horrid boy. She had hated Wlodek ever since he had spanked her for riding in the woods without letting Magda know. That was last summer; he had thrown her over his knees, pulled up her skirt, and beaten her. The red marks had lasted for quite some time; even now, she winced at the memory. No, she couldn't stand his presence in the empty house!

Inka put on her heavy overcoat and ran down to the station, where she slipped into the crowd waiting for the Warsaw express. The stationmaster didn't notice her, and she boarded the train with the others. She hid in the toilet for a while; when passengers started banging on the door, she came out and moved to the next car. The ticket collector went through just when she was holed up in another toilet, right at the back of the train.

At the station in Warsaw, they asked her for her ticket at the exit, but she clung to the skirts of a peasant woman just ahead of her and managed to get out into the street. Now she had to find her parents—but how? She walked for a long time, afraid to stop anybody and ask the way. Then quite by chance she found herself standing in front of the hospital. She recognized the building; this was where Uncle Andrzej worked as a doctor.

Inka climbed the steps and went into the lobby. She went up to a woman in white with a pretty face. "Is Dr. Rybicki here?"

"No, child, he's not," Dr. Maria Solin replied. "Who are you?"

"Inka Rybicka. I'm his niece," Inka lied without hesitation.

"Don't you have any parents? Where's your mother?"

Inka didn't want to go back to her parents; they would only scold her and take her back to Celestynow.

"I want to go to Uncle Andrzej," Inka said. "He's the only family I have."

"I see," said Maria in surprise. "But why did you come to Warsaw? Didn't you know that your uncle's been working in Cracow for several years?"

Inka shook her head.

"Well, it's all right. It just so happens I have to go to Cracow tomorrow morning, and I can take you to see your Uncle Andrzej."

Maria stroked the blond head gently, and Inka looked up at her, her big green eyes full of distress.

"I wish I had a little girl like you," she told her suddenly. "I have a son who's already grown up, and I don't hear from him much. He's called Andrzej, like your uncle, but I've always called him André, in the French style, because his father had such a passion for the French." As she spoke, Maria was pushing Inka along in the direction of the kitchen.

Old Agata, the cook, beamed when she saw the little girl. "Jesus Mary! Where did you find such a pretty child, Doctor?"

"Under a gooseberry bush," said Maria jokingly. "She's hungry, Agata, so I'm counting on you to feed her well and look after her here this evening. I'll come back for her later, and find her somewhere to sleep tonight."

"You can depend on me," said Agata as she took Inka by the hand.

Inka settled herself into a chair and helped peel potatoes. Agata made her a fine dinner, and they sang songs together; by then, Inka was getting quite sleepy. It was nearly seven o'clock when Maria came back to fetch her. She gave Inka one of the beds in the duty room, said her prayers with her, then tucked her in for the night.

"You know something?" said Maria. "When André was small, I used to tuck him in like this. I was happy in those days, but I didn't know it. André grew up, went to the underground high school, and joined the Home Army. One day the Gestapo came for him and took him away. I got a card from him from the concentration camp they'd put him in. Since then, nothing; and yet I keep waiting, you know, I keep waiting for news of him. I don't know where he is, I don't know anything; I'm all alone, child."

There were tears in Maria's eyes, but Inka never saw them; she had fallen asleep, feeling warm and secure with this woman who had become her friend.

"I'm going to keep her," Andrzej told them. "I've already got her a place at school, and you yourselves have said that Cracow's a wonderful place to live. Don't be so stubborn; it's the perfect solution, and besides, nothing could make me happier!"

They were all dining together at the presbytery: Irena,

who was refusing to give in; Father Marianski, who was trying not to butt in; Helena, who seemed completely indifferent; and Robert, who was taking great care not to make things worse. Inka had stayed in Cracow with Madame Nalkowska, who kept house for Andrzej and his two colleagues.

"Magda won't be out of the hospital before the end of the month," said Helena, "and it'll be difficult to make room for her in Warsaw."

"She could sleep at the presbytery while we're waiting for Magda," Father Marianski suggested, "and then you could make your minds up later."

"No, that's not the answer." Robert glanced at his daughter. Ever since she had admitted to him that she had been expelled from the School of Medicine, he had felt oddly embarrassed in her company. He had poked fun at her zeal for hard work; he had criticized the passion with which she had set about becoming a great doctor. Now he realized that her naive enthusiasm of the past was infinitely preferable to the cynicism that now dominated everything she said and did. He would give a great deal to be able to reach back in time and retrieve some of her old hope and confidence in the future, so that he could inspire her with them now, and erase the look of bitterness from her face.

"But it's not normal," said Irena crossly, "for a nine-year-old girl to live with a bachelor, when she's got parents in Warsaw!"

"Parents," Andrzej repeated. "Parents who live in an apartment too small for even themselves. The little alcove where Helena sleeps simply isn't big enough for herself, much less another person."

"Enough!" Helena suddenly shouted. "What's the good of all this hypocrisy? If I have to, I'll marry Kazik and move out, and that'll settle everything. Kazik's trying to get hold of an apartment right now. Just give me a few weeks, and then you'll have a room free for Inka. Until that time, though, I refuse to have her in my room."

An embarrassed silence fell upon them all.

"You are wrong to keep arguing like this," Father Marianski spoke up. "Maybe it's not normal for a girl of nine to live with a doctor she considers to be her uncle, but then again, what's normal? If Andrzej wishes, and is able, to look after Inka during this coming school year, it would be better to accept it, since that is what the child herself wants. You have to respect her choice. Next summer, perhaps, you can reevaluate the situation. As for you, Helena, I realize how unhappy you are right now, but there's no need for you to treat us like enemies. Medicine's not the only thing that matters, you know!"

Without replying, Helena lit a cigarette. Her eyes met Andrzej's; there were tenderness and resignation in his look.

"Medicine . . ." he sighed. "I don't know how much longer I'll be able to practice it in this country. The other day, a woman refused to be operated on by me because I was a Jew." He looked at the group earnestly. "Let me have Inka for this year. She'll be like a ray of sunshine in the house—and do I ever need some sunshine!"

"In short, then," Irena protested, "you all consider me to be useless, no longer capable of being a mother. You think that Andrzej will be a better mother than I, is that right?"

"Oh, for God's sake!" Robert cried angrily. "We're not talking about you, but about Inka. I think Father Marianski's right. We'll accept your offer, Andrzej, and we'll talk things over again in the summer."

Robert bent his head, and Helena suddenly felt sorry for him. Poor man! Everyone seemed to forget how it hurt him to get around on his artificial leg, how brave he was, and how much self-denial was hidden behind some of his gestures. She herself had been rather cruel to him. But no matter; in a few days' time she would tell Kazik that she would marry him, and then she could stop being a burden to her parents. *In three months, I'm going to be skiing at Zakopane with my brand-new husband. To hell with love; I'll settle for comfort.* She looked at Andrzej. *To hell with love!*

"It's interesting to see how much your little sister looks like you," said Maria Solin to Helena. "The day she sat where you're sitting now, she had the same anxious look on her face."

She paused to pour boiling water into the washbasin. "Now, listen, Helena, I've spoken to two professors and the dean, and I'm quite satisfied they're going to take you back into the School of Medicine next autumn. So I'd advise you to keep on doing a bit of work here, and to wait. This Kazik Skola has got the right idea. Let him use his contacts. You shouldn't make a fuss, protest, fight, or call for an investigation. I'm sorry you have to go through this, but it will only be a few months, at the most."

"An eternity!" Helena shot back bitterly.

Maria was sitting at her little desk; with the light behind her, her face looked surprisingly young. With her blue eyes, blond hair, delicate lips, and long, graceful neck, she looked like something out of a Gainsborough painting.

"Once, I had a husband and a son, and parents whom I loved. Now I have nobody. My husband and parents are all dead, and André's probably dead too. If he were still alive, he'd be a bit older than you. He, too, wanted to study medicine . . ." She looked at Helena. "You've got your life ahead of you! Just be patient until next autumn, and try to get the most out of your work here."

Maria got up. "I think I'll go home," she said. "I'll count on you to go through the ward and make sure that Seven and Nine don't need anything. The number of night nurses is terribly inadequate; two of them, I know, left the hospital recently to work in the homes of people who've got the money to pay them: important, influential people. It's a sad fact that our workers aren't any better off today than yesterday; they still have to take on these illegal high-paying jobs to get themselves a bite to eat."

"That'll change!" said Helena. I don't know if you're aware of it, but the party's approved the reforms put forward by the Economic Council. We'll have independent businesses, run by competent people who'll be appointed by the Workers' Councils, and they won't have to be beasts of burden any longer."

"I'm all for that, Helena, but what you refuse to understand is that the Workers' Councils have victimized people, not helped them: not only that, but they're already being replaced, in some factories, by Workers' Conferences controlled by the high priests of the party, who are even more cruel and ignorant. That's the difference between us, Helena. You're in the party, you read official communiqués; but governments, names, slogans, ideologies don't mean very much to me. I'm a doctor, I treat workers; and ten years after the war, I find they're not living any better, they're still just as poorly housed, and it's all they can do to pay me with a few eggs or a chicken or a little tea or coffee."

She left, shutting the door of her little consultation room behind her. Helena made her way back to the ward, where the lights had just been turned out; she could make out only the rows of beds, and the duty nurse's table with the night-light on it. Down at the other end of the ward, a man cried out; a young nurse turned to Helena nervously, saying: "We've got to get him quiet; he'll keep the others awake."

Even suffering's a collective affair, Helena mused. It doesn't really matter if that poor fellow dies—so long as he doesn't disturb the others.

*   *   *

"Helena—at last!"

Wanda, her best friend, whom she had not seen for several months, hugged and kissed her before rushing off to class. Helena was back at the School of Medicine after receiving a piece of paper authorizing her to reenroll. She didn't know whether she felt pleased to see Wanda again, or even to be back in school. It was clear after her year's absence that she was no longer the darling of the class; in fact, she was barely tolerated by her peers. Some people would even cross to the other side of the street to avoid meeting her face to face.

Her classes were over for the day, and she was on her way to work. She preferred to stay at the hospital, where she at least felt she was appreciated. Kazik was too busy to ask her out, and she found evenings at home unbearable— Robert and Irena never seemed to stop talking about Inka.

"As soon as you give the word, I'll ask Andrzej to bring the little one back," Irena kept saying to her.

Irena was now working as a teacher for a class consisting entirely of the children of party leaders. Provided she handed out good report cards, she earned some money, and reaped considerable fringe benefits as well. She could make purchases in a special shop which was always well-stocked, and was even able to obtain certificates which protected Robert's workshop from tax investigators.

There was no doubt that the family was living better. Robert and Irena had bought Helena a lovely evening dress and two pairs of new shoes, and, to celebrate her return to the university, a little gold cross. Robert had installed a stove and obtained a stock of wood for the coming winter. And her parents had even been able to go to Cracow several times, to take presents to Inka and Andrzej. But still, they always worried about money.

It began snowing just as Helena reached the hospital, and she hurried inside. As she was walking through the lobby, a young man approached her. He was tall and attractive, and wore an odd-colored military coat from which the badges had been removed. He looked at her expectantly with intelligent brown eyes.

"Are you looking for someone?"

"Yes," he answered, "and this fool of a doorman here seems incapable of giving a coherent answer! There's a doctor here, Maria Solin, and I want to know where I can find her. She's my mother."

Helena gasped. "You must be André!"

He nodded.

"I know Maria Solin. She's waiting for you. Oh, how she's waiting for you! Come quickly." She took him by the arm and led him outside to a streetcar. Fifteen minutes later, breathless, and without having exchanged another word, they found themselves in front of Maria's house.

"Upstairs. Fourth floor." Helena pointed, and turned to go.

He hesitated for a moment as he stood in front of the entrance. "Do you work at the hospital with my mother? May I know your name?"

"Helena Stanowska," she replied, holding out her hand. He bent down and kissed her ceremoniously on the wrist, just at the edge of the glove, where the skin was not protected against the cold.

How handsome he is, Helena thought as she took a streetcar back to the hospital. And how happy Maria is going to be tonight.

For a second Helena envied Maria for the love she felt for her son. Helena would never be able to feel anything for Inka other than hatred. Sensing this, Inka did everything she could to win her over. Since she had been at Cracow with Uncle Andrzej, she had written Helena every month. Usually either Irena or Robert read these letters out loud, since Helena never even bothered to open them.

Andrzej chose to love Inka rather than take the slightest

interest in my state of mind, Helena told herself. They're all against me: Andrzej, Magda, my parents, and even Father Marianski, though he doesn't show it openly. I'll never forgive Andrzej and my parents for making me have that child. Never!

They were sitting around the table in Maria Solin's drawing room: Maria, Helena, André, and his best friend, Marek Lobusz, a slender, almost fragile-looking young man with dark eyes and a long, narrow face. Marek had returned from Paris with André, and since he had no family left, he was staying with the Solins. Maria was only too happy to be looking after the two young men.

"So," André was saying, "when these soldiers arrived at the camp to set us free, we could hardly believe our ears. They were talking Polish, not German!"

"It was General Maczek's First Division," Marek added. "We left with them, to go to Paris. They fed us well, and even gave us free liquor and cigarettes. When we got there, we wanted to study, so Maczek's officers helped us get some scholarships. Both of us enrolled in the School of Political Sciences. Those scholarships," he sighed, "were barely enough to pay the rent. It was all we could do to buy ourselves one meal a day. In the meantime, André was sending off letters to the Red Cross, the Displaced Persons Committee, and God knows who else. He kept trying to find you; he firmly believed you were still alive."

"But the worst thing of all," André remarked, "was that at the Polish military mission we were shown letters from families begging their relatives not to come back to Poland. It seemed we'd been condemned to death *in absentia* as traitors."

"Then one day we got a letter from the Red Cross telling us that Dr. Maria Solin was alive," Marek continued. "Unfortunately, the Polish authorities wouldn't disclose her address. So André decided to go back to Poland and find you himself. We went to the consulate and demanded our Polish passports."

"And you know the rest of the story," said André in conclusion.

Maria made no comment as she prepared the tea and sandwiches. "There!" she said. "A feast fit for a king: cheese and hard-boiled eggs."

"Is Paris beautiful?" Helena asked dreamily.

"It's the most beautiful city in the world," André told her, his eyes gazing into hers. "Next to Warsaw, of course."

Helena turned reluctantly to Marek. "Will you be going on with your studies?"

"Certainly not!" Marek laughed. "I'm all through with political science. Yesterday I started the ball rolling to get my party card. I want to take courses in Russian and try to become a journalist for Radio Warsaw, if I can manage it."

"As for me," said André, "I'm not a Communist like Marek, so I don't want a party card. And it's really too late for me to go back to medical school. But I would like to get into journalism, too."

"So you're going to write lies and be at the mercy of censors!" Maria said with a sigh. "Well, you're grown men now, so I won't try to tell you what to do."

The doorbell rang, and both Maria and Helena froze. Marek's face showed no reaction, and André moved calmly to the door; they had forgotten what the occupation had been like.

André opened the door, and two men in street clothes stepped in. Helena's hands began to tremble, and Maria went very pale.

"Your identity papers, please!"

André and Marek took out the papers they had been given in exchange for their passports, and Helena and Maria produced theirs.

"Both of you men report to the UB office tomorrow morning!" one of the men barked, then turned to Helena.

"As for you, comrade, you shouldn't be here. You live in Saska Kepa."

"I came to visit Dr. Solin; I work with her at the hospital," Helena replied defensively.

"Well, we'll let it go just this once, but you'd better leave right away. It's after eight o'clock, comrade."

"Yes, I'll go," said Helena compliantly.

The other UB agent was studying the apartment. "You're very comfortable here, Comrade Solin," he remarked. "Two rooms and a kitchen, and a full bathroom, too. That's quite a lot for one woman."

"My son and his friend are living with me."

"They're not registered here, so they've no right to be sleeping in your apartment."

"They went to the militia station yesterday, but they were told to come back some other time."

"We'll check that," he murmured insidiously, then turned his attention to André and Marek.

"You were a long time in the West, comrades. In no hurry to get back, were you?"

"We were students in Paris."

"That's no excuse. There are universities here."

He nodded to his partner, and they began searching the apartment. Knowing what would happen if they resisted, Helena and Maria held the two young men back, shaking their heads warningly. The agents emptied the drawers, the library shelves, the cupboards, and the suitcases stacked in a corner. Within seconds the drawing room and the adjoining bedroom were in shambles.

One of the agents found some books in André's suitcase; he spread them out on the floor and began examining them carefully. They were in French, so all he could do was to keep turning them over and over in his hands, until finally he gave up in disgust and threw them at André's feet.

"Bring these to the office tomorrow, comrade," he

ordered. "The whole suitcase. As for you, comrade"—he pointed at Helena—"you're coming with us!"

André stepped forward to protest, but Helena pushed him gently aside. "May I make a telephone call?"

"To whom?"

"My friend Kazimierz Skola, who works in the Ministry of Justice."

"Ah!" said the other agent. "Yes, we know him. Are you his fiancée?"

"Yes," replied Helena, noting André's look of pained surprise.

"Can you prove it, comrade?"

Helena opened her handbag and brought out the card Kazik had given her in case she ever ran into any trouble.

"Okay," the agent conceded. "Just this once, you can go home late. You can even sleep here; we have no objections. Good night, comrades!" All of a sudden, they seemed in a hurry to leave. The door slammed behind them. A piece of plaster came loose from the ceiling and fell to the floor.

The four of them remained where they were and stayed silent for a while, as though afraid the two men might return. Then Maria started picking up the books and the other things that lay scattered everywhere.

"You'd better sleep here," she said to Helena. "It's too late to go home."

"No," Helena objected. "My parents will be worried, and they won't be able to sleep a wink all night."

"Come on, Helena, I'll go with you," said André. "Marek will help Mother while I'm gone, and by the time I get back everything will be shipshape again."

He led her downstairs, and they began walking side by side along the gloomy street.

"So, you're engaged," André said slowly.

"No, it's not true," Helena confessed. "I just said that to stay out of their clutches. Kazik's an old friend of mine from school. He's a party officer and works at the Ministry of Justice."

"You don't know how glad that makes me!" André smiled at her, and she smiled happily back.

They were on the bridge now, with the loose boards of the sidewalk shifting beneath their feet. The moon was shining over Saska Kepa. He put his arm around her, and she turned to look at his handsome face, which was so close to hers. The unpleasantness of what they had just experienced at Maria's apartment seemed far away.

Questions, and more questions.

"Why did you go to Paris, comrade? What did you live on? Who gave you your scholarships? And why did you come back to Warsaw?"

André had to report to the UB office every week, and agents kept coming to his mother's apartment. Marek was interrogated separately, and his appointments at the UB office were never on the same days as André's.

The happiness André and his mother had felt upon being reunited was wearing down under the strain of the interrogations. André would sometimes wake up in the night and hear his mother sobbing. Not knowing how to comfort her, he would pretend not to have heard her, and then lie awake for hours staring at the ceiling.

At their neighborhood grocer's, the Solins had been told that they would no longer be served, because they had no party cards. In desperation, André took up illegal currency trading. His partner, a man he had met in a café in Nowy Swiat, was glad to pool his knowledge of the business with André's skill with foreign languages. Together they would hang around in fine hotels and haggle with French and American tourists to exchange their francs and dollars for zlotys, convincing the foreigners that their rate was the best. The profits made from the transactions were enough for André to buy groceries at various shops around town; once André even had managed to buy some Russian caviar. His mother and Marek were not aware of his activities, which, if discovered by the authorities, would land him in prison for many years.

Marek was coping in his own way with the situation. For him, hardships were the price that had to be paid for the victorious march of the people toward perfect socialism. He didn't like the visits to the UB, but he saw them as a necessary evil. In his view, a socialist state had to be vigilant and protect itself by every means against its potential enemies. In the meantime, he continued to look for people who might be able to get him into the party, and he was assiduous in his attentions to a certain influential woman at Radio Warsaw, in the hopes of convincing her to give him a job.

"You must understand," he explained to Maria, "that as long as we set ourselves against those who hold party cards, nothing's going to change. One has to be a member of the party, go to meetings, influence those who have the power to make decisions, and gradually bring about change. To stay on the outside is giving up, or at worst, committing a kind of treason. One must step in and fight."

Maria smiled agreeably and said nothing. She was too worried about the practical concerns at hand to think about politics. The visits from the UB agents were a nightmare, and she was beginning to get anxious about André, who always had too much money in his pocket.

Helena was the only one who managed to cheer her up. Maria knew that André and she were in love, although she didn't understand why Helena seemed to go out of her way to avoid being left alone with him. In any case, she was careful not to interfere with the relationship.

In fact, Helena was troubled by her feelings for André. She knew she had fallen in love with him, but she also realized that she could never bring herself to tell him about her past. How could he possibly love her, knowing that she had been raped, and had a child as well? She told herself over and over again that she was not worthy of his love.

Irena and Robert had become quite attached to André. He often dropped by Robert's workshop to give him a hand with his work, and the two of them would talk for hours on end. Helena found this growing friendship between André and her father very distressing. She was afraid that her father might tell André about her past, and that André would never speak to her again. As though he had guessed her thoughts, Robert drew her to his side one day and assured her otherwise. "Don't worry, I'll never talk to André Solin about your personal affairs. You're a big enough girl to do that on your own. It's a matter between the two of you, and it's none of my business. But if you'll let your old father express his opinion, I feel you would be better off telling him the truth. If you really love each other, then he deserves that from you."

Helena went to her room and lay in bed pondering her father's words. She could hear Irena practicing on the small piano that Robert had managed to get for her.

Irena had also offered advice to Helena: "If you feel you want to spend the rest of your life with him, then he's the one. Don't let him go, no matter what!"

André was the only person she really wanted to be together with for always. But he was also someone she admired so much that she was constantly afraid of showing herself to be inferior in his eyes. The mere thought that she was going to see him was enough to brighten her day, but in his company she always experienced a kind of anguish. She worried that she was not intelligent or interesting enough for him. And there was the issue of her past.

There was a knock at the door, and Helena sat up abruptly. Irena had stopped her playing.

"Is anyone here? It's Kazik."

"Kazik!" Helena jumped to her feet. It had been a long time since Kazik had come to see her.

"I really can't stay," Kazik said after greetings had been exchanged. "Would you like to go for a walk, Helena? It's very pleasant outside."

"Good idea," Helena agreed. "I can't stay out too late, though. I have classes early tomorrow morning."

On the street, Kazik turned around several times to make sure they weren't being followed. Helena couldn't help laughing at him.

"It's no joking matter!" Kazik murmured. "I've been engaged in some very top-secret business since I saw you last. For one, I was a member of the delegation that met with the Russians to negotiate terms concerning relations between us and their soldiers. We managed to wring a major concession out of them. Russian soldiers on Polish territory will no longer enjoy the absolute immunity they've had up until now. If they commit robberies, rapes, and other crimes of that nature, they'll have to answer for them in court, and be sentenced by our judges, just like any other citizen."

"And while you were deciding the fate of the world," Helena broke in, "I was subjected to a search by the UB agents at Maria Solin's. I had to mention your name to save myself."

Kazik's face grew hard. "What happened?"

Helena told him the whole story.

"Those two jokers are going to spend a few months in jail," said Kazik angrily. "As for André and Marek, I'll make arrangements to ensure that they won't be bothered anymore. This Marek sounds interesting. Tell him to come to my office the day after tomorrow, in the morning. If he's as good as he sounds, he'll have his party card, and even a job at Radio Warsaw. We need people like him: young, honest people who want to help build socialism. We'll never make any progress with the kind of parasites we have now. For example, a man came to my office the other day. He'd been summoned to court for some minor traffic offense, nothing serious. Now, completely by chance, he happened to recognize the judge. They'd been together in Siberia, in one of the labor camps. Our so-called judge, a Russian, by the way, had been sentenced to life for two murders! He had escaped while being transported from one place to another. How he managed to reach the Polish frontier, all alone, in winter, I simply don't know. But the fact is that he used the papers of one of his victims, a Polish lawyer, to make a career for himself in Warsaw as a judge. Just imagine, a Russian murderer, barely able to read and write, sitting on the bench in a Polish court and deciding the fate of others! Of course, after investigating the matter, I managed to get rid of him without any fuss. He resigned, and off he went."

"But he should have been tried and sentenced!" Helena protested.

"Should have been, should have been!" said Kazik crossly. "It's easy to say that, but I can't afford to stir up that kind of trouble. Don't you understand, Helena? It's for you I'm trying to keep my hands clean. For you, for me, for our future together." Helena winced, and said nothing.

Suddenly Kazik seemed very tired. "It's late, I'd better take you home. When are we going to see each other again?"

She thought for a moment. "If you're free next weekend, we could go out to Celestynow."

"Splendid! I'll get a car, so we can take your parents and any friends you want to bring along."

At the door, Helena hurried inside to avoid a long good-bye scene. She knew she was leading Kazik on unfairly. He thought she was free, and hoped to make her his wife one day; he had no idea that she was in love with another man. Yet, Helena enjoyed being loved by Kazik, who expected nothing more of her than to be his pretty and charming companion. With André, love was a challenge; it was important that she be bright, that she please his friends, that she become a great doctor, like his mother. With Kazik, it was all so easy.

I'm being dishonest, Helena told herself as she went to sleep, to let Kazik think everything is fine between us, when I'm madly in love with André. But how can I tell him? And how can I bring myself to tell André about my past? Oh, if only Mother and Father could understand my problems. But I'll never be able to talk to them about this. I'm so alone. Oh, how alone I am!

6

ANDRZEJ RYBICKI WAS in a good mood as he walked home from the hospital. He always looked forward to seeing Inka's smiling face, which in the past few years had become a source of great joy for the other three occupants of the house as well.

Originally Madame Nalkowska, the housekeeper, had suspected that Inka was Andrzej's illegitimate daughter. But gradually she came to see Andrzej as the kind uncle of a child whose parents didn't want her around—for whatever reason—and, having no children of her own, soon took Inka under her wing.

Dr. Jozef Kalina had come from Lvov in 1957. At first he had found it hard to express himself in Polish; during the war, and the years that followed, he had been compelled to serve in a hospital where only Russian was spoken. Small and thin, with a face as sharp as a knife blade topped by a mop of white hair, he was a tough, silent old man. Yet Inka's youthful presence had an effect on him; he began to open up to the others, little by little. He even helped Inka with her math homework every night, with a gentleness and patience that surprised everyone.

On the other hand, Andrzej's other housemate, Dr. Wojtek Rzeplinski, was quite talkative and easygoing, despite the fact that he had been a prisoner in a German concentration camp and had lost his wife and children to the war. He was tall and thick-set, and looked like a bear; he was also an excellent surgeon, and Andrzej admired his work immensely. Wojtek took Inka to Wawel Castle every Sunday, or to eat pastries at Michalik's. He always swung her up on his shoulders when they went out, despite Madame Nalkowska's protests that Inka was too old for it.

Inka will have many happy memories of this place, Andrzej thought tenderly. I did right to insist on bringing her here with me. It's not always easy for her, of course, but it would have been a lot worse in Warsaw, with Helena.

No one was home. Inka was at school, and his two colleagues were still at the hospital. Madame Nalkowska was no doubt shopping for food; the problem of finding something to eat was even more serious in Cracow than in Warsaw. It was months now since there had been any meat, and besides, the mad hunt for a pair of shoes or a coat for Inka had become a priority for all four of them.

Andrzej lit a cigarette. Suddenly his stomach contracted in a painful spasm, and he fell against the wall, trying to catch his breath. This was not the first time it had happened to him. For more than two years now he had been treating himself for a stomach ulcer, but he had never had it examined by another doctor. He suspected, deep inside, that it was some incurable illness, probably cancer, and decided it would be useless to try to do anything about it.

Doubled up with the pain, Andrzej dragged himself over to the sofa. Someone had forgotten to turn off the radio on the little table, and he found himself listening to the closing sentences of a speech. Wladyslaw Gomulka was the speaker; he was talking about the Jews, the dangers they represented for the People's Poland, and the necessity of neutralizing their influence.

Andrzej gritted his teeth to avoid crying out in anger. Then the pain returned, more excruciating than ever. He fell from the sofa and hit his head on the concrete floor, losing all sense of time and space as he lapsed into unconsciousness.

Inka had been told that the school she had been attending for the last five years was the best in Cracow, but sometimes she found it hard to believe. The National Education Commission's High School Number 10 had fewer sports and cultural events than the other schools, and far more hard work. And because there had been no uprising in Cracow, the leaders were the same as in prewar times: old, stern, and indifferent to the festivities and celebrations other schools held for the various important anniversaries of the People's Poland.

"Take advantage of your education, and don't grumble!" Madame Nalkowska told her, while Uncle Andrzej said that Inka was lucky to have been spared the curriculum Helena had followed in her day, when she had been at school in Warsaw.

But there was something much worse, something Inka took care not to talk about at home.

"Your parents don't want you!" a big freckle-faced boy had shouted at her one day during recess. "And your uncle's a Jew!"

Inka's reply had been to pull the boy's hair as hard as she could. A fight had followed, but she had been the one to get the bad-conduct mark.

Another time, the girls in her class had tried to prevent her from entering the classroom. She had waited for the professor, and then slipped inside at his heels. Upon reaching her desk, she had found writing all over it: "Jewess, filthy Jewess!"

Inka realized Uncle Andrzej would be very distressed if he knew what was going on, so she said nothing. In the meantime, he attributed her lack of a social life outside the house to her age.

"You're too young," Uncle Andrzej had explained to her. "Wait a little. In two or three years' time, you'll have a whole regiment of lads courting you, and your old uncle will have to protect you!"

That evening, as Inka walked home from school, she wistfully watched groups of students heading for the Café Rio, a favorite hangout. No one ever asked her to go; nor did any of the boys ever take her to Planty Park, where young couples in love strolled hand in hand. She noticed that some people from her class were heading in her direction; she turned away and quickened her pace, so they would not see her.

Inka got back to the house just before six o'clock. While she was fumbling in her handbag for the key, a red-eyed Madame Nalkowska opened the door and took the bewildered young girl in her arms.

"Your Uncle Andrzej is in the hospital," she said. "He's very ill. Dr. Wojtek and Dr. Jozef are looking after him."

Inka was speechless.

"Dr. Jozef's promised to come and get us so that we can go see him. Now, have something to eat while you're waiting."

"I'm not hungry," Inka replied. "I'm not hungry at all."

The people Inka loved and became attached to always went away and left her. That's what had happened to her with Magda, at Celestynow, and now it was going to be the same story with Uncle Andrzej.

"If Uncle Andrzej has to stay in the hospital for a long time, you're going to let me stay here, aren't you? I don't want to go away!" There were tears in Inka's eyes, and Madame Nalkowska was moved by her distress.

"Of course, darling! Of course you'll stay here with us.

Besides, your uncle's going to get well and come back to us. Everything will be all right, you'll see!"

Madame Nalkowska stroked the blond locks. She would have liked to tell Inka that she would move heaven and earth to keep her there, that Inka was the light of her life and her only consolation in the grayness of her day-to-day existence. But how does one say such things to a little girl of fifteen?

Inka was praying silently as Madame Nalkowska began plaiting her hair: Dear God, make Uncle Andrzej get well quickly. I promise to pray properly at Mass and not daydream ever again, if only you'll arrange to make Uncle Andrzej get well and come home to me.

The little room was almost completely dark. On either side of the bed, the church candles were slowly burning down; they lit up Andrzej's face and hands, which held a crucifix. Death had smoothed away his wrinkles so that he looked younger, and his features wore a look of indifference that Irena had never known in him while he was alive. Seated beside Robert, she tried to pray, but she kept getting swept away by the flood of her memories: the war years, her loneliness and fear, and the smile of this man, always so ready to give her courage, now gone from her forever.

It had happened in the spring of 1943. Andrzej had come to bring her some underground newspapers for distribution, and a can of cocoa he had managed to get for Helena. He and Irena were sitting side by side, talking in whispers so as not to wake Helena. Suddenly, a little after midnight, there was a loud noise, and the house shook. They had rushed to the window; in the distance there was a fire blazing up into the sky.

Andrzej had put his arms around her shoulders. Pressed against his chest, Irena had been overtaken by a fit of trembling. Very gently Andrzej had turned her toward him and covered her face with kisses; but just as she was about to return his embrace, she had thought of Robert. Pushing Andrzej away, she had dashed madly for the stairs.

That was the night on which the Russians had dropped bombs on German-occupied Warsaw.

For Irena, the memory of that spring night remained graven on her mind. For months afterward she had felt ashamed; and then, later on, that feeling had turned to regret. Especially during the uprising, when she thought she would never see Robert again, she would reproach herself for the absurd chastity of her body. Yes, she could have loved Andrzej, belonged to him, and known with him a physical passion that Robert could never give her.

But instead, she and Andrzej had lived together as friends. He had been her protector, the one person without whom she would have found it impossible to raise Helena, keep waiting for Robert, and face the dangers of every succeeding day.

I'll never be able to thank him now for what he did for me and my little ones, Irena thought. I thought I'd have plenty of time to show him my gratitude, but I was wrong. And now, it's too late! She hid her face in her hands and began to weep.

On the other side of the deathbed Helena was on her knees, deep in thought. She was recalling Andrzej's last words to her in the hospital room: "Helena, tell me you don't regret having brought Inka into this world. That little girl's so beautiful, and she deserves so much to be looked after, protected, guided. Helena, promise me you'll take care of her. . . ."

"I promised you, Uncle Andrzej, and I'll keep my word," Helena murmured as she rose to her feet. "You can rest in peace." She bent down to pick up Inka, who had fallen asleep on the floor, carried her to her room, put her to bed and covered her, then tiptoed out of the room.

Out in the corridor, Helena collapsed against the wall
and began sobbing. Uncle Andrzej was gone, and he had
taken with him a part of her memories, her youth, and her
dreams. What was left was for her to honor his last wish.
She would have to learn to love Inka somehow, and assume the duty she had thought herself to be free of once
and for all. As for André Solin, if he truly loved her, then
he would have to accept her past, and Inka's part in her
life.

Helena went back to Andrzej's bed and began praying.
In the flickering candlelight she saw the suffering on her
parents' faces. For the first time she realized that she was
responsible for this man and woman, her father and mother,
who must be able to count on her, as she had counted on
them in the past.

Madame Nalkowska dressed quickly and went outside
to fetch some wood and water for coffee. She felt Dr.
Andrzej's absence most strongly in the morning, when she
prepared breakfast for the household. He used to come
into the kitchen just as she was striking the first match,
take it from her hand, and get the stove going in no time,
whistling a tune as he did so.

"Poor man, may God preserve his soul!" Madame
Nalkowska said to herself. She had decided that he should
be buried in her own family vault, in the Catholic cathedral,
right next to her brother: he would be better off there
than anywhere else; the old Jewish cemetery had no care-
taker and was in a terrible state. She had also arranged for
a plate carrying his name, the dates of his birth and death,
and the very simple inscription: "Here lies a man who
knew how to be kind."

The kettle started boiling, and almost immediately Dr.
Jozef came in, followed by Dr. Wojtek. Madame Nalkowska
left them in the kitchen and went into the next room,
where the Stanowski family was keeping vigil. She crossed

herself, and knelt for a short prayer; then she woke Irena and Robert and the girls, who had gone to sleep in their chairs. In a few seconds they were all seated around the kitchen table. Madame Nalkowska put out some bread and strawberry jam, which had actually been made with beets.

"We must go and see the grave-digger," she said. "I've got a chicken ready for him, and a dozen eggs. He's an honest man, and he'll do a good job. They brought the coffin yesterday evening. It's not new, but it's in good condition. It's a high-quality military coffin."

"I'll reimburse you for all your expenses," Robert murmured.

"No, no, it's all paid for already!" Dr. Jozef protested. "He was our friend. Really, you can't refuse us this, it's the least we can do."

"What does it matter?" Inka suddenly cried out. "Uncle Andrzej's dead, right next door, and I'll never ever see him again!"

There was something so heart-wrenching in the girl's voice that they all turned toward her. Dr. Wojtek got up and took her by the hand. "Come on," he said, "we'll go and get some flowers. Your Uncle Andrzej loved flowers. That will make you feel better."

Sobbing, Inka followed him obediently.

"Go and put his things in order," Madame Nalkowska told Irena, "while I get myself ready for the funeral. The priest will be here any minute now."

Zofia Nalkowska went across the kitchen and shut herself in the little cubbyhole, where she changed, daubed her cheeks carefully with what little lipstick was left in the tube, and did her hair. In the room next door, they were preparing to put the body into the coffin, the big black second-hand coffin, which was to serve as Dr. Andrzej's last resting place.

*   *   *

It was a fine warm day. Irena opened the window and leaned out to look at the festivities on the streets. Robert was listening to the radio, waiting for the usual speeches.

Exactly twenty years ago this July, he had been preparing for his third escape attempt from the prisoner-of-war camp. Twenty years! There was nothing to celebrate in a failed escape attempt, but down there in the streets they were all busy parading like idiots in honor of the twentieth anniversary of the People's Poland. They were welcoming their masters!

Nikita Khrushchev and his stooges had arrived and were on their way to take their places on the stands. The Polish officials, with Gomulka at their head, were bowing and scraping like the lackeys they'd become. The radio began broadcasting the speeches, and Robert strained to listen.

"The present production potential is nine times greater than it was in bourgeois Poland. The industrial production per capita in this country has reached sixty percent of that in Great Britain, France, West Germany, and Italy, while in the days of bourgeois Poland it never reached more than seventeen or eighteen percent . . . Despite a terrible war, despite all the destruction, we have succeeded in eliminating unemployment—"

"What a catastrophic farce!" Robert cried as he turned the radio off. "To listen to them, you'd think we were all rich and happy, when in fact we can barely get enough water." For the past week, Irena had had to go to a pump several times a day for water; there was always a long line, and it was an exhausting task for her. Robert was ashamed of not being able to do it himself, because of his leg.

Irena turned around. "Helena will be back soon," she said. "Then we can find out how things went in the heart of the city. There's not too much to see here." She felt a bit envious of her daughter, who could participate in any demonstration or march she wanted to. Robert would never forgive her if she went to join Helena; he despised crowds, and he found holidays, particularly this one, irritating.

At that very moment, Helena had just joined Kazik at the corner of Jerozolimskie Avenue. In the sunshine, everything looked very pleasant; there were flowers everywhere, and the whole atmosphere was joyful and enthusiastic. But Helena was unable to fall in with the general mood.

Kazik took her arm with a smile. "Right now, I've got to join the others for the speeches. There's a place reserved for me in the stands, and you're coming with me!"

"No!" Helena objected suddenly. "I won't go up in the stands; that wouldn't be honest. You believe in all this, but for me it's different."

"Don't talk nonsense, Helena! That's pure defeatism. It must be that André Solin of yours who's putting all these crazy ideas into your head. You shouldn't see so much of him."

Helena tensed at the mention of his name. "But I don't see him very often. He's too busy looking for work."

There was bitterness in Helena's voice, and an unmistakable note of reproach.

"I'm doing what I can for him, and you know it! Besides, why can't we ever go out without having to talk about him?" Kazik frowned. "Ah, here's the car. Get in, Helena."

It was a long black convertible. A uniformed chauffeur got out and opened the door; Helena climbed in and settled herself into the soft cushioned seat. With her white tailored suit, her big hat from the milliner on Wiejska Street, and her Italian shoes, bought on the black market, she felt like a queen.

"You're beautiful, Helena," Kazik murmured at her side, "and I'm happy to be able to show the whole world what a lucky man I am."

Helena gave him her most radiant smile. The car was moving quite slowly; someone threw a red carnation, and she caught it in midair. She remembered the feeling of

solidarity she had experienced in 1956, when she had
listened to Gomulka's speech, lost in a crowd not unlike
this one. But this time, it was different. She seemed to
have won something intangible, moved up a step, gained
the right to be admired and driven around in this superb
limousine.

The car came to a stop. Kazik said a few words to the
militiamen outside, who let them pass, and they drove a
little farther until they came to the stands. He was in high
spirits, welcoming the admiring looks Helena inspired. He
was proud to be with her, proud of her beauty, her charm,
and the grace of her every movement. Helena responded
happily; with André, this type of male pride merely irritated her, but with Kazik she found herself enjoying it.

After the speeches were over, they drove to a mansion
hidden away in a huge park, to attend a special banquet.
They went up onto the terrace, where Kazik introduced
her to a group of people; inside, they found a buffet
waiting for them. It was a long table covered with a white
cloth, displaying hams, cheeses, salads, fruit, vodka, and
wine. They were served by waiters in white jackets and
gloves, just like in the foreign films, Helena thought. She
ate with enjoyment; she had never seen so much food in
her life, and she found herself thinking that contrary to
what she had always been taught, luxury was not necessarily repugnant.

The vodka and wine flowed, and the whole company
was gradually becoming merrier and merrier. At the far
end of the hall, the sliding doors were opened, and the
orchestra began to play. As if in a dream, Helena let
herself be swept away onto the dance floor in someone's
arms; then he was gone, and there was another. She forgot
about Kazik and André, and all of her problems; she felt
exhilarated. But the feeling lasted for only a moment;
Kazik cut in, gripping her hands in his.

"We've got to leave at once!"

"Oh, no, not yet!" Helena protested.

"Do you want me to leave you here alone?"

Helena suddenly realized she knew no one else at the party.

"Let's go," she said dejectedly.

He took her hand, and they went out by the little side door, past a drunken militiaman who called out: "Oh, surely you're not leaving already?"

"I'm afraid so," Kazik replied firmly. "This lady's not feeling well."

Why was he lying? What was going on? As they got into the car, Helena was bursting with questions, but Kazik signaled her to keep quiet, pointing to the chauffeur. At the next corner, he told the chauffeur to stop. Then he made Helena get out, kissed her hand, and got back into the car, leaving her stranded there, alone and bewildered, with her beautiful Italian shoes that were killing her feet and not enough money for a taxi.

It was dark by now. Helena walked to the nearest streetcar stop, ignoring the hostile looks her tailored white suit was attracting. When the streetcar came, it was packed and she had to fight her way in.

"Out working, are you, darling?" someone yelled out. "But I bet a pretty little ass like yours brings in a good bit of money, don't it?"

Helena reacted without thinking, and slapped the man as hard as she could. He slapped her in return, and at the next stop he pushed her roughly outside. She found herself on the sidewalk, her skirt torn and her nose bleeding. She had lost her shoes and hat somehow. Gripping her handbag tightly, she struggled to her feet and leaned against a lamppost.

"Had a drop too much to drink, darling?" Two militiamen were at her side, sly grins on their faces. "Come on, sweetheart, let's see your papers!"

They examined her papers for an unbearably long time,

making humiliating little jokes, before they let her go. Barefoot, and barraged by jeers and whistles, she made her way across the bridge and stumbled home.

Her father opened the door for her, and she hurled herself into his arms. Her parents didn't ask her any questions. Robert brought her a cup of tea, and between sobs Helena told them the story. Irena washed her face with a damp cloth, while Robert stroked her hand.

"Something serious must have happened," Robert concluded. "Kazik would never have left you like that unless he absolutely had to."

Robert turned out to be right. The next day, Kazik appeared in his workshop just before closing time.

"Come," he said. "I'll walk home with you." They walked along for a while side by side, in silence; then Kazik began talking in a voice so low that Robert could hardly hear him.

"They tried to kill Khrushchev and Gomulka. There was a bomb hidden on their route, a homemade bomb. The car in front of them was blown up, and three people died. I've got to go now. Not a word to anybody except Helena. I'm terribly sorry, but I've very little time. We've absolutely got to find some suspects; doesn't matter who, just some suspects."

Kazik disappeared, and Robert felt a shiver run down his spine. He was well aware that an attempt to assassinate Khrushchev and Gomulka could lead to massive arrests. It was an excellent opportunity to arrest and condemn intellectuals who had nothing to do with the whole matter.

When he reached the house, he threw a pebble at the window; this was the family's signal to come down at once. A second later, Irena and Helena were at his side, and he quickly repeated Kazik's story.

"Kazik came and told me all this. He heard about it during the reception yesterday, and he wanted you to understand why he behaved the way he did, Helena."

"My God," Irena murmured. "Perhaps we'd better start buying flour tomorrow, and anything else we can find in the shops, just in case."

They spent half of the night listening to broadcasts from the BBC and from Radio Free Europe, hoping to hear some more information, but it seemed that the news of the attempted assassination had not leaked abroad, there was nothing in the newspapers either. Helena went to check the television set in the shop window on Marszalkowska Street, but all she got were programs on the great festivities for the twentieth anniversary of the People's Poland.

As the weeks went by, the silence seemed to the Stanowskis more ominous than if something terrible had actually resulted from the incident.

7

"I'VE FOUND OUR man," said Marek slowly.

He and Kazik were walking along the edge of the woods. It was a hot day, and the air was fragrant with the smell of pine needles.

"Are you sure he's the one?" Kazik asked.

"Absolutely certain. He's an old man, quite senile. I think his parents are dead, and he's got no family in the village. He was in the neighborhood at the time of the assassination attempt—looking for mushrooms, he says. They don't care for him very much in the village, so nobody's going to stick up for him."

"The perfect culprit," said Kazik approvingly. "What's his name?"

"Stanislaw Zbrzycha. He's a practicing Catholic, like the rest of them."

"No Ukrainian or Soviet background, or any other problems of that nature?"

"No, nothing special like that, I've seen to that. It will be an easy job. There's a shed where he keeps his gardening tools. All we need do is plant some evidence in it to make it look like there was a homemade bomb put to-

gether there. I'll do it myself, so that I don't have to bring
my men into it; it would be better not to have any
witnesses."

"You've thought of everything." There was a touch of
irony in Kazik's voice. "Let's go and have a look at him. If
everything is as you say it is, we can have him arrested
this afternoon. Do you think you can plant the necessary
stuff in the shed while I go and question him?"

"Yes, I think so, provided you can give me an hour."

"No problem."

Kazik put his jacket around his shoulders and walked
several steps ahead of his companion. Marek was doing
very well at his new job as the head of a Citizens' Volunteer Militia unit, and Kazik was glad to have had some
part in getting it for him. Now, if only he could carry off
this mission without any slip-ups!

"Will you give me a lift in your car?" Marek called to
him.

Kazik turned around and shook his head. "It would be
better if we weren't seen together. You'd better take your
bike and get over there as fast as you can. I'll meet you in
Warsaw a week from now at the Krakowskie Przedmiescie
Church, around five P.M., for a follow-up report. At that
hour, there's not much risk of running into anybody. Good
luck to you!"

Kazik got into his car and drove off. Marek's directions
were quite clear. He found the hut very easily, and
Stanislaw Zbrzycha himself was sitting on a little bench
outside his door.

The poor man, thought Kazik. I've got to fix it so that
they don't execute him. He'll do a few years in jail, and
then I'll see that he gets released.

Meanwhile, Marek was pedaling along the sanded road
as fast as his legs would take him; he had very little time
to get everything there and put it in place. He had yet to
feel completely comfortable about the job he was about to

do. He knew that it was for the good of socialist Poland, though. Moscow had threatened to suspend payment of the money the Polish government had borrowed to increase agricultural production, unless the person responsible for the assassination attempt was found quickly. And without more food, public discontent would grow, and there would be trouble.

Besides, Marek was well aware of the fact that if this job should succeed, he might be able to ask for Radio Warsaw after all.

Stanislaw Zbrzycha looked in astonishment at the militiamen surrounding him. He had no idea what was going on. They put handcuffs on him, heaved him up into the truck, and pushed him down between the two men already seated inside. It was dark, and Stanislaw couldn't make out their faces.

The militiamen had interrogated him and pushed him about, and although he had tried his hardest, he couldn't remember what he had been doing in the woods that day. At first he thought he had been looking for mushrooms, but now he was no longer completely certain. However, he was quite sure that the things they had found in the toolshed hadn't been there before, and that he had never seen them or touched them.

Stanislaw had a terrible headache and could no longer think straight. Luckily, Czeslaw Radjewski had seen him being taken away. Czeslaw was a good boy; he would look after the house and wouldn't let any prowlers come and take the vegetables from his garden. Yes, that was lucky.

The truck drove off into the night, and Stanislaw groaned softly, wishing the pain in his head would stop.

Everything had gone badly from the start. Early that afternoon, Czeslaw Radjewski had gone to see Stanislaw Zbrzycha. He had knocked on the door, but the old man hadn't answered. It was at that moment that Czeslaw had seen a man coming out of the toolshed, moving very cautiously. Czeslaw had realized that he was probably a thief and decided to follow him. The man had a bicycle, and Czeslaw had had to run at top speed in order not to lose sight of him. The man had stopped in front of a house, gone in, and come out again carrying a heavy sack on his back, which he had then taken back to Zbrzycha's toolshed on his bicycle. Czeslaw had run madly after him and hidden in the grass. When the man had finally come out of the toolshed and started to leave, Czeslaw had started to follow him again, but just then a black car and a truck had pulled up and several men had gone into Zbrzycha's house. They had come back out with Zbrzycha, prodding him in the back with revolvers. Czeslaw had watched them go into the shed and bring out some objects, which they had held under Zbrzycha's nose, shouting. Around nightfall, they had pushed Zbrzycha into a truck, in handcuffs.

Czeslaw decided to do what he could for his old friend. He went back to the house to which he had followed the strange man earlier. The man was still there now, tidying the bed and obviously getting ready to go. Czeslaw watched him for a moment, with his face pressed against the window, then made up his mind to confront him. The door was not shut. He pushed it open and went inside, but at the same moment, the man swung around and aimed his revolver at him.

Czeslaw tried to knock the man down, and they fell to the floor struggling. But just as Czeslaw had almost succeeded in crushing his opponent beneath him, a shot rang out. Czeslaw released his grip immediately; the man lay still, very pale and barely breathing. Overcome with fear, Czeslaw dashed out of the house and started running down the road.

*   *   *

Marek could not remember how long he had lain there before his assistant from the Citizens' Volunteer Militia had found him and taken him to a hospital.

The doctor examined him very carefully. "You were pretty far gone," he told Marek. "The bullet went through your lung, but I've managed to get it out. You've been lucky so far, but your convalescence is going to take some time. Have you any family? Anyone we can get in touch with?"

Marek hesitated for a moment. He couldn't get Maria Solin and André involved, so he had no choice but to have the doctor contact Kazik.

Marek wrote Kazik's name and telephone number on a sheet of paper, then fell back weakly against his pillow.

Helena ran as fast as she could. She was supposed to meet André at the Café Roksana; he had something very important to tell her, he had said. She was already half an hour late when she reached the café and found André at a corner table.

"Helena, at last! I was afraid you weren't coming. Oh, Helena, I've got such news for you—for us both! Quick, tell me: do you love me?"

Helena stared at him in surprise. "Yes, André, I love you, but . . ."

"But what? Listen, darling, I've wanted for so long to ask you to marry me, but up until now I didn't dare. I had no home to offer you. But now that's all changed—I've got an apartment! We're going to get married, we're going to be together." He paused. "That is, if you'll have me. I know I don't have a job yet . . ."

He leaned forward and took Helena's hands in his own. She saw the silent pleading in his eyes.

"Whether you have a job or not doesn't really worry me," she said carefully. "But there's my past, André."

"We don't have any past. Our lives began that evening

when we met each other in the hospital. It doesn't matter to me what you may have done before then."

"Yes, darling, but I wouldn't want you to feel that I'm hiding things from you which you may not be ready to accept."

"I accept anything and everything in advance. Even if you should tell me that you used to work in a brothel, that wouldn't change anything. I love you as you are."

Helena thought for a moment, then broke into a smile. "Yes, then, André, I'll marry you."

Helena would never forget that moment. André's face exploded with joy, and he pushed the table aside to take her into his arms.

"Come on, I want to show you our new home," he said, taking her by the hand.

He was so impatient that they nearly got run over as they crossed the street to the taxi stand. In the back seat of the taxi, he started kissing her wildly and Helena couldn't help but notice the taxi driver's shocked look in the rearview mirror.

"Kids," he muttered as they got out and ran off laughing.

Before them was a brand-new housing project, built on an unfinished park dotted with young trees and piles of sand and soil.

"Up these stairs." André pointed. "We're on the third floor."

At the door, André picked her up and carried her into the big, tastefully furnished room. There was a window that looked out over the park. "There's a kitchen, and a bathroom too," André said excitedly. "The gas works, there's hot water, and most of the time the central heating works. We're going to have a bed, a real one, and fresh linen. And in the kitchen there are pots and pans and dishes."

Helena was stunned. "How did you find this place?"

"Through a businessman. He's been transferred, so he's

not coming back for two or three years. He agreed to let
me have the apartment because he knew how much I
wanted it. The apartment's still in his name. No paperwork,
no problems, no visits to the Cooperative, nothing; we'll
just pay the rent at the office a few yards away. He's a
Frenchman—that's how he managed to furnish the place
so nicely. The French have great taste. Don't you think
it's fantastic?"

"Are you sure this arrangement's going to work? It's not
legal; your Frenchman doesn't have the right to hand an
apartment over to us like this without getting approval
from the Cooperative."

"Don't worry about it, it's all fixed. The employee in
charge of the records has had his palm greased."

"You must have spent a fortune to get him to do that!
Where did you get the money?"

"I have my ways." Not wanting to tell her about his
illegal currency trading, he quickly changed the subject.
"So, Helena, when are we going to get married? Tomorrow?"

"We'll go to Celestynow this weekend. Father Marianski
will be very glad to marry us."

Helena admired the deep blue carpet, the beautiful
Chinese screen that separated the bed from the rest of the
room, and the bookshelves filled with French books.

"We'll have all these to read during our honeymoon,"
said André. "We're going to hide away here, just the two
of us, with the books, and the view of the park, and each
other."

Helena had never known such a feeling of oneness with
a man.

"Happy?" Robert asked Irena.

She nodded, smiling. "Yes, of course I am. Everything
went so well, and Helena looked radiant. I like André
very much. And now that Helena's room is free, Inka can

come live with us. Finally, after all these years, we're going to have her here."

"I know she'll be glad to come back here," Robert added. "It hasn't been the same for her at that house without Andrzej."

Irena winced at the sound of Andrzej's name. It was spring, and outside, the trees were covered with new leaves. During the wedding service, Irena had thought only of him. Seeing Helena and André together had evoked pent-up memories, and she had asked herself once again the question that had tormented her for years: why hadn't she yielded to Andrzej that April night long ago?

And now it was too late. Andrzej was dead. Between Robert and her there was only a tender sort of friendship. She loved Robert, and yet there were times when she would lie awake at night thinking of Andrzej. Like a schoolgirl, she would try to conjure up his image in her mind, to capture the delicious confusion she had experienced in his arms.

"You're not listening to me!" Robert's words interrupted her reverie.

"Yes, I am. I'm just . . . tired."

"Do you want to go to bed?" he asked immediately, with infinite concern in his voice.

He opened the divan and got out the sheets, pillows, and blankets. Irena undressed and washed her face at the washstand. Suddenly the lights went out.

"Don't worry, I've got a candle," Robert called out to her. He knew how frightened she was of the dark. He lit the candle and took her in his arms.

"My darling!" he murmured. "My sweet Irena . . ."

He led her over to the divan, helped her under the covers, then lay down beside her, holding her close against him. Comforted by his presence, Irena fell asleep. Robert moved away from her very gently and sat up. He could not stop thinking about last week's unexpected visit from

the tax inspector. Suddenly they wanted five years of back
taxes from him, when they had been telling him all along
that he wasn't required to pay taxes. What was he going to
do?

Nickel by nickel, he had saved a thousand American
dollars. They were hidden underneath the divan on which
he was lying, and he could change them the next day; on
the black market, he could get a hundred zlotys to the
dollar. But that wouldn't be enough to pay what they were
demanding: two hundred thousand zlotys. And it would
be out of the question to ask Irena to sell her piano and
the little engagement ring he had given her years ago.

He looked at his wife's sleeping figure. Irena would be
better off without him. She could get married again, to a
man more resourceful than he was. A man with both his
legs. A man with a real job. A man who would be a father
to little Inka. A man—

No, Robert told himself. I'm going to fight this thing to
the bitter end. I'll get the money somehow, and a better
job. I owe it to both of us.

Helena got up first and went to the kitchen to make
breakfast, taking care not to make any noise. With a bit of
luck, she and André could leave for Celestynow without
waking Marek, who was fast asleep on the floor.

She lit a cigarette. André doesn't realize how much he
expects me to put up with, she thought bitterly. I realize
Marek is his best friend, and has no family to stay with,
but how can the three of us go on living in this one room?
Now, Kazik would never have put me through something
like this—

And that wasn't all. Three weeks after their wedding,
Helena had been busy hanging curtains when there had
been a knock at the door, and a strange girl had barged
into the room. The girl had been dressed in tight jeans
and a white fur jacket.

"Where is he?" she had demanded.

"Who's 'he'?"

"Gilbert, of course."

That was how Helena had met Dosia, the mistress of the French businessman who had sublet the apartment to André. Dosia had met Gilbert at a bar when she was sixteen. That first evening, he had taken her out to dinner, and they had gone dancing. Afterward he had given her money.

"Take it!" he had said with a laugh. "In any case, with the black-market rate of exchange, young girls like you cost much less in your country than they do in mine!"

In the beginning, Dosia had not understood, but she had soon come to realize that he had made himself her "patron."

"He was honest," she had told Helena, her eyes filled with tears. "He told me he was married and had two children. We lived here, in this apartment, for several months. Then he went back to France. He came again shortly after Christmas, with his suitcases full of presents."

She had paused. "He didn't stay for long, though. And what's more, yesterday a man came to see me at the shop where I work. A Frenchman, like Gilbert, but old and fat and bald, a member of the French Communist-party delegation. He brought me a letter from Gilbert, in which he recommends that I do whatever this man wants, because he pays well. You realize what that means, don't you? Well, I sent that foreigner packing, and I said to myself that perhaps Gilbert was at the apartment. So I came to see if he was here or not. I don't want to make trouble, but are you sure you're supposed to be here?"

Helena had hastened to explain that she was married to André and that they were the new tenants. She had not dared to be rude, mainly for fear of being reported to the management. After all, their sublet was completely illegal, and André had no idea how Gilbert had gotten the apartment in the first place. Not totally mollified, Dosia had left.

Helena was pondering the unpleasant incident as she sliced bread.

"Good morning," André murmured from behind her. "Let's leave right away, so we can take our time on the road."

They drank their tea standing in the tiny kitchen, and then quietly left the apartment. It was a fine, warm day outside. They got into the car and drove in silence. They reached the outskirts of Celestynow earlier than expected; Helena's family was not expecting them for several hours.

"Why don't we go for a walk, just the two of us?" André suggested.

"Good idea!" Helena agreed.

André pulled off the road and parked the car. A few yards away lay a path that disappeared into the forest. Helena suddenly felt happy; she and André had few opportunities to be alone together with Marek at home, and a walk in the woods seemed like a wonderful luxury. She walked ahead on the narrow path, humming softly.

Through the thin material of her dress, André could see her long slim thighs. Above them lay the dark triangle veiled by her panties, and her firm round breasts. He felt desire mounting within him, and he longed to take her right there, in the middle of the forest. Grabbing her by the shoulders, he drew her to him and kissed her passionately. In her surprise, she resisted for a moment; then she yielded, without really knowing what was happening to her.

They slipped down onto the mossy carpet between two trees. André was no longer fully sure of what he was doing. His hands caressed her soft skin, his lips crushed hers. Then he took her roughly, with a violence she had not known in him before. Helena moaned, sending his desire for her to greater heights. Clasping her even more tightly, he prolonged the moment, so that the memory of the pleasure he was bringing her should be imprinted on her mind forever.

Helena lost control of herself and became another being, a being for whom nothing could be more important than the movement of their two bodies interlocked so perfectly together. For the first time in her life, she felt she really belonged to a man, and she wished to keep him inside her forever. A shudder ran all through André's body, and after a moment he rolled off her, to lie by her side. Helena held him tightly, as though she were afraid to be parted from him. Above their heads the treetops stood out against the background of the blue sky.

Their hands met and their fingers interlaced. Neither of them dared break the silence; they did not know what to say after what they had just experienced together.

André ran his fingertips lightly over Helena's arm, and immediately desire rose within her again, but just at that moment they heard the distant sound of voices. Helena stirred, sat up, and began adjusting her dress and hair.

André jumped to his feet and held his hand out to her to help her up. "Darling," he murmured, kissing her one last time before moving off.

Helena shuddered, as though her body could not stand being separated from his. He put his arm around her waist until the path grew so narrow that they had to walk single file to the main road.

"I hope I didn't hurt you," said André as he started the car. "I don't really know what came over me. That must have been an enchanted forest!"

They laughed, and he reached for her hand. "I want to have a child by you," André said suddenly. "A little girl, who looks just like you."

Helena winced, and her hand stiffened in his. When the car drew up in front of the presbytery, Helena got out very quickly to avoid André's questioning eyes.

Irena and Inka were inside, busily getting the meal ready. In the garden, Robert was sitting in a big wicker chair, chatting with Father Marianski. Helena kissed her father.

"Your roses are lovely," André said to Father Marianski, hoping to please him.

Father Marianski had aged considerably. In fact, he had never completely recovered from the time he was arrested, and his ensuing illness. His tall figure was no longer as upright as it had been before, and there were deep wrinkles on his face.

Robert lit his pipe. "We were discussing philosophy," he said. "Now, André, what does the verb 'to live' mean to you?"

" 'To live' is to fight, and to resist," said André slowly. 'To live' is also to have freedom to know, to be liberated as much as possible from unimportant day-to-day concerns, so that one can learn greater things."

"For me, 'to live' is to love a woman and be loved by her," Robert said.

"Who said that?" called Inka, leaning out of the kitchen window.

"Your old father," Robert answered with a laugh. "Ah, if youth only knew, if age only could!"

"You're not old," protested Inka. "Now, come and eat; supper's ready."

"Oh, by the way, Marek is back," André told Robert. "They took care of him at the sanatorium, and now he's able to function. And thanks to Kazik, he was able to get a job at Radio Warsaw. He's living with us for the moment, or rather, he's camping out on the floor, on a mattress Helena brought from the hospital."

"Speaking of Kazik, what's become of him? We haven't seen him for months. He must be too important nowadays to visit us," said Robert.

"Oh, he's very busy," André replied. "As far as I can

tell, he's a sort of liaison officer between the ministries, or
something like that. He's got a fine car, a little house at
Zakopane, and an apartment out toward Wilanow. He
travels a lot, and rarely comes to Warsaw. By the way, he
helped me to get my job reporting for *Trybuna Ludu*. I'm
very grateful to him for that."

"Good day!" Magda was coming toward them carrying a
basket, with Wlodek following close behind. "Master Robert,
it's good to see you. How are things going with you in
Warsaw?"

"Not too well, Magda. I've been forced to give my
workshop over to the authorities to settle my tax debt. So
I've been doing my work in the apartment."

"Wlodek!" Inka called out. "Come here a minute. We
need a strong man."

Wlodek rushed forward, obviously happy to be of help.
He and Inka carried the table out into the garden, while
Helena and Irena brought out plates piled high with salads.
There was potato salad with bits of cucumber, cooked beet
salad, and a big bowl full of carrots. There was also an
earthenware pot of cheese. Magda put her basket down on
the ground and took out a big loaf of black bread, still
warm from the oven.

"I've got some butter, too," she announced.

"Homemade!" cried Inka. "The best in the world!"

"What have you done to your hands?" Wlodek asked
her as he sat down beside her on the grass.

"Oh, it's nothing!" Inka's hands were covered with
scratches and cuts. "I work in a canning factory near
Wilanow. It's the mandatory workers' training you have to
go through after you've graduated from school and before
you go to college. Most of my friends get out of it by
getting their parents to pay someone to go and work in
their place, or with a phony medical certificate. But I
didn't want any unfair favors; I wanted to fulfill my obliga-

tion myself. Besides, I know what it feels like to work eight hours a day, six days a week."

Father Marianski said grace, and they began eating. Inka passed the plate of beet salad to Helena; their eyes met, and immediately Inka turned away. Inka had been avoiding Helena since the day Father Marianski had taken her out with him for a walk in the fields and told her the secret of her birth.

"That means I don't have a real father," Inka had murmured.

"But you do!" the priest had protested. "And don't ever say anything like that again! It would hurt Robert and Irena far too much. I think you should make an effort not to show them that you know. I thought it over a long time before deciding to tell you about it, but it seemed to me to be better that you should find out from me."

Since then, Inka could no longer think of Helena as her sister, but as her mother who did not want her.

"Times have been bad for the church," Father Marianski was saying. "Last week, four professors at the Catholic University in Lublin were arrested. It's still not known where they were taken or what they were accused of. In Cracow, three nuns have disappeared, and we've been waiting for news of them for months. It's more than likely they, too, are in prison. Cardinal Wyszynski was supposed to go to Rome, where he was going to try to get some sort of funding for our churches, but they've refused him a passport."

"Won't there ever be an end to this?" Irena sighed. "When Gomulka came to power, we thought our troubles were over. How naive we were!"

"Let's go in," Helena said uncomfortably. "It's beginning to get chilly, and besides, it's not very smart to be talking about this sort of thing outside, where people might hear us."

"What are you afraid of?" Inka asked sarcastically. "You're the only one of us who is safe. They never arrest doctors."

"Come now, Inka, that's not nice," Robert scolded.

"Never mind," Helena murmured. "Inka's right. I don't have much courage left these days."

Inka and Irena collected the plates in silence and disappeared into the kitchen. Father Marianski fetched a pair of scissors and cut some roses. Magda went to help the others tidy up, while Wlodek took the table indoors. Robert stayed in his armchair.

"You know something, Father?" he said. "I think it would be a good idea for you to give me descriptions of the professors from the Catholic University who've been arrested, and the three nuns who've disappeared. I could talk to Kazik about them; he may be able to help find them."

"That's an excellent idea," Father Marianski replied. "Wait here for a moment, while I go to my desk. I made some notes which you might find useful."

Father Marianski went off, and Robert got up. His leg was hurting very badly; he leaned for a moment on his cane, not daring to take a step.

"Something wrong?" Irena called to him through the open window. "Wait for me, I'm coming!" She rushed out, took him by the arm, and helped him forward. He kissed her cheek, and she smiled at him.

Once they were in the car, Robert put his head on Helena's shoulder and went to sleep. Inka leaned her cheek against the window. She was thinking of Wlodek. He was clumsy, and shy, but he had about him the quiet strength of a man accustomed to living on the land. When she was with him, she felt that life was simple, peaceful, calm. And he had a way of looking at her which made her feel she was pretty and intelligent. Yes, Inka very much wanted to see Wlodek again and go walking with him in the fields. He was no longer the same boy who used to frighten her in the old days, when she was a child. It was true that he didn't have much to say, and wasn't brilliant like André, but he was handsome with that tall, slim figure of his, his broad shoulders, and his blond hair.

It was late when they reached Warsaw. André dropped Irena, Robert, and Inka off at Saska Kepa.

"You know," Helena said to him as they drove off, "I really think Marek should find himself a place to live. I'm finding it harder and harder to put up with our little threesome."

"What do you want me to do, throw him out? The way you're talking, you make it sound like I should send him on his way tonight."

André was obviously in a bad mood, and Helena didn't pursue the subject. When they reached their apartment, Marek was not home yet.

"Let's go to bed," said Helena. "I have a big day tomorrow at the hospital, and I'm exhausted."

They got undressed and got into bed. André couldn't go to sleep, and for a long time he lay on his back feeling resentful of his wife for no particular reason.

Razowa could not manage to keep warm. She had covered herself with everything she could lay her hands on, but she was still shivering.

I must have a fever, she thought. Oh God, am I going to die all alone here, in this hole?

A rat was scratching around in the corner and Razowa pulled her shawl around herself protectively. She thought of her sons, wishing desperately that she knew what had become of them.

"Nineteen-sixty-eight," she said out loud. "How many years does that make since the war ended?"

She tried to count, but got confused and had to start all over again. Her feet had lost all sensation. She tried rubbing them, but it was no use; she couldn't feel anything. Should she call for help? Yet the few friends she had didn't own a telephone, and she wasn't about to call some curt UB agent who would be interested in talking to her only if she had information to report.

Now her arms were growing numb. It didn't hurt; quite the contrary, in fact. Razowa felt a strange sense of peace coming over her, which was broken only by a distant ringing sound. Was it the telephone, or sleigh bells? No, it couldn't be that, there weren't any sleighs in Saska Kepa any longer. In the old days, when she was still young and living in the country, she used to go to church with her parents in a sleigh. They would dress up in warm clothes, hitch up the horse, and ride off to midnight Mass.

"Almighty God! Forgive me my sins . . ."

Razowa's lips moved very slightly, and then were still. She had stopped breathing, and the room was completely silent except for the telephone.

At the other end of the line, Kazik replaced the receiver. He found it odd that Razowa wasn't home at this hour. Besides, he had an important letter to show her. Her two sons were alive and well in Lvov. But what an irony of fate! It had taken twenty-three years to trace them in a town which used to belong to Poland and was now annexed by the Russians.

Kazik put his files away and left his office. He returned the guard's salute automatically and went out into the small lot where his car was parked. He spent several minutes trying to get the key into the lock, which was frozen. On the bridge, he had to stop and clean his windshield with his sleeve, since the windshield wipers weren't working and he hadn't been able to find replacements.

At Saska Kepa, he turned right and stopped in front of the house where Razowa lived. There were a few pedestrians on the street, and he parked his car right under a lamppost. People did not hesitate to steal whatever they could, whenever they could, and he had no desire to come back and find his tires gone and his gas tank empty.

I must be growing old, Kazik said to himself. I'm always expecting the worst to happen. It's absolutely ridiculous! I ought to get married and stop living alone; it's making me paranoid. Helena . . . Ah, Helena! She didn't want me. She preferred that little journalist, who's so obsessed with French culture, who thinks he's changing the world because he manages to get some interviews with a few minor officials.

He reached Razowa's door and knocked, but there was no answer, and the door was locked. It was only eight o'clock; he decided to try again tomorrow, and take the opportunity to pay the Stanowskis a visit. Kazik got back into his car and drove off, cheered by the thought of seeing Robert and Irena again.

He was in luck. They were in, chatting with Inka, who was knitting a pullover.

"I'll make some tea," said Irena cheerfully. "There's some cake, too. You've come just at the right time!"

"It's a long time since we've seen you," Robert added. "You know, we miss your visits."

Inka took Kazik's coat and hung it up; then she drew up a chair and gave him a radiant smile, so like Helena's that Kazik felt a pang in his heart.

"How are things?" she inquired.

"Oh, fine!" Kazik replied. "I work a great deal, and I don't have much time to myself. But I am planning a vacation, in Hungary, on the shores of Lake Balaton."

"What a good idea! It's a magnificent area," Irena said, a touch of envy in her voice.

"Why don't I take you all with me?" Kazik exclaimed suddenly. "My car's big enough for the four of us. I know a little house there, hidden away among the trees, which we can have for the month of July. Would you like that?"

"What about your parents?" Robert asked.

Kazik looked embarrassed. "My parents have left."

"What do you mean, left?"

"Well, it's quite a story. My mother has a cousin who has been living in America since before the war, somewhere near Pittsburgh. He and his wife wrote several times, and offered my parents a couple of airline tickets. At first they didn't want to go on such a big trip, but I insisted. My parents are both retired, so it was really a unique opportunity for them. Anyway, I think they're having a wonderful time; they had planned to return this summer, but from their letters, it sounds as though they're going to stay there a bit longer."

"You must be feeling awfully lonely," said Inka gently.

Kazik laughed. "Come, now, I'm an old man. I'm used to the solitary bachelor life." He sipped his tea. "Tell me, though, Inka, would you like to go to the theater with me? I've got two tickets for Mickiewicz's *Ancestors*. They say this production's quite good. What do you think?"

Inka paused. "It depends on what evening. I've got a lot of work at the university just now."

"What are you taking?"

"I'm taking a year of biology, and then I'm going to do a degree program in agronomy."

"And does mademoiselle propose to become an agricultural engineer, or a landed proprietor?"

The four of them laughed at that, and Kazik and Inka made a date for the following Saturday.

"We'll have an early dinner at a restaurant, and then we'll see the play," Kazik promised, as Inka, flushed with pleasure, held his coat for him.

8

INKA FELT LIKE a queen. Until now nobody had ever taken her to a big restaurant with white tablecloths and crystal glasses. In the old days, in Cracow, Uncle Andrzej used to invite her to Wierzynek's once in a while. But that was so long ago that she had almost forgotten the taste of the wine and good food. And with Uncle Andrzej, people hadn't turned their heads to look at her, as they did now. She was glad for her beautiful new dress, which Irena had made just for the occasion.

"Did you know Uncle Andrzej well?" Inka asked Kazik.

"Yes. He was an outstanding man, but unfortunately, he was Jewish, and that's not a very easy thing to be in this country nowadays."

At work, Kazik knew an informer who took pleasure in systematically tracking down Jews, and this irritated him. Every time Kazik told the man he was wasting his time, he would retort that after all, in Stalin's time, the secret service had included many Polish Jews who had been trained and indoctrinated in Moscow.

"There is so much prejudice in the world," said Kazik slowly. "What's the good of endlessly rehashing old history and old hatreds?"

Inka nodded solemnly.

"But enough of serious subjects, Inka. Let's talk about something else. Tell me, how is your family?"

"Unbearable sometimes. They're always discussing the war, the resistance, the camps, the Warsaw uprising. My parents love recalling old memories, and when Helena comes . . ." She paused. "Each year, I have to go with them to the Powazki cemetery to take part in the demonstration in honor of those who died in the uprising. We all march carrying those little candles in our hands; it's so morbid! I prefer thinking about the happy things in life: dancing, walks in the country, lovely houses like the ones in American films, skiing at Zakopane. Mama says I'm selfish."

"You're not selfish," murmured Kazik, taking her hands between his own. "You're young, and alive, and beautiful."

Inka blushed. Later, as he escorted her out of the restaurant, she felt pleasantly unsettled as he slipped his arm around her shoulders.

The theater was crowded, but the attendants promptly led Kazik and Inka to their seats in the front row. Inka felt like an empress.

The lights dimmed and silence fell just before the red velvet curtain rose. Inka's heart was racing with excitement. Kazik took her hand in his as the play began.

"All is darkness, all is silence, who will come? Who will come?" chanted the chorus. Inka sensed a strange tension in the audience; she tried to ignore it and immerse herself in the play.

During the intermission, the crowd spilled out into the lobby, where they formed groups and discussed the play. There were many students among them.

"It's a play that's become completely topical again," a young man said to Kazik. "When it was written, it dealt with the oppressive Russia of the czars, but it also applies to the Soviet imperialism of today." Kazik didn't introduce him to Inka, and hastened to move away from him. With a nervous gesture, he lit a cigarette.

"Something wrong?" Inka asked, but he just shook his head.

However, after the second act, the audience stood up and applauded wildly. The scene looked like a demonstration: people were shouting and cheering as loudly as they could, and someone at the back of the hall started yelling, "Liberty! Down with Moscow!"

Fearing trouble, Kazik hastily led Inka to the exit at the side of the stage. They went down a corridor, passing some of the actors who had not yet had time to change out of costume. An employee opened a door for them, and they were outside.

"This could be very bad," Kazik murmured. "They'll ban the play, I'm certain of it."

On the way back, Kazik seemed agitated, and remained silent. But when he dropped Inka off in front of her house, he held her and kissed her on the mouth. She closed her eyes, savoring the feeling; nobody had ever kissed her like that before.

"I'll be back," Kazik said softly. "If you want to see me again, I'll come and get you." Then he turned around and was gone.

Irena and Robert had already gone to bed. Inka took care not to crumple her dress as she undressed; then she slipped into bed. Never before had she felt such pleasure at the touch of the cool sheets on her naked body; it made her think of the love and happiness that Kazik would surely bring her.

Everything happened very quickly. In the hall, the students started shouting as the militiamen and the plain-clothesmen moved forward into the crowd, striking out with their batons. Inka fell, and couldn't manage to get back up. Someone kicked her and grabbed her by the arm, and she found herself being shoved into a black van filled with people.

The demonstration had begun shortly after class had ended. The students were protesting the closing of the theater at which Mickiewicz's *Ancestors* was playing. But no one had thought that the militia would step in.

From inside the van, Inka could hear the shouts of the crowd. "Young swine, Jews, traitors!"

One of her comrades crawled to the door at the back of the van, which was still wide open. He pulled a handful of coins from his pocket and threw them at the people standing on the other side of the campus fence.

"Proletarians, beggars, slaves!" he shouted. "Pick up your alms and shut your drunken mouths!"

A militiaman struck him with the butt of his revolver and the young man fell back, bleeding from the mouth and groaning softly. At the same time, the doors were closed, and the van moved off. Inside, the students huddled against each other and fell silent. After what seemed like hours, the van came to a halt. The students got out, surrounded by militiamen who spat on the ground as they passed by. Inside, the men and women were segregated.

"Undress!" a woman in uniform ordered Inka.

Inka had never been more humiliated in her life, having to take her clothes off in front of all the others, feeling the woman's hands on her body, showing that there was nothing hidden between her legs, inside her mouth, under her tongue, beneath her arms. Inka was trembling from head to foot, and she had to grit her teeth to avoid breaking down and sobbing. Then the woman tossed her some clothing: a tubular garment which she had to slip on over her head. Inka saw that once all the women were dressed in this uniform, they became almost unrecognizable. They were no longer individuals.

They were locked up in a big cell, where they were greeted by the other prisoners with jeers and coarse laughter. Inka knew that her parents would be waiting and worrying about her. How could she let them know? The papers and the radio stations wouldn't say anything about the incident; nobody would know where she was. Inka knew that they could keep her here for months before the story managed to leak out.

Determined, she fought her way to the bars, through which she could see the guards standing on the other side.

"Open up!" she shouted. "Let me out!"

Slipping her hand between the bars, she grabbed the edge of a guard's sleeve and pulled as hard as she could. The man turned and hit her hand with a club. The pain was so intense that Inka staggered back. Behind her, someone started shouting for a doctor. Inka saw red drops trickling down her clothes; she realized that she was bleeding, and then she fainted.

"It's time to get up, darling!"

Inka opened her eyes. Magda was standing over her, smiling happily, and sunlight was streaming in through the window.

"Is it late, Magda?"

"It's after six!"

Inka jumped to her feet. "I'll be ready in ten minutes," she said, "and then I'll go and tend the hens. I'm sorry I overslept!"

For two months now, Inka had been working with Magda, and she was going to stay there until the winter. After what had happened, she did not want to go back to Warsaw.

First of all there had been the long days in the infirmary. They had put her hand in a cast, because the guard had broken two of her fingers. Kazik had come to see her there; he had brought her cheese and honey, and promised her that she would be out soon.

Kazik had kept his word. One morning the guards came and took her into a room, where she was given back her clothes and made to sign a piece of paper. Then finally she found herself out in the yard, where Kazik was waiting for her in his car.

As soon as they had cleared the gates and were outside the prison walls, he took her in his arms. Driving with one hand, he cradled her like a little girl, so sweetly and tenderly that Inka had cried.

"I can't stay in Warsaw," Kazik told her. "I'm leaving for Prague this evening. I'm going to take you home to your family. They're going to take care of you, and everything will work out all right, you'll see. But how pale you are, my poor darling."

At the house, Robert and Irena had been waiting for her on the street. They had literally carried her inside.

Helena had also been very good to her. So that Inka wouldn't have to go to the hospital, Helena had come to the house every day to examine her. They had been afraid that the cast might have been badly applied in the prison infirmary, but when the time finally came to take it off, Inka had recovered the use of her hand almost immediately.

Inka had been overjoyed to have the use of her fingers once again, but her good mood had not lasted long. At the end of April, she had been notified of her dismissal from the university.

"You're not the only one," Irena had said in an attempt to console her. "This has happened to a number of students. Wlodek has been thrown out of the Institute of Agricultural Economics; that's much more serious. He's a man, and he's much older than you. Besides, you never know. The government just may end up exonerating all the students who demonstrated."

Robert had also tried to comfort her. "Come now, Inka, have a little courage. Think of the professors. Several of them have been dismissed from the staff. That's even worse for them than it is for you. They had to study for many years to get their degrees, and then their jobs.

They've spent their whole lives teaching, and now they've lost the right to do so, and have to start again from scratch. Some of them have even had their apartments taken from them because they're professors. You're young and you have many options. And you still have a home."

"Look at me," Irena had added. "I have no degrees, and yet I'm just as smart as the next woman. Women can get by in other ways."

Inka had shaken her head and said nothing. Her parents simply didn't understand her; to them her being dismissed from the university was trivial compared to other, more universal problems. But to Inka it meant everything.

Kazik had not come back to see her. Inka received a beautiful postcard from him, from Prague, which she kept on the nightstand Robert had made for her.

Inka had started to feel weaker and weaker, despite the vitamins that Helena had given her, and she spent all her time in bed, depressed and constantly tired. That had gone on for a couple of weeks, and in mid-June they had decided to take her to Celestynow. As soon as she arrived at Magda's, she had felt better immediately.

Inka turned all this over in her mind as she tended the hens, which were cackling loudly at each other. It was a fine warm day. She searched carefully for the eggs, put them in her basket, then took them back to the house. There were more than usual, and Magda would be pleased, which made Inka feel very happy.

"God, how simple life can be," she said to Wlodek, who was harnessing up the horse in the yard. But Wlodek was not in a good mood.

"Speak for yourself! With the threat of nationalization hanging over our heads, and having to constantly worry about shortages of seed, fertilizer, and machinery, how can you say life is simple? But enough complaining, we have work to do. We've got to pick some lettuce and turnips and get them over to the cooperative today. Are you going to help?"

Inka nodded. "I'll get rid of this basket and be right with you."

Inka quickly showed Magda the eggs, and ran back to Wlodek, who didn't like being kept waiting. She jumped up onto the seat, and Wlodek urged the horse forward.

Along the road, the horse's shoes made a merry clip-clop on the pavement, but then there was an unpaved stretch where the wheels sank slightly into the sand. When they arrived at the field, the horse's coat was shining with sweat. Inka got down.

"I'll come and pick you up when I've finished at the other field," Wlodek said. "Don't waste time!"

Inka started pulling up the turnips, shaking the dirt off, then stacking the big round vegetables on the jute sacking she had spread out by the side of the road. The sun was hot, and she was soon perspiring; since there was nobody around, she unbuttoned her shirt. Little by little, fatigue slowed down her movements; she tried to go systematically down the rows on her knees, but her back began to hurt her. Still, it felt good to work hard out in the open instead of being cooped up in a small apartment with Robert and Irena. She loved the meadows and the fields, and best of all, she loved being with Magda and Wlodek.

He came back for her just before noon; this time, he seemed happy.

"You've done good work," he said as he helped her load the cart, which was already half-full with the vegetables he had picked. "If you like, we'll eat before we go to the cooperative. My mother prepared a little hamper for us."

They sat down on the ground beside the cart, in the shade. There was black bread, cheese, and a bottle of water. They ate for a while in silence.

Wlodek drank from the bottle, wiped the rim with his sleeve, and passed it to Inka. "Listen, Inka, I've had a job offer. A friend of mine wants to take me to Gdansk with him to work on the construction sites. I'm very tempted. You know, I can earn a fair bit of money doing that kind of work." He paused. "It all depends on you, though. If you stay here with my mother, I can accept; if you go back to Warsaw, that's something else again. I don't want her to stay alone on the land. If they do decide to nationalize, single women will be the first to get thrown out of their homes."

She looked at him thoughtfully. "I'll think about it. You see, the idea of going back to Warsaw doesn't please me very much. Back there I feel so useless, whereas here . . ."

"You'll find the winter long."

"That doesn't bother me in the least. And Father Marianski will be happy if I help him with his catechism classes for the children. Perhaps I'll also find some work to do at the Regional Committee; they don't really trust me, but they need people to do office work, and I know how to type. Who knows?"

Wlodek nodded. "Good! We'll talk about it again soon. I don't want to rush you."

Inka wrapped up the remains of the bread, and they started back along the sandy road. When they reached the cooperative, Wlodek began to unload the vegetables.

"We won't unload it all," he told Inka in a low voice. "We can sell the rest in Warsaw for five times more than we'd get here. Leave it to me. If you're tired, take a rest. They take more time weighing the turnips and lettuce, and then paying us, than we took picking it all and bring-ing it here." He added, smiling, "I'm glad you're here—it's fun being with you."

For Wlodek, who was not very communicative, that was the highest of compliments. Inka stretched out on the grass with a sigh of contentment, glad for the chance to relax. She stared at the clouds, vaguely aware of the sound of people chatting all around her, and wondered what

Kazik was doing. And yet the thought of him seemed much less important now than it had a few months ago.

When Wlodek returned, Inka jumped to her feet and greeted him happily. He returned her smile, and they set off under the envious stares of the peasants who were still arguing with the inspector. It was after six when they got back to the yard where Magda was awaiting them.

"Come quickly!" she said. "We have to go to the presbytery right away, to listen to Father Marianski's radio. There's bad news from Prague."

At the presbytery, Father Marianski was in the kitchen, busily turning knobs to pick up the transmission from the BBC in London.

"Sit down," he murmured. "It seems things aren't going well in Prague. And don't talk; they're jamming the waves, and the reception's worse than ever."

They sat shoulder to shoulder, as close to the set as possible. At first there was a series of crackles, then a voice, then more crackling, and then finally they began to make out some words.

"Soviet tanks have entered Prague. The Polish Army is assisting in the task of pacification—"

"My God!" Magda cried. "Our boys from Poland—it's not possible!"

"Shush!" Wlodek protested, but his mother seemed not to have heard him. She hid her face in her hands and burst into tears.

"Our boys, our soldiers, our army, in Prague! Almighty God, what a disgrace!"

"They forced them to do it," said Wlodek. "It's not their fault."

"If only the Soviets don't cause as many deaths as they did in Budapest in 1956!" Father Marianski remarked anxiously. "Let's pray. It's all we can do for them."

Inka put her arms around Magda's shoulders. Kazik was in Prague, she remembered; what could he be doing down there? A feeling of suspicion and mistrust came over her. But in order to avoid being ungrateful to Kazik, who had always been so good to her, Inka got on her knees and tried to pray.

The last of the office workers had left, and Marek gave a sigh of relief. Alone at last, sitting at his desk with his papers, his discs, and his recordings. He loved this moment, which made him feel he was dominating the world by the simple fact that he was working late in the huge Radio Warsaw building. He had done an excellent broadcast on the Warsaw uprising, which he had recorded with Ula, an old girlfriend who happened to be passing through Warsaw, and it had gone out on the air that evening.

It had been good to see Ula; it was years since they had last met. They had known each other from childhood. They had lived on the same street and seen each other constantly, since their parents had been good friends. Ula's father had been a lawyer, like his own. During the occupation their parents had been in the same resistance unit, and had been together when they were arrested by the Gestapo, tortured, and murdered. They never broke down and talked, and they died under interrogation in the Pawiak prison. When the Gestapo came looking for them, Ula and Marek were away from the house; when they came back later, they both found themselves orphans, with little idea of what to do or where to go. Ula was thirteen then, and Marek fourteen; it was the end of July 1944, a time which neither of them would ever forget. Their local resistance commander put them into "safe houses"; then came the Warsaw uprising, the surrender, and deportation to the prisoner-of-war camps in Germany. When liberation took place a year later, Ula had happened to be in a zone occupied by the Allies; and, like Marek, she had gone to the West, to Paris. She studied there, and eventually married a man called Dupont, an engineer. They lived together for a few years, and then were divorced.

Hurt and lost, Ula had tried to reverse the passage of time by going back toward her past, toward her roots, toward Poland. This was her first trip to Warsaw in twenty-four years. In her hotel room she had heard Marek on the radio and had gone to see him.

He had shut himself up with her in the studio and gotten her to talk into a microphone about their joint experiences during the war and the occupation. Ula was a fluent speaker, and he'd been able to make an impeccable recording. She left Warsaw the next day, and hadn't been able to hear the broadcast. She'd been very sad at the airport, although back in Paris she had a good job waiting for her in a travel agency, and friends as well. Marek hadn't told her he was sleeping at André and Helena's in their tiny apartment, staying in his office at nights to be able to write in peace. He had wanted to look like a winner in her eyes.

Thinking about her, Marek filled his pipe, went and fetched the bottle of brandy from the cupboard, and poured himself a glass. Then he used a little key to open his desk drawer, and took out a file. It was the manuscript of his novel. He was busy making the final corrections; the following week he was to take it to the publisher who had accepted it, subject to approval by the censor.

When my manuscript's published, Marek told himself, my friends are quite capable of suspecting me of being an agent in the pay of Moscow. In fact, it would be better if I had them read it first.

Marek sighed, got his briefcase, put his manuscript inside, took a little key from his pocket, and locked the case. He told himself it was time to go home, but he really had no desire to go back to the big room where André would greet him with false cheerfulness intended to hide his disappointment at not being able to spend the evening alone with Helena. Half an hour more, to let them finish their meal, Marek decided. He turned the radio on; it was time for the BBC news, and the reception here was better than at André's place. There were a few crackles and a few bursts of static before he could hear the announcer's voice.

"Soviet tanks have entered Prague, supported by army units from Russia's allies . . ."

The radio crackled, but Marek was no longer listening to it. He picked up the briefcase which held his manuscript and left. He needed to find André and Helena, or just somebody to talk to.

"Am I disturbing you?" Maria Solin half-opened the door of Helena's office.

Helena looked up. "No, no! Please come in."

"I've come to ask you something. Our Committee's received a request from a young woman who claims she knows you very well. It's a problem that's rather worrying me. She's pregnant, and her pregnancy's already too advanced to be terminated, but she's absolutely insisting on it. She's got to be brought to her senses."

"What's her name?" Helena asked. Her little office suddenly seemed to close in on her.

"I don't remember her surname, just her first name: Dosia. She's tall and slim, and fairly good-looking." She paused. "Look, the girl's waiting out in the corridor. Can you see her in here and try to talk some sense into her? Oh, don't look at me like that! I know you think I'm old-fashioned, but all these abortions make me sick at heart. There are far too many of them, and then, it's so often the same ones who come back again. And we're short on antibiotics, penicillin, streptomycin, and even surgical thread, and I feel that the sick have the right to be cared for before these girls who come crying to have their pregnancies terminated. From both social and humane standpoints I find that a waste of energy and resources."

Helena shook her head. "I don't agree with you, as you well know. For me, abortion is both a social and a medical necessity. Women have a right to decide whether or not they want to have a child. They shouldn't be forced to give birth like animals and raise children they don't really know what to do with."

"And yet, you're a practicing Catholic," Maria objected quietly.

"Please forgive me," Helena murmured. "Despite my religious principles, despite all the economic contraindications, I do feel that women have a right to be helped and cared for if they want it. Look, I agree with you it would be better to give them contraceptives, but we don't make them in this country and we're not allowed to import them, it seems, because of their cost in foreign currency."

"Let's leave it, shall we?" said Maria in a conciliatory tone. "I'll send the patient in to you. See you this evening, my dear."

Helena lit a cigarette nervously, then went and fetched Dosia and brought her into the office. As soon as the door closed behind her, the girl began sobbing.

"I didn't want to tell the others, but you know my story, Doctor. I don't even know who the father of this child is. For some months now there have been a lot of Gilbert's friends coming by to see me, and since I needed the money, I've been sleeping with them all. If I don't want them to stay the night, I can kick them out at any old hour; they've only got to go a few yards and they're back at their hotels. Gilbert doesn't write to me anymore, and nobody seems to know when he's coming back. So I don't want to bring this bastard into the world. You understand, don't you?" It wasn't Dosia talking about her bastard, it was a young, young girl—almost a child—who was begging Dr. Andrzej Rybicki to spare her the long months of waiting, the big belly, the humiliation. . . .

"It's too late . . . you'd be running a big risk," said Helena, but it was no longer she who was talking to Dosia; it was Uncle Andrzej.

"I don't care if I die!" Dosia sobbed. "My life is worthless anyhow. I'm a prostitute, and you can't be a prostitute and a mother at the same time. Help me, I beg you, help me!" Dosia looked very pathetic, with her pale little face framed by a mass of disheveled hair.

"I'll examine you," Helena said, to gain time.

Dosia wiped her nose. "And another thing. If you don't agree to help me, I'm going to report that you're illegal occupants of that apartment, which Gilbert got hold of no less illegally," she shot at Helena.

Just as Helena was about to reply, there was a knock at the door. It was young Dr. Skiba. Unlike the rest of his colleagues, he was an atheist, the only one on the hospital staff; he was also a member of the party, and he made no secret of it.

Helena quickly gave him a brief summary of the case, while Dosia was already starting to throw pleading glances at him. Skiba was an obstetrician; he could take having to make such crucial decisions, and he'd do it all the more willingly because he didn't give a damn for the members of the Committee.

"All right, kid," he said to Dosia. "I'll take care of you. I've never let a girl carry a load she didn't want; I always manage to get rid of it for her somehow. I'm a good-hearted lad, and I love every pretty girl in the world. I know how you feel, kid; these little troubles happen so quickly! Come along with me."

Dosia thanked him effusively, threw Helena a look of hatred, and left her office with Dr. Skiba. Helena breathed a sigh of relief. Luck seemed to have sorted things out.

But not for long. That same evening, just as she was

about to leave the hospital, Helena got a call from the head nurse. Dosia had been operated on that afternoon, but had reacted badly to the anesthetic and died instantly. No information on her file. No family. Helena knew her, it seemed. Did she know who should be informed?

No, Helena knew nothing, and she was in rather a hurry. The militia should be informed. What, Dr. Skiba didn't want that? Okay, well, that was his business. Helena hung up the receiver and slumped down in her chair. Her legs refused to support her, and she was sweating profusely.

I've got that girl's life on my conscience, she told herself. I'm responsible. I've just taken part in a criminal act contrary to all the rules of practice. I'm unworthy to be a doctor.

At that moment the head nurse came in the door. Helena sat up and tried to regain her composure.

"Here's the card of that patient who's just been taken to the mortuary," the nurse said matter-of-factly. "Since you were the only one who knew her, they'll probably come to you for her effects. I've put everything in a big envelope— her watch, keys, rings, and handbag—and I've locked it away in the lost-property cupboard. Here's the receipt."

"Thanks," Helena said in a hollow voice, taking the little ticket which dangled from the end of a string. She threw it quickly into a drawer, as though she could not stand to touch it.

"Are you ready?" Maria Solin was standing in the doorway.

Helena got up and followed her without a word. They left the hospital and walked off side by side. André had kept the car that day, so Helena had to go with his mother to meet him at the Journalists' Club.

"That Dosia is dead," Maria said slowly. "And you're quite wrong, my dear, to hold yourself responsible. All Dr. Skiba had to do was refuse to carry out an abortion.

He's the obstetrician, not you, and it was up to him to comply with the Committee's decision. He deserves to go before the Disciplinary Commission, but because he's a member of the party, there's every chance that no action will be taken. It's a scandal, but that's the way it is, and I'm certainly not going to worry myself about it. I ought to, because that young Skiba's a real butcher who doesn't deserve to be called a doctor; but I'm going to leave it to others."

"It's not Dr. Skiba who should be suspended," replied Helena, "but I who should lose my license to practice. It was I who presented the patient. I'm the one who's responsible for everything."

"Come now, Helena! You're being ridiculous, child!" Maria protested.

"No, let me talk!" Helena was almost shouting. "What do you know about me? About my motivations? My personal experiences? I never told your son, but you should know that I have a child. Inka's not my sister, she's my daughter. Dr. Rybicki, my very dear uncle, forced me to keep the child. I was thirteen, and I'd just been raped by some drunken Russian soldiers."

"Stop it, my dear," Maria murmured gently. "It's no use telling me all that; your past doesn't concern me. Besides, you're hurting yourself. That poor girl could have found Dr. Skiba on her own. You really had nothing to do with it at all. You're a general practitioner, and it's not your area."

"I've never dared tell André the truth, but tonight I'm going to do so," Helena said in a hollow voice.

Maria took her by the arm. "Why do you want to make him suffer? What he doesn't know can't hurt him. You're behaving like a guilty woman who thinks that if she confesses her sin to someone, she'll unload some of her remorse onto him. But since you're not guilty, my dear, that won't help you. You know, men have this stupid pride, and there's no point in wounding them. I just want to tell you one thing, if you'll allow me. As long as one follows a line of conduct, be it good or bad, but precise and clearly defined, then one can overcome anything. As soon as one starts reasoning, and playing with human lives, one never knows where it will lead to. Doubtless that's why you regard me as being out-of-date, because I oppose abortion as strongly as I can, while you, by seeking absolute justice, are forced to find new paths. My dear, it's difficult to reinvent values which meet people's needs."

"But it's essential!" protested Helena.

"Perhaps," Maria sighed resignedly, "but that young girl could have survived labor, whereas abortion was nothing but a death sentence."

Helena shook her head. "Go and meet André alone," she begged. "I'd so much like to go home, go to bed, and not think of anything anymore."

"All right, my dear, but promise me not to do anything stupid."

"Come, now, how could you imagine a thing like that?"

Helena kissed her mother-in-law and left. She got in a cab, and when she got home she went upstairs as quickly as possible and turned the key in the lock.

Marek was sitting on the floor in the middle of the room, busily emptying a bottle of brandy. When he saw Helena, he tried to get up, but couldn't manage it.

"Wait!" Helena told him.

Abruptly she kicked off her shoes, threw her coat over a chair, went to the little kitchen cupboard for a bottle of vodka, and sat down on the floor beside him. Face to face, their legs crossed, and staring into each other's eyes, they both raised their bottles and drank straight from them. They had no need of words; they felt attuned to one another.

"I drink to Czechoslovakia!" Marek cried between two hiccups, while Helena muttered on and on about Uncle

Andrzej, suicide, prostitution, Dosia, and Soviet tanks in Prague. Marek suddenly crawled over to his bed on all fours, and came back carrying a briefcase. The case was ugly and dirty, and the imitation leather had cracked almost everywhere, but Marek opened it with infinite care. He took out a sheaf of paper and stacked it neatly in front of him.

"Come on, Helena, help me!" he said. "We're going to have some fun and settle some accounts at the same time. This is the year I came back from Paris; I'll take care of that. Here, you take Chapter Two—yes, go on! Don't hesitate; it deals with the murder of an innocent man."

"Have you killed somebody?" Helena asked, looking at him in confusion.

"As good as. Tear it up, I tell you! Don't argue. I don't want my thoughts and memories living in a briefcase, like in a prison."

She tore up the sheets Marek handed her and threw the pieces in the air. "Prison! You men'll never know what prison is. It's not bars and cells and guards. It's here, in our bodies. It's the belly; do you understand? We're imprisoned because that *thing* is moving about inside. Body . . . prison . . . freedom. Freedom is not to be the slave of what's growing inside. You understand, Marek? Our country's just a huge belly, a woman's belly, which can't manage to get aborted. The baby's dead. It's a corpse she's carrying, but the poor thing hasn't been lucky enough to have a miscarriage. You understand . . ."

A hiccup, and then another. Helena was weeping now. Once again she was thirteen and walking along a road that had no ending. Her body felt heavy. Uncle Andrzej was talking to her about love. The really ridiculous thing was the easy way in which males who had never lived in that prison, the prison of the body, could force women to undergo it and live through it.

"There's nothing left to tear up," Marek said with an

exaggerated sigh as he threw the last shreds of paper into the air.

He grabbed at the table with his left hand and the lamp fell off and broke. In the darkness Marek thought he could hear the beating of his own heart; but instead, it was footsteps coming up the stairs.

"What on earth's going on here?" André stood at the doorway.

"Prison," murmured Marek. "You see, we're all in one big fraternal prison. That's why they're called the brother countries of Eastern Europe."

André found a candle and lit it. Then he carried Helena, who kicked and fought, over to their bed, where he laid her down and covered her. He went back, dragged Marek over to the divan, and took his shoes off.

"What's all this paper?" he asked out loud, although he knew neither of the other two was capable of answering.

André had a horror of disorder, so despite his fatigue, he picked up the torn sheets, crumpled them, and stuffed them into the briefcase together with the two empty bottles. He went outside; in the yard there was a big wooden bin for garbage, and, groping in the dark, he got it open and carefully emptied the briefcase into it. Then, with relief, he took in a deep breath of fresh air and went back up into the apartment. Somewhere, behind one of the doors on the first floor, a dog barked as he passed.

André couldn't find the keyhole in his apartment door, and lit a match. There was no point in knocking; both of them were fast asleep now, and they would never hear him. When he finally managed to get the key into the keyhole, he went inside, got undressed and into his pajamas. Then he blew out the candle and lay down beside his wife, who was murmuring incomprehensibly in her sleep.

What am I doing in this damned country? André wondered. Right now, I could be working somewhere in Paris, and spending my Sundays at the Louvre. It's not much fun being born Polish, so when one does have an opportunity of getting the hell out and going somewhere else, one shouldn't let it slip. Why the devil did I come back? He turned to look at Helena. Tomorrow I'll suggest to her that she come with me to Paris. We'll ask for passports, and we'll start all over. I can always find work in France as a janitor!

"They've signed!" Kazik kept repeating these words over and over again, like a prayer. The official party was over. Chancellor Brandt, accompanied by Scheele, his minister for foreign affairs, was due to leave Warsaw that same evening. Poland's western frontiers had been officially recognized by the Federal German Republic in this month of December 1970, twenty-five years after the war.

Kazik got into the heavy black car with its shiny black coachwork. It was snowing. He made himself comfortable and lit a cigarette; he was going to the Grand Hotel to pick up the German officials who accompanied the chancellor. He was to take them to the outskirts of Cracow, where they were going to spend a week. They were being put up in the hunting lodges, but very fortunately it wasn't the season. Kazik hated hunting. The last time he had been present at a hunting party, the Germans had shot some unfortunate stags, and Kazik had thrown up. It had been a disaster.

He shook his head and tried to think of his upcoming vacation in Celestynow: Inka will be there, and she'll have to give me an answer. If she says yes, we'll get married in January. All I have to do now is get the German delegation off my hands, sleep for two days, and write up that file that has to be submitted to the Central Committee on the fourteenth; then I'll buy a present for Inka, another for her parents, and the shawl I promised Magda, and fix up the rosary I found for Father Marianski. And then there's the two big boxes of chocolates I got for Helena. Everyone's going to be pleased.

In the front of the car, the driver and the UB agent seated beside him were silent. Kazik could see their bare necks, their close-cropped hair, and their broad shoulders.

He hadn't been able to see Inka for several months now. He had sent her postcards. When he had been down at Celestynow during the past summer, they hadn't been alone for a single moment. He had tried to get her away into the fields or woods, but it was no use; Magda was always at their heels. Poor Inka! She wasn't made for this hard and thankless work, but she was stubborn. She had even taken the first steps to get a plot of land of her own. Perhaps that was more or less inevitable, after what had happened to her at the university.

Kazik had tried to intervene, but to no avail. They just didn't want to listen. Perhaps things could be fixed up later on, and Inka could go back to school, but she refused to wait. She was young and wanted everything, and she wanted it right away.

Kazik felt his palms go moist. Just the thought of Inka filled him with an impatience he found it difficult to control. I love her, and I want her, he told himself. It's funny, how things turned out. I loved Helena desperately, but it seemed to me there was such a gulf between us, such an insurmountable barrier, that I never even fought to make her mine. It's nothing like that with Inka. But she is younger than I am, and those fifteen years between us may be an obstacle.

Kazik shifted in his seat so that he could see his reflection in the rearview mirror. A handsome face, and curly hair. You won't regret it if you marry me, Inka my darling, he thought. You'll be the best loved and best coddled of women. You won't live in a small room, or spend your days slaving away in a hospital, like Helena. How could I have been so stupid! I deceived myself into thinking Hel-

ena had done right to become a doctor; it took me years
to realize a woman's true place is in the home. We'll have
lots of children, Inka and I.

Kazik finished his reverie as he got out at the Grand
Hotel. In the hotel lobby he smiled at the pretty blond on
the other side of the counter; she was an excellent agent,
whom he had known for years. To the left of the door
there were armchairs and sofas covered in black leather.
Kazik sat down opposite two men who seemed engrossed
in reading their newspapers. There were more agents in
this hotel than clients, he thought, and it cost a fortune to
keep them all going.

"Hi there, Kazik!"

He started in surprise. André and Marek sat down
beside him. "You don't have to wait much longer," said
André. "They're on their way down."

"What are you doing here?" Kazik asked, barely conceal-
ing his annoyance.

"Just our jobs," answered Marek, with a little ironic
smile. "André did a brilliantly successful interview, and
I've got a recording that's not too bad. Thanks for letting
us know these important guests were available. Without
you, we'd still be kicking our heels in the waiting rooms."

"Oh, don't mention it! Just a little favor between friends,"
said Kazik.

"I'd like to see you tomorrow, if possible," André said to
Kazik in a low voice. "There are some disturbing rumors
going around."

Kazik lit a cigarette, and with an almost imperceptible
gesture drew his attention to the two men sitting opposite
them, their faces half-hidden behind newspapers.

"I'm busy tomorrow," he said. "Come and buy some
cigarettes." They got up and walked a few paces out into
the lobby.

"Is it true they want to raise the price of meat?" André

asked in a low voice, hardly moving his lips. "That's madness!"

"The Old Man has decided."

"Is he being pushed by others?"

"Possibly. In actual fact there are several of them behind this."

"Can I say so in my article?" André asked.

"It all depends on how you present it," Kazik answered. The German officials were coming out of the elevator. "Excuse me, but I've got to go!"

Kazik greeted the three men, and they all went out together, with the porter bowing very low as he opened the door for them.

"Please get in," Kazik said in German. He went around to the other side of the car and spoke to the UB agent in a low voice: "Inside, in the lobby, there are two journalists. Do you know them?"

"Yes," the agent replied. "André Solin and Marek Lobusz of Radio Warsaw. I've just been told."

"I want to know what they've picked up. They did an interview with our guests and made a recording. I'm interested in the recording—*extremely* interested. Fix it so that I can have it tonight at home. I also want to know what our guests do after they come back to the hotel. If they have girls sent up to their rooms, get their names and addresses."

"You can count on me," said the agent as he opened the door ceremoniously for Kazik.

9

A CROSS THE STREET, the newspaper kiosk was on fire, and the windows of many of the shops had been smashed in. Wlodek retreated to the back of his room and sat down on the narrow bed, burying his face in his hands.

"Coward, coward, coward!" He was almost shouting the words. "I'm nothing but a coward. The others are out there battling with the militia, and here am I, hiding away thinking only of my own security. Oh, God, how can I go on living with such shame? I've got to go out there!"

Wlodek got up and began looking for his cap, but a piece of paper on the nightstand caught his eye and distracted him. Inka's letter. He picked it up and read for the hundredth time.

Dear Wlodek,

Magda's not very well, and I'm looking after her as best I can. We're expecting you for the holidays. I've done a lot of thinking. You asked me to tell you if I thought I could spend the rest of my life working on the land. Yes, Wlodek—that's what I want to do.

Inka's photo, which he had managed to sneak before he left, was there beside the letter, in the cardboard frame he had made. He stared at her lovely eyes, her mouth, her long braids. He was not ready to risk losing it all yet: Inka, the land, Celestynow. He threw himself onto his bed, rolled over onto his stomach, and buried his face in the pillow. No, he wouldn't go out; he was a coward, and that was his true nature.

Wlodek got up, rummaged through the nightstand, took out a pencil and a piece of paper, and began to write. Outside, night was falling, and he had to light the lamp. He wrote:

Dearest Inka,
   If anyone attacked you, I'd fight. But down there in that crowd's no place for me. They think they're going to change something, and I don't. So why? Who for? For what purpose? Listen, Inka, I'm no hero. I'm a peasant, the son of peasants. If you really want to have me, you have to know what I am.
   I've never dared to tell you this, but I love you more than my life . . .

Wlodek shook his head, then crumpled the paper up into a ball and threw it into the wastebasket under the window. There was no more paper in the drawer, only the little notebook that Inka had given him before he left. He tore out a sheet of paper and started again:

I don't know how to write. I've never learned to talk with an open heart. But all the same it's easier to write this to you than it is to say it to you—

A loud noise made the walls shake, and Wlodek ran to the window. Down below, tanks were rolling slowly along the deserted street; they looked like huge prehistoric animals.

There was no light showing on the other side. Wlodek put his light out and began mechanically counting the

tanks, which kept coming. He switched on the radio for
some sort of an announcement as to what was happening,
but there was only music. He considered briefly the idea
of walking to the station and getting on a train for
Celestynow, but he knew there would be no trains running.

"We're surrounded," the foreman had told him as they
were leaving work. "We're caught in a trap. They'll shoot
us all!"

The music had stopped, and Wlodek could hear the
announcer's voice. "You will now hear an appeal from
Comrade Kociolek: 'Comrade workers! Those manipulated by counterrevolutionary elements have forced the
closure of the work sites, but we are counting on the
courage of the working class. Tomorrow morning, Thursday,
the seventeenth of December, you will all go to your
posts, and together we shall oppose those who seek the
ruin of our country. Tomorrow . . .' "

Wlodek didn't listen any further. If work was to start
again the next day, it meant that order had been reestab-
lished and that he could leave. He would go to the work
site in the morning, and as soon as the sirens went off in
the afternoon, go to the station. The train would stop at
Warsaw, where he would have to change trains; after a
few hours' wait, he would take the express for Lublin.
On the second day, at noon, he would get off at the little
station in Celestynow. The railwaymen would wave to
him; they all knew him down there. There would be snow
on the tracks, or perhaps just a few lumps of ice stuck to
the sides of the rails. He would hurry across, and set off
down the main road, trying not to break into a run.

Wlodek didn't dare put his lamp on again, and started
groping about in the dark, getting his things together. For
weeks he had had everything ready: an amber necklace
and a little silver ring for Inka, an apron for his mother, a
cake of soap bought on the black market, two pairs of

stockings he had managed to get hold of by bartering with a sailor, a bottle of vodka with herbs in it, obtainable only in Gdansk, and a pot of caviar. The caviar had cost him a lot, but he had been very pleased to get it. Some Russian sailors had sold it to him for two almost-new shirts.

Once the knapsack was packed, Wlodek sat down on the stool near the window. In the street below, the tanks had halted, a long string of mastodons that blocked the horizon.

Blocked the horizon? Who had said that? A writer, a poet, or perhaps Father Marianski? No—it was Inka who had said to him one day: "There's no use our struggling. Everywhere, the horizons are blocked. It's only here, on the land, that one can still see into the distance, as we could before."

It was odd how he remembered each word perfectly, each gesture, each moment they had spent together. No doubt about it, that was love. There was an art in not forgetting anything, in gathering everything together, bit by bit, and hiding it away somewhere, in order to draw upon it later on, when one was alone.

The window started shaking again. In the street below, the tanks were on the move. Wlodek bit back a cry of joy; they were retreating! Everything was settled, then. It was five o'clock in the morning; it was time to leave for work. Wlodek made himself some tea, poured water into the washbasin, and washed himself. The water was boiling, and that gave him confidence. The simple fact of nibbling at a slice of black bread baked by his mother, and drinking tea, helped him to recover a certain amount of calm. Wlodek shaved, brushed his hair, and picked up his knapsack. That afternoon he would draw his pay and leave Gdynia, never to return. He had made his decision. With what he had saved, he could last until the spring, and do some renovation work at the house. The shed wasn't heated, but with a good thick winter coat on, he would be all right; anyway, it wouldn't be any colder than the work sites, where the concrete floors froze one's feet. And his shed would be well-swept, and well-equipped, and would smell of fresh-cut wood, while the work sites were filthy and full of rats.

The street was littered with garbage, bits of wood, and shattered glass. Wlodek walked quickly, passing other workers who, like himself, were headed for the work sites. There was silence everywhere; people were afraid of provoking the militiamen stationed at the corners of the streets, who kept the muzzles of their automatic rifles aimed at the passersby. The wind was so cold it burned the skin and made one gasp for breath.

The closer he got to the site, the more militiamen there were, but the tanks seemed to have gone, and this reassured Wlodek. A bus stopped and he got on. There were a lot of people inside, all workers, packed tightly against each other, silent and uneasy. A sense of fear hung heavy in the crowd, enough to make one's throat contract.

The driver went straight past the next two stops, and this in itself was enough to increase the tension. Normally, there would have been a lot of grumbling, but nobody protested now; it was as though they had all lost the use of their voices. Yet there had been people waiting in the street to get on, and there had still been a little room for them on the bus. To have stopped would have been more humane than leaving them there in the morning cold.

It was beginning to get light outside. The bus came to a stop, and they all got out. There were army units stationed in front of the Commune de Paris naval yards. Wlodek wondered what they were doing there. But at that very moment, the silence of the morning was shattered into a thousand fragments. First there were shouts, and then the volley of bullets. All around Wlodek, men collapsed like marionettes. He threw himself to the ground in a reflex action and hid his head in his arms in an attempt to blot out all sight and sound. "Jesus Mary," a woman screamed, "they're going to kill us all! Run for it, run for it, quick!"

Wlodek cautiously raised his head. All around him there were bodies, and people shouting. Then a pair of arms grabbed him, dragged him up, and threw him into a truck. He was surrounded by Polish militiamen who cursed him as they took him away.

"They killed three hundred," said André, "and arrested hundreds of workers. A simple misunderstanding. The previous evening, Kociolek launched an appeal over the radio, asking the workers to go to work the next day, while the army got the order to fire, to protect the installations in the Commune de Paris yards against vandalism—or so they said. Oh, Mother, it's just too frightful!"

Maria Solin realized her son was trying not to let her see how upset he was; he was standing in front of the window with his back to her.

"And that's not all. From what Marek and I managed to find out, that very same day—the seventeenth—army tanks drove into the crowd gathered in the main square in Szczecin. There were two hundred dead. What irony! The broadcasts from the BBC in London and from Free Europe give more details than we can get here in Warsaw. What I've just told you is top-secret; there's not a word of it in the papers or on the news. People here don't know a thing! That's 'objective information' for you! Marek and I have asked if we can go to Gdansk, but we've been refused."

Thank God, Maria thought. I don't want to lose him a second time.

The sound of the telephone made them both jump. André answered; it was Kazik. "Take what you need. Marek and I'll be along to pick you up right away. Yes, we're going!"

André hung up slowly.

"They want me urgently at the office," he told his mother. "I may have to be away for several days on the job. Will you tell Helena?"

"You're going to Gdansk," said Maria in a toneless voice.

"Look, Mother, there's no need to be worried. We're no longer at war. It's just a few unimportant disturbances, that's all."

André, once more in control of himself, didn't give her any chance to react. He kissed her on both cheeks and left. Maria had managed to slip four pieces of chocolate into his pocket, a present from one of her patients. She could still hear the noise of his footsteps on the staircase; and then there was nothing, just the oppressive silence. She shook herself. During the occupation, she had been an officer in the Home Army; and now, when everything was crumbling into ruins, how could she just sit idle in her chair and worry about her son? They must need doctors over there, and there must be some way of getting past the militia. She leapt to her feet, grabbed her medical bag, threw a few necessities into a briefcase, and left the apartment. Downstairs, she managed to find a taxi, and rode to the hospital.

Helena was in her office. "I'm coming with you!" she told her mother-in-law. "You can't refuse me that. I've got a car, and if you go by yourself you'll only get turned back. We'll get through in a car; by train, it'll be much more complicated. And let me arrange things here. I know a certain Dr. Skiba who won't dare to refuse me anything!"

Helena went up the stairs three at a time. She passed an old woman clutching the banister with one hand, while in the other she was carefully holding an army mess tin. Patients who had no family to bring them food were condemned to go hungry. What little meat the hospital received went to the kitchen staff. The patients also had to live with dirty linen, barely acceptable hygienic conditions, and nurses who expected "tips" for carrying out the most elementary services. It was not surprising that "accidents" occurred, but then again, nobody seemed to care; the families kept quiet, and so did the doctors. Nobody had bothered to find out why a certain Dosia had died in the operating room, and apart from Helena, Dr. Skiba had nobody to fear. Curiously enough, Helena sensed the link between the conditions at the hospital and the events taking place in the naval dockyards. It was time somebody had the guts to protest. The intellectuals had failed, but perhaps the workers would succeed. There were thousands of them, and sheer force of numbers must count for something.

She found Dr. Skiba doing his rounds on the second floor. "Dr. Solin and I are leaving," she told him. "We need a pass, and you can give us one."

"What sort of pass?" asked Skiba in surprise. "Where to?"

"Come quickly, and I'll explain it to you."

Helena dragged Dr. Skiba into the office of the director, who was on vacation, and dictated the wording of the pass to him: "In response to the request of the doctors of Gdansk, Dr. Solin and Dr. Stanowska are to proceed there as quickly as possible. The appropriate authorities are requested to give them every assistance on their way."

"But you're out of your mind!" said Skiba crossly.

"Not at all, dear colleague! It's urgent, and you're an understanding person. You're a warmhearted man. You love women, don't you? Nurses, patients—and your colleagues too. Surely you can't refuse me this little favor . . ."

Helena's voice was sugar-sweet, and her allusions were scarcely veiled. Silence fell between them, and then Dr. Skiba murmured: "There's really no need to get so excited. I won't refuse you anything, so I'll sign this for you. But I warn you, this paper will mean nothing to the militia, and they won't let you through."

"That's my problem!"

Skiba signed the paper. Helena took it and blew on it to dry the ink; then she handed it back to him.

"Now put the official stamp on it, and make a note that we'll be gone for a couple of weeks or more," she instructed him.

"You have a curious sense of your responsibilities," Skiba objected as he banged the stamp down onto the sheet. "Our medical strength here is already very reduced for the holiday period, and I just wonder who's going to look after the patients."

"You are, of course!" Helena called out to him as she hurried off down the corridor.

Once they were in the car, Helena told Maria what had happened, and they both had a good laugh about it.

"I wonder why André didn't take us with him," Helena remarked. "He seems convinced that only men can take action, while women—whether they're doctors or not—must confine themselves to daily drudgery."

Helena drove fast and well. The car sped along the freeway, and no militia or army units were to be seen. Fortunately there wasn't too much snow on the route, but now and then the surface became slippery, and she had to slow down.

It was cold, and there wasn't much sign of life in the villages they went through. At Torun, everything was quiet, and traffic seemed perfectly normal. To save time, they stopped at a baker's, and Helena bought some rolls and a big hunk of cream cheese. The line was relatively short, and she was in and out of the store in no time. "I feel in fine form," she announced as she got back into the car.

They went through Chelmno and Grudziadz; at Malbork, there was a militia roadblock. The car came to a halt, and the militiamen pointed their machine guns at it. Helena got out the paper signed by Dr. Skiba, and two militiamen read it slowly.

"A damned funny idea, sending women," said one of them. "Your certificates?"

Helena gritted her teeth and gave them her and Maria's cards.

"Women ought to be looking after children instead of running about on the roads," the other militiaman said. "Leave medicine to men!" He addressed this remark to Maria. "All right, you can go, lady doctors!"

"Filthy swine!" Helena swore. "And those are the ones who deafen our ears with speeches about women's rights in the beautiful People's Poland. Equality, oh yes, when it's a matter of slaving away in a factory, but inferiority when it comes to getting into line to buy something to eat or scrubbing floors. Our jobs are housekeeping, raising the children, and taking care of other domestic problems. Furthermore, even at the factory it's the women who are given the worst jobs. The foremen are all men. The devil take them!"

"André spoke of two hundred dead," said Maria slowly, as though she hadn't been listening. "If that's true, there must be hundreds of wounded. I just hope they let us enter the hospital; they're quite capable of letting them all die, without attention, so that it doesn't get known that they've carried out a massacre."

The nearer the car got to Gdansk, the more traffic they encountered. Trucks filled with soldiers kept passing them; the soldiers waved gaily in their direction, but neither of them had the heart to return their waves. They reached Gdansk after nightfall. The streets were filled with militiamen and soldiers, and the car made very slow progress; they were stopped three times by the militia.

When they got to the hospital, Maria went up to the first doctor she met. "We've come from Warsaw to help you," she said quite simply.

"How did you manage to get through?" the doctor asked in astonishment. "Thank God you're here! Do you have a pass?"

"Yes."

"Splendid! We'll leave for Gdynia straightaway. They're very short of doctors there. Do you have a car?"

"Yes."

"Good! I'll come with you. Let's go!"

Now it was Maria's turn to ask questions, and in a few words he explained the situation to her. "There are hundreds of wounded at Gdynia, and also at Sopot and Szczecin. The Gdynia hospital seems to have overflowed; the militia keep bringing more and more people in. There's evidently been a lot of arrests, but the prison dispensary doesn't answer the telephone, so there's no way of finding out if they've got wounded there, or what they're doing. But both of you must be tired out after that long journey," the doctor finished anxiously.

"No, no!" protested Maria. "You can count on us. We're in excellent shape."

She wanted to add that during the Warsaw uprising she had had no sleep for several days, but she stopped herself in time. There was no point in annoying Helena, and besides, this doctor was really too young. During those days he must still have been only a child.

When they reached Gdynia, the doctor directed Helena; they had to take back roads because many of the main routes were blocked by army tanks. They were stopped and interrogated and their papers checked. The streets were deserted, and there were no lights in the windows. The town seemed plunged in a deep sleep, submissively obedient to the curfew ordered by the authorities.

At the hospital, the corridors were cluttered with wounded lying on army stretchers. Militiamen were walking about in the wards, and nurses were scurrying about in all directions; the whole scene was one of indescribable disorder. Maria took off her coat, got her white smock out of her travel bag, and went to wash her hands. She was calm, tranquil, efficient—just as she had been during the Warsaw uprising, a quarter of a century before.

In the doorless toilets André was throwing up. The spasms brought tears to his eyes, set him coughing and spitting, and sent waves of pain up into his skull. Every time he was inside a prison it was the same story. But this time he had to regain control of himself as quickly as possible. Kazik had advised him to interview as many imprisoned workers as he could, and try to set them free.

"Tell the director the UB has ordered you to take them away with you—a secret order. If he doesn't believe you, ask to use the telephone, and call me at this number. There will be a truck waiting for you outside the gate. All you've got to do is get them into it and bring them to this address. Choose the young ones who seem to you to be particularly panic-stricken, those who've never been in prison and have no criminal record. You understand?"

In fact, André hadn't understood, but Marek, who was with him, seemed to know more about it. "Look, André," Marek had said, "they're anxious to recruit agents right away who can be used in another strike. Future voluntary *agents provocateurs*, who act out of gratitude, and are by definition less costly and more efficient than the usual paid agents. In the old days, you know, there was a third category available, the 'ideological *agent provocateur'*—I myself used to fit very nicely into that category, incidentally—but nowadays that particular species has almost disappeared."

André made no reply to this, since he didn't really know if Marek was joking or making a confession. Marek had changed considerably. He was no longer the gay, amusing companion he had been in Paris; now he was uncommunicative, bad-tempered, and sarcastic.

André shook himself, looked at his reflection in the little cracked mirror, mopped his forehead, and went out. The guard was waiting for him in the corridor and took him to the director's office, where Marek was drinking tea and listening to the director's explanations.

"I'll let you meet the ones who came in yesterday," the director was saying. "I can't swear they've got no records; we haven't finished checking them out yet. In fact, we're swamped; last night we had to add several more beds. But what can one do? Nobody could have expected such an increase in the prison population. Anyhow, they're waiting for us in the big hall on the ground floor, so come along."

"That means," said Marek as he got to his feet, "that we're not going to go around the sleeping quarters and the cells?"

"No, no," protested the director. "That would take up too much of your time, comrades!"

If only he doesn't insist! thought André, whose stomach was beginning to contract again, but Marek seemed intent on visiting the prison.

"In short, the people we're going to see have already been selected, to some extent, by yourself?"

"What are you getting at, comrade?" protested the director, who was obviously worn out by a long, sleepless night and barely managing to keep his temper under control. "There's no way I'm going to show you *all* the killers, *all* the assassins, *all* the thieves. Another time, if you really want it, but today—forget it!"

The guard had gone ahead to open the doors. There was the squeaking of unoiled hinges, and the jangling of the big bunch of keys against the bars.

"This is even more sinister than in the movies!" Marek said jokingly.

"Prison isn't a four-star hotel, and the people we get here haven't come for a well-earned rest!" The director

sounded irritated, and quite clearly couldn't stand much
more of Marek.

"Radio Warsaw newscasters are cantankerous types,"
said André, to unruffle the director's mood. "Don't pay
any attention to him!"

The big hall where they went was much better maintained than the administrative wing. The floor had been
freshly washed, and the walls looked as if they had been
repainted recently. They sat down behind a long table,
with the guards standing beside them, while the prisoners
came in one after the other.

Kazik had advised them to ask each prisoner his age,
and the number of years he had worked on the sites, and
André stuck to these two questions, which he asked in as
neutral a voice as he could manage. It was Marek who
decided which prisoners should be chosen, and ordered
them to go and stand at the other end of the hall.

Suddenly André found himself looking at a familiar face.
It was Wlodek, Magda's son. Without waiting for Marek's
reaction, he said: "Go and stand over there, comrade!"

André prayed fervently that Wlodek wouldn't say
anything. But Wlodek had understood in a flash that he
had had an unexpected piece of luck, and in order not to
give himself away, he lowered his head and looked fixedly
at the toes of his boots. At the same moment, the guard
slipped André a little piece of paper, almost imperceptibly.
André immediately concealed it in his hand, and opened it
surreptitiously under the table. There were five names on
it, and as though by chance, the five men named appeared
before them in order, one after the other. That was the
end; there was no more room for any of the others. That
was what they'd been told: a maximum of ten. They got up
and went out. But as they were saying good-bye to the
director, André had an idea, which he put forward at
once.

"We'd also like to visit the prison infirmary. Some of them might perhaps be transferred to a hospital."

"There are no wounded," the director lied. "The infirmary's empty. The few sick we had were sent back to their cells last week. *Au revoir*, comrade. Incidentally, that's an unusual name you have—André Solin. Are you of French origin?" Disconcerted, André explained his father's French bias, and then left as quickly as possible.

Outside, the men were already in the truck, and the driver motioned to them that he was ready to go. André and Marek got into the car Kazik had sent, and followed the truck. André tore a sheet out of his notebook and wrote: "Magda's son is in the truck. We've got to set him free before we arrive. Look out for the driver." Marek nodded to show he understood, tore the sheet into tiny pieces, and stuffed them into his pocket.

They drove through streets filled with soldiers and militiamen, but there were also women with shawls over their heads, carrying bags, mess tins, little baskets. These were the wives and daughters of the prisoners and the wounded, who were hurrying to bring them something to eat. Would the men be allowed to see their relatives? Would they be given the simple food their womenfolk had prepared for them with their love?

During the occupation, André recalled, the Germans had accepted parcels brought by the family for the prisoners in the Pawiak prison. On receiving the parcel, an official would consult the list of prisoners on the desk before him, and when a name no longer appeared there because the person had been executed during interrogation or had been transferred to a concentration camp, he would simply say: "No longer here."

The truck stopped in front of a house set back from the road, outside of town. André and Marek got out of their car and went over to it. Besides the ten men they had already selected, there were five others inside, and the driver gave them a wink; he was obviously in league with the guards, who had taken the opportunity of freeing some of the people they knew. The eternal complicity of the Polish people in the face of the force and violence of those in power was amazing.

"You, comrade," Marek said to Magda's son, "get into the car, next to the driver, and wait for us."

"And above all, not a word!" André managed to murmur to him. "Say nothing, whatever happens."

Wlodek nodded and got into the car, while the others went inside the big gray building.

"You're not wounded?" the driver asked Wlodek. "You were lucky! It was a real butchery. Here, have a cigarette." The driver opened the door and spat. "But it's not over yet. The strike committee at Szczecin's very well-organized. They're in complete power at this moment; they've even got their militia, and they've thrown out the killers of the Voluntary Workers' Militia Organization—the ORMO— along with those who are in uniform. They've burned down the party first secretary's villa. The army tried to stop the crowd, and there are many dead and wounded, but it doesn't matter. Comrade Gomulka hasn't got much longer left. What a nice Christmas present that will be!"

Wlodek inhaled the smoke from his cigarette. After all that had happened to him, he felt incapable of thinking. One single idea kept coming back to him: he had saved his nest egg because he had taken the precaution, before leaving for work, of putting the money under the inner soles of his boots. He had hesitated before leaving his room; then he had remembered that his father had always advised him, when he had any money on him, to keep it hidden. Old-style peasant wisdom, but it had worked.

"Let me have him! I beg you, let me have him!"

Helena finished doing the dressing while the woman on

the other side of the window kept her face pressed against the glass.

"I know her," said the nurse. "They're decent folk. You ought to help her, Doctor. If her man stays here, one never knows; they can transfer him to prison, or perhaps even shoot him."

"Do you feel strong enough to walk?" Helena asked the wounded man.

"Even to run!" replied the worker.

"Okay," said Helena. "Nurse, the rest is up to you."

"Thanks, Doctor," the nurse murmured, taking the man by the arm.

"But all the same, he needs an overcoat or a jacket or something. It's cold outside. You can't make him go out in pajamas and on bare feet!"

"Don't worry, I'll take care of it," said the nurse with a laugh. "It's my problem!"

Women, young and old, slipped along the narrow passages between the beds to visit their wounded men. They rarely spoke, but instead stood by the beds and looked at the wounded with expressions of indefinable sorrow. Helena and Maria found it very difficult to explain to these courageous women that they had to take back the food they had brought, because their wounded weren't allowed to eat. They always answered that they had brought good soup, made with potatoes and some bones they had managed to get hold of, and a soup like that would put anybody back on his feet, and certainly couldn't do anyone any harm. There would be tears in their eyes, but neither Helena nor Maria had time to comfort them. There were many wounded, and others were still pouring in—men at first, then women and even children.

Helena and Maria had been assigned one room to share, in which there was only a single bed. Helena had no nightdress and slept naked, which embarrassed Maria. Helena realized this, and laughed at her.

"Come now!" she said. "It's really time you got used to it. It's easy to see you've never been in a prisoner-of-war camp, as I have. We were perfectly comfortable about nudity, I suppose from being made to strip as a matter of routine for inspection and taking a common shower every month. Frankly, for a doctor, you have some attitudes toward modesty that are beyond me. You're used to examining patients, aren't you?"

"That's not the same thing," Maria protested, blushing. "Not the same thing at all! And besides, I'm your mother's age, and you're my daughter-in-law."

"So?"

"Oh, nothing—tradition, I suppose. I never slept in the same bed with my mother-in-law. It's true, those were different days. A woman of fifty was an old woman, respectable and respected, whereas nowadays—"

"You're not an old woman!" Helena said warmly. "You look much younger than your age, and besides, you're a doctor—that makes an enormous difference."

"Why? Is my body affected by my professional status?" laughed Maria, recovering her sense of humor.

Suddenly there was a knock at the door, the two women quickly put on their robes. It was the head doctor, who excitedly reported that Gomulka had resigned for reasons of health. The Central Committee had met at Natolin on the previous Sunday and accepted his resignation. Cyrankiewicz was no longer prime minister, but he was going to be given another post. New men were coming to power: younger people, better-trained, more interested in administrative problems than in ideological slogans.

"Plus ça change, plus c'est la même chose," said Maria with a sigh. "History repeats itself, but this time it's Gomulka who's on the way out, and Comrade Gierek who's moving in. I'm absolutely certain that in a few days—if it hasn't happened already—he's going to warn us

against a Soviet intervention. We'll be reminded of Budapest, and Prague, and we'll be forced to believe in an absolute, total, and unhoped-for renewal, which we'll have to earn by staying on our best behavior so as not to annoy our friends in Moscow."

"Edward Gierek's not Gomulka," Helena protested. "He's spent a long time in France and he's lived in a democratic country, whereas Gomulka was educated in Soviet jails. That's completely different."

"That's all very fine, but we're not in France," Maria said crossly. "Both of you must understand that Poland is Poland, a country which has a common frontier with Soviet Russia. Neither Gierek nor Gomulka can do anything about that, even if they wanted to."

"You're a pessimist!" said the head doctor. "Gierek's just promised there'll be no reprisals against the instigators of the strike, and everyone will get paid. The Russians won't intervene, and we're going to have a new team in power. And Dr. Stanowska's certainly right: Gierek knows the West. He'll know how to give our economy an impetus, reorganize our services, and surround himself with advisers who aren't complete imbeciles."

"I'm tired," said Maria suddenly. "I'm very happy looking after brave people, but discussing the future of this country is beyond my powers. It makes me feel as though there were a hundred years of mistakes and deceptions behind me. I don't believe in anything or anybody any longer."

"Oh, come now," the head doctor chided, and proceeded to take a small bottle of brandy out of his pocket. "This is Russian brandy, because the French stuff's too costly for me," he said with a laugh. "But we'll drink all the same to Gierek's arrival and to new times."

Helena drank her brandy without a word.

"We're leaving tomorrow morning, if you don't need us any longer," said Maria.

"I shall miss you, but I won't keep you," the head doctor agreed. "We've got good reason to hope that everything will calm down now and that the staff will even be able to enjoy Christmas. The tanks left town last night, and we've been promised there will be food in the shops. If we can believe the radio, this is the first year there will be dried prunes for the traditional Christmas compotes, and raisins, so that our wives can make proper Christmas cakes. But let's get back to more serious matters. I've spoken to Warsaw and tried to get plasma for transfusions; they claim they haven't got any. We'll have to mobilize the students and ask them to give blood."

"I'll look after that as soon as I get back," Maria promised.

The head doctor took his leave, and the two women prepared to go to bed.

"We must try to find André, all the same," Helena said.

"We'll see about that tomorrow," Maria agreed, as she snuggled under the coverlet. "Excuse me, but I'm really exhausted. For me, there's nothing more tiring than hope, especially when one knows in advance that the whole thing's just a sham."

"We want to know everything about them; it's essential to find out how far the ringleaders went in their contacts with foreign countries. Knowledge of the facts is power. The Old Man was taken by surprise because he was cut off from his sources."

Kazik listened to his boss in silence. Times had changed; the top brass was much more talkative now than in the old days. A year ago, he would never have been given such detailed and precise orders.

With a conspiratorial wink, Kazik was dismissed. As he walked to his car, he couldn't help noticing the beautiful grounds, with tall trees and exotic flowers, and wishing Inka were here.

Inka! The painful memory of last Christmas Eve was

still with him. Kazik had gone to Celestynow in spite of all
the work he had to do not only in Gdansk, Gdynia, and
Szczecin but also in Katowice and Warsaw. He had taken
risks to see her again—Inka, the only woman for whom he
was always ready to throw caution to the winds. They had
all been there: Robert and Irena, Helena and André,
Maria Solin, Marek, Father Marianski, and Magda with
her ill-starred son. And he, that peasant Wlodek, had
been the hero of the party! Inka had had eyes for nobody
but him, talked to nobody but him, showed interest only
in what he said or did. She had barely deigned to acknowledge Kazik's presence as they shared the consecrated wafers,
as was the custom at the midnight meal on Christmas Eve.

Kazik had been able to stay for only that one night, and
left the next morning. He was staying at Magda's, and
when everyone had gone to bed after the midnight Mass,
he had slipped along to Inka's door and knocked gently.
His heart had beat wildly when he saw her; God, how
beautiful she had been in the light from the little lamp in
her long dressing gown!

"I love you!" he had blurted out. "I never know what's
going to happen to me from one day to the next, but I've
got some money hidden away, and whatever happens,
you'll have whatever you want. If you like, we'll go and
live abroad. I'll fix it!"

He had taken her hand, and she had not resisted, but
her fingers had not responded to the pressure of his palm.

"You used to quiver in my arms before," he had told
her to her face. "You, who wanted me then as much as I
wanted you. You let me hope for all sorts of things, but
now you look at me with those blank eyes and treat me
like a stranger! There's a name for that sort of behavior,
you know."

Sweet, ignorant Inka had blushed deeply and started
apologizing. Yes, said Inka, she should never have given

him the impression she was ready for love; but now it was different. It seemed to her that—

Kazik hadn't been able to hear her out to the end. He was far too intent on humiliating her and hurting her. It was a painful scene. Inka had hidden her face in her hands as he told her that only whores behaved like that, provoking men and making them believe they loved them. He told her that she had been interested only in his apartment, his car, his connections, and his brilliant career. His nerves completely frayed, he had gripped her by the shoulders and threatened to kill her if she were to love another man. But his threat had had the opposite effect of what he had intended. The gentle young girl had been transformed into a lioness beneath his very eyes. She no longer sought to excuse herself, and defended herself fiercely.

"You can kill me here and now," she had shouted at him. "Because I'm in love with another man, and if he wants me, I'm going to marry him. Is that clear enough? He is simple and honest. He's got no gold, no car, but his hands are clean!"

Kazik had refused to hear another word. He had seized her in his arms and started kissing her like a man possessed. Her tight-closed lips had yielded beneath the pressure of his, and her tensed body crushed against his own had seemed to welcome him for a moment; but then he had felt her nails digging into the back of his neck, and had stepped back. Standing stiffly in front of him, Inka had raised her hand and slapped him across the face as hard as she could.

Since that night Kazik had slept around a lot, with girls picked up in cafés, women encountered in the street, prostitutes met in hotels. He knew that, in his profession, this was dangerous; women could pick up bits of secret information disclosed in sleep, which could easily ruin an officer's career. But Kazik just laughed all that off. He swore to himself that he would get to the top, and then snap his fingers at Inka, her family, and that boorish peasant, Wlodek, and that nothing would stop him. His need to have women in his arms was stronger than reason.

It was a beautiful, warm morning when Kazik reached the outskirts of Lodz. He decided to stop and have something to eat. His father, who had been a textile worker here in his youth, had told him sometime before of an ultrachic café in which no mere workingman dared set foot. Kazik tried to remember the name of the café: Frascati, Tivoli—yes, that was it, Tivoli! The car jolted along over the cobbled road surface, which had never been properly paved. Another of socialist Poland's failed promises, thought Kazik ironically, then stopped to ask for directions.

"Ah, Tivoli! It's a bit farther on, down the road, right on the corner where the trees are," a passerby offered.

Kazik drove on, stopped the car, and got out. He had never been in Lodz in all his life, and all he knew of the city was from his father's reminiscences.

"It's the Polish Manchester," he used to say. "An industrial city, one of the first built in Poland. It's ugly, and it's smoky, but it's very rich!"

"It *was* rich," his mother had interrupted. "But it's a different story nowadays."

Kazik looked for a table among the trees and sat down. The lawn was dead, as were the flowerbeds and shrubs that used to shield the customers from the stares of passersby. The legs of the rickety chairs sank into a sort of morass of dust, cigarette butts, and bits of paper, and the bare tables were an ugly grayish-white.

Kazik called for service several times, with no result. He got up and went inside the empty, dusty café, where he found a fat girl in an apron swilling beer from a bottle.

"Are you closed?" Kazik asked.

"No, of course not. I'm here, aren't I? What do you want?"

"Coffee, and some bread and cheese, if you've got any."

"I can make you some tea and bring it out to you, but that's all we've got at the moment."

Kazik took out a hundred-zloty bill and put it on the counter. "I said bread and cheese and coffee, and make it snappy! I've no time for joking, and I'm hungry."

The girl understood. She put down her beer bottle and went out, while Kazik went back into the garden, sat down at the table, and opened his newspaper. *Trybuna Ludu* was particularly boring that morning. The waitress brought coffee, a roll, a piece of butter, and a slice of yellow cheese which sweated tiny drops of fat in the sun. Kazik used his newspaper to cover the dirty table and began to eat. Really, this Tivoli bore little resemblance to the paradise his father had told him about. Kazik threw some crumbs to the sparrows huddled on the next table, and looked through the list of addresses he had been given the day before. He would have to hurry if he had to go and see them all.

Once again the car jolted its way along the bumpy road. A little farther on, a pretty park ran along the right-hand side of the road. Kazik checked the number of the houses. Yes, this was it. A big gloomy gray building, exactly like all the others. They were the former workers' houses built by the textile-industry magnates before the war. The stairwell, dirty and decaying, was in urgent need of repair and a coat of paint. Parts of the ceiling had come away, leaving big blackish patches. The doors of the apartments were scarred, the walls were covered with illegible graffiti, and the bells didn't work. Kazik knocked three times, and finally the door was opened.

"Is this where the Machlik family lives?"

"Yes, where else?" the woman replied. "Come in."

"I've come to talk to you about your husband."

"My husband's not here; you're wasting your time."

Kazik dropped down into a chair. The room, so carefully arranged, reflected one stark reality: utter poverty. Here there was nothing fancy, no ornaments, no extra furniture. There were only beds covered with gray-brown coverlets, four rickety chairs, and a table marked with a triangular burn where a hot iron had been left to stand too long, some knife cuts, and an inkstain.

"Would you like some tea?" the woman asked.

Traditional Polish hospitality, thought Kazik as he watched her. She was poor as a church mouse, but she was ready to share what little she had.

The woman took off her apron, wiped her hands, and sat down opposite him. Kazik noticed she had lost two fingers on her left hand.

"Did you have an accident?" he asked.

"Yes; those fingers stayed in the machine. Still, I was lucky not to lose the whole hand, or even my arm. The foreman managed to switch the thing off in time. These things happen; you know how it is! They say it's our fault because we're not skillful enough, but that's simply not true, believe me! I've been working for several years, and I've got a good deal of experience. The machines are old, worn out, and badly repaired. The safety devices are only checked after there's been an accident, and they're not always checked even then. But anyhow, it's no use complaining. We've just been told we're going to be able to retire at fifty-five. For me, that means I've got only twenty years to wait, while under Gomulka I would have had thirty."

"You're only thirty-five?" Kazik asked in surprise.

"I am indeed, my fine sir, and I know very well that I look fifty. What do you expect? We slave away six days a week, and we work long hours. I start at five in the morning, and I never finish before three in the afternoon. That's a long working day. There have also been accidents, and illnesses, and children. But enough, you didn't come here to listen to me talk about my misfortunes."

"On the contrary, I did!" protested Kazik, who suddenly felt ashamed of his job, of his past, of himself.

"Well, if you want to know everything, the worst thing is that my man's in prison and I don't know when they're going to let him out. And with my salary of fifteen hundred zlotys a month, I can't go on much longer. I've sold everything, and I've even taken subtenants in; that's why there's all these beds here. With two kids and my old mother who's got nothing but her pension, I've got to look out for myself. Things didn't look too bad at the start. I really hoped they were going to let my man out; but now they want to bring a case against him. I don't really know why; he's been there for six months already."

Suddenly Kazik had an idea. "Have you got an advocate?"

"A what?"

"A legal defender, someone who's capable of taking on your husband's case."

"What am I supposed to pay him with? If my man had killed someone, I could have had a lawyer appointed by the court. Real criminals can get those things, it seems, but my husband hasn't done anything criminal. He's 'antisocial,' and for that one has to find a private lawyer and pay him a thousand zlotys or more."

"I'm an advocate," said Kazik in a hollow voice. "And I know some colleagues who'll defend your husband for nothing."

"It's very nice of you to try to cheer me up, but with all due respect, I don't believe you. In these parts, you see, men of the law, learned people, don't talk to the workers. We don't know each other, we don't meet each other, we don't even know what the other side looks like. You people busy yourselves with the big problems of socialism; we're here just to work in the factories. How do you expect anyone to be interested in my husband's case? Men of the law have to earn their living in their own way, and we have to do the same in ours."

She's right, thought Kazik. We don't know each other, we don't understand each other. But I, Kazik Skola, didn't come from stock any different from that of this woman sitting opposite me. I'm the son of a worker, and I surely must be capable of understanding the whole situation, and changing it. I must be capable of that, and I'm going to do it!

Kazik stubbed out his cigarette. His mind was made up.

"I smoke too," the woman said suddenly. "But I can't afford it any longer. I rolled the last of my tobacco the day before yesterday."

Kazik put his pack of cigarettes on the table. "Here's something to get you through the summer. No, don't refuse me! And here's some money. I didn't steal these thousand zlotys. I earned them honestly—well, in a way that's generally held to be honest and that doesn't land one in jail. However, I'm going to ask you for something in exchange, something that'll help you and others look after themselves a bit better. You can turn me down, and I'll go away without arguing with you, but that won't do you and your friends any good. You must understand me; this isn't a piece of blackmail, it's an offer. My father was a worker, and he worked in this very city in days gone by. I really owe him something, and that's partly why I'm doing this. You can help me, so don't say no!"

Despite himself, he was moved by a powerful emotion, and the woman seemed to realize this.

"I don't know who you are or what your name is," she said. "But you have an honest pair of eyes. I always judge people by their eyes, so I'm going to say yes. What is it you want?"

"A meeting of women whose husbands or sons have been arrested, injured in an accident at work, or denied part of their salary. A meeting of people for whom good lawyers can do something. Have I made myself clear? In fact, what's needed is not one single meeting, but several,

in small groups. Otherwise, your friends could find themselves in trouble with the militia. And you must tell them
to keep their mouths shut about it. Choose women who
you're quite sure won't talk. I shall be staying in the city
all week, and I'll come back and see you this evening with
the lawyer who will be looking after your case and others'.
I'll be back around six; is that all right with you?"

Now it was she who was moved by emotion, but Kazik
gave her no time to thank him. He had to hurry; he had to
go and meet Witek, a former colleague at law school who
was now in practice at Lodz, as soon as possible, and then
he had to make another half-dozen visits like this one in
order to cover himself. Kazik's boss was perfectly capable
of checking up on how he had occupied his time, without
even following him, and there was no guarantee that a
plain-clothes agent wasn't at that very moment pacing up
and down in front of the building, waiting for him to come
out.

Kazik went over to the window and glanced quickly at
the street; seeing nothing out of place, he took his leave.
From then on he had one objective. "I'm going to show
them all what I'm capable of," he murmured to himself as
he started the engine. "I'm going to organize a chain of
friendship. These people will have lawyers in every city.
They'll stop feeling isolated and abandoned. I'll find lawyers everywhere—men and women who're ready to defend them for nothing. That's the true solidarity of a
people: the most knowledgeable of them being there to
help those who need it. Maria Solin will dig me up some
doctors to act as experts in injury-at-work cases; she teaches
at the School of Medicine, and her students adore her.
Kazik, you old swine, at last you're going to be able to
apply the principles of communism, and to the letter!
Poles of every walk of life and every profession, unite!
This is Marxism revised and corrected, socialism with a
human face—and an excellent way of no longer feeling

ashamed when I look at my face in the mirror every morning as I'm shaving. And it's all at the UB's expense. What a splendid joke!"

Kazik drove off like a whirlwind, leaving a cloud of dust behind him. For the first time in a very long while he felt strong and happy, and sure of himself.

10

I T HAD RAINED that morning, an early-summer rain that
had left the country roads muddy and made the big
cities look depressing. However, near noon the wind
had chased the clouds away, and the sun had already started
drying out the roads.

Irena was in high spirits as she put on her new dress,
which was a little too thin for the season, but very becoming.
It was a present from Kazik; he had written to his parents
in the States and they had sent it to him. It was made
from some fantastic material as smooth and slippery as
silk; it never creased, and could be washed like a pocket
handkerchief. Women must have an easy life over there,
Irena told herself. White suited her very well, and the
contrast made her old black raincoat seem quite new.

Robert had gone to spend a week with Kazik. They had
gone to visit workers' families. What an odd idea! Irena
had tried to question them about it, but neither her husband nor Kazik would give her any further details.

Robert had been gone three days now, and Irena, who
wasn't used to being alone, was finding his absence hard
to bear. At the beginning, she had been quite pleased to

be on her own and to be able to pass the time as she wished. She had promised herself to do all sorts of things— play the piano as much as she liked, sew, clean the apartment, and read—but she hadn't managed to put all her ideas into practice. She had slept a lot, hadn't touched the pots and pans, and had been too lazy to make herself proper meals. And now here she was on this fine Wednesday morning hurriedly getting dressed because Helena and Inka would soon be coming to pick her up. They were going to a very elegant restaurant in Wilanow. She couldn't possibly embarrass them, but she no longer knew what was being worn these days, and what was in style.

Of necessity, she and Robert didn't go out much, due partly to lack of time, and also to lack of money. Robert was economizing; he was obsessed by the idea that he would die first and Irena would find herself penniless. It was no use her giving piano lessons; what she got paid for that was never taken into account. Robert insisted she spend that money as she pleased. He wanted her to look elegant, and yet that was no small expense.

Two days ago Irena had gone to buy some eau de cologne and toothpaste in one of the special shops where one could buy imported products with dollars. But there had been a crowd, and disagreeable salesgirls, and Irena had felt humiliated at being obliged, in her own country, to buy goods which could be paid for only in foreign currency.

The customers around her seemed fascinated. Men and women, young and old, had kept touching the items, which had carried foreign tags and labels, with a sort of respect that bordered on fetishism. The bars of Swiss chocolate had been a big success, as were the bottles of scent, the cakes of soap, the electric kettles. Irena had looked at everything, considered buying some cologne, but then, instead of waiting her turn to be served, had gone away with her ten dollars intact. Now she was regretting

it, for all she had in the way of eau de cologne was a little
bottle of rubbing alcohol perfumed with lemon.

She looked at herself carefully in the mirror, and noticed,
not without a feeling of pleasure, that she looked young
again with her old beret worn at a jaunty angle on her
head and hiding her white hair. She would get the cologne
another time.

Ah! There was Helena blowing her horn.

"We've got some surprises for you," said Inka as she
helped her into the car. "But we're not going to tell you
now, we're going to save them for dessert."

In the restaurant at Wilanow, Helena slipped some
money to the maître d', and they were seated immediately
at a table beside the window. It was pretty, with a colored
tablecloth, a little vase with two carnations in it, and a
view. Irena was enjoying the atmosphere and didn't much
mind what she had to eat. What counted was the setting,
the luxury, the well-trained staff who seemed to enjoy
serving them. In the restaurants where she sometimes
went for a snack, everything was dirty and gray, and the
people who frequented them seemed as gray as their
surroundings. Here Irena found the people sitting at the
tables elegant.

"That's a pretty beret you're wearing," Inka told her,
sensing that Irena needed a compliment to feel completely
at ease.

"Have you noticed my new dress?" Irena removed her
coat with a very feminine gesture, as she had done in the
old days with Robert. Helena and Inka uttered little cries
of admiration; even the maître d' seemed to notice how
well the dress suited her. He leaned over her to point out
what dishes on the long menu were available, and she
thanked him with a smile.

"Now, my surprise first!" Helena announced. "André's
leaving for Paris tomorrow. I didn't want to tell you earlier,
because right up to the very last minute I didn't think he

was going to get his passport; but now it's a *fait accompli*. All the formalities have been completed, and not only that, but I've been given my passport and visa at the same time. I'm going to join him at the end of the month. We'll stay in Paris till Christmas, and—get this!—not as poor people having to look for cut-rate lodgings, but as official delegates. Well, André at any rate, and I'm included as his wife. Our job's to prepare for Gierek's visit; he's going to France next year as the guest of the Republic."

"It's too good to be true!" exclaimed Inka; she was entranced by the news.

I shan't see her for months, Irena thought. And it's not even certain she'll come back. Once they're in Paris, André could easily find some sort of job. He's such a capable fellow; with his knowledge of French, he could even be a journalist there.

"And what about your work at the hospital?" she asked tonelessly.

"I'm going to take a sabbatical, and perhaps with a bit of luck I can study certain methods of treating skin diseases in Paris. I'm interested in that."

"Hey, it would be wonderful if you discovered something new!" said Inka dreamily. "You could become a second Marie Curie-Sklodowska! Just think how this would sound: 'Helena Stanowska-Solin has just found a cure for cancer, thanks to her remarkable research work carried out in French laboratories'!"

Both of them burst out laughing, and Irena did her best to seem as enthusiastic as possible.

"I'll send you lots of pretty things—dresses, shawls, and perfumes," Helena went on. "And when I get back, I'll tell you everything so that you'll feel you were there with me, day after day. I promise I'll send you hundreds of postcards. All of Paris, all of France, in pictures—and in color, too! Will that make you happy? But don't say anything about this. For the moment, André's mission must remain confidential."

"We'll be silent as a tomb," Inka promised. "But as a bit of good news, it's the best I've heard for a long time in this family. Normally they would have sent André alone and never have allowed you to go with him. That's something we could never have hoped for. It makes one think that they've stopped being afraid people will choose to leave and simply not come back."

"I agree it's quite exceptional," Helena admitted with an air of false modesty. "But all the same, André's got a very good reputation in the world of journalism, and when he said he wouldn't go without me, they really had no option but to agree."

"Now it's my turn!" Inka announced. "I'm getting married!"

Irena started involuntarily on her chair and exchanged glances with Helena, who was frowning.

"Who's the lucky man?" she asked.

"I'm marrying Wlodek, and I'll go on with farming. Father Marianski's going to marry us in four weeks, just long enough for the formalities to be completed, whatever they are. The date's fixed, and Magda's started getting ready."

"You want to marry Wlodek?" Irena asked in an astonished voice. "Are you certain it's not just an impulse? He's older than you . . . he hasn't got the same interests as you . . . and he's—"

"He's wonderful!" Inka broke in angrily. "What are you so shocked about? Weren't you always telling me that in your day girls used to marry men ten years older than they were because they preferred men with jobs to young boys without a penny to their name? All right, he's a peasant, so what? You and Father and Helena—all of you used to tell me Magda was part of the family, didn't you? I like life in the country, because it's the only way that lets you have real freedom. I depend on nobody, and nobody depends on me. I shall never be forced to stand in a line to buy milk for my children. I shall never have to beg to be allotted a shabby room. I shall never be reduced to eating in cafeterias. Furthermore, you'll have a place to come when you're old; you can come and live with me. Wlodek's building a new wing on the house right now. There'll be our room, a bathroom, and a room for you and Father."

"Thank you," Irena murmured in embarrassment.

"Evidently I'm to be excluded," Helena protested, half-serious, half-teasing.

"Certainly not—what are you thinking of! You won't be able to come to our wedding because you'll be in Paris." She paused. "It's going to be a somewhat unusual marriage. In the autumn, Wlodek's going back to Gdansk to work in the naval shipyards, and I'll be alone for the winter. We want to buy a good tractor, and some other machinery as well. For that, we need money, and plenty of it. Before, we were forced to deliver fixed quotas, but now, as of next April, we're going to have contracts with the government, and they'll give us the right to buy equipment. And then, when I have a baby, I'll get the same free care as you did. I won't have to pay for the doctor or the hospital or all the follow-up care, as poor Magda did, in the old days, when she broke her arm."

"It's odd," said Irena pensively, "that at different times and for different reasons, both of you cleared out of Celestynow. Helena said she would never live in a hole like that where people keep watching and checking up on each other. As for you, you used to claim the country was nothing but a prison where everyone was dying of boredom. Ah, well, now you're tying your whole life to this same place. It's no wonder I'm worried about it all. Are you sure of your feelings for Wlodek?"

"I don't want to seem impertinent," Inka replied, "but

you never asked Helena all these questions when she decided to marry André. Yet the situation then was definitely more disturbing. He had no stable job, and they're still living with Marek in a single room. Now I'm going to have plenty of breathing space, and room to work in. So Wlodek's not a journalist and doesn't speak French, but he's got a strong pair of arms, and thanks to him, I know what it means to be a woman, a real woman!"

"Oh, my," sighed Irena. "If I understand you right, it's too late to change your mind."

Helena stared out the window. Was it possible that Inka, little Inka, was pregnant? Anyway, pregnant or not, it made no difference. She was going to marry this primitive, half-civilized creature Wlodek, and within a few years they would no doubt find that they had nothing in common. Inka would become like all country girls, old before her age, worn out by hard physical labor.

For her part, Inka bit her lips and kept silent. If Helena dares say a word, she said to herself, I shall simply scream! What does she know about the tenderness of a man like Wlodek, the happiness of being in his arms, of working with him? She's just a cold, competent machine, determined to make her mark as a woman doctor at whatever cost. She'll never understand that living means loving, because in fact she's in love with Kazik, and not with André. Only Kazik, the son of a worker, doesn't stack up to André Solin: a doctor's son, just back from France, a handsome boy who brought with him some of that dreamland, the West, that everyone imagines as some sort of paradise, since they can't go there and see it for themselves.

There was cheesecake for dessert, and coffee. Irena lit a cigarette; it was some time now since she had last done that. Her pianist's hands, with their tapered fingers, fluttered about nervously.

"I'll let Robert know," she told Inka, "and I'll take care

of your dress, if you'll let me. You're going to have a white
wedding, I hope?"

"If you'd like me to. I haven't actually thought about it."

"What a strange generation!" Irena sighed. "In our day,
that was very important. I had friends who threw themselves at the first suitor who came around, just to be able
to wear a white dress, a veil, and a tiara of orange blossoms.
Oh, one last question: may I tell Kazik about your marriage and invite him to the wedding? For some time now
he's been coming to see us quite frequently, and Robert
goes visiting needy families with him."

"Of course!" Inka agreed. "Kazik can come to my wedding if he wants to."

Helena tried not to think of what Inka was getting
herself into. At least, marriages were no longer forever,
were they? If Inka found herself unhappy with her Wlodek,
all she had to do was drop him and move to Warsaw,
where she could live with Irena and Robert.

Smiling, Helena paid the bill. For her, life was fine, and
full of promise; the time for tears and remorse was over.
I've tried to love Inka as best I can, as Andrzej asked me
to before he died, but there's nothing in common between
us, she told herself. Inka doesn't love me, and finds it the
hardest thing in the world not to show it. Well, in two
weeks' time I shall kiss them all good-bye and go aboard
the plane. When I land, there will be a whole new life,
and I'll be able to send them parcels to keep them happy.
I shall have a clear conscience at last!

Father Marianski moved with long, rapid steps, and
Kazik found it hard to keep up with him. They were
walking along a path that ran between the trees as far as
the clearing. The forest was superb; it was exceptionally
warm on this October day, but here, under the canopy of
the trees, the protective shade kept the air fresh and cool.

Tadeusz Marianski was worried. Observers—strangers

to the village—had been coming to the local Council's meetings and following the debates. There was some question, it seemed, of regrouping, and forming larger councils, so the few powers enjoyed by the members of the existing councils were thus in danger of becoming even more diluted.

"You've no cause to be alarmed," Kazik reassured him. "For the moment, the changes are all for the good. You mustn't be a pessimist and think that things aren't going to get better for us. On the contrary, there's already more stock available in the shops; also, the church is no longer being attacked in the press, and there's every chance things will continue that way." He paused. "How's Inka?"

He'd been waiting to ask that question for some time now, and the answer meant more to him than everything else. Father Marianski smiled imperceptibly and began chattering. Inka had gotten married to Wlodek the year before. It had been a beautiful ceremony, but in the long run the real question was how she was managing to get along alone with Magda. Some workers who had known Wlodek at Gdansk had come down, and they had persuaded him to go back there; since then, he had spent the winter there working and taking refresher courses.

"Off the record," added the priest, "I must tell you that I myself am worried about him. He takes a great deal of interest in the workers; he goes to all the meetings and organizes discussion groups, and I get the impression that he's not doing all that just to please the authorities. He's already been interrogated twice by the militia up there. He pretends it's nothing serious, but he didn't sound very confident when he was telling me about it. I think he's hiding something from Inka, but she senses it and is worrying herself sick."

"Do you think I can go and see her?"

"Of course you can! Go over this evening; that will

please Magda, unless you would prefer that I ask them to come to the presbytery?"

"I don't have much time," said Kazik hesitantly; then he shook his head. "No, I'll pay them a visit another time, but I'd like you to give her something. I've arranged for her to be granted the land which formerly belonged to Robert and his family. It's not a very large field, and it's been lying fallow for years; but all the same, I think she'll be pleased. I've got the papers in my car, and I'll give them to you before I leave. There's also Robert's house; it's falling to pieces, and even the tramps don't seem to want to camp out in it any longer. She could either have it torn down, or perhaps try to save two or three rooms. It would be a good project for Robert and Irena to get involved in. Since Helena left for Paris, they've been feeling very lonely."

Father Marianski was delighted. "What a marvelous suggestion that is! But are you sure you got it honestly, my son? Um, what I mean is, without exploiting anyone, without . . . um, actually, I don't really know *what* I mean."

"Oh yes, Father, oh yes! Don't worry yourself! Besides, it's in my own interest. Robert's collaborating in an undertaking I'm engaged in with certain other people. I'll explain to you what it is, only this has got to be under the seal of secrecy. Nobody must know about it. Do you understand me, Father?"

"I understand."

They had reached the clearing now, and Father Marianski sat down on a tree trunk. Kazik stood facing him, and they stared at each other for a moment or two.

"You're aware that at the time of the strikes there were victims. Women were left to take care of themselves and their children while their husbands were in prison. Well, officially all the strikers have been released, but in reality many of them are still in prison. I've managed to organize a group of lawyers who are trying to intercede in these cases, and we're also collecting money for the families. Robert's agreed to help me. He keeps the accounts, meets certain people, and even pays visits to the families. I'm assuming that nobody's going to come and bother him. Helena and André are well thought of; he's got a job in our embassy in Paris. All that counts, you know. Now, I want to avoid making any call on the church, so there'll be no special collections, no drives for gifts in kind, just a little discreet shove from behind. See Robert and give him advice when he needs some help, because I myself am caught up in some rather sticky business, and I don't know how it's going to turn out."

"Give me a cigarette," Father Marianski said. "You fire this news at me, and you want me to behave as though the whole thing was going ahead quite smoothly all on its own. Do you realize that I don't even know where you work, or what you really do? No, no protests! I'm well aware that you're a lawyer in the Ministry of Justice, one official among many others. Only you don't seem to be like the others. I've known you forever; you used to come and see me at the presbytery before you were dry behind the ears, so I trust you. All the same, tell me a bit more about what you want from me."

"Thank you for your trust, Father. You'll have two contacts in Warsaw: Robert and Marek, who's still living in Helena and André's former apartment. They won't call you, and you mustn't communicate with them by telephone. In any case, Robert hasn't got a phone, and Marek's could very well have been tapped. So definitely no telephone conversations. At a pinch, Robert can call you from a public phone booth, but be careful. Just take his message, and don't ask him any questions. Marek will come and see you. You'll go for a walk together, and he'll tell you what they need: money, a safe meeting place, supplies, or some family to take a child in for a few weeks. I can't foresee anything else for the moment."

"Right," the priest agreed. "I understand. As long as there's no question of asking me to hide arms under my bed, I agree to all the rest. Now let's talk about you. What's happening to you?"

"That's not so easy to explain. I've done a lot of things—handled a good many files, settled some fairly ugly cases—and along the way, I've made some enemies. I've also got certain people on my conscience; you know that better than anyone else. It was to you that I made my confessions at the time. Now, with the changeover, and with Gierek and his team in power, they want to eliminate me. But they simply can't arrest me just like that; I've taken precautions. They know that my files have been hidden away well enough to reappear no matter what happens here or abroad, and that those files will bring about the downfall of certain party bigwigs and cause a scandal. In short, their only way out is to compromise me."

Kazik put out his cigarette and immediately lit another one. Father Marianski sat with his head bent slightly forward; he looked deep in thought, but he was in fact listening with unflagging attention.

"They've just arrested a murderer, a real hard case. He was trafficking gold between West Germany, the Urals, and Poland. He was caught in a trap, and he killed a militiaman and a UB agent. The case against him is a hundred percent solid, and they used it to make him give details about his so-called accomplices. They forced him to denounce people he doesn't even know. This was why he 'remembered,' among other things, having met me in Berlin with a Yugoslav agent. The agent's dead and buried, and can't give evidence to the contrary, but it leaves me implicated. No, don't worry about me, I can defend myself. I've got an airtight alibi. They don't know it, but I can prove that on the day that this swine claimed he saw me with the Yugoslav agent, I was in the arms of a pretty girl several kilometers away from Berlin.

"Oh, forgive me, Father, you mustn't take these little pranks of mine too seriously. So tomorrow I've got a meeting with a judge whom I've known a long time and who owes his job to me. Unlike the others, this man believes he owes me a debt of gratitude, and he's prepared to help me. It all depends on how badly they want to have my hide; if they want it badly enough, they'll succeed, but if it's just a question of compromising me and making me lose my job, I'll get away with it. I'll leave the ministry of my own free will, and I'll get a job with a firm of lawyers. Only it's quite possible you might find the whole thing written up in the papers, you see, and you might come to the conclusion that I'm not only a somewhat dishonest sort of person, which you know already, and have known for ages, but that I'm a traitor! I value your friendship, Father."

"I understand," Tadeusz Marianski said as he rose to his feet. "One more thing. What am I to tell Inka when I give her your . . . your papers?" The priest stumbled over the words in his desire to avoid using the word "present."

"Just say it was sent to you from Warsaw for her, from the ministry or the authorities. That's all you know about it: a gift from Gierek, perhaps, for the Stanowski family, in recognition of services rendered to the country by their son-in-law, André Solin. Try also, if you can, to put that idiot Wlodek on his guard. He's not tough enough and he's too naive to be able to stand up to the machine. I assume he's trying to broaden the organization of official trade unions. That's an excellent idea, because in spite of all the promises Gierek made in 1970, nothing at that level's been changed yet; and although they've promised to carry out reforms after this year's congress in November, they're not going to do it. At best, a few old stick-in-the-muds will be fired, and tactfully replaced by others. My

information is that there will be fewer intermediaries between the councils of the business associations and the
national Council—but in practice that means nothing. If
Wlodek's being supported or even manipulated by others,
he's got some chance of getting somewhere; but by himself
he stands no chance, believe me. So try to get in touch
with him and talk to him, face to face."

"He's promised to spend Christmas here," said Father
Marianski, "but if he doesn't come I've no other way of
getting in touch with him."

"Do you think he'd trust Marek?"

"Certainly not. He's a loner, and he distrusts intellectuals like Marek who work for Radio Warsaw and carry a
party card; he insists they're bound to be thieves and
racketeers like all the government bunch. You know, above
all, Wlodek's an honest man."

"If Marek brought him a message from you, would that
change things?"

"I imagine it would. I'll think it over."

"In short, Father, you also distrust Marek, and it's only
natural. Listen, I know a way to convince you. He's busy
writing a book, about our situation, which he'll never be
able to get published here. If he let you read his manuscript,
would that change your attitude at all?"

"Perhaps. I'll see. But I can't promise anything in
advance."

"This distrust is heartbreaking!" said Kazik angrily.
"Listen, if I get arrested, you're going to spoil everything.
Robert and Marek must count on you. I beg you, Father,
do understand! This is the first time we've managed to
show the workers that they're not alone, that the professional classes are supporting them, and that they can
collaborate with them. We're busy doing our best to create solidarity. That's absolutely essential if we're going to
achieve any real reforms. Without it, we'll never succeed
in changing our damned system."

"A little while ago, you said the new outfit *wants* to make improvements, but now you're contradicting yourself," said Tadeusz Marianski with an ironic smile. "How do you expect me to understand you?"

"They're less puritanical, more open-minded—and they've also got some trump cards in their hands, which Gomulka didn't have. First of all, there's the atmosphere of détente between the Kremlin and the West, and there's the possibility of borrowing from abroad, which has been partly agreed upon, for the construction of the giant Katowice complex and the plans for the construction of the pipeline."

"What pipeline?"

Kazik hesitated for a moment, looked around to make sure they were alone, then drew close to Father Marianski and murmured softly, "They've found oil and natural gas in Siberia, but they need money to develop them. The West has a guilty conscience where Poland is concerned; after all, they handed us over to Stalin at Yalta. So Gierek, with his good manners, his knowledge of French, and his air of distinction, has a better chance of obtaining loans from the French and the Americans than anyone else within the brother countries. Moscow prefers to let Warsaw run into debt rather than to do it directly themselves. Gierek makes an excellent intermediary for them."

"My head's in a whirl," said Father Marianski. "You know too much, Kazik, and I just wonder how you manage to keep everything straight in your mind. Okay, I'll trust your Marek, since you want me to; and I'll help you as much as I can. Now, run along, because I need to think this whole thing over."

They reached the main road, passed by the cemetery, and stopped in front of the church.

"Go on in for a moment," said Father Marianski. "It'll do you good."

The smell of burnt candles permeated the empty church. Kazik knelt down, put his head between his hands, and

tried to pray. He didn't succeed, but the peace and silence calmed him considerably. So what if he were arrested,
condemned, hanged? After all, what was his life worth?—a
single man for whom nobody was waiting. In any event,
sooner or later, his present way of life would land him in
prison.

He shook his head. No! I'll keep fighting to the bitter
end! he thought as he rose to his feet. I'm not going to be
condemned for nothing. When they take me, I'm going to
be quite sure that others are going to carry on the fight in
my place. I'm going to show them all that there's a way to
be free of the Soviets and to help people live better,
without causing any butchery. I, Kazik Skola, a worker's
son from nowhere, am going to transform this country and
show these long-winded intellectuals that the workers are
the only force for true revolution, because it is they who
represent the masses. Let Marek go on scribbling books
which will never see the light of day; all I need is this
priest—as a man of the church, as one of us.

Kazik crossed himself, slipped some money into the
collection box, and went outside. Out of respect, Father
Marianski had waited for him out front.

"If anyone asks you what I was doing here," Kazik
advised him, "tell them I brought the papers for Inka
because I wanted to be certain they were in good hands.
And don't let yourself be intimidated! These documents
are official, the thing's perfectly legal, and nobody can
pretend otherwise. The signature at the bottom of the
pages is that of an individual who will not deceive me
because he knows he risks the gallows if he double-crosses
me."

Kazik took the file out of his car and handed it to
Father Marianski.

"I'm going to pray for you," said the priest. "And try not
to forget that . . ."

"That what?"

"That you're a Christian, and that as such you have to have some self-respect."

"I promise!" Kazik cried as he started his engine. "I seem to remember you like giving heavy penances, Father, to those whose confessions you hear."

The car drove off, and Tadeusz Marianski entered the church. I'll pray, he said to himself, and I'll think all this over afterward. It'll be easier then!

It was snowing and white flakes were dancing on the other side of the window. Gazing outside, Robert puffed on his pipe and began to cough.

"Something wrong?" Irena called from the kitchen, where she was preparing dinner.

"I'm so happy!" Robert answered. "I love this house."

Irena came into the room and stood next to him. "Poor darling, you've learned to be happy with very little!" she murmured as she stroked his hair. "These two rooms don't really look very much like your parents' house, and we're living in quite a different age."

"Look!" Robert cried, pointing out the window. "It's exactly the same landscape as we saw from this window in the old days. What a lovely country ours is! The walls, the floors, the furnishings—none of that is important. The essential thing is this landscape, this countryside, this field that we're going to be able to cultivate next year, and the fact that we're both alive, you and I, and are together. I could never thank Fate enough for that. I was being stifled in Warsaw between those gray walls, those dust-laden streets, and the daily hell of the stairs. I didn't want to worry you, but it often happened that I couldn't get downstairs without clinging to the banisters like an old man. I've grown younger in these two rooms, where all I need do to get outside is push the door. I'm no longer afraid of one day finding myself shut up within four walls. Back there, in Saska Kepa, I was the prisoner of a stupid staircase, while here I've become a free man."

Irena nodded. "I realized that the staircases tired you, and I often asked myself how long you'd be able to manage, but we had no chance of finding anything better. It was a real miracle that Inka was able to get this ruined house and put it back into shape. I'm very happy to be here with you, too. I feel I'm doing something much more useful, giving piano lessons to Father Marianski's pupils, than I was during the last year we were living at Saska Kepa. And then, we've got Inka and Magda here, and I believe both of them need us. I don't understand how Wlodek can leave them alone without even coming back for Christmas. And they have three days' leave from the shipyards for the holidays!"

"I've already told you, Wlodek's got no alternative," Robert protested as he turned away from the window to face his wife. "He's making progress, he's taking courses, and he sends his salary to Inka. I really don't see what more he can do. You women, you're insatiable! You're always demanding more and more."

"Inka demands nothing," Irena sighed. "But is it normal to live the life of a single woman at twenty-six years of age? I don't care for all these activities of hers. Do you think she's acting sensibly in being the local Rural Youth delegate to the Warsaw Congress?"

"She's got a perfect right to do whatever interests her."

"In theory. But the Rural Youth Association's actually just a bunch of young people who joined the party to justify their lack of gusto for work. Instead of doing the plowing, they leave that to the old folks, and run meetings where they exchange slogans and commonplaces."

"The library Inka organized functions very well, and the young folks of Celestynow go there and take out books. That's already something," Robert objected. "For my part, I'm satisfied the little one's doing good work, and I'm very proud of her. Stop worrying! In any case, she's due back tomorrow from the Congress, so we haven't got much longer to wait. You fuss over her too much."

"Oh, no," Irena sighed. "You know very well that all these communal movements, all these organizations, serve solely to manipulate and discipline the young folk more easily. It's a means like any other to stop them from thinking and questioning, under the pretense that they're educating them. A fine education! For some of them it's a way of profiting from the advantages their party card brings them, and for all of them it's a form of brainwashing."

"You must understand, darling, that in our country individualism's a luxury that only old folk like you and me can allow ourselves. The young folk have to amalgamate, create a solidarity among themselves, and make joint decisions on what they want to build as their future. Otherwise the government will lead them like sheep to the slaughter. Come, Irena, I'm dying of hunger; since I'm never going to be able to convince you, we'd do better to eat than argue!"

He sat down at the long wooden table and Irena brought two bowls of soup. She lit the lamp and sat down opposite Robert, but they had hardly begun to eat when there was a knock on the door. It was Inka.

"Good evening!" she cried happily. "Is there anything for me? I've brought some good news, so I deserve a reward!"

Irena jumped to her feet and threw her arms around Inka. "Sit down, I'll set a place for you right away. I've got some nice cabbage soup, some potatoes, and even a bit of herring. So, tell us everything. How was it? You must be worn out, poor darling!"

"What about that Congress?" Robert asked. "Did it go well? I suppose your speech was brilliant, and that you got lots of applause after reading something that's been censored by a dozen party members! No, don't be cross, I'm just pulling your leg. Anyway, you look like you're in good shape."

"I must talk to Father Marianski about the Congress," Inka said, suddenly very serious. "Actually, it's not all that complicated. Instead of discussing our problems, and the needs of young farmers, we started by voting on a change of name. From now on it'll be the Association of Socialist Rural Youth, with the word 'Socialist' added to the previous name, the Association of Rural Youth, which has been in existence since 1957. Apart from that, the talks were predominantly about the Russian Revolution, the Soviet experience, and the importance of building a true socialism. All the speeches had been prepared in advance, as usual, and I had a lot of trouble asking certain questions. When I asked if we were going to receive an increase in aid to buy tractors for the cooperatives, they cut off the microphone. The people in the room didn't understand anything. I shut up; I was afraid there might be trouble. One never knows . . ."

"I don't understand why you find it so surprising. That sort of thing's perfectly normal. A rigged congress, collective brainwashing, and you, my naive little daughter, still insist on believing in Santa Claus! I'm just happy they didn't do you any harm." Irena placed a bowl of soup in front of Inka. "Eat, it'll do you good."

"I really believed they wanted to get something done. They'd promised to supply us with more machines, more equipment, but when we asked them to be more precise, when we tried to talk about our needs and the way in which they could be met next spring, they started talking to us like in the days of Gomulka about the purity of the socialist doctrine. International doctrine, you understand, which mustn't be tainted with national considerations." She paused. "But I won't give up; that's defeatism! On my own, I can't make the people at the meetings understand what's going on, because they'll merely cut off the microphone and then nobody will hear me. But if those who think like me manage to form a group, and while one of us is talking, the others make sure the microphone is working, then we have a chance of making ourselves heard. They can intimidate individuals, but not a mass of men and women who have the guts to oppose the party leaders."

"Brilliant!" Robert said, stroking Inka's hand tenderly. "You're young, so go ahead and try it. Irena and I have done our part; it's your turn. I just want to remind you that Helena had her party card when she was nineteen, I believe, and it didn't last."

"At that age Helena was merely a young girl who got a lot of amusement out of the youth organizations," said Inka ironically. "Even now, despite the fact she's a doctor, she still doesn't understand much about the demands and necessities of a collective action."

"Fine!" Irena interrupted. "Now that you've said all this, may I read you the letter we've just received from Helena?" Without waiting for a reply, she went over to the drawer and took out a long envelope, removed the sheets of paper, and began reading by the light of the lamp:

My dears:

I'm taking advantage of a French friend who is on a trip, to send you this letter, and another one for André's mother. For once, I'm sure it'll reach you intact without having been read by anybody. My friend doesn't know Polish, and since she's on an official trip, she won't be searched at the frontier. Paris is certainly the most beautiful city you could ever dream of. The years go by, but I'm always finding something new to look at. But it's no longer quite the same thing it was at the beginning. Do you remember how I hoped then to work my way into the French community and make myself some friends?

In fact, it'll soon be two years that we've been here, and all that I have are some acquaintances. I meet French people at embassy receptions, and I find them very brilliant, but my life and my loneliness are beginning to get me down. It's quite out of the question for me to visit the Polish immigrants; to them, I'm a representative of the regime they detest, and a profiteer, too, which is even worse!

I see Marek's friend Ula fairly frequently. She's a Polish girl who married a Frenchman and then divorced him. She works for a living, but since she's a single woman, she meets me more readily when André's not there, which happens much too often for my liking.

The worst thing of all is that as time passes, I find I'm seriously asking myself what I'm doing here. I've learned French, I read a lot, and I'm taking some courses, but professionally I'm doing nothing. My medical experience isn't enough for me to practice in Paris. I've spoken to André about it many times, but he won't listen to me. Worse still, he considers me ungrateful. I have a lovely apartment, a maid, money, dresses, jewels (they're paste, but beautiful). Next month, we'll be going on vacation, no doubt to Spain. What more could I ask for? Well, it's very simple: to find myself back in my little office at the hospital, discussing a case with Maria Solin, and looking forward to seeing you at the end of the week. I want to live! Here, I don't live, I exist. It's very comfortable and interesting, but I'm nothing but an eternal foreigner.

Inka gave a yawn that nearly dislocated her jaw, and Robert noticed it.

"Do you want to go and lie down, poor darling?"

"Her life over there doesn't sound much fun," said

Inka. "I was wrong to envy her when she described the lights on the Place de la Concorde and the view from the Trocadero."

"Let me just finish the letter!" Irena insisted.

> Here, I can buy as much good cheese, poultry, shoes, dresses, and hats as I like. With what André earns and our entertainment allowance, our budget's not too tight. However, every time I go out shopping, I find myself less happy when I get back home than I did in Warsaw, when I was lucky enough to come across a bit of meat. It's too easy here! And then again, I keep feeling remorse whenever I think of you—

Inka put on her coat, pulled on her thick man's gloves, and kissed Robert on both cheeks.

"Well, till tomorrow, then!" she said. "Go to bed—both of you look tired out."

It was cold outside, but the snow had stopped falling, and the stars were twinkling brightly. Inka walked briskly, thinking how good it would feel to have Wlodek's arms around her waist.

She missed his male body, hard and insatiable. Sometimes at night she lay awake for hours on end tormented by desires she didn't want to acknowledge. "Our country is more important than the two of us alone," Wlodek had said to her as he kissed her good-bye, and at the time, she had agreed with him. But now things weren't the same, and she could feel a sense of revolt growing within her.

I only have one life, Inka said to herself, and in the country, one grows old quickly!

The road that led to Magda's house was all white, and the snow creaked beneath her heavy boots. There was a light in the kitchen window; Magda hadn't yet gone to bed.

Inka pushed the door open, and felt the heat of the

room. Magda hurried to help Inka off with her coat, and asked the eternal question: "Are you hungry? Do you want something to eat?"

"No, no, I've eaten already. Don't get up. I'll tell you everything there is to tell." She moved closer to the fire. "The shops in Warsaw are much better stocked than they were last year. You can actually get meat! I've brought you a little present. I bought some wool in a private shop, and I'm going to knit you a—"

There was a loud snore, and Inka turned around. Magda was asleep, hunched forward over the table with her head resting on her folded arms. Inka smiled tenderly as she took Magda by the shoulders, raised her to her feet, and led her to her bed at the back of the room. Magda muttered a few words as Inka undressed her, then stretched and began snoring again.

Inka turned off the light and sat in front of the fire, her body motionless and her thoughts confused: I'm twenty-six. Wlodek's far away, and I'm constantly alone. We have no children, and I'm not sure we're ever going to have any. How much longer must I wait to find a little happiness?

Inka felt particularly happy on this spring day. She got up very early and slipped out of the house without waking Magda. Ever since the days of her childhood, she had loved walking along railway tracks, and at six in the morning she could amuse herself by jumping from one tie to the next without fear of being watched.

Inka breathed in the familiar smell of trains—a mixture of soot, oil, and coal—and dreamed of the long trips she would take with Wlodek one day, to far-off lands. Suddenly she heard a train whistle and experienced the infantile fear that brings pleasure in its wake, the last-minute rush from the top of the embankment to the fields below. As she stepped halfway down and crouched against the sandy soil, her lungs were filled with the hot blast from

the locomotive and her ears rang with the deafening din of
the wheels pounding on the rails.

Walking back to the house, she felt peaceful and relaxed.
It wasn't until she was almost at the door that she saw the
two militiamen.

Inka broke into a run. Magda was there, already putting
on her shawl. The militiamen took them both to the
station, and there, in the dark little room, they gave Inka
a big parcel: Wlodek's effects. They told her, with no
attempt at tact, that he had been killed in an accident. No,
they didn't know any of the details. The officer thrust the
official notification at Inka, a big sheet of paper covered
with stamps, and told her to sign it.

"If you want further details, comrade, you'll have to go
to Gdansk," he added curtly.

Outside, Irena, Robert, and Father Marianski were waiting for them. News spread quickly in Celestynow, and
they had heard that Inka was at the militia station. Inka
was trembling from head to foot and couldn't speak. It was
Magda who showed them the documents they had been
given.

"We're going to Gdansk," Robert decided. "Marek will
take us in his car; he's at the house now."

An hour later, Marek, Robert, and Inka were driving
along the main road. The two men were silent; they didn't
dare turn around to face Inka. She was holding Wlodek's
effects on her knees, still wrapped in their brown paper,
and did not weep at all.

In Gdansk, Marek managed to obtain a hotel room,
thanks to his Radio Warsaw identification card. Once in
their room, Robert made Inka swallow some sleeping tablets Helena had sent from Paris; they were very effective,
as Robert well knew, since he so often had sleepless nights
himself.

"Go to the naval shipyard," he told Marek. "I'll stay

here with the little one. She shouldn't be alone when she wakes up."

Robert installed himself in an armchair and fixed his stare on Inka's pale face, half-hidden under the mass of blond hair. This was how he had watched over Helena in the old days as he waited for Andrzej; many years had passed since then, and yet he remembered it as though it were only yesterday.

Robert had no idea how long he watched over Inka, or even whether he slept. It was very late and the room was in total darkness when Marek's key turned in the lock. Robert saw at once that he was drunk; he could barely stand on his legs, and Robert had to support him to keep him from falling onto the bed. Without a word, Robert dragged him over to the alcove where the shower was installed, and pushed him under a jet of cold water.

"Hey!" Marek protested, but he began coming slowly to his senses.

"Okay?" Robert asked.

"I think so," Marek sighed as he dried his face with his wet sleeve.

Robert threw him a towel and went back into the room, gripped by a feeling of discouragement. He lit the little night-light and dropped into the armchair near the window. Inka was still asleep.

"Are you capable of talking now?" he asked Marek, who had taken off his jacket and shirt and was trying to wring them out.

"Give me a cigarette!" he said at last, sitting down on a chair beside Robert. "Is she asleep?"

"Yes, you're lucky!" Robert murmured. "I'd rather be the only one to see you in this state at a moment like this."

"Good!" said Marek as he inhaled smoke from the cigarette. "First of all, the official version. It was an accident at work; the crane hook was defective, and at the

very moment that the load slipped off, Wlodek was standing right underneath. He never knew a thing; his body
was literally shredded by the impact. They've buried him.
I got the authorities to agree to a judicial inquiry; it wasn't
easy, but I made them do it. It's not the first time you and
I've been involved in a case like this. Inka will get the
miserable pittance they dish out by way of compensation,
a tiny little pension, and perhaps even the certificate of
honor awarded to the widow of a man 'killed on the field
of battle in the fight for socialism.' But there's worse."

Marek went to get a glass of water for his hiccups, and
came back rubbing his neck with a towel.

"When I came out of those fine gentlemen's offices, I
met a man. He took me to his home, where another man
was waiting for us."

"With some vodka, I assume!" Robert interjected.

"Yes, lots of vodka. Here's what they told me. They had
known Wlodek in 1970, but at that time he wasn't very
communicative. Later on, it was they who came looking
for Wlodek to get him to go back to work at the naval
shipyard. They needed him, because he was better
educated, and because they could trust him. At first,
Wlodek didn't want to do anything, but in the end they
persuaded him it was his duty to the men who had died in
1970. After that, they organized discussion groups together,
groups that were completely independent of control by
the unions or by anyone else. They were of the same type
as those we organized with you and Kazik, and, of course,
with the same objectives: defense of the rights of workers
injured in accidents at work, or fired without cause, or
jailed on various pretexts. Unfortunately, that idiot Wlodek
didn't trust us. He acted on his own with his group, but
he wasn't strong enough to stand up to the UB agents.
They started off trying to infiltrate the group, but they
didn't succeed; so then they began using threats against
Wlodek—but he refused to listen. They used various kinds

of intimidation against him, and the men mounted a sort of guard around him. They took turns getting Wlodek in the morning and taking him back home in the evening. A young boy went to live with him, to keep guard over the apartment. Two months ago, they tried to fire Wlodek, again without success. His immediate superior was against it, saying Wlodek was the best employee he had on his team. In short, they had no choice but to cause his little 'accident.' "

Marek emptied his glass of water in one gulp; his hiccups had started again and were making it difficult for him to continue speaking.

"The problem," he said, "is that nothing can be proved. The equipment's so poorly maintained, so rusty and old, that they can always throw the accident theory in our faces. Furthermore, nothing that the men said within those four walls will ever get repeated in front of a judge. These men have families, and they'll never dare open their mouths. They're good types, all the same. They're passing the hat around to collect money for a commemorative plate on Wlodek's tomb. That may seem like little, but it's actually quite a lot, because they're all living on starvation wages with their wives and kids."

"Dear God!" murmured Robert. "I really am an idiot. If I'd had any idea of the risks that Wlodek was running at the shipyard, I could have helped him, warned him. But all he ever talked about was the money he was earning, the repairs he had to make on the barn, and things like that. Even Inka didn't know what was going on. Nobody did!"

"What are we going to tell her?" Marek asked quietly.

"Nothing. Nothing at all! Wlodek died in an accident, do you understand? That's dramatic enough as it is. Inka must never find out that her own husband didn't have enough confidence in her to tell her what he was really doing in Gdansk."

"Poor devil!" Marek sighed. "No doubt he wanted to protect her. That way, if he'd been arrested, Inka wouldn't have had any secrets to confess."

"The poor devil, as you call him, is dead and buried, while the little one has to go on and live her life. Tomorrow morning we're going back to Celestynow. There's nothing more for us to do here, not with her, at least. Go to sleep now. I'd rather stay awake. No, don't argue! I'm very comfortable here in my armchair."

Without a word Marek stretched himself out on the other bed, while Robert kept watch until daybreak, when he woke Inka.

"We're leaving," he said. "It was an accident, my dear, a defective crane. There'll be an inquiry to make sure it doesn't happen again, but for our poor Wlodek, it's too late."

Inka was strangely calm. "I want to see where he died, his room, and the place where they buried him." Robert had no choice but to agree.

Marek forced her to swallow a little tea in the hotel restaurant before they left. Marek drove in his damp, crumpled suit, with Robert beside him, and Inka was curled up on the back seat. As though in a nightmare, she visited the naval shipyard, where the union representative and Wlodek's boss moved around her like two fat spiders. Words flew back and forth: "he died on the field of battle in the fight for socialism . . ." "an unforeseeable defect" . . . "a frightful accident, the whole shipyard is mourning." Flowers, a bunch of carnations, were brought out. Inka pushed them aside and got back into the car.

"Now we'll go to his place," she told Marek. "It was a good distance away from his work, yet he never complained about it in his letters. He never complained. He said nothing, just sent me all his money."

The room was on the third floor. Wlodek's roommate was there. He handed Inka a big bouquet of flowers, but

she didn't even notice them. Standing in the middle of the
room, she looked around it for a long while in silence,
then went out onto the landing while the young man tried
to show her where Wlodek kept her photo, which he
looked at every night before he went to sleep.

Inka clung to Robert's arm. "Let's go to the cemetery,"
she begged him. "Take me there quickly!"

They set off; this time, Marek had to ask his way several
times from passersby. When they reached the cemetery,
they saw the iron fence, the sea of crosses, the chapel, and
the grave-digger who came to meet them. The plot of
freshly turned earth was there, right at the end of the
pathway on the right, all muddy and waterlogged. Inka
walked quickly, and Robert found it very hard to keep up
with her. Marek and the grave-digger stayed in the rear.

"Darling," Robert begged her, "let go. Have a good cry;
it'll make you feel better."

Inka didn't answer. She sank to her knees before the
spot where they told her her husband lay buried, and
prayed. Pictures started passing before her eyes: Wlodek
driving the cart, Wlodek reading a book in front of the
fireplace, Wlodek and she on the motorbike, her arms
around his waist. All that was finished. Never again would
he hold his hands out toward her, never again. Why, dear
God, why?

It began to rain. Cold drops blown by the wind struck
her face. Wlodek's saying good-bye to me, thought Inka.
He's advising me not to abandon Magda and the farm.
Those are the only things that matter to him. Our marriage had no importance while he was alive, and it continues to have none now that he's dead. Just the land, the
damned land! Enrich the land, fertilize the land, invest,
buy seed, hire equipment. The land, his only love, in
which his body now lies forever!

                    *   *   *

"Are you going to sign this manifesto?"

There was a note of supplication in André's voice. A group of people had gathered in Maria Solin's apartment for a meeting, and the room was hot and filled with cigarette smoke.

"Yes, we're going to sign it," said Robert calmly. "It's the only way of showing we're still on our feet. Their plan for the new constitution is treason, pure and simple, and not to protest against it means giving formal recognition to the one-party system. Even more, it means abdicating our natural sovereignty, since they want to include a statement in the text to the effect that our foreign policy must depend on our indissoluble fraternity with the Soviet Union. We would be agreeing implicitly that citizens have no rights, that the party is the single instrument of the state's authority, as arbitrary as it can possibly be, and that the government and the party are responsible to nobody."

"Yes, yes!" André cried angrily. "I've read and reread the text of the constitutional amendment; I know it by heart. But in the long run, all we're going to get in return for our signatures is visits from the militia, house searches, workers being laid off and sent to jail, and a series of political prosecutions. We're going to be regarded as dissidents, and surely you know what that means in practice?"

"I don't see why we have to behave like cowards," Helena remarked calmly. "In 1952, when they brought in the constitution imposed by Stalin, I was too young to understand: but now, twenty-three years later, I have no excuses. They can't put us all in jail. There are thousands of people who will sign this manifesto."

"Wait a minute!" A small man named Jacek, who had come with Marek, jumped to his feet and walked over to Helena. "We've decided there will be two types of militants active within the movement: those who will make an open show of things and be ready to get themselves arrested if necessary, and those who will do their utmost to live undercover and stay on the sidelines to help the others. I believe doctors run less risk signing a petition than journalists do. So I agree with Helena—but also with André. It's obvious we lack good doctors, and the authorities are going to think twice before they deprive themselves of their services, while it's not the same for a journalist. So I propose that Dr. Solin and Dr. Stanowska sign the petition."

There was a long silence; then Maria went over to the table and added her signature to the big sheet of paper that lay there. "You don't know how happy I am to be able to help you in some way," she said.

Helena smiled at her; there was a sort of friendly complicity between the two women. Helena signed in her turn, then made way for the others. The tension in the room gave way to a feeling of relaxation; there were jokes, and laughter, and banter. André was the first to leave, and Helena accompanied him. On the staircase, he took her hand.

"I apologize," he murmured. "I think I disappointed you."

"No, no!" Helena protested halfheartedly. "You're in process of building a career; it would be most ungracious of me to criticize your behavior. I signed for us both, and that's all there is to it."

It was cold, and André shivered in the elegant overcoat he had bought in Paris. He wished he were a thousand miles from Warsaw, somewhere in the French countryside, where life was simple and good.

"Tomorrow," said Helena, "I'm going to start looking for presents. It'll be Christmas in a week's time, and we'll go to Celestynow. I hope Marek won't get drunk and that we can all go together in his car. You ought to talk to him. He really is drinking too much. Is he having an unhappy love affair?"

André shook his head with a frown as he turned the key in the lock and switched on the light. Helena followed him into the tastefully furnished drawing room and cast her eye over an expensive painting that she hated, the big sofa, the low tables, and the trinkets.

"I paid a great deal for all of this," André said suddenly, "and I don't want to lose it."

"You're growing old, my dear," Helena said bitterly. "My parents and your mother seem to me to have more imagination than you do. I'll never be able to stop thinking that one small bomb would be enough to destroy all of this. I saw the ruins of my grandmother's house, which had been a beautiful place, and my parents' house, and many others. No doubt that's the reason I can no longer become attached to things. When I'm in an apartment, I always get the impression it's just a temporary shell which will disappear one day, like a stage set. Only people matter, André. Things have no importance; their tomorrows are too fragile."

"People die, find themselves in prison, change," André remarked, "while the things one owns are, in spite of everything, the measure of success, especially in Poland, where it's so difficult to get hold of them. Do you dare tell me you're not happy to own a television?"

André's voice took on a note of aggression, which angered Helena.

"Seems to me we earned it together," she said. "And if instead of living in France with you, I could have been practicing my profession, I could have bought myself lots of things."

"Do you regret having lived in Paris?"

"Oh, regrets aren't worth discussing, but I'll never do it again. I found it a humiliating experience waiting for you day after day, twiddling my thumbs while my family was here slaving away like convicts."

"So you would have preferred to live the life of a peasant like Inka here, rather than to strut about in the embassy drawing rooms or visit Versailles? Why don't you admit the truth? You're completely out of your mind, my dear, and a hypocrite as well!"

Helena faced her husband, and her voice trembled. "Yes, if you want to know the truth, I'd have preferred to spend those two years looking after the sick, tilling the land, or working at anything, no matter what, here, at home. You reduced me to the role of a doll, which I tried to play as best I could so as not to damage your career. Only, you see, very often I found myself asking if it was all worth it, if your intrigues, which seemed more and more shady to me, and your relationships with Gierek's entourage, and your business lunches, and all the rest of it, really amounted to a worthwhile life! I put you on a pedestal so high that I hardly dared raise my head to look at you, and now I have the impression that you're nothing but an unscrupulous careerist, a man ready to do anything to get a little comfort and a little money. In a normal country, in the West, maybe that's the right way of going about things, but here in Poland it's indecent!"

"Stop shouting, my dear," André said very calmly, pouring himself a Scotch. "Anger makes you ugly. You've never known what you wanted. At the beginning, I found that charming, but now it just bores me. You've been a Communist, then an anti-Communist, and here you are now making yourself out to be a national heroine because you signed a manifesto. We don't have many things in common. You didn't want to have any children, which is rather surprising in a doctor. You used to dream of discovering Paris, but you reproach me for having taken you there. You had had enough of living in a tiny room, and you used to moan about it; but now you accuse me of everything under the sun because I managed to get a decent apartment. You used to admire the way I maneuvered in diplomatic circles, and you used to encourage me, but this evening you're hurling insults at me and accusing me of underhanded behavior. Well, just imagine how proud I am of the confidence our government shows in me. After all, thanks to the loans we've managed to arrange, life in Warsaw is much better than it was in Gomulka's day. True, things aren't entirely perfect, but we're making progress."

"We're making progress down the road to slavery," said Helena sarcastically. Then, suddenly tired, she stubbed her cigarette out and got up. "I'm going to bed," she announced. "I'm falling asleep."

"One moment," André objected. "I've something important to tell you. I've been offered a job in Great Britain. Until now I've hesitated because of you, but since you don't seem particularly keen on living with me, I think I'll accept. I'll be away several months, and you'll have time to think things out quietly. When I get back, we'll decide what to do."

Helena had put her nightdress on. She felt strangely detached from everything, and André's half-ironic, half-triumphant expression didn't impress her.

"You do as you please," she said with a yawn. "Your career always comes first. I'm sure a long stay in London will do you a great deal of good. When's the happy event going to take place?"

"Immediately after the Christmas holidays, early in January, or in February at the latest."

"Perfect," said Helena, grabbing a pillow and settling down on the sofa.

"You want a separate bedroom?" André asked.

"Yes. Now that we've got a bedroom *and* a drawing room, that's a luxury I can permit myself. Go and use the bathroom; I want to turn the light out."

"Good night," said André. "But remember, my dear, it's easier to give up one's place than it is to get it back."

Helena made no reply. Under the wool blanket, her

body relaxed. It was over; she had practically admitted that she no longer loved this tall, slim, elegant man who was her husband. Tomorrow she would start looking for presents and preparing for Christmas; then there would be the new year, which would perhaps bring her the courage to leave André and make a fresh start. Yes, she thought, it's been an eternity since I last had the courage to be honest with myself. I'm going to make a nice little solitary existence for myself. I'm going to work a lot, and I'm going to . . ."

Helena fell asleep without managing to work out all her future plans in detail, and without even noticing that André had slammed their bedroom door in an outburst of anger.

11

MAREK SAT DOWN at his desk, marveling at how good it felt to have a room of his own, to be able to write in peace.

In one flowing gesture he swept up the daily paper, swallowed a glass of vodka that stood beside his typewriter, and began running his nimble fingers over the keys.

In January 1976, amendments to the modified constitution were proposed. This was a major victory; the party had yielded to the pressure of a group of intellectuals and of the church. In the spring—to be precise, on the seventeenth of May—we all met again. Kazik Skola and I were there. The National Polish Party, the NPP, was formed. We drew up a manifesto in which we noted that after thirty years of Communist rule, cynicism and demoralization ruled everywhere, and negated the most far-seeing attempts at reform. To support the movement and bring it to the attention of the public, we decided to publish an underground paper. Thanks to this paper, I learned all the details concerning the events of the month of

June. I learned that at Ursus, the workers had welded the train wheels to the rails and brought international traffic to a halt so that we would finally stop sending the Soviets our ham and butter, of which there was never a trace to be found in the Warsaw food shops. I knew how many people had been killed and arrested at Radom, where the workers had organized a general strike and demonstrated in front of the local party authorities. I knew that thousands of workers had lost their jobs, that many had been sent to jail without any due process of law, and I had a long list of addresses.

During that year, I spent all my weekends visiting families, either on my own or with others. In the following spring, they began releasing people, but several of us got caught by the militia. Kazik was arrested several times, and so was I. They generally let me go after forty-eight hours, but Kazik did a month in jail. And then on the seventh of May they killed one of our people in Cracow, a student named Stanislaw Pyjas. The Archbishop of Cracow, Cardinal Wojtyla, organized a procession to protest against this murder and to commemorate the young man's sacrifice, a procession which marched through Cracow under the eyes of the militia and the UB agents. You can't arrest several thousand people marching behind their priests. And as long as that's the case, we're invulnerable!

Try to understand, dear readers! While all this was going on in Cracow last spring, nobody in Warsaw outside our own little group knew what was happening. That was a good example of "disinformation," and I believe the people abroad, in the West and in America, are quite unable to grasp what that means. We need more organizations, more underground newspapers, more information. Maria Solin understands that, while Helena Stanowska-Solin thinks we're dividing up our forces to no useful purpose. In any event, both of them form part of the Movement for the Defense of the Rights of Man—the ROPCIO— which has also started publishing its own underground paper. But we still need more; we want to top *Trybuna Ludu*'s circulation if we're going to be able to defend this country against dissolution.

Marek reread the last sentence, lit a cigarette, and went back to work.

This dissolution started a long time ago—in 1945, and at the time of the liberation. The Germans were leaving, the Russians were arriving; our allies, we were told, but it was whispered that these were the same officers and the same men who had occupied part of Poland in 1939, around Lvov, with the agreement of a certain Adolf Hitler. Yet Poland was obliged to accept these Soviet regiments, who started swarming over the country and toasting with us the victory over the fascists. They brought with them Poles, both Christians and Jews, who had been trained in the camps of Siberia; it was these Poles who organized the services of the UB, the secret police, so that now we can be arrested and tortured, interrogated and sentenced, all in Polish!

We were poor, the country was in ruins, and we had no option but to accept. But afterward, why did we continue to align ourselves with the Russians? Why did we think Gomulka was going to change anything, when his hands were tied? Why wasn't the KOR—the Committee for the Defense of Workers— formed after the workers' riot in Poznan and the students' demonstration in 1968? Why?

Well, dear readers, here's my explanation. It's because the intellectuals, our only hope for change at the time, were powerless. Intellectuals are by definition isolated individuals, and have no striking force at their disposal other than their words; it's only when their words get under people's skins that they have any significance.

Yes, the intellectuals are powerless creatures who dream of comfort while pretending the opposite. They find it hard to survive in prison, where there are no individual cells, or to live in a small room and have to struggle to buy a cake of soap. The workers and the peasants put up a better resistance, but they're afraid, and they find it hard to communicate. Yet they are the ones who represent the masses. One can always liquidate several thousand intellectuals, or even "buy" them, but it's very difficult to do that with millions of workers.

The NPP was born because Kazik Skola, I, and many others learned how the workers' families lived, spoke, ate, acted, and reacted. We had to go to them, listen to them, and try to help them without alienating them, in order to get them to accept us. We had to teach them all that instead of treating us as "comrade doctors" or "comrade engineers," it was preferable to treat us as friends, and to use each other's first names. That took more than thirty years, but since then, that solidarity, that friendship between us, has been indissoluble, as it was in olden days when we were facing death during the occupation and the Warsaw uprising.

Only now, dear readers, it's no longer a question of dying, but of creating for ourselves a vital space in which we can stand upright, and where there will be enough room for thirty-five million members of our family.

Marek stretched, and got to his feet. It was after midnight. The next morning, he had to leave early; he had a course to give at Zbrosza Duza, in the Grojec area.

He swallowed another glass of vodka and started undressing. Before turning out the light, he carefully hid his manuscript in the false bottom of his suitcase, together with a ream of white paper he had stolen from Radio Warsaw. At that time, paper was rare in the shops, and one simply had to take it where one could find it.

Stretched out on his bed, Marek suddenly began laughing out loud. He remembered the crazy night when he had taken the key from the pocket of one of Radio Warsaw's female employees who was in charge of the photocopier, then spent hours watching her sleeping while his friends secretly photocopied the latest edition of an underground evening newspaper which couldn't be printed because the militia had raided the workshop and arrested everyone inside. The girl, who was a UB agent, like most of those in charge of office photocopiers, had woken up and assumed Marek wanted to make love. To escape her advances, he had had to explain to her that he had taken a vow of chastity.

Marek poured himself a final glass of vodka. He felt pleasantly drunk. Outside in the night, heavy trucks rolled by on the highway. They're taking our bread to the East, he said to himself angrily. Instead of helping the workers, publishing underground newspapers, and organizing universities, we'd do better if we inspected the trucks, trains, and boats to show once and for all where our meat, butter, and cereals are being sent to. I've simply got to talk to Kazik about it. He's got some good ideas, and since we're going to end up being hanged in any case, it might as well be for a good reason.

Kazik knotted his tie carefully. He had washed his hair and spent a lot of money on a nice bottle of eau de cologne, and he had polished his car until every strip of chrome shone brilliantly.

Here I am, forty-five, and I'm behaving like a schoolboy, he told himself. And the worst of it is that it's giving me the greatest pleasure to do so! I've been putting off this meeting with Inka for months, for fear of spoiling it all, but this evening I'm going to take a chance. She must tell me either yes or no. I can't go on dreaming and waiting forever.

Inka had arranged the meeting at the Budapest Restaurant. She was spending the weekend at Helena's; it was October, and there wasn't a great deal of work at the farm, so she was able to leave Magda on her own for a few days. These little trips to Warsaw were good for her, and Helena really looked forward to seeing her; since André had left on his mission to London, Helena seemed to have become closer to Inka. Besides, they were working together with the ROPCIO group; both of them were giving courses to the farmers.

Kazik went downstairs, checked his tie one last time, put on the brand-new raincoat he had bought during a visit to East Germany, and got into his car. He sighed and started the engine. He was afraid of being late; the light rain forced him to drive more slowly, and there was heavy traffic on the road. Parking was forbidden in front of the Budapest, but just a little farther on he found a place.

Inka had not yet arrived. Kazik began pacing up and down the sidewalk. It was raining and cold, and a nasty wind blew down his collar. He turned it up, only to turn it back down at once, thinking that it might look inelegant.

"Good evening!" said a voice at his side. "I'm sorry I'm late. I had to wait a long time for the bus."

"How beautiful you look!" Kazik murmured as he gazed at Inka's face, which turned red beneath the blue hood of her raincoat.

"Come now," she said with a laugh. "You're becoming

nearsighted; you'll be needing glasses soon! So we're going
to the movies, are we, to see this fantastic film everybody's
talking about? I hope we can get seats!"

Kazik pulled himself together. "Of course we'll get seats!
You're going out with *me*, and I always take care of things.
Do you want to eat before or after?"

"After, if that's all right with you, but I'm afraid there'll
be nothing open."

/   "Don't worry, I know a little private restaurant where
they'll feed us even after midnight. Besides, they've been
warned already, and there'll be a real feast waiting for us."
He took her arm. "So, off we go to *The Man of Marble*.
You'll find Andrzej Wajda's created a masterpiece. It's
surprising they've let this film be shown. The censors
made him change the ending, because in the original
scenario the hero died during the events at Gdansk in
1970; but it doesn't matter, it's fantastic just the same.
People are waiting in line for hours to get in to see it, and
tickets are being sold on the black market."

"What a charming prospect!" said Inka jokingly. "And
with this rain, it's going to be a great success!"

"Don't worry, I know the usherette, and we'll be going
in by the back door."

Kazik kept his word. At the front of the theater the line
waiting to get in stretched back to the corner of the street,
but Kazik took Inka in through a little lane. He whispered
to the attendant for a moment, and then, without any
waiting, they found themselves inside the theater, which
was in darkness.

There were two empty seats near the end of the third
row. They pushed through to these, ignoring the protests
of those they disturbed on their way past. It made them
feel like a couple of schoolkids on holiday. Kazik helped
Inka off with her coat, and their hands met. Inka found
her fingers trapped in Kazik's palm, but she made no
attempt to withdraw them.

Inka felt very much at her ease like that, leaning lightly against his shoulder. It was years since she had felt so relaxed—no, it was *centuries* since she had experienced this kind of intimacy with a man. How on earth could she have felt dislike for Kazik in the old days, before her marriage to Wlodek, when now he seemed so attractive to her?

They had missed the opening of the film, but they were immediately gripped by the plot and the performance of the actors. It was not merely a film; it was a slice of their lives passing before their eyes, as though the past were becoming the present. Kazik especially recognized moments he had lived through before.

At that time, there had been Helena, and Inka had still been a schoolgirl. As a matter of fact, it was with Helena that he should have come to see this film, but the idea of inviting her had never even crossed his mind. Helena had killed something inside of him; it was as though a whole chapter of his life had been obliterated. Between Dr. Helena Stanowska, the wife of André Solin, and the young girl with whom he had been to school, there was no longer anything in common. If I'd married her, we'd have been divorced, Kazik said to himself. How do people manage to stay together for years on end? You marry a young girl, you see her day after day; but each of you develops separately, and not necessarily along parallel lines. Then suddenly you discover you're faced with a stranger with whom you can't go on living. If Inka agrees to marry me, we're going to have children—lots of children. That's the only bond one can forge between two human beings. A couple without children has only the present; the future doesn't belong to them at all.

Inka was so fascinated by the film that she forgot where she was. The actors on the screen became real men and women, made of flesh and blood, and she identified totally with them. When the film was over, she had to shake herself to recover from its spell.

They left the theater, got into the car, and drove to the restaurant.

"You must have a very difficult existence working on the farm," said Kazik as he helped her out of the car. "Aren't you tired of working from dawn till dusk?"

"The land is my wealth and my strength," replied Inka. "The land is like love; it calls for a human relationship, as between individuals."

"Love," Kazik repeated, like an echo.

They were sitting opposite one another in the little restaurant, with its decor from another age, creating an effect of unique and antiquated charm. Kazik hesitated a moment longer, then made up his mind.

"Inka," he murmured, "I've never stopped loving you. I know I've hurt you in the past, because I was so unhappy I no longer knew what I was saying; but I've grown since then. If you want to turn me down, go ahead! Don't be afraid. I shall respect your decision and remain your friend. But I warn you, whatever you do, whatever you decide, that I shall never stop loving you. Honestly, I have tried to forget you, but I didn't succeed. I come to you empty-handed. The situation's changed; I run the risk of being arrested at any moment. Inka, I've no time to wait. Can you love me? I've got something for you in my pocket, and if you promise not to be cross with me . . ."

There was a tender smile on Inka's lips, and she didn't withdraw her hand when he took it in his own. Kazik put a little package on the table and pushed it over toward her. Inka took it gently, untied the ribbon, opened the white cardboard box, and took out the silver ring upon which was set a piece of amber. The golden stone shone in the light; it was an unusual piece in which there was a small particle of alga, or grass, or perhaps a little piece of shell, which looked like a tiny imprisoned flower. Inka slipped the ring onto her finger. She stretched out her long, narrow hand, so like Irena's, to admire the effect; then she raised her head, and her eyes met Kazik's.

"You know, Kazik, day after day, night after night, I've thought of you. I think I've always loved you, but you didn't need me. You were so strong, and Wlodek was vulnerable; I had a place in his life. You wanted to buy me, like an object—a little more precious than the others, but an object just the same. I was afraid of you!"

"Oh, come, darling!" murmured Kazik. "That's not possible—"

"Listen, Kazik! For a long time I was a child; for a longer time than most others, no doubt. Now I'm an adult, a woman. I can allow myself to tell you things which formerly I wouldn't have dared to admit even to myself. For me, you've always been the invulnerable one, but at the same time, the one to whom one can tell everything, both the best and the worst. You see, Wlodek could never accept the fact that I'm the child of—"

"Sh!" said Kazik, leaning toward her and brushing his fingers very lightly across her lips. "Father Marianski told me about your real mother long ago. There's no need to talk about her. The past is dead. Darling, do you want us to get married?"

"Yes, Kazik, on the condition that you tell me you need me and that you're not a superman. I'm not asking you to tell me all your problems. You'll tell me about them if you want to, and if you prefer to keep silent, that's your right. Just let me help you, and swear to me that when we're married you'll never leave me alone."

"You want to live on a farm, and you know very well that I'm involved in something and that I can't abandon my friends. Darling, give me just a little time, a few months at most. It won't be long. Then I'll come and fetch you, and I'll never leave you again. Or, if you prefer, you can live with me here, in town."

"So, we'll wait," Inka agreed. "But I want to have children and enough time to raise them and see them grow. Can you understand that?"

"Yes," said Kazik slowly. "But promise me you'll wait for me."

"I swear it!"

"Oh, how I'd like to kiss you!"

"Then why don't you?"

"Here, in front of all these people?"

"Helena says that in Paris lovers kiss on the public benches in the parks. It's time we stopped being such prudes!"

Inka leaned forward slowly, and their lips met. There was a shy tenderness in Kazik's kiss; in Inka's there was an element of abandon and passion he hadn't expected, and then he forgot where they were and took her in his arms.

At that moment the cloakroom attendant burst into the room like a meteor. "They say Cardinal Wojtyla's just been elected pope in Rome!" he shouted.

"It's not possible!" murmured Kazik.

"Perhaps it's a propaganda trick," said someone at the next table.

"Quick," said Kazik. "Let's go! We can still get to my place before the BBC news comes on."

Outside in the street, Kazik found it hard to drive, and when they reached the door of his apartment his hands trembled and he couldn't get the key to turn in the lock; Inka had to open the door for him. The lights were on, and there was music coming from the radio.

"Is there someone here?" Inka asked.

"No, it's just my way of warning off any UB characters who might be tempted to try a discreet search during my absence."

Kazik took off his coat and helped Inka off with hers. They heard the announcer's voice over the radio: "Attention, here is a special bulletin. The Polish Cardinal Karol Wojtyla has just been elected pope. This is the first time in the history of the church that a Pole has acceded to the throne of St. Peter. I repeat, the Polish Cardinal Karol Wojtyla—"

"The world has just given Poland the most beautiful, the most marvelous of presents," said Kazik. "The best present in all of our history."

"My God, it's not possible!" said Inka excitedly. "What station are we on? Oh, check it, Kazik, check it quickly!"

"No, darling, it's not propaganda, it's the BBC in London, so it's the truth!"

The telephone started ringing, but Kazik made no attempt to lift the receiver. He turned to Inka, his arms folded across his chest, and began reciting the poem of Juliusz Slowacki, the great Polish poet of the early nineteenth century, whom they both loved:

> Amid the trouble, amid the strife,
> God has struck a mighty bell.
> This time it is for a Slav that he has
>   laid open the throne of the new pope.
> He comes already and will share out the
>   forces of the earth.
> Under the effect of his words,
> Our blood will course through our veins.

Inka placed her hand on his shoulder. "We must call Helena. The ROPCIO should be the first to comment on this incredible news in the next edition of our paper."

"But I tell you the KOR should announce it before you," objected Kazik.

The BBC's broadcast from London came to an end, and the radio was transmitting only random sounds. Kazik changed the dial, trying to pick up one of the Radio Warsaw stations, but he had no success and switched the set off.

"Wait!" said Inka. She took him by the arm, drew him over to the window, and opened it. A cold wind filled the room, and she pressed herself against Kazik instinctively. Far off in the night, bells could be heard ringing.

"It really doesn't matter much which newspaper announces this wonderful news tomorrow," she said slowly. "This evening, it's the church that is telling us that our collective destiny is lying within its hands, and that's a symbol that expresses our truth better than any words could do. Come, we can't stay here alone! We've got to go and meet the others, we've got to be together and share this immense, incredible joy. We've so often lived together through despair that this time we simply have to share with others the most marvelous news of all time!"

Cheeks red with excitement, Inka grabbed her coat, but at that very moment there was a knock on the door. It was Marek, arriving with a group of people she had never met before. Instantly the apartment was filled, and everyone was laughing, singing, kissing, shouting happily. Only Kazik stayed in his corner, repeating Slowacki's poem in a low voice, as though he was trying to extract the prophetic truth from every single word:

> Under the effect of his words,
> Our blood will course through our veins.

Marek went over to him, and Inka followed, and then the others joined in a chorus, repeating the phrase until it rang through the room like a solemn promise.

It was three days since Father Marianski had been able to sleep. This had happened to him before, in the old days, in prison; but then the reason had been physical suffering and anguish. This time it was something else: he was in the grip of a crazy joy. Everything had not been in vain, after all! Surviving the occupation, the camps, the tortures, and everything up to and including the poverty and the shortages had been somehow necessary for the country to merit the great honor of having a pope born on

Polish soil. God, in his pity, had offered this reward to his people, who never ceased seeking their liberty and their independence. Deep gratitude welled up within him, and instead of praying with the usual words and phrases, Father Marianski thanked the Almighty with his own words, which came from the bottom of his heart.

And then there was the invitation for him to direct a group of pilgrims who were going to Rome to witness the holy father's coronation. Even more, he had been offered the opportunity to choose someone from among his parishioners, for whom the journey would be paid.

"It's a privilege I don't deserve," Father Marianski had told his bishop, but the latter had refused to listen to him.

"It's been more than two years," he had said, "that you've been giving courses, not only to the children who've been coming to your catechism lessons but also to the students from the Catholic University of Lublin. You're writing a book on the history of the Polish church during the postwar period, and you're working all the harder in that you have to travel frequently between Celestynow and Lublin. You've also lost many days in militia posts. Don't you think all that deserves a trip to Rome?"

Since that conversation, Father Marianski had suffered from the usual attacks of nerves. He was certain they wouldn't give him his passport, or that he wouldn't get a visa, or that the plane wouldn't take off from Warsaw airport. In fact, how could one possibly imagine that in Poland a priest could obtain his passport in only five days? Quite impossible! Even high party officials had to wait longer than that.

As might have been expected, the person the priest had chosen from among his parishioners was Magda. The loss of Wlodek had noticeably affected her. Since his death, she had not regained her propensity for laughter, nor her gaiety, nor even her physical strength. She was no longer full of spirit, but listless and sad, toiling away from dawn until dusk because the only thing left to her was the land.

When he told her she was going to Rome with the pilgrims, she had thought at first that he was kidding her, and right up to the last minute she couldn't believe that such a wonderful thing could happen to her, even on October 20, when they were climbing up into the bus and on their way.

Helena and Maria were waiting for them at Warsaw. Both of them also came out to the airport the next evening and brought some money for the pilgrims. Father Marianski didn't want to accept any, but Magda took what they offered her.

"We'll use these to buy you some souvenirs," she decided, "so that you'll feel that you went with us."

This was the first time either of them had been in an airplane, and this in itself was already quite an adventure.

"Are you afraid, Magda?" Father Marianski asked her as he helped her into her seat.

"Oh, no! Why should I be afraid?" said Magda indignantly. "If something happened now, that would be the best possible death I could ever wish for."

Tadeusz Marianski had run across several of his students on the plane. They had eaten together, and talked in low voices into the night so as not to disturb those who had managed to drop off to sleep.

There was quite a crowd waiting for them in Rome: Polish emigrants, clergy and laymen, and Italian priests. There was a lot of hugging, and shouting, and singing, and exchanging of the latest news on the next day's ceremony. Father Marianski was taken to the convent where he would be staying, and spent another sleepless night there, in anticipation of the next day. Magda was lodged elsewhere.

The pilgrims left very early and packed themselves into St. Peter's Square to await the hour of the coronation ceremony. Above their heads fluttered the flags they had brought with them, and the names of Polish towns and villages written on broad ribbons in letters of gold. Among the crowd, the black cassocks stood out among the beautifully colored traditional costumes of the various regions of the country, the white jackets and the hats of the mountain folk, the embroidered shirts of the peasants, and the costumes the miners put on for special occasions.

Father Marianski realized it was impossible to go and look for Magda. He was stuck among his group of students, right in front of the altar. Then, almost immediately, the bells began to peal, and the new pope, John Paul II, appeared, surrounded by cardinals.

Magda felt her heart beating then as it had never done before. All her sorrows, all her misfortunes, were forgotten in the face of this boundless happiness. Along with the others, she began praying for this man, clad in white—praying that no evil should befall him and that he should live a long life.

One after another, the cardinals drew near the pope, and among them was Cardinal Wyszynski. The crowd of Polish pilgrims stood there waiting; it was then he came, their Cardinal Wojtyla, now their Pope John Paul II, a man among men, a human being of flesh and blood. He came toward them quite simply, like a man coming to greet people who loved him; there were no more barriers between him and them, because he smiled at them all, and his smile was full of friendship and joy.

At that very moment Father Marianski was carried by the crowd toward the holy father. It all happened very quickly, but for the rest of his life he would never forget what he felt when Pope John Paul II passed so close to him. He felt he was being recharged with energy, a sort of electricity which filled him with life.

A Mass was then held for the pilgrims. Gathered in a huge hall, they sang as they awaited the holy father. One after the other, the cardinals bowed before the pope, who took them in his arms. Then the cardinals rose to their feet and began taking their leave, while the pope came down among them with his hands outstretched. The ceremony turned into a family gathering. The holy father kissed the children, exchanged a few words with those nearest the central aisle, while people crowded together to get closer to him, and he passed among them confident and happy.

"We'll never be the same after this," a woman murmured, passing close by Father Marianski as the crowd began flooding toward the door after the pope had left.

Tadeusz Marianski was to think over those words often during the future, although at that time he paid them but scant attention.

Outside, the lights of Rome were glittering. They were expected back at the convent for the evening meal, but Father Marianski was so fatigued that instead of eating he went to bed at once. He still had three days left, and he had promised to show Magda the churches and museums of Rome. However, the next day he learned to his utter stupefaction that she had left at dawn, without waiting for him, with a group of women. Magda, usually so frightened of unfamiliar places, seemed to have no fear of getting lost. In fact, Father Marianski managed to find her only when it was time to go home, as they were climbing into the bus leaving for the airport.

In the plane, Magda was seated down the row from where Father Marianski was sitting. She seemed transformed, rejuvenated, relaxed, and calmer. He went and chatted with her immediately after takeoff.

"The years to come will be different from all those we've lived up till now," she said to him seriously.

"Why's that?" he asked her with a smile.

"Because we're going to be forced to show ourselves worthy of our pope, and that's going to be no light affair," Magda answered.

At the Warsaw airport, the customs officers let them

through without searching their baggage, but several UB agents and militiamen in plain clothes bombarded them with questions:

"It seems the pope spoke Polish; is that true?"

"Is it true he didn't want Cardinal Wyszynski to go down on his knees before him?"

"Is it true that people in the street clapped when you went by?"

"Did the Italians know you were Polish?"

"Is it true there were Polish flags at the Vatican?"

The young priests were careful to obey the advice they had received before they left, to talk as little as possible. On the other hand, the older priests and nuns got a lot of amusement out of being the center of attention.

Thanks to him, thanks to our Cardinal Wojtyla who's become pope, thought Father Marianski, now we're one big family. Politics are secondary; oppressors or victims, we're all living the same joy and the same hope!

For Marek, that winter of 1979 was particularly painful. He worked himself to the bone, drank hard, and lived constantly on the edge of despair. Writing was his joy and reward for all the meaningless jobs he carried out at Radio Warsaw; yet he still found it painful to reread his manuscript. He was continually making corrections, sometimes doing entire passages over again, and then throwing his work into the wastepaper basket, swallowing glass after glass of vodka.

In February, however, he was able to write the words "The End" at the bottom of the last page, and took the manuscript to show to Helena. At Easter, when he went to Celestynow, she told him that she had finished reading his manuscript and that it was a book that must be sent abroad, because it would never pass the censors in Poland.

When he returned to Warsaw two days later, he arranged for a friend to smuggle the manuscript to Paris to

Ula. Then he eagerly awaited her answer, which arrived at
the beginning of May, a week before the pope's visit to
Poland. Ula wrote:

I've received your manuscript, and I read it through
nonstop in one night. I'm ready to translate it as
quickly as I can, and approach the publishing houses.
However, don't expect to make any money or become well-known here. Your book's sensational from
every point of view, but you must understand that in
the West they try to ignore certain realities. There's
a prejudice here, and it's no use explaining to them
that Poland is under Moscow's thumb. But how can I
explain it to you? I don't have your talent, and I
don't know how to turn words into dynamite, as you
do in your manuscript.

I hope to finish it this coming winter. Will you
give me a free hand, or do you wish to review the
French text, choose your own publisher, and so on?
I suggest you come to Paris and stay with me. You
won't have to spend a cent, and I'd be so happy to
see you again.

Marek reread Ula's letter several times. She's being
stupid, he told himself. How can she imagine I want to
become famous, make a lot of money, and see my book in
every library in the world? All that matters to me is that it
be translated and published.

He wrote this to her, in not one but two letters. He
managed to entrust the first one to a Radio Warsaw girl
who was leaving for Paris, but since she was completely
featherbrained, he didn't sleep for a week, imagining that
she had forgotten it in her handbag, tossed it into a
mailbox without a stamp, or even dropped it in the street,
where it would be cleared away by the street cleaners.
Finally Marek decided to send the second letter by a
stewardess on LOT, the Polish airline, whom he had

interviewed in the past for a broadcast. After thinking it over, however, the stewardess had handed his letter over to her superiors instead of putting it into a mailbox in France, as she had promised.

Marek decided to go to the post office. On the telegraph pad he wrote a message to Ula: "THE LILACS ARE BLOOMING IN WARSAW, THANKS FOR YOUR LETTER, LIFE'S WONDERFUL," then handed the form to the woman on the other side of the window. Reluctantly she leaned over the message and began reading it; then after a long moment she raised her head and asked him: "Is this really what you want to say?"

"Of course!" said Marek irritably. "What do you find so surprising about it? Isn't it true that the lilacs are blooming in Warsaw?"

"Wait a moment," the woman instructed him. She went away, then returned with another employee, older than she was. The two women stared at Marek. They had adopted a severe air, and seemed worried.

"You're certain you want to send this?" the elder woman asked him. Marek insisted, and finally they took his money without saying another word. It was only after he had left and was already back in his office that he realized that the text of his telegram might be taken as an attempt to transmit secret information in the form of a code. Since they'll never find the key to a code which doesn't exist, Marek said to himself, my telegram may never reach its destination. What an ass I am.

That morning there was an unusual amount of activity in the corridors of Radio Warsaw. There was a lot of advance preparation going on in connection with the pope's visit, and everyone was on edge. In his office Marek took calls, prepared a list of records that were to be played during the evening broadcast, and tried not to think anymore about Ula and his manuscript. Then there was a long telephone call from Helena, telling him the roads were closed because it was feared that all of Poland would be heading to Warsaw. That meant that her parents, Inka, Magda, and Father Marianski would be unable to attend the High Mass John Paul II was going to conduct.

"They'll see it all on TV," Marek consoled her, "and much better, too."

"It's not the same thing," Helena objected.

Marek had scarcely had time to hang up before three of his coworkers barged into his office. They were furious; the director had been up to his tricks again. He had cut the time that should have been reserved for commentaries on the pope's visit, and two employees—a producer and an announcer—had been fired suddenly, without any explanation.

"It's highly probable that I'm on his black list, too," Marek murmured. "He's been making me job offers, which I've turned down."

"Oh, splendid!" said one of the journalists with a knowing air; and immediately the two others were seized with mistrust. They left his office, bringing the meeting to an abrupt close and giving him an odd look as they left.

Marek decided to get drunk that evening. He had been happy to finish his manuscript, but once he had sent it off to Ula, he felt a sort of emptiness. He missed those nights spent at his typewriter.

After his broadcast, he bought a bottle of vodka, which he emptied to the last drop as soon as he got home.

Did Helena sense how lonely he was? After the pope's visit, during the months of June and July, she had spent a lot of time with him. Sometimes they went to Celestynow together; sometimes he called for her at the hospital and took her out to dinner.

"You've got to stop drinking," she kept telling him. "Your liver can't handle such quantities of alcohol. Even if you don't get drunk and don't make scenes in the street, sooner or later you're going to suffer the consequences.

You've already been in a sanatorium, and you know what it means to be ill, so think about yourself a little!"

In the end, Marek managed to get his drinking under control, not only thanks to Helena but also because of the pressure of the events around him.

Everything happened very quickly. Toward the end of August, he and other members of the KOR had completed the text of the declaration announcing the birth of a new party. On September 2, an underground manifesto announced the creation of the Confederation of Free Poland, the KPN; its objectives were listed—basically similar to those of KOR, but also proclaiming the beginning of a decisive struggle, a political struggle directed against Moscow.

Although Marek had participated in the birth of this party, he had not immediately realized the consequences of his action. All the other organizations, including ROPCIO and KOR, dissociated themselves from KPN, and in November Marek began receiving visits from the militia and being followed. Sometimes his telephone would ring ceaselessly; but when he picked up the receiver, there would be nothing but silence at the other end of the line. Sometimes, when he came home, he would find traces of a search. Marek slowly found himself living a veritable nightmare. More and more frequently he took to spending the night in his office to avoid having to go home, and he jumped every time the telephone rang.

His friends from KOR stopped visiting him, and Kazik could not be found. Only Helena continued to see him, although he had told her everything during a long walk in the forest at Celestynow.

"Get out of KPN," she had told him then. "Not only is it dangerous, but it's also completely unrealistic. Political action of that nature is premature; the objective is to force the party to make reforms. Now, no level of the party, no organization, can accept the challenge you're presenting them with. Moscow will intervene at once, and you and your group will simply plunge the country into a bloodbath."

"Moscow will intervene sooner or later, and it's not the West that's going to stop the Russian Army from firing on the population of Warsaw. We might as well show our colors clearly and carry on to the end, carry on as far as we possibly can."

"I'm never going to find myself in agreement with KPN's policies," Helena objected, "and when they arrest you, it'll be impossible to defend you. I just hope Kazik thinks the same as I do."

"He can't be found these days, but that doesn't really matter. So let them arrest me, and let's get it over with! Anything's preferable to this war of nerves. I'm at the end of my tether!"

Marek wasn't willing to listen to Helena. He no longer had the courage to deprive himself of the one and only support he still had, and which had become his *raison d'être*. Within the KPN group, he worked, he wrote, he distributed underground newspapers; he was alive! To leave it would mean vegetating from day to day, since neither KOR nor ROPCIO wanted anything more to do with him.

"Leave," Helena had advised him. "Go, no matter where. Take a vacation."

In January, when the countryside was buried in snow, Marek decided to do just that. He got Radio Warsaw to give him leave and went off to Tykocin, a charming little village, where he managed to rent a room from some farmers. He had told nobody where he was going, except Helena, who had agreed to look after his mail. From then on, Ula would have to write to him at this address. According to her last letter, she had not finished the translation of his manuscript as quickly as she would have liked, but she was aiming at finishing it in the spring.

Marek's room was on the second floor, above the kitchen.

Slowly the family adopted him, and he began coming down for the evening meal, which they all ate together. The wood crackled merrily in the big cast-iron stove on which there was always a pot of excellent potato or cabbage soup simmering.

But Marek's money was running low, and besides, it was no use trying to write; it simply wouldn't come. It was as though everything he had to say had been said already; he couldn't even manage to write articles for the underground newspapers any longer. He grew discouraged, and shut himself up in his room in front of the window, staring out stupidly at the falling snow. A month later, he returned to Warsaw.

He left the train and set off on foot through empty streets. When he got to his door, however, it was almost immediately opened by a man who looked as though he had just gotten out of bed. He was a big, disagreeable man, and he laughed as he told Marek he was living in Marek's apartment with his family, and had no intention of letting him in.

"But you can't do that!" Marek protested weakly.

"Your apartment was empty, comrade," said the stranger, "and in any case, it was far too big for a bachelor. Two rooms; that's just right for a family. I've got a wife and four children, and we were out in the street. So go and complain to the cooperative, or, if you prefer, to the militia, and see what they say to you. We haven't stolen anything. Your belongings and all of your books are with the janitress."

The door slammed shut in his face, and Marek barely managed to get his hand out of the way before it was crushed. No, he had no wish to go and discuss matters with the janitress, who was a UB informer like so many others of her profession; so he left immediately. It was over; he was well and truly out in the street, and the only thing he could do was go and sleep in his office. What had just happened to him was hardly exceptional. Many people who had come to be known as "squatters" moved like this into empty apartments, thanks to information supplied by another tenant on the same floor or by the janitress. To get rid of them meant making approaches to the authorities, which could go on for months, if not years, and which involved the risk of the case's coming before a tribunal.

At work, he met a journalist in the hall who pretended not to have noticed him, but Marek was too tired to worry about it. On the second floor, there was no one in at this early hour of the morning, and he reached his office without meeting anyone else. There, too, however, a surprise awaited him. There was a woman sitting at his desk. Marek thought for a moment there must have been some mistake, but she told him quickly that, yes, it was *her* office now, since Marek had been replaced. It was true that he had been granted a vacation, but there was too much work and it had been necessary to fill the gap. No she didn't know where they had put his things, but he certainly could find out from the administration office, which would open, as usual, at ten o'clock.

Marek went to the cafeteria, ordered tea, and drank it in little sips, which did him good. He left his suitcase with the cashier and turned up at the administration office at half-past ten.

The secretary gave him an embarrassed smile. "I've got some money for you," she told him in a low voice. "It's for the month of February. You've been laid off because you had to be replaced immediately. That's all I know, and I'm very sorry for you. It's scandalous how they can lay off people like this, but that's the way it is. What can you do?"

"But things aren't done that way!" Marek protested. "I want to see the boss. They grant me a vacation to which

I'm entitled and then kick me out without any warning whatsoever. It's crazy!"

He had scarcely finished speaking when the door at the back of the office opened and the head of his section beckoned to him. Marek stuffed the envelope of money into his pocket and went into the boss's office. The boss didn't ask him to sit down.

"Isn't it true that you've been getting visits from the militia?" he asked with a baleful glare at Marek.

"Yes, that correct. They came to search while I was away, and I don't even know whether it was the militia or the UB. For that matter, I've not been accused of any crime as far as I know, and it could well have been a mistake on somebody's part."

"That's quite possible," the boss agreed, "but when the same error happens for the second time, that's enough to justify my concluding that you represent an undesirable element. And when all's said and done, a man whose apartment's been searched can't be entrusted with the microphone and allowed to make contact with the public. That's all I have to say to you, and if you don't like that, that's too bad. You understand?"

Marek nodded and took his leave. He had only one desire: to sleep. All his aggressiveness, all his capacity for indignation, had been exhausted during the long months lived in fear and uncertainty. With his suitcase in his hand, he went to the Grand Hotel, where he showed his professional card, which entitled him to a key. His room was small but comfortable. Marek threw himself onto the bed fully dressed and fell asleep almost immediately, unaware that downstairs at the reception desk a man who had followed him since he had left the Radio Warsaw building was at that very moment giving orders about him to the registration clerk.

*   *   *

Maria Solin was boiling water for coffee. It hurt her to stand, and she was sitting on a little stool. It had been a very hard winter. The radiators on the second floor had burst, and they had to turn off the heating to do the repairs; but since there was a shortage of piping, the tenants had been obliged to wait. The workmen had finally come, but it was the end of May before the repairs had been completed. Fortunately, Robert had sent her a little electric heater he had managed to get for her; otherwise she would have had to sleep at the hospital. However, since the other tenants had also managed to find electric heaters, the electrical system hadn't been able to accommodate them all, and there had been one breakdown after another. Maria had gotten ill—first of all of a cough, which became chronic, and then rheumatism in her legs.

With the warmth of summer, the cough became less debilitating, but Maria couldn't always manage to walk. Her legs hurt her atrociously, and traveling in packed buses, morning and evening, did nothing to help.

Helena's car was undergoing repairs, and it was probable that it wouldn't be back on the road for quite a while. They couldn't get hold of the parts they needed; they had been ordered from somewhere in East Germany or Czechoslovakia, but it was obvious they wouldn't arrive before the next winter.

Supplies in the shops grew scarcer and scarcer; there was even a shortage of bread, which made life extraordinarily difficult. Maria herself found it not too hard to make do with one meal a day at the hospital, but then there was Marek to think about.

The kettle started whistling, and Maria got up from her stool, wincing from the pain. She made two cups of tea, got out what bread she had left and the margarine, then went into the next room and knocked on the door. She had given Marek her bedroom, and slept in the room she used as her drawing room and dining room; that way, if the militia came, she had some chance of saving him, provided they agreed not to search the apartment. There was no answer from the other side of the door, so she turned the handle quietly and opened the door.

"Come on, Marek," she said. "Get up, breakfast's ready!"

The body buried under the blankets shifted.

"I'm coming," Marek answered in a voice husky with sleep. "I'll be there right away."

Maria sat down at the little table covered with a white cloth. Marek staggered in.

"Did you sleep well?" he asked politely. "I'm sorry I slept so late this morning."

"Nonsense, Marek!" Maria protested. "I'm happy to see you get some rest. You also need to put on weight."

"Why, for God's sake? To run around like a mole in your house? Now that things are finally moving and we have a chance of getting some reforms, I'm cooped up here in your apartment, depriving you of the use of your own bedroom, and feeling continually in the way. I'm a prisoner within these walls, and at any moment I could find myself in a real prison from which they wouldn't be in any hurry to release me."

"Have a little patience, my dear! Instead of getting all worked up, you ought to be writing."

"Writing," Marek repeated sadly. "No, it's not a matter of thinking things over and writing articles, but of action; and here I am paralyzed, incapable of making myself useful. I've even reached the point of regretting that I escaped from that bloody hotel when the UB came to arrest me. I would have done better to have waited for them and gone with them quietly."

Maria shook her head. "Stop getting so worked up. You'll make yourself ill. I've got to go now, and it worries me to leave you alone in this state. Try to have a good day, Marek! I've left soup in the saucepan; all you have to do is reheat it. You have to eat."

Maria took her leave. She walked to the bus stop, leaning on her cane; it was raining, and the wait at the stop seemed particularly long to her. Helena was waiting for her at the hospital, very tense and nervous.

"Things are bad in Gdansk," she told Maria as she shut her office door. "I'm going there. It's impossible to find out what's happening without actually being there."

"But the roads are closed," Maria objected.

"A patient I examined this morning, a taxi driver, is ready to take me there. It'll cost a lot, but I have enough money, and since he's got family at Szczecin, he's sure he'll get through."

"Well, since you've decided to go, get going!" Maria didn't have the strength to argue. Besides, she knew Helena, and was aware that when she'd set her mind to do something, she would never change it. "I'm going to see my patients," she said. "When are you leaving?"

"Around three o'clock. The driver can't make it before then."

"Okay, but come and say good-bye to me, will you? I'd willingly come with you, but since I find it hard to walk, I'd only be in the way. Ah, in ten years I've become completely useless, just about ready for the graveyard."

"Oh, come now, what nonsense!" Helena protested.

The morning passed very quickly, and then at noon Helena left the office to go and eat in the cafeteria. As she crossed the main entrance hall, a man's voice called her name: a familiar, warm voice, which Helena recognized immediately without having to turn round.

"André!" she cried. "André, you're here!"

He came toward her, his hands held out in front of him; he took her in his arms, and a long silence fell between them as they held each other.

"I love you," said André. "I've come back to get you. No, don't say anything. Please forgive me; I was wrong.

Just wait a few days and let me show you I'm no longer the same as I was."

"Why have you come back just now, when things are so bad here? It's not sensible!"

"There was nothing else I could do. Things were going well for me in London. I've even started writing for the English newspapers. I hoped to convince you to come and join me, but then came this strike at Gdansk."

"I'm leaving for there this afternoon," Helena told him.

"Good idea!" said André. "Will you let me come with you?"

"You must need some rest after your trip," Helena protested—weakly, because the last thing she wanted to do was to part company with him. All along, she had been waiting for him, but she hadn't dared admit that to him. "Come and see your mother," she said, and they walked side by side down the corridor.

"You know what this reminds me of?" asked André. "My return after the war. Do you remember? We saw each other for the first time in this hospital, and you took me to see my mother. You're just as beautiful now as then." He paused. "Helena, could we start all over again?"

"Perhaps," she replied. "I don't know yet. But you shouldn't have come back. Your mother was so happy to know you were safe in London. She's having a difficult time at the moment because of her health and certain other problems. Well, we'll talk about it later; for now, try not to show her you find her changed. That would only hurt her."

"Helena," André continued as they stopped in front of Maria's office, "is there anyone else in your life?"

"A whole crowd of men," said Helena jokingly, happily noting the anxiety in his eyes.

Maria was sitting at her desk. When she saw her son, she tried to get up to greet him, but she couldn't manage it. Helena gave André a push, to spare her mother-in-law the humiliation of admitting that her legs could no longer carry her. André seemed to understand; he dashed forward and took his mother in his arms.

"You're back! You didn't stay over there?" she cried. "That was very foolish of you, but I'm very proud of you! You don't know how proud I am."

As he and Helena left for Gdansk, Maria made a surprising gesture: she blessed them. It was so unusual for her to do such a thing that they felt quite moved.

Everything happened quickly after that. They got in the taxi, which was waiting outside, and the driver drove off immediately. Out on the main road, he began accelerating to a dangerous speed; it was obvious he was in a hurry to rejoin his family and give them the provisions he had managed to procure in Warsaw, even though the shelves in the grocery stores were practically empty.

They reached Szczecin late at night. Until dawn, they stayed with the driver's family; he refused to let them go and look for a room. Finally, about eight o'clock in the morning, the driver decided to go on to Gdansk.

People were walking along the streets on their way to work. A bus strike was in effect, and there were no means of transport, but the passersby didn't seem to mind. It was a fine day, and relatively warm for the season. At the gate to an overpass, the militiamen were stopping cars and demanding to see identity papers.

"I can't go over there," said the driver. "That could lose me my taxi permit. I'll park a bit farther on, and we can walk to the dockyards."

The three of them got out and walked to the street that ran alongside the naval dockyards. There were plenty of people around them, both men and women; some were throwing cigarettes, loaves of bread, and apples to the strikers, who waved to them and smiled. There was an atmosphere of gaiety in the air. On the walls were photos of John Paul II, the copy of a letter he had written to

Cardinal Wyszynski, poems written by the workers, and a leaflet on which the strikers' ten demands were printed. People stopped to read them and then moved away. One woman had tears in her eyes; a man laid a bunch of flowers on the ground, then changed his mind and threw it up over the wall. Behind the barred gates of the yard, which had been shown in every newspaper in the world and on all the television screens, the strikers were maintaining order. A little farther back, on the stairs which led up toward the offices, there were also workers, both men and women, guarding the entrance.

Helena moved forward without hesitating.

"Do you need a doctor?" she asked. "I'm at your service."

"No, not yet," said the men who gathered around her. "Are you from Gdansk?"

"We've just arrived from Warsaw."

"And are you going back there?" asked a young workman who seemed to be one of the leaders of the guard team.

"Yes, this evening."

"Is everything still calm in Warsaw?" he asked in a low voice.

"Yes."

"We'd like to know what they're waiting for before they support us—the people in Ursus and elsewhere."

"Can I have some pamphlets to take them?" André asked.

"There are no copies. The men spent the night copying them out by hand, and they were all distributed early this morning. The photocopier's broken, and there's no more paper. We're managing things the best we can, but I can tell you it's no party! We're even sleeping on the ground, on concrete. But it's not too serious; morale's good, and that's the main thing. Wait a moment—I'll try to find you a pamphlet all the same."

He disappeared through the door leading inside, while a young girl standing next to Helena asked, "Are you from the KOR?" A small sign of comradeship, a smile exchanged like a present.

"I'm part of the ROPCIO," said Helena.

The young worker returned with a folded sheet of paper in his hand. "Here's the last information bulletin," he said. "You promise me to have it photocopied and distributed in Warsaw? Our main problem at the moment is communication. The KOR people who ought to be arranging it have been arrested. Polish journalists have been ordered not to mention us. They came to the meeting yesterday, but there's nothing in today's papers. We've decided not to let them inside any longer. Only foreign journalists are allowed into the yards; they at least publish, though in foreign newspapers, not in ours. Now, they've got to know in Warsaw and Lodz what's going on here; that's extremely important! Go back to the big main gate. There's a loudspeaker there, and they'll be announcing the latest results of negotiations with members of the government. Unfortunately, it's not a very efficient loudspeaker, and you've got to be quite close to it to hear well."

"My God!" André murmured as he walked beside Helena, while the taxi driver went off to recover his car. "These people don't even have paper to print their communiqués on, and yet all the world is talking about them. It's the victory of courage and determination over oppression."

They got back to town and bought what they could find—cigarettes, handkerchiefs, and even some pieces of smoked eel that a man was selling in the street—then went back to the yards and threw them up to the strikers sitting on top of the walls.

They decided to return to Warsaw. Helena was worried about Maria, who was alone there, with Marek hidden in her apartment. They drove quickly, stopping only for gas. Helena became more and more nervous; it was as though she had a presentiment of misfortune. It was daylight when the cabdriver finally dropped them in front of Maria's house. They went upstairs and rushed through the door. Maria was paler than usual, and looked exhausted.

"They arrested Marek yesterday afternoon, while I was out. He doesn't have a strong enough constitution to withstand being in jail, and he's at the end of his nerves. I'm afraid he'll merely make his case look worse. He's quite capable of standing up to the UB agents and provoking them into finishing him off all the more quickly."

"We've taken the animals to the slaughterhouse," said Magda. "There was nothing else to do. After these two years of poor crops, I'd have had to let them starve to death."

"Poor Magda," Robert murmured consolingly. "My problem is my potatoes. I planted several rows of them, but the ground's so muddy they're drowning."

"You've got to get them up as quickly as possible," Magda advised him, "otherwise they'll go bad. It's true they won't be full-grown, but it's better to have them small and spotted than not to have any at all."

Irena listened to their conversation with half an ear. Sitting at the big table, she had a pile of newspapers in front of her, snipping out articles and arranging them in stacks.

"They're busy writing history!" she kept repeating. "Those 'Solidarity' boys don't realize they're carrying out the most surprising of peaceful revolutions. For once, even our newspapers are managing to escape censorship to some extent, and are interesting to read!"

Since October, Irena had organized a chain of newspaper suppliers. She helped to distribute *Trybuna Ludu* and the weekly *Polityka*, and there were also the foreign papers which André got for her, which she patiently translated with the aid of two dictionaries.

"Look!" she cried to Robert. "Just look! According to

this West German paper, the Soviets managed to obtain credit and technical assistance from the Europeans to develop their oil deposits, which have lain untouched till now. In exchange, they've promised to supply Europe. You realize this means that anytime Europe does something to make Moscow unhappy, all Moscow has to do is shut the tap off. It's diabolical! The Europeans don't even realize that they're about to part with their freedom."

Robert listened to his wife politely, but didn't seem particularly impressed by her remarks. The only things that mattered to him were his garden and his field, which he could see from the window. With the arrival of the cold weather, Robert had also rediscovered his taste for puttering about. Sometimes he would make a chair, a cupboard, or some other piece of furniture, and at other times he would patch up and repaint odd corners of the house.

"I'm going to sell everything," Magda said again. "I haven't got the strength to go on any longer, and Inka won't be staying here with me forever. There are no spare hands in the country; the young folk prefer to go and work in the factories. And the prices they give us for our products are very low, and the milk subsidies they've promised us are just ridiculous."

"Come, Magda, you mustn't get discouraged; we saw lots of this sort of thing during the occupation. Surely you remember those times!" protested Irena.

"Oh, yes!" Magda sighed. "But I was much younger then, and I had growing sons; while now there's only our Inka, who does what she can. I can make do with very little, and with what Father Marianski gives me for the housekeeping, I'll be able to make ends meet. Other people have done the same thing. They've sold out, and they've found it hasn't left them worse off—quite the contrary."

Magda sighed deeply, and for a moment silence fell over the room.

"Now, now," protested Irena, "I'm quite ready to spend hours discussing crops, and hardships, and the price of meat, and how difficult it is to make vegetables grow, but listen to this! Lech Walesa's said that if they let us organize ourselves, he'll turn Poland into the Japan of Europe. Our production will astonish the world. Isn't that wonderful? At last we've got a man who's neither a defeatist, nor a cynic, nor corrupt. Everyone wants to follow our Walesa: the workers, the peasants, and the intellectuals."

"I just hope you're not going to be disappointed," murmured Robert as he polished a freshly cut plank. "Nobody knows how all this is going to turn out. Right now, Marek's on a hunger strike in prison. 'Solidarity' will make a fuss about him on television and in the newspapers, but what can they do to save him?"

"Yet somebody's got to have the courage to talk about independence," murmured Irena.

"Life here in Poland consists of never forgetting what's feasible and what isn't!" retorted Robert.

Irena had no time to answer him. There was a knock at the door, and Father Marianski walked in. His cassock floated around his body, which had grown thinner and thinner. But he seemed to be in excellent form. Irena was delighted to see him; Father Marianski understood her much better than Robert did, and always shared enthusiasm over press cuttings, which he read attentively.

"I've got problems," he said. "The militia chief's two children arrived this morning for the catechism course. I did my best to welcome them warmly, but the other children were very unpleasant to them; nobody wanted to sit next to them. As if it were *their* fault that their father's a militia officer! Nobody can be more cruel than children."

Irena made tea. All three of them sat close to the radio, and Robert turned the dials. They did their best to discuss calmly the great events that were shaking Poland, but in fact they were only too conscious that they were living through moments that were historic.

The voice of the announcer was almost drowned out by static. "On the question of possible intervention of the Soviet Army, Lech Walesa replied: 'I see no reason why a friendly country should interfere in our interior affairs. Since when does one have to fear one's friends?' "

"If they come, we should defend ourselves!" cried Robert. "We shall defend ourselves to the end. This time, there'll be no deportation to Siberia. All they'll be able to load into cattle wagons and transport to Russia will be the dead! What they did in Lvov in April 1940 won't happen again. Never again!"

Inka washed her hands and changed her blouse. The day was over; she had finished milking the cow and cleaning out the henhouse. Magda had gone down to the village, and Inka was alone. She looked at her reflection in the little mirror; her features were drawn, and her face had a sad expression.

Would Kazik come for her, as he had promised? It had been months since she had heard from him! Was he in prison, like Marek? No, she would know about that. It was no longer like the old days, when people just disappeared. The prison staff put out regular lists of those who'd been arrested for political reasons, and the Solidarity people never failed to protest any injustices. True, they had done nothing for Marek; but all the same, if it were Kazik, who belonged to the KOR, it would be different. Had he gone abroad without bothering to tell her? After all, there was nothing to stop him from going to live in Paris. In Ula's last letter to Helena, hadn't she said that she was prepared to accept any of Helena's friends who wanted to leave Poland? Inka was thoughtful as she tried to recall certain phrases of the letter which Helena had read out loud to her. Ula had written:

You understand, I'll never manage to get rid of my remorse for having stayed here instead of returning to Poland and sharing those years after the war with you all. I'm ready to do anything to help you, because I'm ashamed. It's not I who am doing you a service; it's you who are giving me back a reason for living. I'm tense and on edge all the time, and I listen to the news as though my own existence were at stake. The people around me—both French and Polish immigrants—say to me with concern: "Poor you, you have family over there." And I reply to them, like an imbecile: "Yes—thirty-five million Poles!" Can you understand that one's individual destiny remains linked, whatever one does, with the collective destiny, when it's a question of a people having to struggle for their survival and their rights?

Helena had also received a letter from Kazik's parents, who wanted to send her money and parcels:

We have a bad conscience when we go shopping in the supermarkets they have here. In the newspapers and on the TV, they tell us—and even show pictures— of people lining up in front of the Warsaw food stores. I really want to come back and be with you during these times which are so important for the future of us all, but Kazik won't have it. He doesn't write often, and in his last letter he threatened not to see us if we ever decided to return to Warsaw.

These letters had made a big impression on Inka. After all, these people had courage; they lived abroad, a long way away. They could very easily forget us all, thought Inka, in the comfortable conditions they're enjoying, and snap their fingers at what's happening to us here.

It was raining outside, and the sky was heavy with a gray mist. Inka brushed her hair slowly, then began preparing the evening meal. Just as she was lighting the fire in the kitchen stove, the dog began barking. She opened the door and peered outside. In the distance, she saw Kazik, his leather jacket covered with rain, his hair wet and plastered down over his temples.

"Kazik!" Inka cried as she ran to meet him. The rain soaked her face and bare arms, and her legs sank into the mud, but she was aware of nothing but the man who was holding his arms out to her. She pressed herself against him, panting for breath.

He lifted Inka off the ground, laughing merrily; then his lips met hers, and Inka felt as though the whole world was spinning around them. She wondered briefly whether she had ever known such happiness, but Kazik's presence put all thoughts and questions out of her mind, and she abandoned herself in his arms as he carried her into the house, covering her face with kisses as he went.